I0636403

Meridian

FEVER & FRAY

AURELIA T. EVANS

Fever & Fray
ISBN # 978-1-80250-529-0
©Copyright Aurelia T. Evans 2023
Cover Art by Kelly Martin ©Copyright April 2023
Interior text design by Claire Siemaszkiewicz
Totally Bound Publishing

Published in 2023 by Totally Bound Publishing, United Kingdom.

Totally Bound Publishing is an imprint of Totally Entwined Group Limited.

FEVER & FRAY

Dedication

For those who don't know who they are

Chapter One

She'd only taken her sweater off because she was too warm.

Now she wrapped it around her like a cross between a cloak and a shield as she stood in front of the receptionist, waiting for the young work-study student to acknowledge her from whatever she was scrolling through.

"Yeah? What?" the student said, still not looking up.

Nova shifted on her wedge heels. "Father Marcus told me to wait in his office."

The assistant rolled her eyes and shrugged toward the line of offices for interdenominational staff. "The door's open. You don't need my permission."

Nova nodded, even though the girl couldn't see her, then hurried to the office labeled with Father Marcus Cane's name. The hall was modern in design, but the office had been paneled in dark wood and decorated in the vein of an old-school study. The scents of woven hardcover books and leather from the chairs entombed her.

She lowered herself into the chair nearest the door, right under the air vent. Although she tucked her sweater even more tightly around her, it wasn't thick enough to block the cold.

Anything to keep her sweater on.

The room where they did their Saturday evening worship services was sometimes too cold during the summer months, but once the weather started to cool down, there was that awkward set of weeks in autumn and spring when it wasn't chilly enough to turn on the heater but too cool for the air conditioner to kick in.

When a modest college crowd crammed into a too-small room with no air circulation, it was bound to get too warm before someone decided to manually turn on the air.

While the worship band had played the seventh praise song in their set, everyone had stood, those freer with their bodies waving their hands in the air like Pentecostals while the frozen chosen of the Methodist and white Southern Baptist set had awkwardly swayed. The Saturday evening service served primarily a Catholic crowd, with a Catholic Communion—the Protestants took theirs during Wednesday and Sunday services—but they remained casual enough to welcome anyone who wanted to come in evenings instead of having to wake up early on Sunday morning. They used the same praise band for both Wednesday and Saturday services and borrowed music majors for the more traditional choir on Sunday.

All that body heat, all that closeness with the chairs crammed together... It had been a perfectly natural thing for Nova to remove her thin sweater. It wasn't like she'd had a spaghetti-strap shirt underneath. The tank-top straps were at least three fingers wide. She'd checked before she'd bought it. The neckline was modest enough, although she always had some cleavage. Short of a turtleneck, there was nothing she could do about that, and it wasn't cold enough for turtleneck sweaters. Her skirt passed a high school dress code's muster by a whole foot of fabric, but there wasn't much of a dress code in college, where as long as you weren't naked, they wouldn't kick you out. Still, she was practically nun-like in comparison to what some of the other girls in the makeshift sanctuary wore.

It wasn't that nobody had noticed the boy trying to slip his hand over her ass during the praise songs or the way he'd kept acting like she took up too much space and his elbow just couldn't help but brush the side of her breast. Everyone beside and behind them had probably witnessed that. But when she'd slapped his hand, that's when the situation had become a problem — and only because the slap had been so loud in the otherwise-silent crowd during the homily.

One of the counselors — volunteers from the University of Texas-Meridian campus staff — had made the boy move, but Father Marcus had stood and actually interrupted Father William's message to tell Nova to see him after the service.

Her chest had ached as she'd lowered her head and nodded, crossing her arms over her breasts — not that that helped at all. She'd just wanted them all to stop looking at her.

Always the eyes... Nova couldn't walk down the street alone in a bulky coat that covered her whole body without feeling the eyes. She'd consider herself paranoid, but it wasn't always just eyes. Ever since she'd turned twelve years old, she'd been inundated with wolf whistles and catcalls. The years before puberty had hit were a distant dreamlike memory — a time when strangers had called her 'pretty girl' and given her little extra treats and attention but had never ogled her as though their gazes were fingertips.

A girl got tired of it after a while. Free drinks or desserts now and then were nice, but people seemed to expect that they paid for something else.

When she'd been twelve, her parents had yelled at the people who'd scammed on her. Around the time she'd turned fourteen, something had changed. Her mother and father had sat her down and told her she was growing up and needed to start taking responsibility as she became a woman. Her father wouldn't let her out of the house unless she'd been suitably covered. *Modesty*, they'd called it—no jeans that showed the shapes of her legs, no tight-fitting or low-cut tops, no tank tops. They'd have put her in a Catholic school with ill-fitting uniforms if they could have afforded it.

Perhaps she would have been less resentful of their totalitarian rule over her closet if it had done anything to dissuade the gazes, the hands, the taunts that had made her afraid to leave the house alone. Perhaps that was why, once she'd enrolled in UTM, she'd started buying clothes to wear that didn't wear her, although she still stayed relatively modest. If people were going to bother her anyway, she might as well let her skin breathe, and if people—if *men*—were going to tell her how good she looked, she might as well look good to herself. Right?

All those justifications she'd made in her head for her shopping spree once she'd settled into the dormitory, away from her parents' control, suddenly seemed weak and small...like her.

She sat in the office with the door open, her legs pressed together instead of crossed. Her father had once told her that when women crossed their legs, it made them look like *those* kinds of secretaries. Her skirt hem rested well below her knees, even while sitting, although it was thinner and flowier than her old skirts had been.

Shivering under the air vent, she hugged her stomach, which was playing cat's cradle with itself. She hadn't done anything wrong, so why did it feel like she'd been sent to the principal's office?

She'd been sent home from high school twenty-one times for skirts that were too tight in the rear, according to her teachers, and the dress code had specified no super-tight clothing — although it had failed to clarify what constituted 'tight'. She'd tried to explain that if she didn't tie them tight enough, they'd fall right off, but she'd been sent home anyway for being a disruptive influence. Other times, she'd been told her shirts were too low cut, even though there'd been girls around her with lower-cut tops, as though her real crime was having bigger boobs.

She'd never been rebellious, had always tried so very hard to please, but since her first major adolescent growth spurt, she'd still developed a reputation as a troublemaker. She'd eaten her lunches alone and made straight As, but she didn't think any one of her teachers remembered her report cards — just the number of times they'd ignored her raised hands in class, the times they'd told her to go home to change or go to the office for one of the oversized T-shirts they kept to shame dress code violators.

All her friends, girls as well as boys, had dried up in middle school. She'd had a few boyfriends, the kind she couldn't bring home because her father always said she was too young to date and needed to focus on school, but a pair of people found a way, anyway.

However, the boys never stayed long. Either they got what they wanted from her and were done or she didn't give them what they wanted, hoping they'd stay under the assumption that she'd give it to them eventually.

Girls seemed to think she was competition, particularly when it came to boys, including all the ones she didn't want. Nova was always a threat, even though she tried to be as unthreatening and fairy-princess nice as she could. It never got her anywhere, and middle school had been a special brand of hell, so she'd stopped trying to make friends by high school.

She and her roommate didn't even talk, despite having majors and church services in common. Nova might as well live alone in the minuscule dorm.

This was her life. This had always been her life. It was as normal for her as brushing her hair and putting on lip balm in the morning.

Other girls had long-term boyfriends who, even in their horny teenage years, didn't paw at them all hours of the day. Girls could be friends with other girls, even whole groups of them, without claws coming out. Boys . could hang out with other girls without incessantly asking if they wanted to make out behind the gym or drive home with them.

There was something wrong with her, something wrong that she was doing. She just hadn't figured out what it was yet. She was afraid to talk about it with anyone, even during confession, where she detailed how she got in trouble but never asked the priests *why*, afraid they'd have no other answer for her than 'Eve's sin', which was no help to her.

She couldn't help having been born a woman. She just wanted to know how to survive it.

Maybe Father Marcus could explain it to her when he arrived. And if he knew that she *wanted* to be good, *wanted* to be pure, *wanted* to be everything short of a nun for the rest of her life, maybe he wouldn't punish her for being the reason why he'd interrupted the homily.

As the clock hand inched toward thirty minutes after the hour when the service should have concluded, Nova closed her eyes and prayed an Our Father. She didn't feel comfortable with Hail Marys anymore—prayers to a maiden when she wasn't technically a maiden. She'd say them when she was told to, but in secret, and whenever she thought of Mary, her soul seemed to shrink in fear.

Although why she thought she could go straight to God when she couldn't even go through a saint was beyond her—all those women celebrated for going to such great lengths to preserve their virginity unto death. And she'd just given hers up in a fruitless attempt to get a guy to finally like her for more than her body, get it out of his system so that maybe he'd see her for what she really was.

It never worked. Maybe it did for some girls, but not her. Once the boys tasted what they wanted from her, she was chewed-up gum, mucky and unsticky tape, if you believed the sex education videos their health teacher had made them watch when they'd reached the reproductive unit. The boys were completely sated, and she was left wanting more, wanting deeper. Was it such a terrible thing to want to be held, to be touched, to be loved, to feel like she was important? But they used her as though she wasn't even there at all.

If she'd been lonely in her preschool and elementary days, Nova thought she wouldn't be quite so lonely now. As it was, she'd never gotten used to having people around her who were only after one thing.

"What are you doing here so late, Ms. Harvey?" Father Marcus asked out in the hall.

"Just waiting for you to come back, sir, to see if you needed anything else from me," the receptionist said.

"Go on home. I'm sure you have other things to do tonight."

"Thanks. Oh, you have someone in your office. She said you told her to be here. Should I stay?"

"No. This shouldn't take long. Thank you, Ms. Harvey. Have a good night."

"You, too, Father Marcus."

The receptionist's footsteps, muffled on the carpet, headed away, while a stronger gait made its way to the office door. Shadow blotted out the light from the hall.

"Have you been sitting here in the dark this whole time?" Father Marcus said in surprise when Nova stood up at his entrance. He switched on the standing bank lamp next to her chair. It didn't cast out all the darkness, but it illuminated Father Marcus' weathered face and a gentler expression than he'd given her during the service.

"Yes, sir."

"Why? I wouldn't penalize you for wasting electricity or anything."

"I don't mind the dark," she said.

"No, I suppose you don't. Please, join me at my desk."

Nova picked up her satchel purse and followed Father Marcus to the two wingback chairs in front of his desk. She took the left. She expected Father Marcus to settle behind the desk and stare disapprovingly at her, but he leaned against the front of his desk instead.

The lamplight reflected in his glasses, concealing the direction of his gaze

"You're not wearing a nametag," he said. "What's your name, young lady?"

Nova and nametags were time-honored nemeses. When she put one on her chest like everyone else, an adult usually gave her a stern look and told her to stop calling attention to her breasts. When she put it on her stomach like some of the girls who didn't like to grope their own boob, they told her to stop calling attention to her midriff. When she put it on her skirt, they told her to stop calling attention to her legs or her lady parts. When she put it on her forehead, they told her to stop being a clown and grow up. At this point, she'd given up and hoped that people wouldn't notice or care that she refused to wear nametags anymore.

She stared down at her hands. "Nova Mendez."

"And you're a freshman this year, am I right? I can't remember seeing you in services last year."

She nodded.

"How old are you? Seventeen, eighteen?"

"Almost nineteen, sir. I'm old for my year."

"Almost nineteen," he murmured, as though savoring the word. "Well, at your age, I'd expect you to know better."

"Excuse me, sir?"

"Oh, you're demure now, aren't you? So you know what I'm about to tell you. Stand up, Ms. Mendez. I want you to take off that sweater. Go on. I'm going to demonstrate something to you."

"Father?" In spite of the chill in the room, her body flushed hot beneath all her clothes. The sweat under her arms smelled sour to her when she shifted.

"Please, Ms. Mendez, take off your sweater and stand up for me. There's a point I need to make that's important for you to learn."

Nova slowly stood up and pulled her arms out of the sleeves of her sweater. Father Marcus held his hand out, then snapped when she hesitated. Nova dropped her sweater into his hand. He set it on the desk behind him.

"Now, I know that girls — young women — your age like getting attention, any kind of attention. The world tells young women that their only power is in their sexuality, then they act surprised when women flaunting their bodies ends badly. I know it seems like an undue burden forced upon you to adequately cover your body when the world only gives you so many options to do so, but it is your duty, as a woman of God, to not deal in matters of pride and vanity, to preserve your purity, to maintain your modesty. There's a reason why adultery is written into the Ten Commandments as one of the most devastating betrayals that a person can engage in with another person. Do you know why we tell young women to be modest?"

Nova nodded, struggling to swallow past the obstruction in her throat. "Because we belong to God first and our husbands second. We dress modestly to respect God, respect our husbands and respect our brothers in Christ, to help them not to stumble."

"See?" Father Marcus stood with a warm smile. He was well into middle age, but it was a good smile, taking the edge off the storminess of his bushy brows and deepening the lines at the corners of his eyes. "You understand perfectly. It's especially difficult for teenage boys and young men. The slightest glimpse of certain accentuated areas of your body are enough to make them commit adultery in their mind with you, and because you invite their eyes, you commit adultery with them. So tell me, Ms. Mendez... I know our services are less formal than you might be used to, but why did you choose to wear something like *this* to Mass, of all places?"

He passed his hand over her shoulder. Where his fingers met bare skin, the little hairs on her body stood up with a localized shiver that only made her flush harder. He trailed his touch down her bare arm.

"Even the tightness of your shirt is enough to make a man stumble." He stepped even closer so that she felt his heat as he loomed over her. Nova was petite in stature. Father Marcus was tall, easily twice her size.

And he smelled...different. He didn't have the scent that had clung to the boys back in high school — gym socks, corn chips, wet hair, whatever they'd eaten last. There was an aged quality to him, as though he'd absorbed some of the dusty, leathery odors of his office.

Nova leaned forward, her eyelids fluttering as she breathed him in. It was completely involuntary, but once she'd done it, it couldn't be undone. She entered into the pocket of his heat, where the scent intensified. He was one of those people who seemed to burn from the inside. Her mother always said Nova was one of those people, too, but it didn't feel like it most days. Tonight, it did. She gasped as her heat met his.

His black shirt over his chest filled her vision, the white collar calling her gaze up as a reminder. She raised her eyes to his. At this angle, she could see them through the reflected light, his pupils wide in the dark room, expression as solemn as though he were dispensing the Host.

"It leaves little to a man's imagination, Ms. Mendez," he said. "I can practically see down your shirt. This was how close the young man was to you, yes?"

"He was next to me."

"He could still see what I'm seeing now. I'm a man of the cloth, promised to the Father, my service to the church, and what I see now makes me stumble. Now, this situation is less than organic. I created it as an illustration. But the young man next to you didn't know what this would do to him."

Father Marcus ghosted the tips of his fingers over her collarbone. Then, swallowing thickly, he lowered them down her sternum to the swells of her breasts over the neckline, the deep shadow of cleavage from the low light in the room.

She couldn't help it. She dragged in a breath, her chest expanding, bringing his touch closer. He scalded her where their skin met. She was aware of everything about him — the blue-gray of his scholar's eyes, the glimmer of silver in his eyebrows and the short, thick hair on his head, the duskiness of late-night stubble, the pores on his nose, the slightly parted lips, the ivory of his teeth between them, the wet undulation of his tongue before he spoke.

"The way you're dressed now, you might as well not bother with the shirt." His fingers trembled before he slowly drew the neckline of her tank top down, down, until the shine of her plain black bra was visible over the top.

"You mean I might as well walk around with nothing on but my bra?" She didn't know why she did it, but she took the hem of her shirt and drew it up. Everything was so sharp, yet dreamlike. This couldn't possibly be happening. It *shouldn't* be happening. Yet her breath quickened, and the sweat dripping down her back had nothing to do with fear.

Father Marcus could have—should have—stopped her. She gave him enough time. But when he didn't, she wriggled the tank top over her head, flipping her ponytail.

He opened his mouth to speak but stopped to swallow. His Adam's apple bobbed above his collar. "You think a bra is enough to block out a man's fantasy? Really, Ms. Mendez, it's an insult to think that little slip of material conceals anything. Look at you. It doesn't even hide the shape of your nipples."

He pinched them through the bra cup. She didn't realize just how close the two of them were until she jumped and her hips brushed against his erection through his loose-fitting black trousers.

Father Marcus stepped back, as though shocked at himself. But he seemingly couldn't tear his gaze away.

When she looked down, she saw that he was right. The bra cups were structured and thick to contain her, practical rather than fanciful in construction, yet the shapes of her hard, tight nipples were clear. Underneath the bra, they rubbed uncomfortably against the fabric.

No, not uncomfortable…unbearable. She didn't want the bra on her skin any longer. She wanted skin on skin, the velvet of heat, the softness of a mouth. She wanted it so badly that she nearly doubled over, wrapping her arms around her belly and whimpering at the sensation of her forearms brushing the skin there.

Father Marcus fumbled behind him for a pair of scissors near his blotter. He raised them in front of his glinting eyeglasses. For one terrifying second that did nothing to stifle her need, Nova thought he might stab her with them.

For some reason, the old Exodus verse surfaced in her head — *Thou shalt not suffer a witch to live.*

But she wasn't a witch. She wasn't actively doing anything.

Am I?

The evening ran around her like a river, drawing her along as helpless as a kitten. It might have seemed like she was moving of her own accord, but she felt as though there was another person inside her doing these things instead.

However, it also felt like that person had been there all along.

"God will forgive me for your temptation," he whispered.

"Is that what I am?" Nova looked up just as the priest clipped the straps to her bra before grabbing the cups and yanking them down. The scissors clattered to the floor as he slid his palms back up, cupping her, holding her high and close. Then he withdrew his hands to watch their weight settle.

Father Marcus passed the back of his hand over his lips. "All women are a temptation to men. Man has been giving in to woman's temptation ever since Adam. But you, Ms. Mendez? My God. Every part of you tempts a man, and you do nothing to save them from the curse of their desire for you."

He grabbed the front of her bra again and whirled her around with him to shove her against the desk, where the lamplight illuminated more of her. He found the clasp in the front and ripped the bra off her, the set of his jaw angry but the rest of his face captivated — utterly enchanted.

The desk edge dug into the small of her back. She gripped it, caught in a whirlwind of uncertainty, fear and lust. "What am I supposed to do? I can't help the way I look. And this evening, I didn't take my sweater off to seduce anyone. I was just warm. I don't try to do this. I try to wear things that cover me. This skirt..."

"The way it clings to you, hugging your hips, your..." Father Marcus swallowed again. "It swirls around your legs like a caress every time you move. And what do you think a skirt really hides? We know what's under everything you wear. Whether you're in sackcloth and ashes or a bathing suit, nothing hides what you are."

"I know what's under all this." Nova bit her lip as she closed a fist in the front of Father Marcus' black shirt and drew him toward her. "Does that mean you might as well not be wearing any of it?"

She started at the middle and worked her way up. His abdomen and chest seemed to leap away from her every time he exhaled, but he couldn't help but inhale again so that her knuckles brushed his chest.

When she reached his clerical collar, he batted her hand away with a sharp slap. Then he slapped her face.

Nova leaned back against the desk, holding her hand to her cheek where it tingled from his blow. For a moment, she was shocked out of her haze, shocked by her behavior, shocked by his.

Father Marcus clutched at the loose clerical collar, pressing it against his chest like a man holding on to the top of a cliff. He dipped his gaze from her wide eyes to her bare breasts enhanced by the golden light, the broad, dark nipples and their tips shifting and quivering slightly with every movement, every breath.

"I'm sorry, Ms. Mendez." He tentatively reached out to stroke her other cheek. "There's nothing you can do."

A groan escaped his lips when he touched her. Suddenly, he crowded her against the desk, pushing her against it until there was nothing for her to do to save her back except to lift herself up to sit on its edge.

She spread her thighs wide as he pushed between them, her skirt riding up her legs to expose more bare skin. His collar fell onto her thigh and tumbled to the side. It hit the floor with a muffled whisper.

"They say the devil was the most beautiful angel of all," he murmured as he leaned over her and kissed down her neck. He cupped the underside of her breast to lift it to his mouth.

It didn't matter that there was a window in the door or that the blinds to the large windows were open, that anyone who might walk in for late-night counsel or to clean the offices would see Father Marcus face-deep in Nova's breasts. And even if they didn't see anything, they would be able to hear Nova as she moaned her pleasure.

She nearly fell back on the desk blotter, except Father Marcus had his arm around her, and she clutched at his neck to cling him closer. Lust vibrated through her, keen as fear, strong as a cocktail of adrenaline and caffeine. As Father Marcus thrust his hips against her, dry-humping with his clothed erection, she wished she could spread her legs even more, but that would mean not wrapping them around his. Liquid heat dripped from her pussy, as hot and wet as Father Marcus' mouth around her nipple, sucking her with all the enthusiasm of a drunk with his bottle.

He pressed his forehead against her breastbone and dragged his mouth from the peak of her breast. It gleamed in the low light and chilled in the air.

"I can't..." he whispered. "I can't..."

He fumbled with the front of his trousers while she stroked his chest, falling back on his desk at last, feeling sick, feeling free, feeling twisted like a knot of bread, feeling like if she didn't get his cock inside her right now, she might spontaneously implode into a shriveled mummy of a girl. With contact, her spirit arched like a cat against a hand over its spine. It was better than anything she'd ever had with those fumbling boys in high school. She might actually get what she wanted this time, what she *needed*.

He knocked her hands away from his chest as he lifted her skirt away from her underwear.

Nova whined, shaking her head against the blotter. Without him touching her skin, she knew he still wouldn't be enough, that he was using her...but she couldn't grasp what was missing. It slipped through her fingers as soon as he nudged her underwear away from her folds.

"God forgive me." Father Marcus clutched his deeply flushed, short, full cock in his hand, the tip leaking thin fluid that made the head shine and her mouth water. With his shirt askew and his pants open, she saw the reality that so many priests like him would deny to the world with their shapeless clothing—that he was a man, thick and alive and desirous, hungry to surround himself with her.

"God forgive me," he pleaded again, but he spoke to her breasts, as though they were the idols from which he sought forgiveness. He brought his cock to her folds, coating the head with her wetness. There was no way she could ever claim that she didn't want this. The proof stained his desk underneath her. "God forgive me, I can't stop her."

"Now, that's just pathetic, Padre," a man said from behind Father Marcus, his voice dripping with disgust.

Father Marcus stumbled away from Nova.

She pounded her fist against the desk when the head of his cock was taken away just a fraction of an inch from entering her, a fraction of an inch from satisfying her—at least a part of her. Not enough, but it would have been better than nothing.

Now Nova was just incredibly aware of the fact that she sat there with her legs wide, her cunt exposed and her skirt hiked up. Her bare torso seemed somehow more obscene with her skirt still on.

She felt dirty—horny and dirty and confused and dead angry that Father Marcus had the audacity to be ashamed of her, to call her the only sin in the room and give her no hope to be otherwise, the hope for forgiveness only for him. She'd done some of the damage, even though it all seemed like a dream. She'd admit that. But she'd far from done it all.

The man emerged from the shadow of the corner as though he hadn't been in the corner at all but the shadow alone. He slouched out, his thumbs in the belt loops of his jeans, no shirt—somehow especially naked in this stuffy office, where even Father Marcus was mostly dressed, albeit disheveled. The man's tousled sandy hair and dark bedroom eyes made him appear even more naturally sexual and carnal than Father Marcus with his erection unabated. He certainly looked as though he knew better the ways of the world than a priest in denial.

"Look at you. She's a ripe plum of a girl, probably tastes as good as she looks, but let's face it, Padre. She's just a college girl, and you're a priest. Where's the accountability?"

Father Marcus gaped at him, holding the sides of his placket together as though he'd forgotten that he could close it.

"*Her* priest, in fact. Yet here you are, half-undressed, ready to fuck her like a sailor, and you're really going with the 'I couldn't help it' defense?"

"Sh-she seduced m-m-me...with her cl-clothes. And-and she t-took off her shirt. I can't be e-expected to—"

"You can't lie to me," the man said. "I saw the whole thing. Damn pitiful. I know you don't get a lot, Padre, so all the tension probably builds up like a bitch, but haven't you ever heard of foreplay? As long as you're blaming everything on her and abusing your authority, couldn't you have given her a smidgeon of consideration in return? A nice, long kiss, say...or perhaps you could have fallen to your knees for a taste of the unholy bread and wine."

Father Marcus finally got enough of his wits about him to button his trousers. Then he started after the stranger, attempting to intimidate, to tower over him. "Who are you to come into *my* office and spout these blasphemies and accusations? You have no idea the context of the situation."

Just before Father Marcus reached the stranger, the stranger advanced upon him in turn, his arms spread to invite a fight if the priest wanted one. The man was shorter but younger, his body tight and fit, buzzing with kinetic energy and an odd grace as he moved. Father Marcus staggered back a step, hopelessly confused behind glasses that no longer made him appear mature and learned. Instead, he looked almost feeble as he fell back into one of the chairs.

"The context of the situation..." The stranger glared down at the priest. "It doesn't matter how fucking sexy this woman is, doesn't matter the magic she carries in her veins. You're still the responsible party here. Don't get me wrong. I'm not judging. I didn't interrupt because I was morally offended and shocked...I tell you, shocked. I interrupted this inept, fumbling bout of despair because I wanted better for her. Judging by the way she took everything you dished out without complaint, she's probably had a steady diet of shame, abuse and guilt slung her way by mindless, depraved animals like yourself."

The stranger grabbed the priest's shirt collar like he was going to pick a fight, but his lips were curved in a smile, his eyes alight with amusement.

"I'll bet she's not the first, is she, Padre? No, you don't have to answer that. I can tell the difference between dreams and memories. You've tasted forbidden fruit while wearing that pious costume before. It's true that Nova isn't a normal girl, but it's hard to really blame her when a normal girl still gets your motor revving so hard that you think you can't control yourself."

"God forgives," Father Marcus said.

"Sure, even a worm like you." The stranger wrenched Father Marcus onto the floor. "Even the things you condemn in others, the Creator forgives. I've always had a few words to say about that. But just because He erases the ledger doesn't mean she'll ever forget the way you treated her, the way it made her feel — or the other 'shes' in your life. What do you say, Nova? Should we leave this shit stain behind while I show you what you've so sorely lacked all these years?"

Nova nervously smoothed her skirt down her thighs, tried to find her sweater and her shirt. Her bra was...somewhere. She just wanted to leave. She was still horny as a toad, but she was too nauseated now to want anything to do with anyone except Ben and Jerry.

The worst part wasn't what Father Marcus had been doing to her. It was knowing that he was wrong to do it...and doing it with him anyway. Wanting it — like the whore that everyone believed she was, the whore that everyone treated her as. All at once, it was as though the clammy hands of every man who'd ever touched her had stuck their hands in mud and caked it on her in slimy handprints. She felt like the mouth of a beer bottle passed around a circle jerk.

"Sweetheart, I would've loved to see you drain this slug dick drier than the Sahara, because then you'd be feeling so much better than you do right now." The stranger absentmindedly kicked Father Marcus' chest when the priest tried to rise from the floor. "No, you stay down there. If I could board you beneath the hardwoods, I'd do it, but for now, I want you as close to where you belong as you can get, Padre."

The stranger held out his hand to her.

"I know who you are, Nova. I've been trolling this campus for years. You're the first of my kind I've found. It's been a real pleasure getting to know you, waiting for the moment you were ready to meet, to leave this life behind for everything you were meant for, made for. Do you want to know what that is? Do you want me to show you?"

"You've been watching me?" she asked.

He closed his eyes for a moment. "That voice. I bet you'd kill in a torch song. Yeah, I've been watching. It's either just as creepy or less creepy than it sounds. I haven't quite figured that one out yet. It's just what I am. But everything will be explained by the end of the night. I don't want to delay your progress another second, sweetheart. Will you come with me? I'll show you a better time than any of these slime trails would."

Nova slid along the edge of the desk away from his hand. Terror ran cold in her fingers and down her spine, but she somehow couldn't look away from him or convince her legs to run.

The stranger tilted his head, his dark eyes warm in the golden light as he stared down at her with…

Is that compassion?

Had any man ever looked at her like that, like anything other than a test, a trial, an obstacle, a prize, a warm place to sink into, a way to get off, an object of shame, a disgusting piece of trash?

"I'll bet you've only ever had boys and horny old men who don't know the first thing to do with a woman, never once showing appreciation for what you gave them—viewing you as a God-given right or a devil-given demon to lead them astray. Am I right? Boys who haven't learned yet to be men and men who haven't earned their title. I, however, won't leave you unsatisfied."

"It's a sin, Ms. Mendez," Father Marcus said from the floor. "It's a sin to have sex outside the confines of marriage."

Nova crossed her arms over her bare breasts. "Like what you were going to do with me? Putting me down the whole time as though it wasn't a sin *we* were committing, but as—"

"As though you were the sin itself," the stranger hissed in her ear.

Nova jerked up, startled.

"Well, it's far more complicated than that, sweetheart. Let me show you. Let me show you what you truly are, what you can be. This world will smother you, unable to handle you, until you learn who you are and how to control it—control *them*. Come with me."

He offered his hand to her again.

She continued to hold her arms over her breasts, but she wasn't trying to avoid his hand anymore. She was just self-conscious in a whole new way. It was as though this stranger was the first person to see her—

really *see* her—as something other than a living flesh sleeve.

"Don't worry about something as common as nudity, love," the stranger said. "Where we're going, it won't matter anymore."

"Ms. Mendez, the consequence of sin is death," Father Marcus urged.

"Everything dies," the stranger said. "But you'll be dust in your grave before we do. Come with me, Nova. Come with me."

She slowly brought her arms away from her breasts.

"God, you're beautiful," the stranger breathed. "The Creator did truly exceptional work with you."

The world spun around her at an ever-increasing pace—or maybe that was just her head. "I don't know you."

"Call me Jules. Actually, call me anything you want, sweetheart. I'll answer to just about anything for you."

"God will never forgive you!" Father Marcus shouted at her as she raised her hand to Jules.

"God doesn't have to forgive her," Jules said. "He made her perfect just the way she is."

A hunger she hadn't realized she suffered for those words reared up like a serpent. She was practically starved for them. Her lips parted to breathe them in, taste them. She couldn't get enough.

Nova slipped her hand into his.

Chapter Two

The window blind panels folded away from the window, and the windows themselves snapped open, sending the cool evening breeze sweeping in with the sound of fluttering pages falling to the floor and sliding on the hardwood.

The autumn air did nothing to chill Nova's skin as lustful heat spread from the place where her hand met his. He wasn't unaffected. They gasped off-rhythm, the sound magnified in her ears until it was almost all she could hear.

Jules tugged her closer to him, heedless of her skirt or lack of shirt as he lifted her. She wrapped her legs around his waist without a second thought. Staring down at him as she clung to his neck, Nova thought there had never been anything so attractive as his lips at that moment. She wanted nothing more than a kiss — his kiss. There had been many tumbles in the backseats of cars, in janitors' closets, under the bleachers — but how many kisses, real kisses that mattered? Could she even fill her hands with the number?

Just as she angled her mouth over his, he spread his fingers through her hair and urged her to tuck her head over his shoulder. Regret threaded every word as he murmured, "All in good time. Hold on, sweetheart."

He leaped onto the desk with impossible grace and strength, then onto the window ledge. He whirled around with his arm around her waist to look back at Father Marcus, who struggled to his feet.

"Say your prayers tonight, Padre. You got an undeserved reprieve. I suggest you go home to your nice, warm, empty bed and don't follow us. Just forget any of this ever happened. Forget Nova Mendez ever existed. I'd tell you not to forget what an ass you are, but asses like you usually forget that pretty easily." He grinned at Nova. "Going up?"

"I know you are," she said, almost shyly.

"Oh, I've been up for a while. And as long as I'm touching you, love, it ain't getting any lower. Brace yourself."

Nova cried out as wings—giant, beautiful black wings—unfurled from two knots on his back that looked like partially healed gashes, at least until the wings erupted from them.

Were those knots there all this time? She couldn't remember if he'd turned his back to her while he'd been threatening the priest. It seemed like she would remember wounds that large and angry. But they disappeared with the appearance of wings, black as a raven and each almost as long as a small bus.

He jumped, his wings storming down to give him leverage as he reached for the drainpipe.

Nova cried out in a combination of fear and delight. She kept thinking they would fall as he climbed up the pipe like a monkey, grasping at protuberances with the skill of a master rock climber, but his wings held him steady and kept them from falling.

If Father Marcus had had any thoughts about following, he must have decided this kind of mess wasn't worth getting stuck in. Nova thought she'd have been peeking out of the window if she'd seen a man grow angel wings and jump out of the Religious Studies building, but when she glanced down, no one was looking up or shouting at them.

There were people on the sidewalks, though. Any of them could idly look up and see massive wings and two half-naked young people climbing a drainpipe like a pair of gargoyles come to life.

Nova dug her fingernails into his back until he paused and groaned into her shoulder. "Nova, sweetheart, save the scratching for the roof. I'm going to come right here, halfway up the building. It won't make your evening less eventful, but it might make me fall a few stories."

"They'll see us," she replied.

"No, they won't. You think that because you can see them, they can see you. But we're invisible now, babe. We could fuck like dogs in the quad and no one would see us if we didn't want them to."

"I don't understand."

"You will. Just a few more stories, and we'll be home free."

"How are you doing this?" Nova asked.

"Does it make it easier to accept if I tell you it's all a dream? The whole world is a dream, and we're the ghosts that move through it."

His arms flexed on either side of her, the muscles straining against his skin as though they would snap through at any moment. They kept rising, but Nova felt like she was falling—falling into a cloud of velvet blankets warm around her, brushing her skin with little electric shocks all over her skin.

"Am I dead?" she asked finally.

"You're coming to life, sweetheart. You wait. After the way the world has starved you like a street urchin, you're going to gorge yourself silly."

Jules vaulted over the roof's edge and rolled onto his back with a playful smile, his wings spread over the gravel on the roof as though he'd fallen there. He cradled her face between large hands, although he wasn't a large man.

"Hey," he said, touching the corners of her mouth with his thumbs.

"What are you?" But her question devolved into a whimper as he slid his hands back into her hair and pulled out the rubber band. Her hair fell to either side of them—thick, dark, good, healthy hair that she'd always liked, but she'd always had to keep it back in a ponytail or bun or comb to keep other people from touching it without her permission. "You're no angel."

"They're not as fun as me." He leaned forward and licked her lower lip.

Nova grabbed his shaggy hair and pulled him away from her so that she could dip down again and sink into his mouth. She muffled his moan with her tongue as she tasted him, possessed him as slow as hot molasses until she thought she would outright melt, just turn from solid to liquid and spill out to every side like a thousand water balloons exploding.

When Jules slipped his hand under the waistband of her skirt and her underwear to stroke her pussy from behind, she did. She arched and cried her orgasm from the rooftop, not caring if anyone saw or heard her, not caring that what she was doing was wrong according to every authority figure she'd ever known—pounded into her head with a dull hammer that she shouldn't want this, shouldn't do this, should save it for a husband who would never happen, since she had yet to meet a man who didn't want under her skirt but not a single one wanted to give her even a fifty-cent ring from an arcade machine.

Jules was under her skirt like the rest of them, but he was different, with the way he looked at her while she wriggled and shuddered out her orgasm, soaking his fingers and her underwear. The fabric was cool when it brushed against her hot, tender folds.

"There you are, gorgeous." He pinched her chin and drew her back down, this time sliding his tongue against hers in a languid but somehow dominant caress as he lifted his hips against hers. She rode the swells of his need, grinding back down against him and whimpering with every stroke of his fingers over her.

She wrapped her arm around his neck as his wings, independent of his shoulders or arms, shifted to push them standing again. Gravity did the work for him, sliding her down over his fingers. He spread and swirled them inside her, all three, stretching her and caressing places she hadn't known she needed his touch. Nova certainly had enough wetness from her orgasm to slick his way.

"I wish you could see yourself." He walked her backward, stumbling, clinging to him to keep her balance while he continued to fuck her with his fingers. Her back hit the leaning roof. The shingles were probably filthy as a smokestack, but she didn't care what smeared on her as he removed himself from her cunt and laid her out like a captive princess against the rough, sandpapery roof.

Gargoyles lined the concrete edges of the roof, their backs to Nova and Jules — although if they could hear, they certainly heard enough to know what was going on. When she looked up the incline of the roof, angels mingled with the demonic-looking gargoyles all along the top. Every university building, not just Religious Studies, was marked with the characteristic New Gothic architecture typical of Angela Cabrera, the Christian spiritualist who had helped found the city's renaissance and had been instrumental in lobbying for a UT branch at its heart.

According to the university's brochure, Cabrera had a team to help cast the sculptures, but the designs were all hers, and every single one of them was unique, made to protect the students, to protect the university, to protect Meridian — according to the stories.

Some of the angels and gargoyles gazed down upon Nova and Jules now, with Classical disapproval on their faces — some cherubic, some fierce, others grotesque.

"Do you feel the wounds on your back yet?" Jules asked. "They've always been there, but it sometimes takes a little time for the scales to fall from your eyes. I speak from experience."

Nova lowered her head from her contemplation of celestial- and terrestrial-bound bodies. "My wounds?"

"Well, I was going to ask you if it hurt when you fell from heaven, but I know it did, and I didn't want to be too cheesy."

"What the heck are you talking about?"

He held her hips as he apparently gauged whether to remove her skirt altogether, given it certainly wasn't keeping him from reaching all the right places underneath. However, she lifted her lower half from the roof, licked her lips as Jules slid her skirt and underwear down her legs. The thin, clingy material of the skirt slithered over her skin.

"I'm talking about the fever under your skin. I'm talking about the way you never belonged. They tried to make you. They tried to fit you into the mold, then condemned you when you couldn't and blamed you for their own weakness around you. Hell, your power right now isn't much more than a trickle, and it's not like you could control it when you didn't even know what it was. I'm going to help you break the dam, though, Nova. I'm not going to make your early days as difficult as mine were. This city is teeming with succubi and incubi like you and me, but they're usually all alone — from birth in a human womb through all the lonely years of immortality after the demon tears through the cocoon of this fragile false form."

"W-what?"

Jules lowered himself into a crouch before her, his wings draped behind him like a winter cloak. He gripped her thighs and stared up as though he worshiped her — not her breasts, not her cunt, not what she could do for him, but *her*.

"If I didn't already know, the fact that I can touch you without you completely losing your mind is enough to confirm that you're a sex demon, sweetheart. It's why men can't be around you without thinking about burying themselves inside you. It's why you can get off with them, even though they think of nothing but getting themselves off. It's nothing personal, which is the problem for many succubi in their early years. Am I right, pet?"

Nova pushed herself up on her elbows. "No. No. Succubi aren't real. They're a story, a myth — nothing more than sleep paralysis and night terrors. My younger sister has sleep paralysis. It's just a dream disorder."

"Then what do you think I am? I don't wear these wings for decoration, and they're not even my only pair," Jules said, amused. "It'll all come back to you, pet. It'll always seem like it belongs to someone else, your other life before being birthed into this one. But there's a point when you won't be able to deny what you are. I intend to help you."

"Help me accept your delusion? Sounds healthy. If I'm seeing what I'm seeing, you must have drugged me, maybe drugged yourself in the process. How else could you have had the strength to carry yourself and me up here?"

Jules rolled his eyes good-naturedly. "Psych majors. You're thinking about this too hard. Your body knows the truth. It knows what it wants to become, what waits just below the surface. Clearly, you're getting too much blood flow to that brain of yours. Let's see what I can do about that."

He kissed her left inner thigh, lifting the leg to bring it over his shoulder, behind his wing so that there was no easy way for her to slide her leg back. Half-reclined on the roof, Nova clung to the shingles and his shoulder, exhaling sharply as he kissed his way to her mound.

"Oh God," she gasped. *Is he really – ?*

Some of the guys had wanted in her mouth when they didn't want in her cunt, but when she'd tentatively suggested that they reciprocate for her pleasure, they'd snorted in disgust or pretended they hadn't heard her in their afterglow.

Nova had heard other girls talking about their boyfriends going down on them, how it made up for some of the other more troublesome parts of sex. Nova liked a cock inside her, but they never stayed long enough, the pleasure collapsing like a punctured tire, and they never asked if it was good for her, just stayed until she was sticky and they had to go to some fast-food restaurant for some jalapeño bites and a soda, so could she leave? They never even offered to buy her dinner.

People took and took and took and took from her, one way or another. Every time they emptied themselves into her — scoffing just as much at the idea of condoms as they did going down on her, asking only whether she was on the pill and shrugging when she said she wasn't — it was as though they emptied her out, too. They gouged at her insides with every insult, every day she sat alone at the cafeteria tables, every pull of her hair, every evening she went home and shut her bedroom door because she couldn't sit in her own living room to watch TV without her parents telling her she was dressed inappropriately — no matter how many clothes she'd put on. It had gotten to the point where she would come out for dinner in her bulky terrycloth robe and go back to her room when dinner was over, even though her mother had said that a robe wasn't respectful at the table.

All this sucked the life out of her, microliter by microliter. She didn't need a doctor to diagnose depression. She was also pretty sure that if this was all some cosmic Harlow experiment on affection, she was like the rhesus monkey they only gave a fucking wire doll to, to nurture her. Her mother hadn't even breastfed her as an infant.

No one ever gave her anything except when they were taking more.

So when Jules ran his tongue through the crevasse of her folds up to the bud of her clit to swirl his wet heat around her, stroking her thigh familiarly, comfortingly, it was no wonder that Nova melted like butter on a skillet once again.

Cries wrenched from her throat as he conjured sensations from her labia and clit that she'd never experienced before, sensations that she'd only ever imagined, yearned for without the words or memory to call upon. Her own fingers were nothing in comparison, the warm blossoming of her arousal nothing but sultry summer heat to this bonfire.

This time, when she dug her nails into Jules' shoulder, he didn't protest, only moaned into her, making her cant her hips from the vibration. She hadn't been prepared for how the low moan would shoot straight up her spine to explode in fireworks in her head.

He wriggled his tongue back between her folds and lapped at her, groaning his pleasure at how wet she was for him to drink from. The shingles rubbed her back and buttocks raw the more she rocked side to side, up and down, moving away and pressing forward against his touch — too much but not enough. She didn't think it would *ever* be enough.

Jules wiped his mouth and chin as he sat back on his heels, his smile cocky and endearing as he looked up at her writhing body, at the tears streaming down her cheeks from pleasure she had never known before. She'd always suspected it was possible, hiding just beneath the surface, but she'd assumed that it was never for her. The church would have amended that by adding 'until marriage', but Nova was no fool. As everyone kept telling her with self-important, self-congratulating nods, why would men buy the cow when they could get the milk for free? She was damaged goods. She'd thought she would never have any more than what she'd always had.

Until tonight. Until Jules. Nova panted, gazing down at him, this crazy man in a convincing wing harness or aided by particularly potent hallucinogens. It didn't matter if he was nuttier than a fruitcake. She was this close to promising him her firstborn child as well as any other fruit of her womb that he wanted sacrificed if he did *that* to her whenever she asked for the rest of her life. She'd let him put his cock anywhere he wanted in exchange for the pleasure of pleasure itself.

How could God make bodies to have such pleasure, then punish them for having it outside such narrow confines, especially for those who could never fit into those confines? Nova hadn't even known how deprived she'd been, how desperate, how wound tight with sexual frustration. Men complained about blue balls and painful deflations, but for her, deprivation left a different kind of discomfort too diffuse for her to put a finger on, a turn of the screws so slow that she hadn't even known that her thumbs had twisted clear around and that they weren't supposed to hurt like that.

"Never gets old, Nova." He climbed up her body, his hands on either side of her. "That's the great part about being a sex demon. Sex never gets old…and it's always good. It's what you were made for—lust, desire, pleasure—pleasure that you can now demand, that you can convince any man to give to you, instead of them just being drawn to your energy. You can have this all the time. You can have *whatever* you want, and they'll give it to you with a smile and thank you for the privilege."

She hadn't known how much her breast needed his touch until he gave her that tender brush of his cheek, although he avoided the nipple, both which were hard as pebbles now. She lifted her hands to tend to them herself, but Jules intercepted, encircling her wrists and pinning above her head to the roof.

"You're not done yet, are you, sweetheart? You can still take more from me. I could make you come a thousand times, and you'd still not be done. That's how many orgasms you need to make up for, after all this time. You can make your men give that to you and more, without them spilling a single drop of their seed on your pretty skin." As he spoke, he brushed her neck with his lips like moth wings, raising bumps on her arms, neck and scalp. "Here's the thing, though. I'm awfully hungry, and you're even hungrier. When you change, you won't be ready for how hungry you'll feel. It'll all come to the surface. I've been feeding all week to prepare for you, but now that I have you in my arms... I've never been much for restraining myself."

Nova strained against his hold on her wrists, baring her neck, arching her back, but he still didn't do anything more than those little brushes of his lips, his clothed hips against hers, her legs tangled with his.

"Then why start now?" she asked.

He grinned. "That's the spirit."

He abruptly released her wrists to run his hands down her arms as he closed his mouth over hers.

Every time Nova thought she was going to take over the kiss, move just the right way for him to lose his control like all the rest and do *something* — something that they both needed but she couldn't find the words for — he wrenched control from her again. She gave a moan as he reclaimed her mouth, the way his whole body seemed to caress her, from his denim-covered thigh pressing against her cunt to her breasts rubbing against his chest, an endless tease for nipples that desired mouth and fingers — something other than what she was getting. He dipped a hand down to rake through her folds and tease her swollen, sensitized clit. There were teeth on lips, sometimes hers, sometimes his.

He shifted his wings to surround them until he must have looked like a massive vulture preying on the dead. *Am I dead?* Could someone dead to this world feel so alive? Her whole life had been such a long, bad dream that she hadn't known she could be this awake.

Nova reached between them and undid his jeans. He wore nothing underneath, so when she shoved them down, she grabbed his firm ass, and he thrusted forward. His erection slid over the front half of her folds as he groaned into her mouth.

"You feel that yet, Nova?" he asked against her lips. "You feel my magic? I feel yours. Your pussy could make grown men beg. Will you beg me, pet?"

"I just want… I just want…" She gasped.

"Yes. Tell me. Tell me what you want from me, and I'll give it to you. Tell me."

It was the strangest thing. She'd said a lot since she'd started lifting her skirts for boys who crossed the line from interested to handsy—those times when it had seemed imperative that she let them in, in hopes that this one would give her what she'd been missing, when all she'd gotten those other times was disappointment. *You want me? Want to have sex with me? Want a better look? You have a place where we can be alone? Can I suck you off? You wanna come inside me?* And they'd said things back to her. Nasty, dirty, obscene things about what she was, what she was meant for, what she wasn't, what a filthy girl she was, how much she liked it—never asking if she did, of course.

She'd never told a man exactly what she wanted from him before. It struggled to leave her mouth with some semblance of naturalness, when her first impulse was to ask. But he was asking her what she wanted. She knew what she wanted, and it wasn't nearly as tentative as her tongue in the telling.

"Fuck me," she whispered, stroking his back and squeezing his ass, as though to assure herself that he was real in that moment. She found the place near his spine with her palm where his right wing began. The flesh- and feather-covered bone was firm as a bed knob, with smooth transition between back and wing, as seamless as shoulder to arm.

"What was that? I couldn't quite hear you, pet. I almost don't believe it's what you really want." Jules kissed the side of her mouth, then delicately licked the corner.

"I want you to fuck me," she said, a little louder. It was easier the second time.

Jules rolled his hips against hers, his cock passing through the front half of her folds and gliding over her clit. "You want *what*?"

"I want you to *fuck* me." She tossed her head back as he thrust through her folds more forcefully in response.

"Make me believe it, Nova. Make the whole university believe it."

"Get inside me and fuck me right *now*," Nova growled through clenched teeth, shaking her head as something inside her snapped free, ripping through her like a wolf rampaging a trail. "Fuck me like an animal. Use me and make me come before you do. Make me come around your pounding cock."

He bared his teeth in a smile like a predator. "That's what I like to hear."

He pushed himself back from the roof, grabbed her shoulders and spun her around. He slammed his hands down on hers to tell her to keep them on the roof, then dug his fingers into the flesh of her waist. With his other hand, he pressed his erection against the entrance of her cunt.

"Always good to be with a woman who knows what she wants." He nipped at her ear before thrusting his good, thick cock inside, where her juices dripped from her like oil.

She gasped, her moan caught so far back in her head that it couldn't escape her open mouth. Not once had it ever felt like this—never this good, as though nerves had awakened in her pussy that had never before existed.

Jules slid his hands up her waist and cupped her breasts, both more than a handful for his large hands, but he didn't seem to mind…and neither did she. He tortured her nipples with his palms, but at least they had something to rub against as he held himself tight against her, his chest to her back. He depended on her to hold them both up, lest they collapse against the roof. It wouldn't be such a terrible thing, but she also liked the control he gave her, as well as the intimacy it fostered.

She'd been taken from behind before. It meant that they hadn't needed to know or acknowledge her as any different from the last slut they'd stuck it into. They hadn't needed to remember that she had a face or a name or any of those complications. They could just focus on the hot body they were fucking.

When Jules fucked her from behind, she didn't feel superfluous, the intruder on someone's masturbation session. He grasped her, clung to her, tightened his grip, pressed his lips to her spine. He didn't have to kiss her like that. It did nothing for him, but he did it anyway, groaning vibrations down her vertebrae as he slammed his cock into her cunt, which tightened around him like a fist that never wanted to let him go.

But she was too soft and slippery to hold him, so he had to keep filling her over and over again to satisfy her need to keep him within her — leaving her only long enough to make her miss him.

It wasn't just another fuck. It was intimate, raw, not two people trying to rub off at different rhythms for different reasons but two people finding the same rhythm, almost becoming one creature with a singular desire greater than just coming.

Nova clawed at the roof, bending but not breaking her nails. She writhed beneath him, filling his hands, shoving back against his cock, feeling like a complete beast and loving every second of it. Her moans weren't anything a guy would see in a porn video, instead guttural growls that raked through her throat. The place where his hips hit her ass and where his thighs hit hers made obscene, dull slapping sounds, and she couldn't get enough of them, even though she was beginning to hurt from it. Physical ache was nothing in comparison to the psychological hollow carved out through the years. The pain made her feel present, alive, and it was such a small thing next to the pleasure he gave her — only made the pleasure sweeter, as though it wore away all the barriers and left her with nothing but pure sensation for its own sake, rather than any kind of expectation or condemnation. He'd stripped away her shields yet hadn't taken advantage of her nakedness, inside or outside. Even when he took from her, he gave.

Nova would do anything for this man. If he asked her to kill for him, she'd do it. She'd already crossed the line, smeared it right out. If vice was the only thing that could make her feel like this and virtue condemned her no matter what she did, what kind of choice was that? Virtue had never done anything for her.

Why had this been so hard for everyone else? Had a little love been so difficult to give, so difficult to find?

When she clawed at the roof, shrieking, the sandpapery shingles tore into curly ribbons that tumbled to the gravel. Nova arched and wrenched back and forth as she came around his pounding cock, clamping down on him like a velvet vise, just like she'd wanted.

It wasn't only her cunt pulling him in. He had to take his hands off her breasts to brace himself against the roof. Her breasts swung free with his thrusts, but her entire existence narrowed to the places his cock stroked. Her body became a giant sucking mouth, drawing not just on his erection or his cum but on something else deeper inside him that was somehow connected to his cock on a metaphysical level.

Jules shouted, his forehead on her shoulder, his hair a sweet, soft caress on her neck, as she *sucked* him in, swallowing and swallowing like the biggest cockslut in the world. She was practically screaming now as wings, wide and weighty yet strong on their own, unfolded out of her back in a flutter of black feathers, like a murder of crows launching from the ground all at once. The blades of her shoulders hurt, as though the wings had truly burst out of her skin, but none of that compared to the bone-deep pleasure of her climax. It kept rolling and rolling through her like thunder through a canyon as she continued to draw that exquisite, energizing vitality from him. The places inside her that had shriveled like raisins after years of systematic starvation suddenly swelled close to bursting. And there were still more reserves yet that needed to be filled.

She couldn't go on. It couldn't keep being this good. Her circuits overloaded, her mind swept blank by a giant hand until her vision went dark. She slumped against the roof, collapsed in complete and utter bliss.

Not yet totally satisfied, but God, it was good to get close.

Chapter Three

Nothing compared to the feeling of waking up to sunset outside his top-floor apartment window.

Eli kicked his legs over the side of the bed and stared out of the sliding doors. His bedroom was supposed to be the living room, but Eli never invited company over, so it made no difference if he wanted his living room to be a bedroom or a fucking garden. The room that was supposed to be his bedroom was his training room instead, conveniently located near the bathroom shower.

His cat, black with a white star on her chest, looked up at him from the foot of the bed where she'd been leaning against Eli's legs through the blankets. Eli just called her Cat. Tiny, effective killer of roaches, crickets, moths and the occasional mouse with high aspirations, she earned her keep in the House of Eli. He was proud of her for every mouse she put next to his boots. He was less proud when she managed to get them inside those boots, and he could match her glare for glare when she tore the legs off roaches and crickets and put them in his bed. She didn't do that much anymore, though.

Cat was the only other living being who saw the inside of his apartment. He sometimes satisfied his need for companionship but never in his own home. This was his sanctuary. This place held his secrets. He paid his rent on time with money from the collective, supplemented by his patron, and never made a fuss. He was the perfect tenant. No landlord had to come into his apartment for any reason, not even for repairs, which he did himself.

His home was simply a place to put up his feet, store his food and keep in shape. The rest of the evening he spent out. Nightfall was his time.

Eli pulled on cargo pants and a thin black sweater. It was autumn, but he wore the same uniform, regardless of season—all black, a nocturnal hunter's camouflage. As he removed the undershirt he slept in and pulled the sweater over his head, the most important of his tattoos was briefly revealed—a single, stylized blue eye near his hip, where it could be covered.

It didn't matter if a person saw it. What mattered was that the demons couldn't, that they didn't know he could see them as what they were, no matter how good their disguises. He could discern the most full-blooded demon flying through the sky or lumbering through the streets, but it was the hybrid demons that Eli really used it for—the ones who lurked behind spells of invisibility and glamours as opaque as fog. The conquest demons thought they were so clever, cuckoos and wasps and spiders who stole into the nests of their prey to conceal themselves in the midst of that which they hunted. Sometimes *they* didn't even know what they were, so effectively concealed were they. But they couldn't hide from him.

The next pieces of his uniform were smaller, just as black and just as important. He strapped on his combat boots after checking first to make sure they were empty of Cat's kills. He slipped his hands into thin leather gloves, supple enough for easy movement, as though there were no barrier at all. The last piece was a cotton ski mask, custom-made for him. It wouldn't have been much use for skiing, thin as it was, but it served its purpose. He tucked his trousers into his boots, tucked his sleeves into his gloves and tucked the bottom of the mask into the neck of the sweater.

Eli wasn't a burglar. He sometimes felt like a ninja, although he would never tell anyone that, because it made him feel like such a dork when he admitted it just to himself. However, neither a ninja nor a burglar would ever don the contraption that he now strapped around his shoulders and thighs. Neither a ninja nor a burglar would ever wear wings.

Eli hunted his prey where they hunted theirs — from the air.

Some demon hunters were indiscriminate, taking prey down as they came across them. Some demon hunters were strictly business, a few incorporated. Meridian was so teeming with dark magic that even the humans who couldn't see most of them noticed after a while, and these kinds of agencies usually had regular discreet work.

Eli was of another ilk — a hunter with only one kind of prey. Some were vampire hunters. Others specialized in werewolves, others in eradicating pestilence demons. Eli hunted incubi and succubi. As with the vampire hunters, it was an especially dangerous task, because it was easy for people going after conquest demons to get sucked into the very world they sought to eliminate. So many vampire hunters had become vampires themselves. So many hunters of incubi and succubi had succumbed to them all the way to the grave.

He prepared himself against such entrapment. When entering a spider's parlor, a man had to think like another spider, not a fly.

He couldn't protect his eyes, but he could protect every other square inch of his body from their tempting touch. The incubi were easier. They rarely did much to him. It was the succubi he really had to be careful around, because what they gave him was so much more than a minor effect. Eli had learned quickly how to think clearly while fighting with a raging hard-on, a skill Eli thought most men could benefit from, even just dealing with non-supernatural ladies, since most of them still had some kind of magic happening that made men stupid. But it wasn't the ladies' fault, and Eli had no sympathy for men who kept their brains in their balls. It was possible to learn control. It just took a genuine wish to conquer desire before it conquered you, and most men didn't care enough to get in the way of their own pleasure.

Eli had little confidence in his own species, but he fought for them just the same. No need to make a bad breed even worse by leaving incubi and succubi unchallenged.

He made sure the sliding door latched securely behind him in case Cat got it in her head to emulate her human. After checking that his silver-coated knives were in their sheaths on his chest straps, Eli reached into the pocket at the knee of his cargo pants and pulled out the artifact.

There were some benefits to one's patron being an inventor as well as an alchemist. It meant seamless machines that bridged the gap between magic and physics. It also meant a discount at the magic store, Book & Candle — one of the few neutral zones in the city that demon hunters mostly tolerated, because they needed to get their real spells and magic supplies from somewhere that took cash and asked no questions, just as much as the sketchier elements of the city did.

But just having an alchemist as a patron — especially one invested in his own inventions that were too magical to ever make him a great fortune — wasn't enough to keep Eli in soup cans and kitty litter. Albert was responsible only for providing him with tools or reimbursing him for some of his practical expenses. That's where the collective came into play. Demon hunter contract pay was rarely regular. Collectives were small groups that agreed to pay seventy-five percent of their earnings into the pool, which would be evenly paid out at the end of the month. This was useful if a hunter had a bad month or an injury. It also incentivized them to pay in when times were good and kills were plenty, because if they got lazy and decided to mooch off the collective for too long and for no good reason, they were usually kicked out by a unanimous vote and thoroughly dissuaded from ever cheating a collective again.

Eli wasn't part of an agency that killed for pay, but there were other ways for a demon hunter to make an income — usually through the help of a shop like Book & Candle but also through underground markets in specialty items. Vampire fangs, werewolf pelts, witches' bones… In the case of sex demons, Eli took claws, teeth, wings, sometimes skin if he could get it to the buyer on time, an incubus' penis or a succubus' breasts, only because it was more difficult to take a woman's genitals without mutilating them. The rest he burned to ash through an arrangement with a crematorium, after which he sold the ashes, or he left any remains to the more neutral pestilence demons. Eli was a big believer in not wasting his kills. He had to make whatever money he could, wherever he could. Most months, a hunter didn't do half bad, but when you didn't do your job for the money, that meant you weren't exactly sipping champagne.

He held the artifact—a little golden wheel, like a skinny doughnut, with spells etched into the top and bottom. As long as it was as hot as fresh bread in his palm, he knew it still worked. He tucked it back into its pocket.

The sex demons flew invisible through the city. Now, so could he. But he could see them, and they would never see him coming.

Aside from good water pressure and fewer vermin, this was the reason why Eli had chosen a top-floor apartment. It certainly wasn't for the view—or for the walk up the stairs.

He launched himself over the balcony rail and spread his mechanical wings.

They were one of Albert's greatest creations, responding to subtle movements of his shoulders as well as intention. It had taken Eli over a year to master them.

It almost made all those years fighting as a foot soldier worthwhile, to see the city like this.

Everything looked so much purer from the air, much more majestic. The mix of New Gothic and aggressively practical contemporary architecture, its trimmed and clean parks and the forest that ran the length of the river that cut through the city, the cemeteries right out of a horror television series... It was easy to forget that beneath all that were Meridian's parasites, human and demon, creeping out at night to feed upon its life's blood.

Eli could spend the whole night just flying, but when it came right down to it, the wings were a tool, a weapon against the enemy horde, and Eli had to do his part to pay the bills.

He swept back around the skyscrapers toward the housing developments—prime hunting ground for sex demons, which meant prime hunting ground for him.

The demons were clever. Even without magic working in their favor, they usually hunted alone and found prey quickly. While sleeping, people were helpless to their own desires. They invited sex demons in between the inhale of their snores. It was a cheat of an invitation—at least vampires had to work for theirs—but it was still genuine. After all, when the repressions and the suppressions of the day were stripped away, who would say no to mind-blowing sex, even if it could kill you?

A good incubus or succubus wouldn't kill their prey, wouldn't invite the scrutiny, but some killed with impunity that nevertheless didn't always raise a coroner's red flag. Unusual heart attacks and brain aneurysms were common in Meridian to the point of being negligible when marked as the cause of death. Local medical scholars had their theories—fracking, electromagnetic frequency, toxins in the water, new drugs, stress from a chronically overachieving populace. Bullshit...every last one.

It was a good thing those geniuses were stuck in that bullshit, though. They wouldn't know what to do with magical problems if they came up and bit them on the ass, wouldn't survive in Eli's world for a hot minute. Of course, non-supernatural problems were still big problems, but climate change just didn't seem all that imposing when you were in a knife fight with creatures of flesh and blood that could kill you now, not in a couple of decades, a century or not at all.

Eli wasn't looking to save the world. The world was beyond saving. But he could save a few people now and then. That was something concrete within his power. It was a hell of a job, but someone had to do it.

Some nights yielded nothing more than tired shoulders, an aching back and sweaty clothes. But if that flutter of wings was what he thought it was, tonight wouldn't be one of those nights.

Eli pulled his wings back and dove. Sometimes, he came across gargoyles doing their good work, but the creature slipped through a closed window as though it wasn't there, and Eli cursed under his breath. Not only was this definitely a sex demon—incubus, from the trousers—but he'd already entered the house.

Eli could throw sleeping gas canisters into a room that would render even the demon unconscious, and the owners of the house wouldn't awaken, but that required an open window. He was stealthy, but his magic tricks only went so far. When an incubus slipped into a closed house, Eli could only wait for him to leave. And a feed made them stronger, not lazy like people, so it was bad news all around. But once Eli found a target, he took it out, even if he waited all night while hearing the sounds of its feed, even if the victim died. Staying on target meant one incubus down, which might be more than he'd get if he soared off to search for another one.

The bedroom had a balcony. The door was locked when Eli carefully tried to open it. He peered through the window to confirm what he'd seen, but he didn't linger in watching the incubus mounting some man's wife as she wrapped her arms around him.

Her moans made it through the window, though. It was a wonder that it didn't wake her husband. Even if it had, the man wouldn't see anything, just his wife in the midst of the mother of all sex dreams. They'd probably even have some decent morning sex out of it if the woman wasn't dead or too drained.

That was another reason to kill the beasts. Infidelity, adultery, fornication, lust, all in a dream where a person couldn't possibly be expected to control themselves, and they certainly couldn't confess to a sin they didn't know they'd committed. That wasn't a problem with Eli so much, since he didn't think that would get a person in bad with the Big Man, but some people thought it did, and maybe they were the ones who were right instead of him. He couldn't know one way or another.

All he knew was that if the incubus was smart, he wouldn't kill the woman. Then Eli could kill him quickly instead of nice and slow in retaliation for life lost.

Eli climbed onto the balcony railing, praying it wouldn't splinter under his weight, and gripped the gutter as he both kept an ear open for when the incubus was finished and tried not to be a party to the act. It just wasn't right to listen.

But when the moans grew increasingly intense, he had to bend down and watch, because he needed to know if the woman died.

After the moans reached their peak, then fell off, the incubus climbed off the woman and pulled on his trousers, like a tryst sneaking away before morning. The woman was replete, her limbs splayed on either side of her.

Come on, come on, come on. Eli squinted through the window. It was hard to see chests moving from this distance, especially under sheets that incubi could slip through as easily as they flew through walls.

The woman turned over in her sleep, drawing closer to her husband, whose back was to her and who snored like a lumberjack. No wonder he hadn't heard his wife's moans. He was already used to a racket in his bedroom.

The important thing, though, wasn't the man's sleep apnea, but that the woman was alive.

Eli could afford to show mercy. He couldn't afford to loosen up. He turned and leaped toward the alley just as the incubus passed through the window again. Eli grabbed the incubus' legs, dragging the demon to the ground and landing on top of him to cushion the fall.

Through clothes, sex demons could still impact a man's desires, but thankfully, this one did absolutely nothing for or to Eli. That made what he had to do much easier.

Unlike many hunters, it wasn't personal for him. Before getting into demon hunting, he hadn't been attacked by a succubus. None of his family had been ravished or ravaged by a sex demon, as far as he knew. None of his friends or acquaintances had been killed. He and his had been blissfully unaffected by the poison of Meridian. He'd encountered hunters before he'd ever encountered what they hunted.

Back then, he'd been a technical writer with a penchant for roughing it in East Texas on weekends when he didn't have to bring his work home. Sometimes, he'd taken a whole week off and roamed west. There wasn't much in either direction, which had been the point.

Then he'd found a bar that catered to hunters. He'd just liked the on-tap offerings and local whiskeys. It had been several weeks before he'd realized what people were talking about around him. In his defense, he hadn't liked bringing his work home, but he'd had no problem bringing it to a bar, so he'd usually worked on his computer during these sessions or watched whatever game happened to be on the televisions.

Once they'd realized he didn't belong, first they'd frozen him out. Then his curiosity had led to him asking questions. Those questions had gotten him into a brawl. Emerging from that brawl victorious had earned him respect...and answers.

So Eli had no vendetta. It was just business — and it was the right thing to do.

Also, it was a fucking rush.

The incubus didn't know what hit him, but the thing about the invisibility spell was that once a person broke the fourth wall, the other person or demon could see him. *Pity*. It would really help him fight if he could stay invisible all the way through it.

Eli grinned at the stunned incubus as it took in Eli's head-to-toe uniform and gleaming golden wings, with wicked tips at the ends of its 'feathers'.

If the creature knew what was good for him, he would turn into his true self, the self underneath the fallen angel guise — with teeth, claws and bat wings like the gargoyles they'd become if they showed an ounce of repentance. But in all his years hunting these things, only three had ever turned full demon in front of him. Either they were that vain or they didn't always know about that other side of them, the evil underneath all the pretty with which they seduced their prey.

"What the hell are you?" The incubus spread his wings to their full span, his teeth becoming sharp and claws emerging from the nail beds. It wasn't even close to his real form, but it got the job done.

Eli didn't respond. You start talking to a demon, you might start thinking it was a person. Some demons — vampires, werewolves, witches — had actually been people once. Those, you could talk to sometimes, especially if they made themselves known to hunters as non-threats. That didn't necessarily mean they were treated as non-threats, but they were granted a kind of leniency as long as they kept their noses clean.

But demons like this? Better to just cut their heads off before they got their hooks in.

Eli pulled out two knives. They weren't the best of weapons because they required close-contact fighting — always a risk with sex demons. But silver bullets weren't always accurate in a gun, although he kept a pistol with silver bullets under his pillow. Knives were more reliable. Nick the skin and the silver wasn't poison like it was for werewolves, but it severely wounded them in a way that demons couldn't heal themselves from, at least not quickly. It hit the really hardcore demons even worse.

The moon reflected in the blades. The incubus stumbled back, his eyes widening as he realized what Eli was. The incubus was smart once again, because he didn't attack. He turned to run, trying to lift off right there from the alley rather than engage.

Eli ran after him and jumped into the air. Flight was harder to manage from the ground, but he had the strength for it. He rocked forward and landed the sole of his boot on the incubus' back, which folded forward at the blow, collapsing him onto the concrete once more.

"I didn't hurt anybody," the incubus begged, trying to stand, but Eli pressed his boot between the demon's wings. "Please. I don't want any trouble."

"You *are* trouble." Taking one of the knives between his teeth, Eli grabbed the handle of the other knife with both hands, then stabbed the incubus in his demonic skull.

The incubus twitched violently underneath Eli's boot.

"Easy-peasy," Eli muttered. "It'll be over in a moment."

The silver sank into the demon's brain. It wasn't enough to kill him forever—although it would kill him for quite a long time—but it allowed Eli to flip the demon over, taking care not to crumple his wings, and stab him in the heart. That was far more difficult than most horror movies made it out to be. If you missed the gap between ribs, it took as much brute strength as it did to stab a demon in the skull. Fortunately, Eli had that strength.

Eli dragged the incubus to the nearest drain, then unbuckled his backpack—a custom job that didn't get in the way of his wings. He was nowhere near one of his buyers, so the skin was out, too big to be preserved well. But he cut off the incubus' wings and bound them to the bottom of the backpack, and there were plastic specimen jars marked with spells in which he could store the claws, teeth and genitals, all intact.

Eli was good at his job, skilled and efficient. He couldn't always afford to take his time. Anyone could come home from a late night at the office at any moment.

But tonight had been a good night—a fast kill, easy money. Another demon down, one more tick in the ledger.

Fire would render the body to purified, valuable ash, but large fires tended to attract attention in the city. That's what the drain was for.

Without the wings, all it took was a few hard kicks to get the body into the drain. Meridian was infested with pestilence demons as well as the creatures that tended to hang around them, natural and supernatural. *Something* would consume the corpse long before it started to stink up the alley for some poor sewer worker to find.

Eli recalibrated his wings for the weight of the real ones swinging from his pack, climbed a fence and leaped off to take flight once again. He could kill one more before he had to head home to unload the goods. He was just one man, after all, and he didn't have drop-offs in every neighborhood in Meridian, nor did he trust another hunter with the fruits of his labor.

With the incubus wings on either side of his hips as he flew through the city, the teeth and claws rattling in their jars, Eli grinned against his mask.

This never gets old.

Chapter Four

Waking up was like climbing her way out of a tub of melted taffy. It didn't help that Nova was ensconced in a feather bed, weighed down by warm quilts that held her fever between the sheets, but it wasn't unbearable.

"Good evening, gorgeous." Jules stood from the sofa, which was situated in front of a TV playing at low volume. He looked like a normal guy. He was even wearing a T-shirt. "Feeling better?"

She pushed at the blankets. "I— How did I get here?"

"I carried you naked through campus. Oh, don't worry. No one could see you. They might have heard us fucking, but they probably thought we were a couple of cats. Campuses are full of strays and ferals. It happens."

"They could *hear* us?"

"No one knew it was you. Isn't that liberating, knowing that you can do whatever you like, wherever you like, whoever you like, however you like and no one can stop you? No one can even see you. All those people who hated or wanted you for your body, I walked you next to them, and they felt your energy. I daresay you'll do some real good business for the local convenience store when people's condoms run low. They'll think of you even when they don't know who you are or what you look like when you come. That'll just be for me. But they'll know, somehow, that whoever they have will fall far short of what they desired."

"So we really—" Nova started to ask, but when she finally got the blankets off of her, they folded down to her waist, where she could see plain as day that she was still completely naked.

She yanked one of the quilts up over her front. She wasn't used to men sticking around after sex. She wasn't used to waking up with them—or having them regard her so warmly after they'd already gotten what they wanted.

"Don't you remember every glorious second? I've been doing this for decades, pet, but I know *I'll* hold what we did right here for quite a while." Jules put a hand to his chest—intentionally dramatic, but at the same time, she didn't get the sense that he was laughing at her.

Something moved behind her. Nova twisted around, wondering if Jules had a dog that she'd been lying on.

She gave a small cry. *Wings.* She'd been sleeping on wings. And those wings were attached to her.

"Ah, yes," Jules said. "I feel particularly smug about that part. Coffee?"

"It's the middle of the night." She was too stunned to comment on the most relevant development.

"It's a new night. You slept through last night and all day. Transformation is a tiring process, and I did work you quite hard."

Nova tried again to get up, but her wings draped loose on either side of her, and although they moved, she freaked out when they did, because she could *feel* them when they moved like that. She could practically sense each new nerve pathway that told muscle and bone she'd never had before to shift. "I have classes!"

"You have wings."

"How do I make them go away?"

"Do you want that coffee?"

"Sure. Whatever." When she concentrated on the wings, she started to get a sense of how she could make them move independently of her arms and shoulders. It was fascinating, although they still didn't feel like *hers*, didn't feel real so much as a vivid dream, like last night. Up close and personal, though, she noticed that her feathers weren't as pure black as Jules'. They were closer to charcoal gray, as though dusted with ash.

"Why would you want to make them go away?" Jules asked as he put the pre-mixed cup into his coffee machine. There were wires all over the walls, extension cords that went into a hole in the wooden floor. The walls were concrete, the room a generous A-frame that ended in rose windows on either side, although there were no panes. Birds roosted in the rafters, but the floors were kept mostly clean, except for a few large feathers that looked like they could be his — or hers.

The details in the windows looked familiar, but she couldn't place them.

"They're kind of in the way," she said. "I can't go walking around naked, but I especially can't with wings. And the wings won't let me wear clothes."

"They work with halter and sleeveless tops." Again, she got the impression that he was secretly joking, but the joke wasn't on her.

"I can't wear those things." She hated the shrill sound of her voice when she was offended. And why she would be insulted by the implication that she was the kind of girl who wore those things when she'd just finished — or felt like she'd just finished — having wild sex with a stranger was beyond her.

"You're confusing 'can't' with 'won't'. Okay, strapless might be harder for a woman of your...bounty. But the right halter would hold you up, if you're talking practical. I only know this because I'm in contact with enough succubi like you who need to plan their stalking wardrobe accordingly. It's both easier and harder for men. We can't exactly go around shirtless everywhere, but it's a lot easier for us to take off our shirts than it is for you. And we're slightly less attached to our shirts than the women are. Well...most of us."

"But I—"

"What are you afraid of, Nova?" He brought her the mug and sat on the edge of the bed. "You afraid they're going to notice you have breasts? Everyone already knows. You could wear a burlap sack and make it look like a pinup costume. You're a succubus. It's your nature."

"But the boys in class won't be able to concentrate. The professors. Everyone..."

"A few days ago, that would have been their problem. But what makes you think you're ever going to class again?"

"What are you talking about?"

"Even if I tell you how to draw your wings back in—and I will, pet, don't worry about that—it doesn't matter. You were attractive before, in the literal sense of the word. You've always been a succubus. You just didn't have enough of your power, and you were unable to control what did make it out of you. Like scentless smoke, any man could breathe it in and get turned on without realizing where the desire came from. Now, you have the full breadth of your power to draw upon, but you're going to be utterly irresistible, no matter how tightly you hold it in. A single touch will make a man your willing slave, and you think it's a good idea for you to go back to your classes as though nothing has changed?"

"I'm used to not touching people. I'll stay out of everyone's way. But people are going to wonder where I am and why I'm not in class. My parents—"

"They won't miss you," Jules interrupted sharply. "They won't mourn your disappearance. On some unconscious or even conscious level, they'll be relieved that you're out of their hands. All the more reason not to care what they want from you."

"What are you saying?" She couldn't help the tremble in her voice. It hurt worse because she knew it was true.

"Deep down, you know they aren't your real parents. Your father isn't your father. Your mother was a carrier, the nest in which some incubus left his seed, which sprouted independently of any human fertilization. You were stolen into their home so that they could raise and nurture you, baby bird, although there's usually tension between parents and a false child. You know what I'm talking about. They sense you're not their daughter, although you took on their features like a mimic. If you never came home, they wouldn't waste a minute's sleep worrying."

Nova's wings fluttered restlessly. God, there it was, the first set of tears swimming over her lower lids. She was so damn embarrassed that this man had to see her cry.

"Fuck, Nova." Jules slid closer to thumb away the tears. "I didn't mean to get so harsh. I just need you to understand the reality of the situation. And because they're not wasting time on you, you don't want to waste your tears on them, right? Everything's going to change, pet. As bad as it was, it's only going to get better now that you know what you are and can have whatever you want. You could make whole cities fall at your feet if you wanted to. Meridian has more competition, but you can go to another town, demand that they adorn you with tiaras to toe rings and they'd do it for you. No more classes. No more fumblings. No more loneliness. No more reaching for nothing but air. You can have everything you've ever wanted and more."

"All I ever wanted was to be normal. You think you can make me normal, Jules? I've got *wings* sprouting from my back."

Jules curled a lock of her hair around his finger. "You don't want to be normal, sweetheart. What you want is to be loved. And you think the only way they can love you is if you're normal. You're so far from right. And I'm going to show you tonight how wrong you are. Don't worry. You'll really like it. I need to feed, too. Maybe we'll find a nice couple shacking up in the dorms where they shouldn't be. That would be a tasty convenience."

"Jules, where are we?" Nova peered through the window. The bed was equidistant between the two windows, so which one didn't matter. However, there was something familiar out of the one to her right, a silhouette of a building that she...

That she walked by every day. It was the Administration Office of the university.

"We're still on campus. What is this place?"

"We're the bats in the belfry of the Art Department," Jules said. "I like it here, and I figured the art folk wouldn't question getting randomly aroused, while the Mathematics Department would look for gas leaks."

Nova looked around at the home he'd made—a huge bed, generous helping of blankets, assorted couches and chairs, a TV that did not look cheap, a computer, a small area with all kinds of portable kitchen appliances. He'd even found a way to get running water, because there was a bathroom in the back.

"What I couldn't scavenge, I stole. What I couldn't steal, I had someone work their magic," Jules said, following her gaze. "I like the little luxuries. So the building uses a little more electricity and water than they budget for. It's only a little, not enough for them to break through the attic to find the door that leads here. I was lucky I was able to fly you up, though, after the draining you gave me. I'd stuffed myself silly for a week, and you still nearly cleared me out. You must have been seriously lacking good sex in your life, love."

"What did I do?" she asked.

"Like I said, the transformation takes a lot of energy. Well, that energy has to come from somewhere. If you'd let that diddling priest fuck you, you would have taken him for everything he had. As luck would have it, you had me, and you can't kill me with your feed. Well, it wasn't really luck, and you can still make a hell of a dent."

Nova crawled back, but she'd already forgotten about her wings, and they got in her way. They twitched from her annoyance. "You're telling me that if I'd let him... He would have died?"

"I'm not saying it would have definitely been him, not the way he was making everything about him and nothing about you. But if not him, then the next guy...or the next. You were right on the cusp of transformation. I tipped you over the edge because I fed your need. And then you fed from me. You probably weren't aware of it at the time, what with the passing out and all, but that's why I walked you home instead of flew. It's been a while since I had sex with a succubus who took so much from me."

She lowered her eyes. "Sorry."

"I'm not. There's nothing for you to apologize for. Everyone's taken everything from you or else you wouldn't have needed so much from me. The rest of your life will be about you taking what's yours. You deserve that much."

Nothing Jules said made sense to her. She gave because other people needed her to give. She didn't take because she didn't deserve to take. It wasn't her place to steal what was his, even though she couldn't remember doing it and wouldn't have known how to stop it anyway.

"You can take it back now." She slowly let the quilt drop down the front of her body, although she kept her eyes lowered. "I don't need it anymore. If you want it..."

Jules dipped his head down and kissed her, cutting her words off. He relished her lips, combing the tips of his fingers through her hair until she was nearly breathless, no matter how simple and practically chaste the kiss was. Her chest aching, she clutched at his shoulder to pull him closer. Jules groaned as he turned his head away.

"Of course, I want you, Nova. But I don't need to feed off you. We can go out and get more. There's an ocean of life out there. Why would I need to take it from *you*?" Jules took her face in his gentle hands. "When we do this, when we feed from each other, it's not going to be like last time. You'll be sated. I'll be sated. Our energies and our feed will be equal. And whenever it's unequal, I'll give you the lion's share, pet, because you need it more than I do, young and new as you are. Maybe if you get enough, you'll start believing you deserve it."

He pressed one more kiss to her lips. Nova whimpered, his touch like moonlight to jasmine.

"God, all that magic," he murmured against her lips. "If only you knew how powerful you are. I could climb into this bed and take you right now, but that's just what you think I should do, take you and take back what was mine. You don't know that if I had you now, you'd just take more from me, hungry little thing. All the more reason why I should take you out."

Jules quickly climbed off the bed, adjusting the front of his jeans before turning back to her. He gazed longingly at her breasts.

"I haven't paid those nearly the attention they're due," he muttered. "But you can always get a new boy toy to do what you like to them. Now, do you want to learn how to pull your wings back in?"

"Clothes?" Nova asked.

"Details, details," he said with a grin. "Don't worry. I raided your dorm while your roommate was out. I have the salient pieces of your property. I left some of it behind, though, including some of your clothes. You can dress however you want now. You can walk straight into any high-end boutique, put on the hottest dress and the most expensive jewelry, walk out and no one will ever know you were there. I can't wait to see you in some of the things I've imagined you in. I stole into a room of someone who has your figure and procured a few items, too. There's absolutely no redeeming moral value to them, but they'll make you feel like a new woman. Trust me."

Jules helped her out of bed. She wanted to bring the quilt with her, but he extricated it from her fists.

"Nothing I haven't already seen from multiple angles. Besides, I got an especially good look while I was bathing you. You were covered with roof dirt, not to mention other things. Both of us were."

Her cheeks flamed. She kept glancing between him and the windows.

"No one can see in," he said. "To them, the window is dark, not even the flickering of the TV light. Just another clever little charm. Now, can you hold your wings out?"

She'd been dragging them behind her, twitching them up a little now and then, but she concentrated, tested the new muscles until she could raise the wings so that they no longer touched the floor.

"There's a girl. A lovely pair. Wouldn't expect anything less. Hold them out, pet. They're strong, just like you are. That's right. I'm just making sure you know how to use them. I know you don't trust yourself to fly yet. You've smudged instinct right out of yourself. I was lucky to be a part of bringing it back last night, but you're…"

He sighed at the way she crossed her arms over her breasts. She could close her legs to hide most of her cunt, but only her arms could cover her breasts — or at least attempt to cover most of them.

"What?" she said. "I'm *what?*"

"Damaged. You aren't the first succubus who needs a while to get used to this life."

"What if I don't want it? What if, after all you show me, I still don't want it."

"You will," he insisted. "But saying you don't want to be a succubus is the same as a spider saying she doesn't want to be a spider. We are what we are, Nova. I understand that's hard for you to understand after working all your life to be something you're not. You're not alone in that. Most people are taught to be everything except what they are. What they are is bad. What they are is evil. What they are, what they were created to be, is depraved and wicked. Instead, let's be this thing that's impossible to attain! No wonder everyone's miserable. No wonder you're even more miserable than average. Do I look miserable, Nova?"

She shook her head.

"Is happiness and contentment a sin, and fear and misery a virtue?"

She shrugged. He was trying to confuse her, but she didn't know how to respond.

Jules took her by the shoulders and stared into her eyes. "Whatever you do, it's what you were born for. You need to understand that. The Big Man doesn't throw the hyena into the Pit for taking down a wildebeest. He doesn't condemn the spider for eating the fly. They call us evil, sweetheart, because we're higher up on the food chain. They'll kill a man-eating tiger because he has a taste for man-flesh, but they think nothing of the rape of their lands and the murder of their beasts. Leave behind everything you've ever believed and fold your wings in as far as you can pull them."

"What?" But Nova had already tucked her wings halfway inside her by the time she realized what he'd asked — like folding a tent into its bag.

"See?" He patted her cheek. "Instinct. Know it. Love it. Reclaim it. Now, you look like you want some clothes."

She refused to even consider the clothes that Jules had stolen from another girl's room. She noticed some of her more shapeless clothing weren't present in her suitcase, but he'd collected her computer and some of her more significant personal items that hadn't been in her purse.

Photographs of a happy family that had managed to look related for the camera, at least for a few seconds. It hurt to see those pictures. She turned them over under her clothes.

Her jewelry box. She hadn't been permitted a lot of jewelry, especially not necklaces, but she had a delicate golden cross necklace from her early teenage years, small earrings, a gold purity ring with a small, unironic pearl set in a circle of diamonds. That had been a gift from her father during her *quinceañera*, a modest party with a few classmates and her extended family. The whole family had chipped in, as though the cost of the ring would constitute a large enough investment in her virginity that she would keep it. They hadn't known that she'd already lost it, and she'd kept that fact to herself. It didn't fit her ring finger, anyway.

She put it back in the jewelry box and continued going through her clothes until she found a long gray skirt and dark gray short-sleeved shirt combination that helped her feel comfortable again. When she tried to add a sweater to cover her arms and hide some of her curves, Jules clicked his tongue.

"We'll just be invisible anyway, right?" Nova said.

"Not at first. I'll teach you invisibility when we get to the dorms. But for fuck's sake, Nova, you're dressed like an Orthodox...something. You don't need a sweater. You're appropriate—whatever that means—and you're fucking gorgeous and sexy, no matter what you wear. You might as well wear what you want, not what you think other people want you to wear."

"Like what *you* want me to wear?"

He rolled his eyes, but she thought he was secretly pleased. When she continued to pull the sweater on, he didn't stop her. "You're going to burn up in that," was all he said.

She'd already gone to hell for taking off a sweater. She'd do it again if she had to. But for now, she just wanted to feel like herself.

Having her clothes on didn't exactly help with that, however. Her wings were nestled inside her, as they always had been, but now she *knew* what that feeling was, and she was all the more aware of it now. Also, along with the pleasant fever and arousal from Jules' kiss, her skin felt different. It all looked the same to her, but *she* wasn't the same, because she had wings in her back, claws in place of nails when she'd torn through the roof shingles and she thought she might have had sharper teeth before losing consciousness. She vibrated at the wrong frequency. Or maybe it was finally the right frequency for her, but the wrong frequency for what she ought to be.

"I feel underdressed now," Jules said. "You hungry?"

"Starving."

He laughed. "Not that kind of hungry. Although you slept all day, so no wonder you're that kind of hungry, too. We'll grab a pie after we feed. It really works up an appetite."

"That makes no sense."

"It will. Hold my shirt. I'll fly us down."

* * * *

Nova was used to people's attention, but not like this.

As usual, the boys' gazes crawled over her like tentacles, but then they'd raise their eyes to hers — seeing her, discovering her, and not just her breasts or her butt or the swing of her hips. They turned to look over their shoulder when she passed them, as though they wished they could follow. They visibly envied where Jules had intertwined his fingers with hers, laying his claim — but claim didn't mean they couldn't fantasize, and she could see on their faces that they did. But they fantasized about *her*, not her body. It was a subtle difference that made all the difference — between them wanting some*thing* and wanting some*one.*

Then there were the girls. Nova was accustomed to glares, especially from girlfriends, or being treated as though she were invisible. But that wasn't the case now. Coeds looked her over, registered her as a woman, sometimes showing admiration or envy, but the emotions never reached the realm of anger at things that Nova couldn't control. Then the girl or girls just walked by. A few of them smiled in cordial, quiet greeting. *Smiled…at her*. How long had it been since a girl had smiled at her where it reached their eyes? Nova didn't think it was just because she held a man's hand — off the market, so to speak.

She didn't know how to handle it. The change was good, for the better. But what was she doing differently, and how could she have done it differently in the past?

And the only answer was that, after her transformation, she was in sync with what she was supposed to be, as though the harmony resonated much better than the dissonance she'd once emanated. And that wasn't anything she'd ever had any control over — which meant there had literally been *nothing* she could have done all those years to make people like her rather than just want to bone her or stab her in the chest with a nail file.

She tightened her grip on Jules' hand. She clenched her other fist as well, digging her nails into the palm. If she hurt Jules, he neither commented nor flinched.

"These are the senior dorms," she said as they went off the walkway and around the corner of one of the towers. Senior dorms meant suites with high ceilings, bigger bathrooms, separation between living space and bedrooms. It wasn't quite the A-frame loft that Jules had made for himself, but it was decent square footage in comparison with the grocery store shelf of her freshman dorm.

"Excellent deduction, Watson," he replied.

"Don't be a smart aleck."

"Then don't tell me there's not some cute senior boy you've had your eye on — soccer star, All-American good looks like a superhero, dumb as a box of bricks, but you've imagined what it would be like to climb that tree at least once."

"No senior fantasy, no. Most of my classes are with other freshmen, getting the core subjects out of the way."

"Damn, that's boring. I guess we'll have to window shop. Ready to learn how to go invisible and walk-through walls?"

"So that's how you got into Father Marcus' office."

"Elementary, my dear."

"Smart aleck."

"What am I, a preschooler?" he said brightly. "Now, use your frustration to shut out your mind. Push your heat out of you, like blowing a really big bubble of gum. You'll feel a chill inside, as though a ghost has entered you. That means the magic is working. Anyone within the heat's sphere will get a hefty dose of lust juice, but that's what you're using it for anyway. You know how to do this, Nova. The demon knows. You just forgot, in all those years of being human."

Nova lost her grip. She thought she'd almost had it, that the heat was moving out of her, but being reminded that she was a demon caught her like a tar pit.

"You were so close," Jules said.

"You called me a demon."

"It's what you are, pet."

"It's not what I want to be."

"Would you rather I just call you a succubus and not mention the d-word? It's a bandage on a birthmark, but whatever helps you accept yourself."

It was a lie by omission, but she nodded anyway.

"Besides, if you really didn't want to be a demon, Nova, you wouldn't be one. Chew on that for a while. Try going invisible again."

"What do you mean by that?"

"Come on. You know the stories. You're a demon because you were once an angel. You won't remember your fall for a long time. Some never do. But you already made a choice. And you can make another one. Because you're here by my side right now and not perched on some roof somewhere, carved in cold stone, I assume that, however you protest at being a succubus, you don't really mean it." Jules nudged her chest right above her breasts, near her heart. "Your spirit is succubus, love, which means you have a taste for what it has to offer. That isn't the end of the world. We serve our purpose, too."

Nova stepped away from him. "Yeah…evil."

"Temptation. Can't have redemption without it." Jules followed her until he could grab her hand again. "How about this, Nova? Give me a month — a month to show you this world, my world, your world, not the world you tried to fit yourself into. The Amish have their *rumspringa*. Angels have something like that, too, believe it or not, like a practice fall onto a very slow trampoline. A little rebellion is good for the soul. It makes you strong when you know what you really want, and that means trying new things now and then."

"Even if they're sins, with the consequence of death? That kind of trying new things?" she shot back.

"It's just a month. Then you can Hail Mary your way out of my life and into a convent or something like that, if that's your dearly departed wish." He released her hand and held his up in a cautious surrender. "I won't hold you back. Scout's honor."

"I doubt you were one."

"Promise, then."

Nova crossed her arms and leaned against the pale brick, narrowing her eyes. How an incubus managed to appear so guileless was a question for the ages.

"If I do this…don't rush me," she said finally.

"Okay, this isn't technically rushing you, but the sooner we feed, the sooner we get that pizza. Your stomach agrees that we should get into that dorm."

"You aren't a smart aleck anymore. Now you're a smartass."

"I love it when you talk dirty. No, I really do."

Chapter Five

After the tension from their discussion, however, Nova lost touch with her magic and couldn't make herself invisible, no matter how hard she tried.

"You're too cerebral about it." Jules pinched her chin with affectionate frustration. "Maybe it would be better to teach you invisibility when you're full instead of hungry. And it would be easier for me to teach it full, too."

"How long did it take you to learn?" she asked, less affectionate in her frustration, made worse by the fact that she didn't know what to be frustrated by — that she couldn't make herself invisible or that she'd agreed to do this in the first place.

He could talk about it in food terms all he wanted. What they were going to do was suck some kind of energy or life out of a man and a woman like psychosexual vampires. That's what they were, when it came right down to it — just another kind of vampire.

She gritted her teeth too tightly to ask if vampires, the traditional kind, existed like they did.

"I didn't learn how to fly properly until after about two weeks. Invisibility came easier. I had that in three days. So don't get too down on yourself. The transformation takes moments. The transition takes longer. Don't worry. I'll take over from here. We'll have to walk, but I don't think you'll be thwarted by a few flights of stairs."

Nova accepted Jules' proffered hand. The touch immediately reawakened her arousal, narrowed her attention to where their hands met—warm, firm, a reminder of better things he could do to her with that hand. Things he had already done. Things she'd only imagined.

"I'd give you a few more rounds, pet, but I think you'll get so much more out of one of the students in there. You're just feeling the effects of my sending out the magic. It makes the air around you as effective as your skin, makes your skin even more potent." He nuzzled her loose hair like a feline. "Let's go get ourselves a treat."

She didn't have her student ID to swipe in order to get in, but they didn't need it, nor did they need to wait for a late-night return to the dorm. Jules walked her straight through the clear glass doors. She didn't even feel them going through her. There might as well have been nothing there.

It was a strong enough shock that her urge to pull Jules against the wall and convince him to take a detour drifted aside—not least because she wasn't sure the wall would hold them or whether they'd go straight through if he didn't anticipate her.

"We can walk through walls and doors, fly through windows and roofs, you name it," Jules said quietly, which confirmed to her that, although no one would be able to see them, they could still be heard. "It's not quite that easy getting into a person's sleep. But you'll see, when we find just the right people."

They dispensed with the formality of hallways. Walking through the dorm rooms fascinated her. It was college, so there were always some people still awake at three o'clock. Every room was built the same, the suites mirror images of each other. The dorm was coed, which meant that one suite could consist of four or five girls, but the one next to them could have four or five guys — more or less, depending on whether they were in another person's room, in a late-night video game session, partying like it was 1999 or the whole room was out. Meridian had a strong night life. Nova was beginning to understand why.

There was a girls' room where one of the roommates slept while the other worked at her computer without any light in the room except from the screen. There was a guys' room in which one guy was ass-deep in another. She watched them intently, caught between judgment and intrigue.

Jules drew her out of the room with a grin. While they walked in the walls between the rooms, he whispered, "I don't think you'd do much for them, pet."

In one girls' room, Bibles had been tossed onto one of the beds while the girls talked among themselves. Probably not a three-in-the-morning Bible study so much as an evening study or prayer group that had become a night of fellowship, in the interdenominational nomenclature. Nova had tried a Bible study group. It hadn't gone very well.

In a guys' room, one of the boys was asleep, but the other was masturbating under his sheets.

At Jules' silent encouragement—and under the compulsion of her own curiosity—Nova eased closer to the boy. The closer she came, the faster his hand went. His face contorted as though in pain. Nova watched him in the darkness with wide eyes. She was used to men treating her as though she didn't exist, even while taking her, but she wasn't used to men really not knowing that she was there. There was a strangely innocent quality to their faces when they thought they were alone, none of the hardness or arrogance she'd always see—or the cruelty, if she was being completely honest.

Nova trailed her fingers over the blue comforter covering his chest down to where he moved his hand. One second, she was touching cotton. The next, her fingers slipped through, the way she and Jules had walked through the walls, and she touched his warm hip.

His eyes flew open, peering through the darkness, but he couldn't see her.

Emboldened, Nova moved her hand to the side to grope his cock.

The boy's hands fell to either side of his hips as he bucked up into the phantom hand encircling his erection, quickly bringing him over his edge.

"The fuck?" he gasped, looking around.

But Nova had already withdrawn, shocked by her own boldness, shocked that he had just given in to an invisible hand that could have belonged to anything at all.

The boy fell back on his pillow, panting. He pulled one of his hands out from under his sheets and rested it against his forehead, shaking his head. "Get a grip," he whispered. "Wow."

Jules drew her away while Nova idly brought her hand to her mouth, where a few spurts of the senior boy's semen had coated her fingers. She couldn't help a moan as she licked it off and swallowed it down.

Turned out it wasn't just her cunt that could feed. Even a little cum was as good as the coffee that Jules had offered her earlier, but it triggered a different place inside her. Not the mind, but the…Jules had called it 'spirit'. If she was a demon, she didn't have a soul—no soul to save, no soul to damn, no soul to make a difference. Did demons have a spirit, or were demons spirits themselves?

"Did you like that?" Jules whispered, wrapping his arm around her shoulders. She turned her head to meet his lips as he walked her into the next room, fighting not to laugh as he clearly tasted the boy in her mouth.

Then he pulled away and smiled widely, his mouth full of too-perfect teeth as he looked down upon the clinch of human limbs tangled on a pair of twin beds that had been pushed together.

It wasn't permitted for boys to live with girls. Married or cohabiting couples had to find off-campus accommodations. But people always found a way around it, usually by keeping an ear to the ground for RA inspections. Sometimes, the RAs were even in on it, either because they didn't have the energy to fight hormones or they had their own secrets to keep quiet.

Suffice it to say, this probably wasn't the only dorm room where a young woman was happily tucked against an equally happy young man. It had taken Jules and Nova three floors to find a pair literally sleeping together, but there were ten floors yet in this one senior dorm and twelve dorms in all. Nova didn't have to be a math major to do the calculation.

"Now, look at that. How sweet, aren't they, pet?" Jules murmured. "You ready for your first feed?"

"What— What do I do?"

"I'm going to let go of you. You won't be invisible anymore. You need to get closer to him. I'll take her." He kissed her neck, then walked around the makeshift king-size bed to sit next to the girl.

Nova tentatively mirrored him, slipping next to the boy. The two of them were cuddled together on top of the sheets. Nova could see everything. The man was husky, his stomach soft, his legs lightly furred and splayed, his cock replete over his scrotum, his nipples brown and small on the chest that pillowed his girlfriend. He looked so...peaceful.

"For a really good feed, a fulfilling one, you have to slip into their dreams," Jules said. "To do that, you need to ask their permission. It's a formality, but a necessary one."

"Why can't we just have sex with awake people?" she whispered.

"People who are awake are doughnuts and ice cream—sweet, delicious, filling but ultimately not what you need. Sleeping people give you everything, their deepest, most unspoken secret desires. But if it's against their will, it's harder to take and not as good for you or them. They have to agree to it. Like I said, a mere formality. I've never had a soul deny me. No one denies something they've always wanted."

Jules didn't say it, but Nova could extrapolate. If she was temptation incarnate, her job was to tempt. The person's job was to accept or decline her temptation. And according to Jules, everyone gave in. She couldn't throw stones. Her own sins lined up like Easter Island idols in her mind, but they seemed hollow now. She wasn't human. She didn't have a soul. And if she didn't have a soul, how could she sin?

And if temptation was what she was made for, how could she resist what those with souls couldn't?

Nova looked down at the boy as Jules touched the girl's shoulder, drawing her away from her lover to display her slender body to the incubus.

Nova stroked her fingers over the boy's face, tilting it toward her. She stared into his closed eyes, then closed her own. With the heat of her magic that drifted out of her like mist, she reached into his unconscious mind. It wasn't a literal door in front of her, but it was *like* a door, and what she did was as close to knocking as she could manage.

She saw the man, looking the way he conceived of himself, clothed, only slightly different in appearance, standing across an empty room from her.

"Hello." She wasn't sure what else she was supposed to say, since he wasn't saying anything.

He seemed embarrassed and awkward across from her. *"Um…hi."*

Just looking at him inundated her with information—His name was Taylor Grimes, and he was graduating at the end of the school year with a major in business. He was thinking about popping the question to his girlfriend, Kim, and he missed his dogs at home, and…

She looked down at herself, in part to disconnect herself from the flood of humanity that threatened to drown her hunger. She was wearing the same thing here that she wore in the bedroom. It wasn't the best outfit to seduce a man, not that she'd ever had any real trouble with her shapeless wardrobe. Still, with a thought, she abruptly changed into a little black dress, no underwear underneath. Somehow, he could tell — and she could tell that he could tell. When she glanced back up at him, he swallowed thickly.

"Do you want me?"

He swallowed again and nodded.

"Let me in?" She held her hand out to him in the blank room of his mind as she leaned closer to him in his bed, her breath puffing against his lips and back to hers, to breathe in his scent — as mouth-watering to her as the smell of baking, for a whole different set of reasons. She didn't quite kiss him, but Taylor stirred on his mattress, twisting and turning over the sheets as though reaching for her with his body.

"Hell, yeah," Taylor breathed.

As she shed her clothes and climbed on top of the boy and Jules did the same to the girl, Nova slipped into his dream, his fantasy, the place where his mind went when he saw what she had to offer him. It was curious, moving through a dream when she wasn't the one sleeping. With her conscious mind sharp, she sensed the tenuousness of the dream reality, so tenuous that she thought she could manipulate it as easily as she sensed the current of emotions, thoughts, wishes, desires, fears and shame running underneath — as though every bit of him resided in this dream, unsuppressed by his waking mind.

He created the fantasy, but for the first time, even though she was the object of that fantasy, Nova was in control — in control of her sexuality, in control of his, in control of everything.

And God, when she stared down at him in his bed and stared at him across the crowded bar of his mind, she was so…fucking…hungry.

He sits at a booth, the table littered with bottles, a mostly finished pitcher and baskets of what once held fried food. He stops talking with his friends the second he catches sight of her.

She stands at the bar, drinking a martini and holding her cocktail pick with the olives still impaled upon it inside the drink.

His first thought is that she can't possibly be here alone. She has to be waiting for someone. She's younger than him, fresh, every lush inch of her firm, high and ripe. No woman who looks like that stays unattached for long.

His mouth waters when she turns in profile so that he gets a good gander at the double shots of her tits and ass. He could ogle that fine body for days. Hell, he's young, no one holding him down, no girlfriend, no mother glaring at him to stop appreciating a woman. He can look to his heart's content.

But as he watches, no one joins her. Some men try, oh, yes. They slip into the seat next to her, but she rebuffs each one, her warm smile never turning icy but her eyes somehow hard as she tells each of the men to leave her alone, scram, take a hike. It makes his heart jolt every time. Ridiculous, he knows, because she's sure as hell not saving herself for him.

Maybe she's a working girl, and they aren't willing to pay.

Nah. He doesn't think he's ever seen a prostitute working a bar this close to campus. He's heard of a few hotels down south of the campus where you can request company, but those are just rumors and nothing he's ever tried, although he's thought about it, of course. He usually does fine with women, though, never needs to pay more than a drink and a dinner when he wants one, and he treats them good, so they treat him good. It's all good.

She's not wearing a bra under that strapless piece of cotton she calls a dress. Even in the dim light of the bar, he discerns the outline of her nipples, and they're not even hard. Also, he's mostly sure she's not wearing panties, even a thong has straps over the hips that would show under a dress that tight.

Oh crap, she's looking at him. How long has she been looking at him while he's been staring at her?

Holy fuck, is she really bringing that cocktail pick to her mouth, closing those perfect, naturally dark lips around each olive, one at a time, sucking the gin with the sharp, salty brine...?

She slides them smooth and slow off the pick and swallows them whole while he watches. He imagines those lips closing so sweetly over his balls, those eyelashes fluttering as she takes one side in, then the other, savoring them in the same way. He's got a regular boner in his shorts, chubbed so hard that he's surprised it hasn't lifted up the table. His friends haven't noticed, either, their chatter faded into silence in the booth.

She brings the rest of the drink to her lips and throws it back, her throat working in an elegant ripple as she swallows. Her untamed hair spills over her shoulders, some locks curling over her prominent breasts like a tease.

The girl pulls a twenty from her cleavage. His mouth goes dry, and he worries he might come as she bends over the bar to give the bartender the bill. If he leans down a little, he thinks he might glimpse the delta of her pussy, but he doesn't want to alert his friends to the ten he's homed in on. For some reason, he doesn't want them gawking at her like he is – like she lets him, as though by silent agreement over the crowd.

She pushes herself up from the bar – God, the bartender probably had a million-dollar view himself – and makes her *way through the crowd…toward him, stalking him through all the people like a lioness hunting through tall grass on the savanna. He can't hear them over the din, but he imagines the click of her tall, black stilettos.*

Yep, definitely no bra. *Her boobs jiggle with each step, and now he can really see the nipples, two dark points against the fabric. She still has her eyes on him, her eyes black through the irises as though in a perpetually aroused state. She's looking at nothing but him. Her nipples are hard like that because of him. And he's hard as a rock because of her. He doesn't think he's ever been this hard or this big in his pants.*

His friends' conversation lapses when she reaches him and sits on the edge of the table, lifting her leg so that her thighs are slightly parted, the dress dragging up her thighs. All he'd have to do is slouch, and he'd see…

She curls her finger into the collar of his button-down shirt. "Follow me."

Even her voice… Soft, shy, naturally husky rather than manufactured, like a moan in his ear.

What is he supposed to do? Say no to that? *A guy would have to be gay not to follow her wherever she took him, which is to a booth for two just a few feet away, miraculously empty in the crowd. She leads him to one of the booth's seats and gently pushes him down.*

The beat of the music changes to something low, pulsing, like his racing heart and the throb of blood in his cock.

There's slightly more privacy in a booth than at a table in the middle of the room, but not much. His friends can still see him. So can other men, who now openly wish they were him, wish she were looking at them the way she looks at him, like she wants to eat him whole.

She whispers in his ear, "I've got something for you."

He didn't think it was possible, but he gets even harder, arousal dominating his body. He feels it all the way to his toes, as though it's building up in his body like liquid. He's almost drowning in it. He thinks that he can smell her, that underneath the stale beer and wine, peanuts, fried bread and the crush of people, he can smell what's between her legs, the scent of pussy that makes him desire a woman's pleasure more than his own.

Right there, for anyone to see, she climbs into the small booth and straddles his lap. Her skirt rides up to the top of her thighs. Her pussy is hot against the front of his shorts.

"Oh God." His eyes roll back, but he still doesn't come. How on earth has he not shot his load in his pants yet? But thank goodness for small mercies, he stays hard, and he lowers his head again to gaze at her magnificent tits. And there they are, both of them, bare and beautiful, the top half of her dress folded down over her waist so that her full, generous breasts bob right in front of his face, the large nipples with their tight peaks driving him mad.

She places her hands on either side of his head and brings his mouth to her cleavage, smothering him with her breasts. It's the best way for a man to die. He grasps them, plumps them against his face as he kisses one, then the other, over and over and over. She moans louder than the music, declaring her pleasure to the whole bar, then undoes his shorts, pushes his boxers away from his massive erection, raises herself up and proves she wears nothing under her dress, because her cunt swallows him all the way down. She's tight and hot as fuck around him, clenching like a sucking mouth over his cock.

His friends cheer. The crowd gawks. Some of them have their hands down their pants, but none of them have the wonderful sensation of their cock being gripped by the most perfect pussy in the world. She's dripping for him, riding at a gallop.

She cries for everyone to hear and know how good his cock makes her feel. "Yes, oh yes, oh yes, yes, yes!"

She takes his hair in her fist, pulls his head back to kiss him as though he's the only way for her to get air. Her breasts mash against his chest, her pussy tightens around him, and she sucks the air out of his lungs. He gasps, gasps in nothing, claws at her back, his eyes rolling back again as he comes so hard that his vision fills with black thunderclouds shooting sparks of lightning.

She wraps herself around him in every way possible and some that are impossible. She draws out his orgasm, stretching the moment into what seems like forever. He shuts his eyes, basks in the bliss, coming and coming and coming until there's nothing left, but she somehow finds more, and the world fades until his life is in her, is her…

Nova lost herself in the kiss, relished the feeling of his bearish body underneath her. She rocked over his rigid cock until she broke away from his mouth and cried out. She didn't want to hold back. She didn't want to be quiet. In his dream, everything she'd done had been for him, which wasn't any different from her usual interaction with boys, but he'd also been captivated by her, at her mercy. He would have done anything for her if she'd asked it of him, which made her that much happier to give him what he most desired—the admiration of his peers, the fantasy of impossibly great sex in the middle of a crowd, a sweet and sultry, sexy, sexual woman who had eyes for no one but him. The strength of his fantasy had been just as potent for her, another reason why she'd been all too happy to dance for him. And God, the feeling of him succumbing to her, burying his cock into her cunt, filling it to its edges, his desperate kiss… She'd had him both in his dream and in his moaning, writhing reality on this bed with his girlfriend wrapped around Jules as he fucked her just as much as Nova fucked Taylor.

Nothing dripped out of her when she finally heaved a contented sigh and lifted off him. She didn't know where his semen had gone, how her body had done it when it hadn't before the transformation. She didn't care, not with how fucking amazing she felt right now.

She spread her fingers over Taylor's chest and massaged him lightly. He was still asleep — astonishing after her caterwauling. She assumed magic kept them asleep, like anesthesia.

Next to them, Jules glanced over at her, his wings sprouting from his back as he slammed into Kim one last time, and she moaned long and low in her sleep. Jules locked his lips over hers to muffle those moans, as though drinking them in.

No, that was exactly what it looked like. His cheeks hollowed as he drank her moans, then seemed to be drawing in something else. His hips jerked as he gave a helpless groan and finally broke away from the girl, panting and holding himself up by his arms.

He glanced over his shoulder at her. "Like I said, never gets old. You're a natural at this, Nova. You repressed everything so tightly, the pressure built up and up, and now you've exploded into yourself. How do you feel?"

The girl's eyes were still closed, her mouth slightly open from the kiss. She rested against the pillows much like her boyfriend, except her chest wasn't moving.

His chest wasn't moving, either.

Nova jerked back, scrabbling away from the bodies. She fell onto the thinly carpeted floor, bruising her ass, before crab-crawling frantically from the bed.

"Calm down, Nova." Jules climbed off the bed to pull his jeans back on. "They're not going to get you."

Because she and Jules had gotten to them first. Nova had killed Taylor. She hadn't meant to. She'd just clung to him, drained every drop of life that she could suck out, because that's what she'd wanted to do at the time — *needed* to do, as natural and automatic as breathing. Not because she'd wanted to kill him.

For the love of all things good and light and holy, was *this* what she'd become?

"Calm down," Jules repeated. "You're going to wake the suitemates. They'll take the moans as sexcapades, but screams of horror might be beyond their rationalization skills."

"I killed him." She stared wide-eyed at the prone body. He still looked like he was only sleeping, but that wouldn't last for long. She glared up at Jules, suddenly scared — because he had that capacity to kill as well. And he'd been inside her. Fed from her. And she'd fed from him. Had she almost killed him?

Perhaps she should have.

"I don't think I was vague in my selection of metaphors, sweetheart." Jules tossed Nova her clothes. "Feel your teeth. Touch your claws. They grew right before you came, just like mine. We could eat their flesh and drink their blood, too, if we wanted — it's all life — but I find it's unnecessary unless I hate the bitch. Also, best not to leave a mark. We can render ourselves invisible, and our fingerprints and fluids evaporate, but bodies stick around and so do bite and claw marks. There's only so much they can chalk up to rough sex."

"I — You — I — I killed a boy," she stammered.

"Predators kill their prey," Jules said, as matter-of-fact as a nature show. "We can control it so that we don't kill them during the feed, but that's a whole other lesson to learn."

"Are you saying you could have told me how *not* to kill him?"

"It's not a good thing to teach early on, hungry as you are. Even if you tried, you need their energy too much. You feel good, right? Even better than when you woke up this evening?"

She did. Aside from the corpse-like cold that spread through her stomach at the revelation that she was a murderer, she felt better than she had in years...maybe ever. The energy of a young teenager jittered inside her—the energy that made limbs ache and twitch and fidget, the constantly shifting attention, the emotional restlessness. But that only made her bone-crushing guilt even more keen.

"I feel like crap because I killed a boy, and you didn't tell me how not to. And *you*...you killed *her*. You knew how not to kill her, but you did it anyway!"

"Shhh."

Jules held his hand up and tilted his head to hear whether she'd woken anyone close by. Then he inclined his head back down toward her.

"I don't know about you," he said softly, "but I don't slather ketchup and mustard and pin lettuce, cheese and a pair of buns onto the hindquarters of a cow so that I have a hamburger, then leave the cow injured but alive as I eat my fill."

"This is different." She pointed at the pair of dead bodies. "These are people. Souls. And they're dying in a state of sin. We're not lions or spiders or hyenas or whatever metaphor you picked out of a hat. We're murderers. God, what did you have me— What have I done?"

Nova backed away, dropping her clothes.

Jules dispensed with stealth as he started after her. "Wait!"

She ran through the balcony window, launched herself over the balcony rail and pushed her wings out, unfurling them from her in a fluttering rush. Then she spread them out to catch her fall.

Nova let go of all thought and let her wings carry her up, away, invisible to all, naked as an animal, to take her away from her crime, from the sin that she'd become.

Chapter Six

He found her perched in the Quad Tree, getting bark in places she'd never had bark before, but she couldn't sit on her wings without losing balance.

She still felt amazing. She couldn't remember the last time she'd felt this alive, when colors and lines had looked this sharp, especially in the moonlight.

Yet she couldn't enjoy any of it, not even that she'd landed in a giant tree after flying halfway across campus.

The Quad Tree was one of the few pieces of Meridian that had been there forever. Most of the trees had been razed for development, but the Quad Tree had roots deep in the city. Students sat on them like benches. The lower branches were protected by state preservationists from students sitting on them — or at least it was against the rules to do so, which meant that a handful of people tried every year before being fined, like the ones caught carving their names into it.

But it was the middle of the night now. No one was going to see her or tell her to get down, and she was higher in the tree than the lower, stronger branches. The draping leaves made her feel like she was in the middle of a swamp, not a city.

She's always liked the Quad Tree. There were dips in the roots where a girl could sit alone without anyone near her, so she'd tucked herself in and read a textbook many times without having to worry about the other people taking an autumn study break around the tree with her.

Now, she was a succubus perched high in the tree where she could see more sky than ground. City lights obscured most of the stars. Sometimes, when her family had left the city on vacation, they'd go out into the middle of nowhere at night, turn off all their lights and just stare up at the stars. Since they hadn't been looking at her, criticizing her for just existing, she'd loved those nights in the dark, when she'd been suddenly aware of how much more was out there beyond their atmosphere. She'd even seen the cloud of the Milky Way. It had always made her sad to come back home and think of people who had never seen such things themselves.

When she looked to the sky tonight, she thought instead of meteorites. Falling stars, some people called them, although that was inaccurate. Other people called them fallen angels. Had she fallen that way— burning through the atmosphere until she'd crashed, diminished, upon the cruel earth? Or lower?

Jules landed on the branch next to hers. "I guess there's not really much more I can teach you, if this is your learning curve."

Nova kept her gaze on where she knew the stars were beyond the city haze. "Just tell me how to keep from killing them."

"Easy as leaving food on your plate. But you're too starved to do that right now. And if you starve yourself more just to keep from killing them, you'll end up killing them all when you can't stand holding back anymore."

She clenched her jaw. "What's your excuse?"

"It doesn't bother me anymore. Besides, think about it. She would have woken up to a post-feed hangover and her boyfriend's corpse next to her. Even if they didn't bring her in for questioning about the suspicious death, she'd be scarred for life."

"At least it would be a life."

"Like your life was a life?"

"Yeah," she shot back. "You know, it wasn't perfect, but I would have found a place for me in it, even if it meant spending the rest of my life alone. At least that would have been something."

A hard set to his face, Jules leaped from his branch to hers and handed her her clothes. "What you are is not my fault. I found you, followed you, helped you transform, but that transformation wasn't because of me. You're not my seed, and I didn't create you or cast a spell on you to make you what you are. I didn't take you away from your perfect human life. With or without me, this is all you, pet. I just thought you might want to go through the transition with some company and help, because that was more than I got."

Nova tucked her clothes against her abdomen, her wings twitching behind her.

"It wasn't as rough as the seven hundred pounds of baggage you're carrying around with you," he said.

"Most of my trouble was practical in nature, the stuff I've been trying to teach you. I can't help with the other stuff, except show you that what you do isn't unusual or unnatural."

"But you said we don't have to kill them."

"I also said that you're going to be killing them for a while. Is this going to be a problem for you?"

"Yes!"

"Do you know how many people would love to go out the way that those two crazy kids did? They talk about dying in their sleep, no pain, no fear."

"When they're old," Nova countered.

"Most people don't get to choose when, where, how or why."

"Most people shouldn't, for themselves or others."

"We're not people anymore," Jules said. "Well, we're people, but what seems human in us is mere camouflage. Like the Venus fly trap and pitcher plants, we entice our prey with lovely things to look at and pretty smells."

"You know what's different between your favorite metaphors and us? Most animals and plants don't have the brain function to develop a conscience or a sense of responsibility."

Jules nodded dryly. "Responsibility. Conscience. Yes. Humanity has those things in spades, don't they? They so responsibly saved one pretty tree so that they could congratulate themselves on the mulched corpses of the rest of their slaughter. Don't talk to me about human morality, Nova. It's absurdly naïve of you, a psych major, to believe humans to be responsible, moral or ethical—especially with their food or with each other. Now, don't starve your stomach on sexual principle, pet. You can ignore me over dinner. Do you want me to get a pizza with meat on it, or are we going vegetarian?"

She glared at him. "I want Canadian bacon, pineapple and jalapeños."

"Weirdo."

"And a milkshake. Chocolate."

"And cheesy breadsticks," he added. "I'll be back in a few. Are you staying here, or are you going to fly to the attic to eat on a couch like a civilized succubus?"

"You're a dick."

"You're welcome."

* * * *

She considered footing him with the food bill, taking all her things, flying back to her dorm and attempting to go right back to her life — sans the Saturday evening worship services.

But Nova looked down at herself for what seemed like the first time. In the past, she'd always limited her time naked because any kind of joy or pride in her body was basically asking someone to do or say something bad to her — to the point where she hadn't been able to be naked alone in her room. She'd hated taking showers for too long, especially when the water felt really good. She'd rushed through and tried not to look or touch too closely. She couldn't even remember if she'd ever been completely naked for any of the boys she'd had sex with.

With bark digging into her butt and almost into her cunt, she inspected her body as though she'd never seen it before, because in a lot of ways, she hadn't. She ran the tips of her claws over her full breasts, her belly, her hips, her thighs, trying to understand herself as a whole rather than the sum of parts. She pulled her wings around her legs to stroke the feathers, to pull on them to make sure they were real. She didn't have a mirror, so she touched her face, ran her tongue over her sharpened teeth.

Nova tried not to feel vain in her consideration — as though acknowledging the existence of her body was an obscenity in itself, that it should be ignored as a mere meat vehicle for the far superior mind and spirit. But that wasn't right, either. Man and woman had been created as physical beings, and hadn't God called that good?

She was confused. She liked what she saw. It was a good body — a healthy body, a conventionally and unconventionally beautiful one, an impossible one, yet here she was. The succubus was real, from nipples to wing tips, every inch of her made to lure men, hunt them, devour them.

With her wings on other branches to steady her, she tentatively parted her legs. After some concentration, she retracted her claws so that she could stroke two lines over her folds and dip her fingers into her cunt.

She was as soft and pliant on the inside as the outside. Everything that she could reach felt normal. No teeth, no inner mouth, just pleasure and a hotbed of magic that awakened when she touched herself like this.

Nova jerked her fingers out and fought to slow her breathing, calm the flush in her cheeks. Pleasure wasn't supposed to come upon a woman so easily.

In so many ways, some would call her lucky.

Lucky.

She inspected the gleam of her juices on her fingers in the moonlight. Then she coaxed her claws out once more.

She wasn't human. She'd never been human. And she'd changed—irrevocably. She could try to go back to what she'd been, but what would happen when she couldn't? As bad as things had been, they could get so much worse.

The next time a guy lost his head over her and dragged her into his car for a quickie, she'd follow him like before. It would mean more to him this time, and when he came and she came, she'd suck more than just his cum out of him. It was no longer simply the irresponsible sin that it had been before, when she'd prayed for forgiveness ad nauseum and worried whether she'd contracted some disease or gotten pregnant this time, although she never had.

They weren't the dangerous ones anymore. And there was nothing she could do about it but try to learn to be less dangerous over time—which wouldn't change how dangerous she was now.

Nova knew what she was. She knew about her power. She couldn't take that knowledge away. She couldn't pretend it wasn't there.

She didn't want to go through this—to *be* this—alone.

And she was still really hungry.

* * * *

Nova didn't talk to Jules for the rest of the night, except to thank him for bringing the food. He'd balked at a Hawaiian pie for himself and instead got a traditional supreme. However, he'd taken a leaf from her book and bought a second shake. He shared the breadsticks.

She reclined on her own sofa while Jules took the other. The food weighed her down, made her sleepy. Every time she settled into some semblance of comfort, the image of Taylor and Kim flashed in her mind. Dinner roiled in her stomach, but she managed to keep the food down.

She'd taken a shower to get the bark off and to scrub everywhere she'd thought should feel vile, but the harder she'd scrubbed, the less clean she'd felt. The actions had lacked sincerity—guilt, but no real desire for forgiveness or repentance.

Nova had finally thrown the sponge on the bathtub floor and twisted the faucet to cold, let herself freeze until she couldn't stand it anymore.

"Besides, if you really didn't want to be a demon, Nova, you wouldn't be one."

She'd shivered while drying herself off, then pulled on a purple nightgown—not one that Jules had liberated from some girl's closet but one from her own dresser. Jules had snorted when he'd seen it. It wasn't flannel, but it wasn't anything close to sexy, either, covering her from neck to ankle. He hadn't otherwise commented, though, just passed her the chocolate shake and her pizza box.

He turned on the TV to some on-demand channel to watch something that she tried not to pay attention to. Her younger sisters had been allowed to watch TV, but her parents hadn't liked her watching it instead of doing homework—or some other excuse. She thought she understood why now—the romance scenes, the swelling music, the simulated sex, the sounds of lips meeting… They got her hot just hearing them.

She reclined on the sofa, closed her eyes and made every effort to sleep instead of listening to the television. Her nightgown confined her, binding her legs together, clutching at her throat and wrists, clinging to her breasts.

Jules turned the TV off.

"No," she said when he tucked his arms under her body and lifted her from the couch like a knight with his lady. But Jules had none of a knight's honor — or armor. He was shirtless once again. In comparison to the boy she'd killed, he was slender, but she found his strength and warmth comforting nonetheless — comfort she hadn't earned. She deserved nothing less than a bed of nails and itching powder for the rest of her demonic life.

Granted, she didn't plan on purchasing those things to make her life harder, but she also hadn't planned on returning to Jules' bed, given how comfortable it had been.

"I'll not have you falling asleep on the couch in this ridiculous nightgown when I have a perfectly serviceable bed big enough for both of us and a few friends," he said. "I'll sleep on the sofa myself if you don't want me here, but..."

He laid her on the folded-down blankets and sat next to her, his hip familiar against hers. He slowly brushed her hair away from her face. Then, as he stroked her cheek, his fingers warmed.

"You're cheating," she said.

"You're in pain. Let me help. You won't hurt me. I won't hurt you. I just want to help."

She scratched her dull nails over the sheets, her body stiff as a board as he passed his hands from her face down her neck, down her body. He traversed the varied terrain as though enjoying the journey rather than anticipating the destination.

As much as she believed she should suffer, she also couldn't convince herself to tell him to stop, not with his magic fizzing over the surface of her skin.

At her compliance, he crawled onto the bed at her feet. The higher he pushed the nightgown over her legs, the more she parted her legs to allow him to kneel between them.

He stopped after pushing the skirt of the nightgown over her underwear, which was eminently practical, nothing pretty, fancy or sexy. He raised a long-suffering eyebrow and sighed. She tried not to laugh. But she did raise her hips when he tugged at the waistband so he could pull them off.

"Remind me to get you some proper underwear as soon as possible," he said. "Ones you and I will be more than happy to have in my way."

"In your dreams."

"I'm going to make you a star, kid."

"They named me after a star self-destructing. I'm not sure I want their aspirations for me, although it seems fitting, doesn't it?"

"Shhh, sweetheart." He stroked his way back up her legs again and settled between them, meeting her eyes over the valley between her breasts.

Her lids fluttered closed when he ran his tongue through her folds, as deliberately as he'd stroked up her legs.

Jules rested his arms over her thighs to keep her legs from moving too much as he settled into a languid feast. He'd already fed, already eaten and he had no urgency, not when taking her slow allowed him to savor all the little things she did under his mouth's ministrations. She could see that savoring in his black eyes, as though she was the most fascinating thing in his world — past, present and future.

Nova arched as he slid a hand up the rest of her nightgown to find the top button. The pearly purple buttons that lined the center of the gown were mostly for show, but still practical. With the deftness of endless practice, Jules worked his way down the row with the same deliberation as he'd worked his way up, worked his tongue through her furrow, into her cunt, then back up to torture her clit with slow, wet, insistent heat.

She felt as though she were rocking in a hot bath, bubbles building up inside her as the water continued to run, not in a crash but a steady stream. Nova pushed against his mouth but left the rest of her pleasure to his will.

He parted the top half of her nightgown. When she breathed in, she filled his questing hand with the breast he'd revealed.

As her soft gasps turned into moans, he drove her harder, faster, more intensely, swirling his tongue around and sucking.

She came for him as he gripped her hips and locked his mouth around her clit, licking her through each sweet wave until tears dripped down the sides of her face and into her hair. Even then, he didn't relent, forcing the orgasm to roll on and on until she couldn't take any more and nudged his forehead to push him away.

He kissed her inner thigh before raising himself up on his elbows and taking her in with a wandering gaze. She rested her head back on the pillow, suddenly exhausted. It wasn't just the orgasm. He'd taken a little out of her, too, but not enough to make her anything other than tired, which she'd already been.

"There." He rolled next to her and splayed out over his side of the bed. "That's the way you should look all the time."

"I think they have laws against that." She started to push the bottom of the nightgown down, but he intertwined his fingers with hers to stop her.

"Not in private. I promise you won't spontaneously combust, and I've yet to have lightning strike me while sleeping naked. This isn't Victorian England. You don't need to protect me from your enchanting ankles or your delicious clavicle."

"I obviously do." But instead of straightening her nightgown, she pulled the blankets over her.

He narrowed his eyes at her cunning. She couldn't help a soft laugh.

* * * *

"Go on," Jules urged her.

This had become a trend—Nova standing outside someplace or someone and Jules coaxing her to do something her parents, priests, teachers, etc. would have thoroughly disapproved of. Earlier that afternoon, it had been walking into the cafeteria and getting them lunch without using her student ID to pay. Jules didn't need her help getting meals. He regularly skimmed from the cafeteria and on-campus restaurants. He just wanted to make sure she could do it. She'd had to make herself seen to get the meals, then disappear so that no one else noticed her, which meant tightly controlling her magic to make her disappearance both gradual and unimportant to the people around her.

Which was a trick, because she was still intensely *noticed* by everyone. She hadn't gotten used to this new, kinder regard. It wasn't exactly the sort given a saint, but she preferred it over hostility and aggression.

Jules had also confessed that he'd exaggerated about the destructive effects of wings on clothing. He'd just wanted to get her into more revealing outfits. She knew now how to keep her wings from tearing through her shirts and dresses — just three ruined shirts before she'd figured it out.

Those ruined shirts and a dearth of wardrobe options had led Jules to bring her to this street, to this boutique store with dresses in the windows that looked like they belonged to high-end escorts, the kind who could fit into a crowd while still displaying their wares.

He'd been working on her to go 'discount' shopping, especially since she still refused to wear the other stuff he'd salvaged. And here she was, blending into the scenery, as remarkable as a draft.

Because deep down, she was curious how she'd look if she put on something as sexy as she was sexual. Hadn't she always been curious? Everyone trying to cover her up while pushing the line on appropriate attire themselves... What was she capable of if she stopped trying to hold herself in?

"What about security cameras?" she asked.

"They lose track of us, too. Magic fills in the blanks, just like it does for people. You act like I haven't been doing this a long time. I have no interest in going to jail for something as petty as larceny, and I certainly don't want you in jail, not right after I've found you."

"It's wrong."

"Not if they never notice. Inventory goes missing all the time. They write it off as a loss. So, unless you want to get a job where your boss regularly sucks the soul out of you rather than the other way around, I suggest you get used to taking the things you need."

"I don't need this," she said.

"Taking what you want, too."

They could argue until kingdom come, but the truth was that she knew she *could* do it. It was a matter of convincing herself that she should—at least once, as confirmation.

"Go on," he said again. "Pick out some nice things for yourself and let me see what you're made of." He nudged her lower back to coax her forward, then walked back to the small, covered seating area for patrons of the outdoor mall to wait for her.

She'd always wanted to go into a place like this, because it seemed to be where everyone else her age and slightly older went looking for an outfit for parties, clubs or concerts. Nova's mother had always commented on the poor parenting of others whenever Nova had asked to go in, but when her younger sister Cara had started buying clothing from similar stores, Nova's mother had never expressed parental mortification at herself.

No one was stopping Nova now.

It was weird, walking through the aisles and around the displays among other people. Sometimes, she made them shiver, sparking a fantasy or two among a few of them that made her think some of the girls there weren't entirely straight, which was something she'd have to process later. She was too worked up about clothing theft to worry about what kind of effect she had on what kind of woman.

Nova didn't even know where to start. For most of her life, she'd shopped for the sole purpose of maximizing coverage and avoiding cling. There was nothing in this store that would work for either of those except a few thin, loose cardigans, and she had no idea what would just work on *her*.

So she started picking things up that approximated her fit and looked like something she'd always wished she could wear, from skinny jeans and cutout leggings to sexy dresses. She filled up her arm with hangers until it ached, and still no one noticed her but for a brush of odd arousal. It was mind-boggling to her that she had this kind of power.

Nova's chest was tight, her fingers cold, her breathing shallow and her stomach twisted, but excitement thrilled through her with dose after dose of adrenaline. She was actually getting away with it.

On the way back to the dressing rooms, she passed by a lingerie section. Probably not the best quality, but she grabbed a few things, including some nightwear that wasn't one of her nightgowns, which Jules only let her wear to bed if she undid most of the buttons so that she looked marginally debauched instead of preparing for spinsterhood.

"These were made for winter and birth control, sweetheart. Winter won't chill you, and you have no need for birth control, since incubi spread the seed and succubi do not bear."

Silk ran enticingly over her fingers like soft water as she spilled lingerie onto the dressing room bench, hung up the rest of her items, then locked the door behind her.

Still nervous and excited, Nova pulled off her usual skirt and shirt and kicked off her sensible shoes. After a thought, she removed her bra as well.

She didn't take off her underwear until she'd tried a pair on over them and decided that she would take them. The lace was more comfortable to her than it looked.

Nova couldn't believe what she saw in the mirror — almost completely naked, just black-lace-edged panties on and the gouges on her back that no one but demons could see.

She looked fucking amazing. She looked…wicked.

After that, it was a matter of figuring out that only one of the bras fit her right. Then she went to town, more and more addicted to pretty clothes with each article. She was on the large side of their sizes because of her curves, but numbers and letters meant nothing to her when she looked like *that* in the right size.

Once she'd discarded the outfits that she didn't love, she ended up with five dresses, three skirts, two pairs of leggings, three pairs of jeans, two trousers and seven shirts, plus the underwear and bra. She pulled the price tags off, checked for security tags, found them on the dresses but ignored them for now, then tucked the price tags into one of the jean pockets. She also left the hangers behind so that she wouldn't make more noise than she had to while leaving.

To minimize what she'd have to carry, she pulled on one of the pairs of jeans that called every kind of attention to her ass and thighs, then a purple shirt that she thought was supposed to be paired with some kind of cami, because the neckline was cut so low that it exposed part of her new bra. She had never shown this much in public. She wasn't used to wearing jeans that fit this well, so she was unprepared for how the seam pressed against her folds, slightly swollen from arousal—not from the presence of any man but excitement at how she knew they would look at her.

After the sales reps dismissed the beeping of the security alarm, Nova strode over to where Jules waited for her. He opened an empty paper shopping bag for her to dump her new acquisitions in before they emerged from their respective concealments.

He started to stand, but she gripped the front of his shirt, pushed him back down and kissed him, moaning as all the delicious tension of the theft released low in her abdomen. Nova didn't give a fuck what disapproving adult might be watching as she slipped her tongue into his mouth to come-hither him closer or as he slid his hands from her waist to her ass. She didn't care what that teenage boy or that dirty old man or that quartet of mid-day mommy shoppers thought of her at all.

She'd done it. The world hadn't ended. She hadn't turned into a disgusting, ugly monster. No one had died. She'd done it—and she could do it again.

When she moved away from his mouth to apply her enthusiasm to his neck, his erection was hot against her abdomen, even through their layers.

"Have I mentioned how amazing you look?" he asked, the question broken with a slight gasp as she bit at his neck, then ran her tongue over the dents, so deliberately that anyone could see her doing it to him.

"Tell me later," she murmured into his flesh.

Then she threw her magic around them, swallowed his groan as she frantically undulated her hips over him, frotting through their clothes because she didn't want to take them off when they made her feel so fucking good. She kissed him, rubbed her cunt and her breasts against him in the middle of the day with people walking all around them. She had to bite his shoulder through his shirt to keep from screaming loud enough for everyone to hear.

Her foundation shifted, everything within her shaken—and not only from her climax or the magical aftershocks of his, like breakers of tide.

It was so much easier when she could just forget, forget all of it—the murder, the transformation, the confusion, the guilt, the shame, the constant need to check herself, control herself, control everyone around her to varying degrees of failure, the relentless lack of love or nurturing environment—hard, cold, cool, collected, chaotic, merciless. Everything was so much better when she lived in the moment, this moment, right now and none other.

"I'm not killing anyone else," she gasped against Jules' shoulder, where her mouth had dampened the fabric. "I'm going to try not to."

"You'll fail," he replied evenly. "For a little while at least. Can you deal with that?"

"I'll get them awake when I can. I'll try really hard not to kill them." *That'll have to be enough. I learned the other stuff quickly. This might come naturally to me, too. If I try hard enough…*

"Whatever helps you sleep at night, sweetheart." He stroked her back, massaging the place where her wings would have been. "If this is how you react to stealing, there are a few more stores I'd love you to look into."

Nova climbed off of him but kept her magic up. "Let's go do that."

"Wait…really?"

"Yes." She forced herself to meet his eyes when she added, "I want more."

"Who are you and what have you done with Nova?" Jules said with a toothy grin.

"Come *on.*" She tugged him away from the bench.

"I'm going to need more bags."

Chapter Seven

This one was a fighter. Eli had landed on her just outside the apartment complex she'd been gliding around, looking for a mark. The complex was surrounded by tall trees, their branches tactfully cut from the lower halves so that no one had to walk their ignorant faces into them and children couldn't climb up. However, suburban entitlement mentality meant that Eli had plenty of room to maneuver, and the succubus had quickly learned that she couldn't just flee to the tops of the trees to get away from him.

Once she'd known how easily he could fly after her, she'd given up trying to escape, furling her wings for ease of movement on the ground. Succubi were often the fiercest fighters, much more of a challenge to him than the incubi — and not just because the females sent their magic out at him like a weapon, because they could never send out as much as they liked. Their real power was in their touch, and he didn't make himself available for touching.

He always figured that was part of the reason why succubi fought harder—plain frustration that they couldn't play him like every other man in their lives, whereas the incubi expected nothing but a fight from him. Succubi also probably fought harder because they had to compensate for size, although not for strength— powerful little demons.

Eli *made* them fight harder, because he gave them no quarter. He wanted succubi just as dead as incubi, and they fetched just as pretty a penny.

The succubus shrieked, indifferent to the hundreds of people in the apartments around them. Eli wouldn't do much more than grunt at a kick or punch, but if the succubus wanted to cause a scene, let her. Most people didn't come out of their safe little habitats unless you pounded on their doors and screamed 'fire'. They rationalized the sound away as an animal fight or favored their own safety over someone else's bad day. At worst, they'd call the police over the commotion, but Eli's invisibility spell would keep him off the police's radar, and the demon's spells would do the same. The grand protectors of Meridian would find nothing and declare that they'd done their jobs, end of story. Nothing to see here, folks.

The demon was a feisty thing, skinny but almost as tall as him, heavy in the application of her claws, which he used his arm guards and armor to block. She was also desperately clever as she scrabbled at his sturdy clothes so she could touch his skin.

He was cleverer. He'd been fighting these beasts for fifteen years. Not one had laid a hand on him, or else he might not have made it this long.

Eli backhanded her, his gloved knuckles striking her cheekbone with a dull hollow sound. She stumbled to the side, hissing.

"I'll have you feeding me the whole length of your tongue and liking it, hunter." She'd withdrawn her wings, so she had to climb back to her feet to launch into a combination kick. One of them connected with his ribs, where he always strapped extra knives. The other nearly hit his masked face.

He grabbed that foot and twisted, forcing her back to the ground. She screamed as Eli stepped on her hip and twisted even more.

They could sound human all they wanted. That was their weapon when they couldn't use lust—a plea for compassion.

His compassion was killing them quickly, if they let him.

Eli slammed his boot into the succubus' stomach, forcing breath out of her lungs—didn't work so well on vampires, but thank God it did for sex demons.

She couldn't try to fool him again with her screams after he cut her throat.

This wasn't an alley where he could be interrupted, and he was close to a buyer. This time, he could take the skin. And succubus hair was in high demand for a special kind of wig. It didn't quite make up for the fact that he couldn't get its wings, but at least the kill wasn't a total waste.

Once the succubus was dead, Eli reaped his harvest.

* * * *

The master of the collective received the majority of the bounty, but Eli's pockets were still well-lined as dawn turned into morning. He went back home, removed and cleaned all his gear, threw out the clothes he couldn't mend, then tended his wounds, did his post-adrenaline workout and concluded with a shower.

After that, he usually ate something before going right to sleep, but today he felt juiced.

There was no rhyme or reason to the good days. It wasn't that he'd fought a succubus or received particularly good compensation for his harvest. He just wasn't ready to go to bed, itched with the uncommon urge for non-demonic companionship — the non-hunter kind, at that. Nothing to warm a bed or the backseat of his truck, just being alone in a crowd, around people who had no idea what hunters went through to keep them safer.

He didn't hang out with regular people as a kind of self-absorbed, heroic 'you're welcome'. He wasn't that conceited. He had a job to do and made a decent living doing it. That was thanks enough for him. Eli liked the ambiance of their innocent ignorance. It reminded him of himself before he knew about the demons. He envied them their non-supernatural concerns, their human foibles, follies and unflagging optimism.

Every so often, he just needed to remind himself why he did what he did.

That, and he often wasn't awake for lunch. He didn't necessarily miss the eight-to-five rat race, but he missed the company. There weren't as many people with his nocturnal habits in Meridian who weren't demon, hybrid or hunter like himself.

Most of what he kept in his closet had been curated for the hunt, but he had a few dependable civvies. Normal felt strange on him, as though he were naked, but he made up for it with a switchblade in his boot and another in his back pocket with his wallet.

When he arrived at the casual dining restaurant a few blocks from his apartment, he asked the hostess if he could be seated at the bar so that he could watch one of the big-screens. There wasn't even a game on. It was just a recap of a game. But it was suitably mindless. *Normal*. For a little while.

It was early for the usual lunch crowd, so there were some brunchers, a father eating with a child young enough not to be in school, a college Bible study group, a book group and a handful of stragglers like him. He ordered a coffee to start, intending to sit back and watch before digging into the menu and complimentary bread.

After a while, others were brought in separately — a girl who looked like she probably went to UTM like the Bible study group, an older gentleman with a woman who was probably his wife and a man closer to his age who'd had the same idea as Eli. At the other side of the bar, he nodded at Eli in solidarity.

It wasn't exactly one of the breastaurants that most of his ilk frequented to watch the same TV, but that didn't mean the view wasn't decent. The college girl was easy as hell on the eyes, and even though she'd brought a book rather than a boy, it looked like she knew it. In fact, the book was kind of a turn-on. Eli had a fondness for the occasional paperback. Instead of bookshelves, he had piles that Cat sometimes knocked over in her quest for a perch. If the girl put on a pair of hipster glasses, the picture would have really been complete, but he didn't hold it against her. He returned his attention to the screen with a light smile.

After he finished his coffee, he asked for another—decaf this time, because he had to sleep in a few hours. The menu had officially transitioned from breakfast to lunch with the sweeping of the second hand on his watch, so Eli also ordered a burger and fries.

As he waited for his meal, his gaze drifted more and more from the TV to the girl, who was drinking orange juice and had also delayed ordering for when the lunch menu became available. She smiled up at her server, a younger girl, who smiled back brightly before walking over to ask Eli if he needed anything else before his food came out. He shook his head.

The girl's pasta dish arrived before his burger, but once his burger arrived, he tried to focus more on his meal, disconcerted by the way that the college girl kept drawing his attention. He wasn't confused or anything. She was quietly smoking hot—not dressed with any ostentatious kind of hotness, but she looked like she could set fire to the roof if she tried. It just bothered him the way the girl *kept* his attention. After all, he usually only gave that kind of attention to women he knew he could have if he wanted them, acquaintance or professional. There was just no *point* to him innocently appreciating a girl who had to be half his age or younger.

At least she looked legal. Although she'd look more legal if she were drinking mimosas instead of orange juice.

Still, he didn't normally concern himself with the doings of young people. Young people were for young people. That girl needed at least ten more years before she was experienced enough for him.

And yet...

Shit, he'd been staring too long, because she'd finally realized someone was staring at her and turned around to see who it was. He tried to act like he'd been engrossed in his fries all along. When he thought it was safe to check — *like a fucking teenager, damn it* — he glanced at her. She was shaking her head with a small grin, but she'd returned to her book.

The game recap and commentary. Lunch. That's what he needed to be focusing on. He divided his attention between the television and his food, refusing to look at anything else.

"Excuse me?"

The girl had approached his part of the bar while he'd been intently not looking at her, and now she was right *there*. Not exactly inches away — she kept a respectful distance — but he got to see her from the front rather than the back, and that view was all the much more appealing, although the back had its good qualities, too.

He couldn't really point to anything specific that made his cock start standing like a gentleman should with a lady. She was only wearing a pair of black skinny jeans and a black and white long wrap shirt that hugged her all the way down to her thighs, complementing her breasts without showing them off, per se, although they showed themselves off, like her hips and her ass and her beckoning falls of loose dark hair over her shoulders. All of it conspired together in a very innocent way to direct blood flow below his waist. So he couldn't actually stand for the lady, no matter that his grandmother would slap his hand with a spoon if she knew he hadn't. He kind of needed the bar top. The poor girl didn't need to know how much the old man was perving on her.

Eli gave a quick officer's speech to his tongue, telling it to behave and not stammer or stutter. He was supposed to be beyond all this, getting flustered over an attractive coed.

"Yes?" He made it through the one word. He prayed he could make it through the rest.

"I asked the waitress whether I could change one of the TVs to another channel, and she said that was fine at this hour, as long as I asked the two gentlemen watching whether it was all right. The other guy said it was, but I wanted to know whether you're really into the show or whether you're just watching to have something to look at."

"Just watching to watch." It had sounded less creepy in his head than when it came out of his mouth. No backpedaling, though. Backpedaling always made things worse. "I mean, you can go ahead and change it. I'm not married to the channel."

"Passing acquaintances or friends with benefits?" the girl asked with a playful grin.

Eli had learned to notice when he was seeing a real face or he wasn't, and she wasn't wearing a lick of makeup. There was no clumpy mascara on those warm eyelashes, not even lip gloss on her dark lips. The flush on her cheeks wasn't blush, either. Was the room just warm, or was she showing interest?

"What?" There went his efforts to act his age.

"Your attachment to the channel. I was trying to make a joke and it didn't work, and for that I must apologize profusely. There might be sonnets of sorry later."

"Sonnets won't be necessary. No, go on and change it to whatever you like." That sounded more like him, although when she smiled at him, her cheeks flushing an even deeper pink, he didn't think he had anything left to keep from making a complete fool of himself in public.

She is way too young for you, you damn horndog. Get a grip.

Bad choice of words. He could really use a grip.

"Thanks."

She practically skipped to the bartender to tell him that he could change the channel to one with reruns of an old medical procedural. He remembered having that kind of energy. He wasn't rickety by any stretch of the imagination, but constant battle caught up with a man. Energy had always been so *easy* back then. And it did wonders for certain parts that bounded with her.

Eli shifted his napkin over the front of his jeans and surreptitiously squeezed himself too tightly, enough to deflate himself a little bit. God, it had been a long time since he'd been so at odds with his dick for no reason.

He spent the rest of his lunch once again trying to ignore the girl while watching the closed captions of the program she'd changed it to. It just figured that they'd finish and pay around the same time. She left first, but he inadvertently caught up with her after paying cash and leaving his tip.

"I hope the channel change didn't disrupt your lunch hour too much," she said as she opened the door for him.

Once again, the voice in his head that sounded like his grandma had a few things to say about that, but times had changed. Everyone opened the door for everyone, because that was polite rather than chivalrous. However, after stepping into the superfluous foyer, Eli opened the second door for her.

"It's a good show," Eli replied, leaning against the door rail as she passed him. "No problem."

Her elbow brushed his forearm. He was intensely aware of the prickles of his hair rising where she'd touched him.

The girl stopped outside the restaurant in the middle of the sidewalk, taking a few deep breaths.

Keep walking. Keep walking, kid, just keep walking.

She looked over her shoulder.

The girl couldn't know what she did to him with those bedroom eyes, couldn't know the things his brain showed him, flashes of scenarios that would probably haunt him when he got home and under the sheets. She was a young woman just starting out in her life. Even if she had some experience, she had *no idea* what she did to him, what he imagined he could do with that enthusiasm and energy, with every inch of her voluptuous body.

It wasn't her fault he was a bad man underneath all his good actions. Everyone was, in their own way. Eli owned his depravity, fought his personal demons the way he fought literal demons. He swallowed against his desire now and smiled at her, a normal smile for a normal girl.

"My name is Nova, by the way." She tucked her paperback into her purse and held her hand out for him to shake.

Eli hesitated for the barest of moments, then took her hand to be kind. He was about to tell her his name when it hit him, really hit him, that she was looking up at him with her dark eyes under the overcast sky, and she wanted him as much as he wanted her.

It was a certainty, in a sweeping glance over her ripe, young body and the way that she held it, the way that she blushed naturally and prettily again, the way she lowered her eyelids, the way that she moved her hand in his, almost like a gentle massage, how she could move her hand over something else.

Eli was equally certain that he was reading everything wrong, that he was just seeing what would serve his fantasy.

Then he stepped toward her, and she stepped back, but not to escape a man's too-long grip. She made no effort to remove her hand from his nor tear her gaze away. Their steps became almost a dance as he pushed forward and she pulled back, both of them in perfect sync in spite of not saying a word as they hurried around the restaurant to the back. It was grimy, as unromantic a place as they came, but it didn't stink, because the dumpsters were kept away from the restaurant, and it was secluded.

She pulled him around her and crowded him against the dusty brown brick. So much for thinking that he might be doing something she didn't like, because the girl cradled his ribs as she pressed him to the wall and stepped closer, insinuating a leg between his. Her thigh nudged the front of his jeans, but not enough for her to tell how hard he was just from her hand in his and the way they'd found themselves back here.

The girl crawled one hand up his chest. With her fingertips on his chin, grizzled from end-of-work-day stubble, she drew his head down to meet her lips. The kiss was almost sweet, a tentative test that she had read him right.

She made such a beautiful sound as he took a fistful of her hair and wrapped an arm around her waist, drawing her so obscenely close that there was no question that he wanted her. She welcomed him into her mouth, met him with just as much passion as he showed her, not struggling at all against his hand as he pulled her head this way and that to change the angle of their kiss.

He just had time enough to realize how she was rubbing herself over his thigh and opening his jeans before he caught her wrists tightly enough to feel the bones grind.

He thought she'd try to get away. Pout. Cry. Things that a girl should do when he hurt her.

She just smiled, her lips even darker, full from the force of his kiss. She bit her tongue playfully but didn't release the sides of his partially opened jeans.

"Do you have any idea what you're getting into?" he asked roughly.

"Funny," Nova said. "I was going to ask you the same thing."

With his hands still tight around her wrists, she drew down his zipper. Alone where they were, it seemed like such a loud sound, inescapably intimate, even though they were still technically in public.

"*Fuck*," he groaned as Nova slowly lowered herself to her knees. "Wait."

Finally, there it was—the hurt and confusion he'd thought he'd call to her expression a lot earlier than this. "Second thoughts?"

"No." Closer to fifth or sixth thoughts. But he still dug into his back pocket for his wallet and pulled out a condom from the three that he kept in there.

This time she could see the twitch of his cock when he got such a close look at that smile. Genuine, bright, wicked as she pulled his jeans open and worked his briefs down over his erection. She tucked them under his balls before giving them a warm greeting with her hot-as-fuck tongue, caressing them with her lips.

Eli fumbled with the condom package. He yanked her away by the back of her neck. "Off."

She laughed, squeezing his thighs, but she settled back onto her heels and licked her lips as he released her to roll the condom over his cock.

With her looking at him like she hadn't eaten a thing in the restaurant, Eli might as well not have wrapped his erection from how intensely turned on he was—by her unfettered eagerness, by her obedience. No, not her obedience…her submission. Cheeky, but her knees on the dirty ground, her only apparent thought to give him what he desired without him even having to ask, but she didn't mind him telling.

This girl. Could he keep her?

"You still have no idea," Eli said. "But far be it from me to say no to a lady."

"I'm no lady." Nova ducked her head, the first sign of shame, but she crawled forward again to wrap her hand around the base of his cock and pump him with the other, exploring him, teasing with how close her mouth got to him without touching.

From this angle, he could see everything he wanted to see of her, short of having her naked—and in a way, the fact that she was fully clothed made this even better. The shadow of her cleavage all the way down to her bra. The curve of her ass enhanced by the clinging of her shirt. Her mouth near his cock, her hands testing its length and breadth, her touch swelling him even more. And those dark eyes, practically black as she impatiently raised them up to his.

He was torturing her as well as himself by holding off telling her to suck him off, in part because he savored how she was really waiting for *him* to *tell* her to do it.

"You look hungry." He tucked her hair away from her face. Such a tender gesture. Such a sweet face.

Suddenly, he grabbed her hair again and twisted it into a close knot in his hand, taking complete control over her head. Her mouth dropped open in a low moan. Her neck looked unspeakably delicate, as though if he shook her too hard, he would snap it.

"How much can you take?" Even though the question came out in a threat, he also really wanted to know.

She gasped when he shook her again to get her to answer. "I guess we'll find out."

He jerked her mouth to his erection and pushed the head into her mouth. She yielded to his cock with a hum that shot straight through him. Her eyelids fluttered as he sank deeper, deeper, deeper, until with a groan her lips reached the bottom of the condom.

Nova met his eyes again as though challenging him as she swallowed around his cock, breathing heavily through her nose. *Is that all you got?*

He shoved his cock all the way inside her, then yanked back for her to gulp in mouthfuls of air. He gave her three seconds before forcing her back over him. She took him in just as eagerly, shaking her head to move down his length like a snake devouring its meal. Not a splutter, not a gag, as smooth as sinking into a woman's pussy.

Eli made it through two more times pushing her mouth down the whole length of his cock before covering his hair-wrapped fist with his other hand and holding her there until his hips snapped forward. He fucked her mouth as she grasped his ass through his loose jeans and moaned with each thrust, as though what he was doing to her was just as satisfying, just as pleasurable, as though it did something for her to be force-fed his cock—which pushed him right over the edge.

She whined as he froze deep in her throat and came, grunting at how his condom practically didn't exist, she was so hot and wet and insistent around him. It made him wonder how much better it would feel if he could take her mouth completely bare.

When he was finished, he pulled her off so abruptly that he caught the tail end of a moan. She coughed, but there still wasn't any gagging, despite how long and how deep he'd shoved his erection down her throat—and he wasn't small. The condom glistened, a thick strand of her saliva connecting it to her lips as though it were a string of his cum.

Damn it to hell. Although his cock had softened some, he wasn't out of the woods yet at the sight, especially with those dexterous fingers pulling the condom off.

"Put that down," he said.

She dropped it next to his boots.

Still with his hands buried in his hair, he hauled her to her feet and whirled them around. His jeans nearly fell off as he caged Nova against the wall with his arms on either side of her head.

Eli panted, shaking his head. He didn't know what to say. Didn't know what a man was supposed to say after he'd so thoroughly debauched, degraded and corrupted someone that much younger than him, someone who didn't deserve it and probably hadn't even known to anticipate it, might not have known how to get out of it. *Sorry* didn't seem adequate.

Just when he opened his mouth to apologize, Nova put her fingers on his lips, then dipped in to kiss what she touched. He desperately kissed her back. In spite of how much he'd emptied himself into the condom at their feet, he swelled again, yearning for more, more of *her*, wishing they weren't behind a fucking restaurant and instead in a nice comfortable bed that would squeak, maybe with a headboard that hit the wall every time he thrust into her.

He didn't normally lose his mind over a woman like this, especially a young woman, and for God's sake, he was over forty. He shouldn't recover this fast.

Breaking the kiss, Eli pressed his forehead to hers.

"I need to go," she said, looking as disappointed as he felt.

He nodded, avoiding her eyes.

"Hey." Nova pulled out a ballpoint pen from her purse. "I never did catch your name, stranger."

"Eli." He tucked his erection into his underwear before carefully zipping up his jeans again. He still couldn't look at her, even though he wanted to—a last goodbye to every lush inch of her, forever condemned to imagination. "Look… I don't normally—"

"Oh, I'm so far from 'normally', too. That's kind of been my life for these last few weeks. Be a shame to stop now." She took his hand in hers and wrote something on the back of it. Then she capped the pen, put it back in her purse and stepped back toward the parking lot. "Hope you take me up on that, Eli."

He couldn't manage to think of anything clever or articulate as she smiled, gave him a parting glimpse of her fine ass, then rounded the corner with the cock-twitching click of her heels.

Eli looked at his hand, then ran the back of his other one over his mouth.

Thursday. 8pm. The Raging Ham. No pressure.

What was she thinking?

What was *he* thinking?

God, he needed a cigarette. He'd never smoked in his life, but he needed one. At best, he'd have to grab a beer when he got home…or two.

He picked up the condom, then walked over to the restaurant dumpster and tossed it into the opening. After jogging back to his truck, he stopped, his hand on the door handle.

"What the fuck just happened?" he asked aloud.

No one, not even himself, had the answer to that one.

After he climbed into his truck, he just sat there in his seat, staring at the invitation on his hand. For a date. He'd just been asked out on a date. By a girl way too young for him who he'd face-fucked behind a casual restaurant.

"Even for Meridian, Eli, you're totally going to hell." He turned on his truck and sped out of there.

Chapter Eight

"What are you so smiley about?" Jules asked as Nova climbed under the covers with him.

"I had a good lunch is all."

"A person doesn't glow like a lightning bug when they've had a good lunch. They glow like that when they've had a good fuck." Jules propped himself up on his elbow and looked down at her with a raised eyebrow. "That's it, isn't it? You had a good fuck."

"Awake and everything."

Jules wrinkled his forehead for a few seconds. He didn't manage to smooth it out quite fast enough.

"Oh. I'm sorry. Were we...*together* together? I didn't even think about that at the time, but now..."

Jules laughed, throwing himself back down onto his pillow. "No. I...no. Sometimes we form families, couples, what have you, but no. It's not in our nature to be exclusive. I just...didn't expect you to jump back on the horse so fast, so to speak."

"Well, like I said, he was awake." Nova wore a pair of panties and a long tank top as a sleep shirt. She was still getting used to sleeping half-naked, even if Jules would still prefer she learn how to forego clothing altogether in their bed, like him.

"Still drains them, pet. You still feed."

"Not when they wear a rubber, apparently," she said, grinning.

He took in her giddiness, then stroked her cheek with his crooked finger. "Don't get too attached, Nova."

She sighed. He kept trying to burst her bubble. "Why?"

"You have control over them. You have power. But falling in love with humans is like winning the lottery. You have to be willing to live a lie, a double life, because they can never know what you are, and you can't stop being what you are. Demons and angels have no business loving humans. We do it on occasion, but we're better off with our own kind. Fewer people get hurt."

"Who said anything about falling in love?" Nova asked. "I met a guy, had a good time, asked him on a date. It was unexpected. It was fun. It was intense. And for heaven's sake, I've never had a date before. I've had spontaneous sex, like I did with him today, but I've never had a date. And he seemed interested in a follow-up. Excuse me for doing what you told me and trying new things I was never able to do before."

"I'm just trying to protect you." He rubbed her arm lightly. "They'll want you more than ever, Nova. How can you be sure that he wants you for you alone and not because of your magic?"

Nova presented her back to him without another word. She should have figured he'd get his needle in somewhere, deflating a perfectly nice bubble of ingenuous excitement.

Jules stroked her spine before resting his arms behind her and settling into the slow breathing of his sleep.

She couldn't explain to him what had happened. On the surface, it sounded like everything else that had ever happened to her — the reaction to her presence, desire that had been etched into his face as though her power was a violent attack, the attempt to rein it in, the mutual attraction at contact, sex before introduction, the rough treatment he'd given her, like a sex slave.

But Eli had checked over and over again to make sure that she wasn't going to run, that she was actually okay with what he was doing. And to her surprise, she'd been more than okay. He'd made her feel present, solid, whole, desired. He'd looked in her eyes while fucking her mouth. His kiss hadn't just been possessive, but at times practically tender.

And he'd had trouble not looking at her before her magic had passed over his skin. It had triggered his actions, but she strongly suspected it hadn't triggered his desire. Magic had made it possible for her to know his fantasies and to fulfill them, but it could only have served as inspiration rather than creation of those fantasies.

She couldn't know that for sure, but she could be sure that he'd been different. She didn't think it was just his age, although she couldn't ignore, to her chagrin, that older men seemed to be her weakness. She'd never thought of herself as that kind of a girl, but then again, she'd never thought of herself as the girl she'd ended up being, either.

His age aside, there was a quality to him that had been just as much of a draw for her as she'd been for him before her magic could reach him.

Nova was too jaded by all the games that boys played to get sex for her to believe in soulmates. However, as a demon, she couldn't deny the existence of fate. She wasn't such a dewy-eyed schoolgirl to believe that Eli was fated for her, but she was inclined to believe that some people were born with more layered attractions to each other. She hoped it wasn't too dewy-eyed of her to believe that, if Eli showed up at the gastropub she'd written on his hand for a proper date, he felt the same attraction, which went deeper than lust.

Nova had to believe that there would be more to her life than stealing and sex, especially after the fiascos, one after another, that she'd had with men over the past few weeks while trying to control her feed. She had to believe that there was something pure left, that she could have some of the things that she'd always wanted — normal things, human things.

Almost human, at least.

* * * *

Nova sat in the canvas folding chair on the balcony, staring through the blinds into the dark room at the young man whose dream had caught her attention. Jules was feeding two rooms down on a girl he'd been working on over the last three nights.

"Three nights, three feeds and they're yours forever. They'll crave you like meth, and they don't have to invite you

in anymore, because at that point, what's the use of that little rule?"

Three nights of a feed was also when he could potentially mate with her, but he wasn't yet inclined to spread the wealth. What he hadn't told Nova, she gathered for herself — that between her transition and his, he probably wasn't in a hurry to give someone else the same experience a couple of decades down the line.

Strange, she didn't even know how old Jules was. He looked like he was in his late twenties, maybe thirties with exceptionally good skin. But he sometimes talked about time as though he'd been around a lot longer. In some ways, that would be par for the course with her, wouldn't it?

The age of the boy inside wasn't the problem, though. Their fantasies were annoying, predictable, juvenile, but at least they were earnest and honest in their dreams, not like when they were awake, when they worked too hard to protect and maintain their delicate egos.

The problem was that she didn't want to kill him.

Killing one was an accident. Two was a coincidence. Three, a pattern. Four made her a serial killer, and she didn't even mean to.

She couldn't do it anymore, especially since Jules refused to pull her back before she came. He insisted that she get as much energy as possible from them, that she kill a few to save more, like an adult telling a toddler to eat all her vegetables, *then* she could have dessert.

Nova also thought he didn't help her stop because he wanted her jaded to it — that after the eleventh or twelfth death, she'd have to get hard or have a complete nervous breakdown that led to eventually accepting the inevitable. Instead, she was losing her taste for feeling full and valuing her hunger. Nova was only a freshman, but even high school health was pretty clear about the signs of an eating disorder. It was a little different when one's source of food was sex, but just as dangerous. After all, it was like Jules had said — if she held back too much, she was only going to go overboard when she got too hungry, the succubus equivalent of a binge.

When she wasn't on the hunt or in the middle of the feed, though, life was surprisingly good. And the only way she could handle it was compartmentalization. She couldn't think about her sins. She spent her days away from the university. She was a different girl out there. Nova liked that girl, even the one who shoplifted with increasingly alarming frequency. It was the sex and murder that felt separate from her, as though she were demon only part of the time — some form of lycanthropy or Jekyll-Hyde binary.

It was the only way she could handle it, but her grip was tenuous at best. If murder became her life, if she lost the stab to her heart and the tears she shed that would degrade long before people found the body, then she might as well not live anymore. Jules could make the cheeseburger analogy all he liked. She felt too human to justify consuming them.

If she could somehow find a way around killing people — and soon — she might just be able to finally *really* live. She'd been a succubus for weeks and hadn't even thought to check her social media or her phone for messages from her family to see if they'd noticed she was gone. That was how little she missed them, although she mourned the family she wished she could have had. Maybe that made her a bad daughter, but they'd been a bad family, too. She was better off without them.

Except for the whole murderer thing.

Nova narrowed her eyes at the sleeping figures inside the room. She wanted to go in. Her skin burned under the sleeveless short dress that she'd worn for ease of access and because, first hunt aside, she wasn't comfortable flying naked or mostly naked yet.

She could taste the edges of their dreams. Their doors were practically propped open for her. Either one or both would do. If she worked it right, she could actually get one of them to sleepwalk over to his roommate's bed, and they could have a lovely little threesome that gave her twice the shot of sexual energy when they came inside her. Perhaps with two men going at her, she'd only drain each of them half as much.

She stood, stepped toward the window. She'd already had several feasts recently. Maybe these would be the ones who wouldn't die…

No.

She spread her wings and jumped off the balcony. If Jules didn't care whether she killed anyone or not, Nova didn't care if Jules didn't know where she'd gone.

What she needed was fast, hard, risky, wakeful sex that didn't involve the other person being any kind of responsible. Which meant…

Nova pulled her wings back into a dive when she hit the cloud of sexual energy, accessorized with colored lights coming out of the fraternity house.

She slipped through the vetted door, then shed her spells so that she could keep her magic close to her, although the rooms were crowded, and her bare arms kept brushing other people. On either side of her rose the light moans and gasps of those she accidentally touched, mostly men, a few women. Other folks on campus were sleeping, but this party was only just winding down.

It wasn't like in the movies and television shows, the close shove of writhing bodies, glowsticks, rampant making out, rampant drug use. Okay, there was some making out. The largest room had music with a thudding bass, and there was dancing, but not like a bunch of spooked sardines. A haze of cheap booze, cheap appetizers and sweat filled the other rooms, but most of the people who weren't making out were just talking, red Solo cups in their hands.

Hardly *The Rape of the Sabine Women*, although Nova detected lies all around her. She'd heard every bad line that meant a boy had begun to realize what a man should sound like when he wasn't being an ass, because the less of an ass they sounded, the more ass they got. But she could recognize a con from a mile away and a horny college boy from even farther, given the taste she'd gotten over the last few weeks.

It wasn't just the men who were lying. Her ears simply caught their lies more easily, familiar as they were. Relationships in general, as far as she could tell, were built on lies first, then carved into something either beautiful or monstrous as the truth chipped away at them.

A boy with a desperate effort at a goatee and too much body spray to mask the fact that he hadn't showered recently came up behind her. "Let me guess…rum and Coke."

"Without the rum," Nova replied. "Please."

"Coming right up."

Nova leaned against the wall with her legs crossed to lure eyes to the dress' brief length, but she wasn't interested in thinly veiled douchebags tonight. There had to be a gem in this rock pile. Nova radiated her heat, drawing out a thin layer of sweat, and closed her eyes against the ripple of it over her skin.

"Here." The boy handed her the cup. "Just the way the lady ordered it. Now, is the lady alone tonight or...?"

"I'm a free agent." After taking a sip of the drink, she jerked back when the rum hit her. "Hey."

"Oh, come on. Nothing wrong with a little fun."

"I was looking for a little fun, but not this kind." Nova handed the cup back to the boy. He reflexively took it to keep it from falling to the carpet when she let go. "And now not with you."

"Aww, man, come on..."

Nova lost him as she took a circle around onto the dance floor, then back to the impromptu wet bar.

"Just a Coke, please." She gave the amateur bartender a smileless, smoldering look that had him fumbling with the cooler that held the soda cans. And he was all thumbs trying to open it. "That's okay," she said, opening it herself with a hiss. "I got it. Thanks."

She was about to leave the wet bar room — with its beer pong and pool and foosball and glowing smartphone screens — when she noticed a boy in the living room near two half-full Solo cups on the mantle, talking with two friends of his. One of them was speaking to a girl who swayed back and forth as she spoke. The one with his elbow on the mantle surreptitiously put his hand in his pocket, transferred something from that hand to the other, then dropped whatever it was into the cup farthest from him.

The girl that the two boys had been waiting for returned. She picked up her cup when the boy did. The boy raised his cup to his lips with a smirk, knowing the girl would unconsciously mirror him.

On her way, Nova manipulated her looks until they were slightly different by the time the five of them noticed her—a brown-haired, blue-eyed white girl instead, just enough to confuse. She took the cup away from the girl, thinner and taller than her and likely older, then edged between two of the boys, one of them the broad-shouldered boy with the roofies, and let her fever emanate as though the lust she carried inside her was an airborne contagion.

"Sorry I didn't come back sooner," she said to the other young man by her side, the tallest of the three. Then, to the increasingly furious and disbelieving expression of the girl whose spiked drink had been stolen, Nova chugged the whole thing down. "Got caught up. What were we talking about again?"

"What the fuck, bitch?" The girl snatched the empty cup out of Nova's hand. "That was *my* drink."

Nova glanced down at the empty cup, then seriously back in the girl's eyes. "You're welcome...and excused."

The girl drew her brows together as she followed Nova's gaze. She huffed in annoyance that wasn't quite what it had been. Then she grabbed her friend's arm. "We're going."

Her friend clutched at the girl's shoulder as she fought to keep from weaving on their way out.

"But I wasn't finished," the boy who'd been talking to the friend protested. He started after the two girls.

"Hey," Nova purred. "There's plenty here for everyone. Think we can find someplace quieter? My eardrums are about to burst. We can dance just as fine upstairs."

"Hell, yeah," her broad-shouldered boy said, with his crewcut and the plaid straining over his chest. "I know just the place."

She drew herself closer by his pockets and carefully pulled out the small baggie of white pills inside it, then brushed her hips against his. He wasn't thinking about drugs anymore, except what he might expect from her in a little while, after what she'd just pulled. "Lead the way."

She had to get upstairs quickly, before the effects started to show and before the alcohol hit her system even faster. She'd only experienced a little pre-legal drinking in her life, because the boys who'd wanted to have sex with her never had to get her drunk first.

Nova wasn't prepared for the buzz of it. What was worse, she didn't know what was the alcohol and what was the roofie, and she didn't know how either of them were going to hit her non-human system. The idea of a succubus getting knocked out by a date-rape drug seemed the height of irony.

But as far as Nova saw it, even if the drug brought her down, she had an advantage over the other girls. She knew what was coming. She knew she'd enjoy it whether she wanted to or not. And she'd get something out of it, *take* something from all three, because all of them were going up the thin staircase now, her boy in front and the two in back ogling her ass and trying to see up her dress.

Better her than someone else.

And if the roofie didn't do her in, Nova had a plan or two in store for these boys. All they needed to do was sleep. After what they'd been planning to do to the other girl and her friend, with what they were planning to do with her, Nova could justify this. She could justify being a few bad boys' really bad day.

With each step she took up those stairs to the third floor, the boys got handsier, and she didn't think she'd have any regrets in the morning. She gradually shed her glamour. The boys didn't care if she changed ethnicity or grew a new set of arms in the process. They were just cheering with the music. Nova had been right — two floors up in the house, and they could still hear the music just fine.

She shivered. Their hands on her, their desires filling the hall like too much musk, her own appetite, the hum of alcohol in her head... Nova rolled her shoulders to warn her wings to stay in and flexed her fingers to tell the claws the same thing.

Her boy led her to a room at the end of the hall. It was mostly taken up by a bed on the bottom and a loft bed over it. He flopped back against the lower bed, spilling his drink on the front of her dress.

"Oops," he said. "Bad, bad Billy. Look what I've done."

"You wouldn't happen to have club soda, would you?" Nova wasn't particularly thrilled that he'd gotten beer on her dress, but at least it was machine washable.

"I got a better idea," Billy said as his friends closed the door behind them. Nova heard the click of the deadbolt. "Hey, Karl, Todd, you guys want a Fuzzy Nipple?"

"I never did know what was in those." Nova stumbled as Billy forcefully turned her around, but she tried to make it seem like she was affected by either the booze or the pill.

Karl and Todd fell gracelessly to their knees, clutching her hips. They each took a nipple into their mouths through her cotton dress, sucking at the beer as though drinking it from her. It took her by surprise, and she pushed on their heads to shove them away, but her touch only excited their lust more, and the warm rhythmic suction over the cold beer also excited her. The bigger guy—Karl, her touch magic told her— fumbled his hand under her skirt. Billy rubbed and squeezed her ass as he laughed at her both squirming to get away and moaning with pleasure at the same time.

Nova was confused. The booze slowed her down. Everything was just moving faster than she'd thought, and they'd all put their drinks on the desk when they'd entered.

"Fuck, she's not wearing panties." Karl grabbed his crotch and squeezed what he found there.

"She's not wearing anything under her dress, the slut." Billy pushed Todd, the thinner boy with a blond, excessively preppy bowl cut, away from her breast, then roughly grabbed the zipper at the top of the dress. "This is what you wanted, wasn't it? You came to this party looking for a good dicking. You need a few good cocks making you leak from all your holes. I can't wait to fuck that pretty mouth of yours."

"Awww, that's what I was going to do," Todd said.

"I found her first. She's mine," Billy said.

Nova kept her fist tight around the bag of pills. There was nowhere to put it that wouldn't be discovered eventually, because now her dress fell away from her breasts and folded down her body before falling off altogether. She staggered, squinting at the three boys, who leered at her completely naked body and slavered like dogs.

"Patience, boys," Nova said, slurring her words. "Plenty for everyone. We've got all night, haven't we?"

"Man, if I'd known you actually wanted this, I wouldn't have wasted my stash," Billy said.

Todd snickered, standing and eagerly undoing his jeans. "They fuck just as well either way."

"Well, we do have a few minutes before she kicks it, right?" Karl said, doing the same. "We'll make the most of it. Like he said, they're just as juicy either way. This one's already dripping." He smelled his fingers and moaned.

"We'll get in a round," Billy said. He advanced on her first.

"No need to rush," Nova said. "Room's spinning enough without rushing. I think I need another drink. What about the rest of you? A drink before you get this ass?" She slapped her right cheek, then smoothed her hand over it to draw their eyes as she opened the baggie with the other.

"I'll drink to that," Todd said.

Nova pretended to trip against the desk and leaned over it. "Whoa," she muttered. While she faked her struggle to maintain balance, she dropped two pills into each of the boys' drinks. If there was such a thing as a roofie overdose, good riddance. She'd take what she could get.

The glint in Billy's cold blue eyes was predatory. "Need help to bed, sweetie?"

You have no idea what you just got yourself into, 'sweetie', Nova thought, staring back up at him.

Perhaps some of that animosity managed to get through, because Billy tilted his head in suspicion. She grabbed the drink she hadn't spiked and fell against him, slipping her hand under his shirt to stroke the trail of hair leading from his navel to his cock under his pants. After that, she was pretty sure he didn't have two brain cells to rub together, with all the blood flowing the other way. He grunted, gazing down at her breasts brushing against his chest.

"Just need the room to stop the carousel." Nova chugged her second beer, thinking with each swallow, *I'm going to regret* this *part in the morning.* She overtipped, and beer ran down the sides of her mouth onto her breasts and stomach. *Why do people drink this shit anyway?*

"Whoa, there." Billy caught her and grabbed his own drink. "We'll take good care of you, won't we? What are you waiting for, boys? Grab a drink and take a seat. I get her first."

"I get your face first." She giggled as he bent down and licked over one trail of beer from her breast. "Better drink that one, boy, before you spill any more on me. I've got quite enough as it is."

"Good point," Billy said, too many teeth in his grin. He thought he was such hot shit—such a lion, as though he forgot that the lionesses did the real hunting. Jules could wipe the floor with all three of these cavemen...and so could she. She could do it drunk, in fact. She still didn't feel too bad, except for a little bit of nausea from the cheap beer, and the room was rocking a little, like they were on a boat.

Billy picked her up and tossed her onto the bed, where she stared at his drink expectantly. He took a few good swigs before putting it on his nightstand. The other boys had already grabbed their drinks, and she thought the levels were lower, although they crowded around the bed and were more interested in the way she caressed one breast and reached between her legs to stroke through her folds. She whimpered a little at the wetness she found between them.

Then she turned onto her side, moaned a little when Billy grabbed her hair. It reminded her too much of when Eli had done the same thing, yet it was *nothing* like what Eli had done to her.

"I think I'm going to be sick." The last beer sloshed in her stomach with remnants of the first one, and from under her fever, cold sweat prickled at her skin. She'd been planning on faking sickness, but now the sickness was real, and with it, reluctance. Even for her, it was difficult to feel sexy or feign sexiness when she wanted to throw up.

"That's fine. It's normal. Just relax." Billy brought her mouth to his erection through his pants. She clawed at his jeans but didn't have her claws out while doing it. "Take it out. You're still awake. I want to see you take it out."

"Can I use the bathroom?" she asked. "I might puke."

"Just do it on the floor. The janitors'll get it." He took one of her hands and brought it to the front of his pants. "Take out my dick, bitch."

Nova struggled to sit up and get away from his grip on her hair, but he yanked her back hard enough to bring tears to her eyes from the pain on her scalp, because he held her hair too far from the base. Eli's hand had been close to her head. His control on her had been effortless, painless.

"Hey, stop. I want to do this. I just need—"

"What you need is my dick in your mouth." Billy released her hair to slap her cheek. It hurt her pride more than her cheek itself. "Now, stop talking and get it out. We didn't bring you in here to talk."

"Oh God, I'm going to—" Turned out even a succubus shouldn't drink too much beer too quickly, because she bent over the bed and retched out the whole contents of her stomach.

Shouting in annoyance, Billy leaped back before it splattered on his feet.

"Ah, gross, man," Todd grumbled.

Her mouth tasted sour and acid burned the back of her throat when she was finished. She coughed, then swallowed. Some of it had gotten on the tips of her hair.

"I think I should go home," she muttered. "I need to go home."

"No way." Billy threw a red towel over the mess and forced her up again by the clean portions of her hair. He had a hand towel in his other hand. He wiped her mouth without tenderness, then squeezed the bottom of her hair where it was dirty. "There. That's good enough for now. Now swallow it."

He'd taken his cock out himself. It was half-hard when he pushed against her lips. She still shivered with nausea, and the last thing she wanted was something in her mouth. She tried to turn her head, but once his cock touched her lips, he was mindless, the cock practically jumping as it swelled.

He crawled on the bed over her, and she collapsed onto her back. He held her down by kneeling over her chest and traced her lips with the leaking tip of his erection. The room was less rocky when she was on her back like this. Nova narrowed her eyes, but he groaned when she ran her tongue over the head. His pre-cum helped, actually, although it wasn't enough to get the taste of vomit out of her mouth.

"Ah, fuck yeah." He thrust his fingers into her mouth to open it and pressed his cock in to join his fingers. She gagged when he pushed down on her tongue, although she didn't actually have a gag reflex. She was giving him every chance to be a decent bad guy, but he refused to take her up on her generous offers, and his friends did nothing to stop him, which was just as bad as helping him.

"Hey, man, something's wrong." Karl grabbed the bottom of the loft bed to steady himself. Todd stumbled, then fell to his knees, holding his head. Both of their Solo cups were empty.

She felt their unconsciousness coming like fog creeping in at dusk. And like fog, she discovered she could manipulate it, move it forward more quickly with magic that reveled in men's sleep. That was a new trick.

Nova grabbed the strings of their unconsciousness and pulled them closer, a fisher reeling in a catch—a good catch indeed. Karl and Todd were easier. Billy put up a fight, shaking his head and blinking rapidly.

"What the hell?" Billy stared at his friends. Then he jerked his head down at Nova, who had taken his erection all the way in her mouth, invigorated by the knowledge that, in spite of her setback, she was going to win this game.

"How does it feel?" she asked, after popping his cock out of her mouth. She propped herself up on her elbows to nuzzle it before grazing her teeth over the shaft, making him jump. And sway. And fall back as she finally got a good grip on his impending unconsciousness. "Oh, I'll give you what you want. I told you you could have this, and you will. But it won't end quite the way you expected."

"What...did you...do?" Billy tried to focus on her. His eyes widened when he realized why he couldn't.

Karl collapsed, making the room shudder. Smaller than both Karl and Billy, Todd was already out for the count.

"I saw what you were going to do to that other girl, what you had probably already done to her friend." Nova cupped his scrotum, her nails turning to claws against the back so that he wouldn't even think of lunging after her, even if he could find the strength. "Turns out I can get drunk, Billy, but I can't get roofied. The first one is annoying. The second is useful. Now, be a good boy and go to sleep like your friends."

Karl was snoring, his mouth open and drooling on the floor.

Nova yanked sleep around Billy with a growl.

"Fuck...bitch..." Then he hit his head on the corner of the support board for the loft as he fell back.

"Don't worry. You will." She gingerly climbed off the bed to avoid the vomit and Todd. Throwing up and the alcohol in her system had left her shaky. "Now, if you'll excuse me, I'm going to use your shower and toothbrush, because I feel gross. I'll see you in a minute."

Chapter Nine

When she walks out of the bathroom, the boys are waiting for her, Karl in the single armchair in the room, Todd leaning insouciantly against the loft and Billy on the comforter. He made the play, so he gets the glory…and the bed.

"See?" Nova holds her breasts up to their gazes as she slowly approaches them, giving them a show. She put her heels back on after showering, and they make her legs look so long in spite of how petite she is. "It could have been like this if you'd been nice."

"What's that about?" Todd asks, massaging his erection through his pants with unabashed enthusiasm, especially when she lets her tits fall so that she can lift them back up, again and again.

"Never mind." Nova pinches her nipples until they are tight and hard. She turns to Karl. "And you, big boy, I know you were dying to see me do this." She raises her breast and lowers her mouth to lick across the top. Then she dips her head farther, tilts her breast up and sucks the sensitive nipple into her mouth. Nova discovered she could do that a few years

ago when she tried out of curiosity. It isn't nearly as hard as trying to kiss her elbow.

"Oh, fuck me." Karl unbuttons his jeans and grabs his full, fat erection as though it will get away from him and go after her if he doesn't hold it down.

"I can't even see anything," Billy says from the bed.

Nova glances over her shoulder. "Nothing at all?"

"Okay, this side's not so bad,"

"Not so bad? Is that a challenge?" Nova turns around with her arm over her breasts and a hand over her cunt in a parody of modesty.

Billy reclines on the bed, his legs splayed and his jeans unzipped but not open. The bulge of his erection pushes the placket up enough for her to see how hard he is.

"What are you waiting for, boys?" Nova asks with a teasing come-hither stare. "A formal invitation? I like lots of boys to keep me warm."

As she climbs between Billy's splayed legs, his knuckles brush her forehead. "Geez, you feel like you're going to burst into flames any second, and you want more? Are you sick?"

"Does that bother you?"

"A gentleman is concerned about the state of his woman," Billy replies.

Nova dips down to mouth over his cock between the fastenings of his jeans. "Yes," she murmurs into him. "A gentleman is. Where does this gentleman want me?"

"What?"

"Well, this lady has a mouth, a pussy and an ass. I didn't bring the three of you up here to go one at a time." Nova nudges Billy's shirt up his abdomen with her nose as she ghosts her lips and breath over his skin. "I want a cock everywhere a cock can be. I want to be stretched, fucked, screwed six ways from Sunday, as they say. I want to come with all of you coming inside me."

"Holy fuck," Todd chokes out as he stares down at Nova undulating her body over Billy's. "Are you for real?"

"Touch me," Nova says. "Do I feel real to you?"

Todd reaches out with a trembling hand and pets her spine as though she's a cat. Nova hums in pleasure at the trail of desire that follows his touch.

"That's right," she says. "A gentleman waits until a woman gives permission, and when the lady gives permission, the gentleman does as the woman tells him. That's how it should be."

She frantically works at the buttons on Billy's shirt until he catches a clue and does the rest himself, yanking it off with impatience. Karl has already taken the hint, even more naked than Nova, who still has shoes on. He's stroking his cock, not that it needs the help staying hard.

Her hand on Karl's arm has him grunting, his fat erection growing even thicker at the touch. Nova licks her lips.

"I think I know how this is going to go." Billy grins at the way she salivates and has to keep swallowing as she stares at Karl's cock, but Billy kneads her breasts to draw her attention back to him. He tweaks the prominent nipples because her gasps make them tremble in his hands. "I've been thinking about that pussy every second you've been in the shower. And if I can't have your mouth on me, I'd like to watch you trying to take that big, fat dick of Karl's. Todd can have this ass." Billy smacks her left cheek so hard she jumps. "But I get your pussy."

"Hell, yeah," Todd says excitedly. He nearly trips out of his briefs.

"Sounds good to me." Nova drags her breasts down Billy's abdomen as she moves to pull his pants and boxers off. "Inspired, in fact. Just the scenario I had in mind."

Billy spreads his arms. "We aim to please."

"Yes, you do. Todd, if you want in my ass, you better get started."

"Get started what?" Todd asks.

Nova slides her hands over her ass down to her thighs. Then she parts the cheeks so he can see everything. "It's not going to lick itself."

Todd recoils. "What…? No. Gross."

She grabs his wrist. "What do you think I was doing in the shower?" she says softly. "In fact, I think you'll enjoy eating ass, won't you, Todd? You like watching a woman lick another woman's ass. Why not try it yourself?"

"How'd you know that?" Billy asks.

"Know what?" she replies.

"What kind of porn he watches."

Nova smiles and bends down to kiss him, tongue first. She dominates his mouth as she strokes his cock with her hand and entices Todd to her with a sway of her ass, so near her wet pussy. She jerks her head up and cries out with a shocked smile when Todd spreads her legs farther and runs his tongue from her cunt to drag her wetness to the hole above it. He swirls his tongue around her with a helpless moan.

Nova's nails become claws in the comforter, but the boys can't see that.

At his first taste, Todd can't get enough. He grips her hips like an anchor as Billy and Karl watch Nova react to his eager mouth, entranced.

"Ooooh, that's good." She reaches down between her legs and rubs herself. She didn't expect it to feel that good, but the longer he does it, the less control she has over her words, until all she can do is moan like a back-up singer to the music downstairs.

"Enough," she manages to say. She grabs Todd by his bowl cut and pushes him back, gasping. His cock bobs in an amusing curve, pre-cum leaking a thread of thin liquid onto the comforter. "Inside. Both of you get inside me. Don't worry, Karl. I haven't forgotten you."

She grasps for his hand, a big football player's hand that swallows hers. He steadies her with that hand but rolls her nipple between three wet fingers, making it harder to maintain her balance as she raises herself over Billy's erection. They need no foreplay, no extra lubrication. Some of Todd's saliva drips down to join her juices as she sinks down over Billy. Her pussy clings to every vein and ridge as she goes down the shaft and seats herself on him, sheathing him with no trouble at all. Billy fights not to wildly thrust up into her, his tendons standing out on his neck. He clutches her waist and her other breast as she groans in pleasure, like she's sunk into a hot bath in January.

Todd sidles as close to her as he can. "Fuck, I'm going to come."

"Not until I let you," Nova replies breathily. She lifts herself up Billy's cock and pushes back down. She and Billy moan in tandem.

"So hot," Billy mutters. "Too hot." But he doesn't try to get away when she licks his stubbled Adam's apple and nips his chin.

"All right," Nova says. "Your turn, Todd. Get inside me. I need you inside. Don't slump. There's not room. The bottom of the loft, hold on to that. Oh yeah, just…like…that."

It doesn't matter who hears as Todd eases his spit-slicked cock into her while she's already full. She gasps, holds her breath, gasps again. She nearly blacks out before she convinces herself to breathe properly. Todd fills her to the utter brim, past what she thought she could handle, but once he's inside, she craves more, wishes he were larger, wishes Billy were larger, wishes that her body could stretch even farther. She tightens her muscles around them, her hips canting reflexively as pleasure goes off inside her, in her cunt, in her fingers, in her neck, in her head, random places that don't make sense, and she can't stop them. She was buzzed from the alcohol, but now her head is clear, the clarity only sharpening the sensations.

Todd jerks into her at the clenching, and Billy starts to thrust involuntarily.

"Still," she hisses.

They freeze, unable to move because of her command. It isn't that they hurt her. It's that they felt too good.

And she isn't finished yet. She isn't full enough. She wants to be stuffed like a Thanksgiving turkey. If she had more boys in the room, she'd stuff them up the three boys' back doors, and they'd like it because she desires it of them. No matter. This will have to do, and do it will. Nova is almost afraid of how intense the pleasure will be, and it alarms her that this isn't enough, that she suspects even the pull of Karl's girth at her lips won't be enough. Especially knowing their end, her own appetites would terrify her if her adrenaline weren't busy with other, more delightful emotions.

"Now it's time for patience to be rewarded." Nova shifts to the side, making all three of them groan from the change in angle. She braces herself on the bed and peers up at Karl through her eyelashes, then traces her lips with the tip of her tongue. "I'm hungry."

Billy moves her wet hair out of the way as Karl offers her his cock, short but almost as thick as summer sausage. Her little mouth doesn't look like it can take such width, but they underestimate her. She drops her jaw like a python and swallows him down.

Karl grunts, his abdomen tightening as he nearly doubles over at having her mouth around him. He's probably never had a girl who can take him in, not like this. She will be his first and last, a goddess in his short-lived memory.

"That is hot," Karl grits out. "My God."

She lifts off the head with a pop and says the magic words, "Fuck me. Hard. Everywhere. Now."

Just do it, *she thinks wildly.* Make me what I am.

Karl shoves his cock back in her greedy mouth, and Todd and Billy grasp all over her body as they try to find a rhythm that works to give both of them the experience they want. Only thin flesh separates them. Their cocks rub against each other as they fuck her. Eventually, Todd grasps the loft slats with both hands and goes at her with just his hips while Billy's hands have her all to themselves, keeping her still enough that neither he nor Todd slips out of her.

The truth is, they can't get out even if they try, but they aren't trying, so they never have to know that the tightness around them isn't just for their pleasure and hers.

Nova becomes something else. Underneath her mostly human veneer, she is a wriggling, serpentine thing, powerful, muscular, contorting and writhing as she takes in Karl's erection and as Todd and Billy fuck her ass and pussy. Her skin goes rough instead of smooth, her teeth wicked, her claws long and curved, her belly smoldering with the building fire that threatens to escape from all the places the boys' cocks stopper her. Her tongue and torso lengthen, featherless wings spreading — all invisible to the boys. To them, nothing appears to have changed, except that her body reaches a boiling point around their erections.

She is the exploding star. She is the falling meteor in the atmosphere. She is the fucking dragon, and these boys are knights who attempted to vanquish her. She has only one use for such men.

Nova clutches at Todd's hip and Billy's head, moving her hips back and forth to shove them deeper and quicken their pace. She isn't going to break just because she's awake and they aren't. Nova thinks it's impossible for her to break. It's them who can't take her, the girl they were going to rape. She's furious as she sucks them into her, tighter and tighter, hotter and hotter, until their groans completely drown out the music from downstairs. They practically shout as they slam into her, and she clamps down so hard they can't move anymore.

Her body milks them for everything they're worth. She ripples around their cocks, drinks them in, wave after wave of invigorating energy that she so desperately needs. Nova doesn't hold back this time. She inhales them, sucks them, absorbs them, drinks them, eats them, burns them to ash inside her.

They shout, bucking their hips with their cocks trapped inside her, until there is nothing left, their last moments far more blissful than they deserve, but the ending exactly what it should be.

* * * *

Jules swung his legs from the rafters with the white-winged doves as she flew in. "You went solo on me."

"Didn't want to kill another innocent boy," Nova said.

"No such monster." He dropped down, clearly prepared to speechify again about how she needed to keep her strength up. He paused, though, taking in the way she walked, carried herself, practically glowed from the fire inside her. "You look radiant...again. There's no way you didn't kill someone to look this amazing."

"I said I didn't want to kill an *innocent* boy." She jerked him to her by the waist of his cotton trousers.

After she'd climbed off the three boys, Todd had fallen to the side like a heavy doll. Karl had dropped from where he'd stood onto the towel that covered her vomit. When she'd checked underneath it, the vomit had nearly completely disappeared, and the towel had been damp but not dry. It was probably dry by now.

She'd glanced back after zipping her dress back on, relishing each slow click of the zipper, and smiled at the orgiastic tableau she'd created. Her wings had furled and her claws retracted after she'd come, but her teeth had still been sharp against her tongue.

They'd looked like they'd had sex with each other rather than a dream-walking succubus. She'd made them dance for her like puppets, the same motions, the same sounds in real life as in their dreams. No one would have heard most of her moans, muffled as they'd been. Someone on their floor would have heard the boys, though.

Add the roofies in their system, and she wished the local police luck in figuring out what had happened.

"*Sweet dreams, boys*," she'd whispered. Unlike Taylor, they'd been ashen, their lips and nails blue. Each of their cocks were still rock hard and likely to stay that way for a while, but they otherwise appeared quite dead. After all, this time she'd been *trying* to kill them.

She hoped it was as hot as her where they were now.

She'd spread her wings and launched through the walls, taking nothing but memories and life taut and lovely inside her, leaving behind nothing but fading shoeprints.

"So you found someone not so innocent," Jules replied, catching on with a grin.

"Some*ones*." She laughed as Jules slid his fingers through her hair, air-dried during the flight, and kissed her hard, walking her back with him toward the bed.

"How many?" He couldn't make it to the bed. He urged her to the floor, pushing up her skirt at the same time. "Oh God, tell me how many. I've never seen you like this."

Nova shoved down his pants and spread her legs. No foreplay for hours tonight. Her arousal was on a hair trigger from the feast. It zinged over her skin, buzzed like a thousand bees inside her.

"Three," she whispered in his ear before licking its edge and catching his lobe between her teeth.

Jules thrust into her without preamble, his shout laced with a deep growl. She planted her feet on the floor and pushed her hips up to meet him. It was fast, harsh, but she wasn't even aching from the pounding she'd already had. It was sweeter here, though, because Jules wasn't under her control and it was all real, not hazed over by the dream she'd been playing in. Also, their fucking was a hell of a lot more intimate. All his focus was on her alone, her focus on him, her limbs wrapped around him hard enough to bruise.

Jules laughed and moaned at the same time when she grew out her claws and raked them down his back as she came, still exhilarated from her justified gluttony. She got a taste of the girl that Jules had taken from, and when Jules captured her mouth and kissed her through his own orgasm, he took a taste of her evening as well.

His climax seemed to last forever inside her, the ice cream sundae to top off her Thanksgiving feast. She'd already gorged herself. It disquieted her that there was still plenty of room.

He hummed into her neck as he slowly relaxed, covering her like a blanket. "I hope you tell me that story some night…every exquisite detail. The glimpse you gave me… I could hardly recognize you, pet."

She traced curls onto his back with the thin lines of blood that she'd drawn. He twitched at the pain but apparently didn't want to move and neither did she.

Nova didn't recognize herself, either. Because this was the first time that she'd taken a life she didn't regret—not one bit.

She thought she was supposed to. Life was precious. A life lived meant more chances to repent. But at the same time, how many other girls had they drugged? How many notches did they already have and planned to add on their bed posts? And how deeply had those souls been carved with a butcher knife because of it? How many had lost faith because of the cruelty, senselessness and helplessness of what those boys had put them through? Somehow, she couldn't mourn the loss or feel guilty for taking them into her, putting their rapacious sexuality to better use.

The trouble was, when one became the clawed hand of vengeance, it all seemed justified until she became exactly what she destroyed in order to destroy it. To kill a monster, she had to become one.

Except she was already the monster. And this time, she wasn't exactly drowning in a river of her tears. Her conscience was usually such a loud, insistent, abusive voice in her head, but it was flat, distant, emotionless now, as though even it couldn't muster the energy for those boys or others like them.

If *her* conscience didn't have a discouraging word, Nova didn't think she'd lose sleep over becoming a nightmare. No one else would have stopped those boys. Nova had seen it time and again, experienced some of the worst that the world had to give girls like her.

Well, now the girl had some teeth. A little power. There were plenty of harmless men out there, and they didn't have to fear her anymore.

But the ones who preyed for fun and profit...

Screw them all, Nova mused, wrapping herself around Jules once more. Then she gave a low laugh that made Jules twitch inside her. *Well, yes. That's exactly what I'll do.*

Chapter Ten

Most people dreaded Mondays, but there was little difference to Eli between Mondays and Saturdays. Demons didn't take days off.

They said that if a person did what they loved, they never worked a day in their lives, but his muscles wouldn't ache so much if it weren't work.

Scotch and soda. A basket of chicken strips. It sure hit the spot at five o'clock in the morning after bagging himself an incubus whose skin he'd been able to salvage. Thank God for the twenty-four-hour bars and coffee shops in Meridian, which usually catered to either demons or hunters or both in some form or fashion.

"How's tricks, Fray?"

"Get the fuck out of my face, Brumley."

Cam Brumley was the cutest little button of a hunter in the whole New Salem bar at any given time, and she took great pleasure in rubbing in every unattached man's face that she was just as good as them and they could never, ever have her. She wore the rainbow bracelet with pride, but not a stitch of irony or camouflage for her happy hunting.

Texas though Meridian was, if a hunter didn't like her, it wasn't because she was a lesbian. Eli was pretty sure that, no matter a person's faith, there wasn't a single straight or bi dude in this hunter bar who hadn't happily imagined her with a woman at one point or another. If they didn't like her, it was because she was as much a gadfly to humans as she was to demons, and she didn't give a flying shit about it.

Brumley kicked her heels against his bar stool. Patent-leather pumps. She actually hunted in those. No one but Cam really knew how. "All those sex demons, and you're *still* not getting laid?"

"More than you," Eli replied.

"If you're getting that much, it's a wonder your mood isn't better. They have pills for that now, you know." She signaled for the bartender to get her the same thing Eli was having.

"Did you need something?" Eli snapped. "I was having a good night. Don't need you in it."

"A good night? I haven't seen you speak more than two words to anyone since you got here. Not a single friendly greeting."

"Exactly."

"That's a sorry state, captain," Brumley said, "when not speaking to anyone constitutes a good day for you."

"And you insist on talking to that kind of person. What does it say about you, considering you came in here alone, too?"

"I'm touched you noticed, Your Grumpiness." She tossed her hair, aggressively curled into blonde ringlets to go with her bright red, pinup lipstick and fifties-style dress.

The woman walked around outside in that get-up and hadn't yet lost her head to some demon horde. Eli understood why evil existed. That had never been a problem for him. What he didn't understand was why there was no justice in the world for costumed, painted clowns like Brumley, still walking around without a proper decapitation. Where did she even put her weapons? Under her petticoat?

"Do you have a point," Eli said, "or did you just get it in your mind to piss someone off and I happened to be in your line of sight?"

"You heard about the university murders?"

"How would I have heard about them?"

"They've been all over the news."

"I don't watch the news." He sipped his drink after Brumley did. She left lipstick stains on the rim of the glass. For some reason, that annoyed him even more than her ordering the same drink.

"They've got the news in newspapers these days. Fantastic invention. I really think they're going to catch on," Brumley said.

"Point. Get to it. Now. Or you're picking up my tab."

"When's your birthday, Fray?"

"I'm leaving now. Thanks for paying."

Brumley stopped him getting up with a firm hand on his shoulder and stood instead. "Happy birthday. Saw this and thought of you. It's not in your usual neck of the woods, but it seemed right up your alley."

She tossed the morning's paper onto the bar in front of him. She'd circled the giant headline with a red marker, just in case he didn't get the hint.

Three Athletes Murdered in Fraternity House

The cutline read, *Young men found with date-rape drugs in system, girl a person of interest in revenge killing.*

That wouldn't have been enough to trigger Eli's suspicions all by itself. He remembered college. Some of the things his friends had done had warranted such a response. They'd stopped being his friends pretty fast once he'd heard what they'd been doing.

What caught his eye were the arrows Cam had drawn a few pages in with the rest of the article.

The mention of a series of isolated deaths that hadn't previously been connected until this higher-profile homicide—a handful of young women and men, all with no apparent causes of death, just like the athletes. The coroner had ruled the athletes' deaths as seemingly natural, the product of cardiac arrest rather than drug overdose. However, they'd also ruled the deaths as suspicious, due to the drugs in their system — wrongful deaths that put the other deaths into question.

Although the university hadn't managed to quell interest in the couple that had died a few weeks ago under similar, albeit drug-free, circumstances, they'd been trying to keep the individual deaths quiet. Each one had been chalked up to freak tragedy as well as the fact that UTM always had a handful of unexplained heart attacks in seemingly healthy students, usually women. This year was the first that men had been included in that number.

There were so many red flags in the article that Eli wondered for the thousandth time how people managed to be so thick.

Natural but unexplained deaths, primarily one sex or the other... In this case, Eli suspected an individual, likely an incubus, who had recently paired off with a succubus, as sex demons sometimes did. There were mixed accounts of who the boys had been with when they were last seen. Eli would bet a month's collective wages that one of the details that the university and police weren't sharing was that the young men and women had been found in states of arousal.

An incubus and succubus were stalking the university, using a college's overdeveloped sense of self-preservation to conceal themselves.

UTM was about the size of an average sex demon's territory. All Eli had to do was find a high spot and look for wings. It was out of the way of his usual neighborhoods, but nothing beat a sure thing when it came to hunting.

Eli looked up from the article. Brumley had waited to leave, watching his hunger with her own.

She patted his cheek. Her nails were the same color as her lipstick. "You're welcome." Then she took her drink and headed back to one of the two-person booths, where she kicked up her heels and talked with someone on her phone.

Eli glared at her, but he didn't have the heart to mean it. He'd just finished a successful hunt, and he had a guaranteed pair of targets for his next hunt.

It would have to wait for Wednesday, though, because he had a date tonight—which meant that he should probably get some sleep so that he could work out when he woke up and get a shower in before dinner.

He couldn't remember the last time he'd had an honest-to-goodness date—maybe back when he'd had a real life instead of this lifetime adventure that dominated most of his time and energy. Eli sometimes got it in his head that, with all his living in the moment, he missed some of the good stuff, like a wife and kids, a retirement fund, a house with its mortgage paid off. Other times, he felt lucky not to be tied down.

But really, it wasn't a matter of whether a man was tied down but what he tied himself down to. He'd chosen this life—attached to little more than a job, an apartment and a cat—just as he'd chosen to accept the date, even though he'd made no promises and the girl probably wouldn't hold it against him if he didn't show.

He *wanted* to see Nova again. He'd replayed their last meeting over and over—sometimes while he was flying, sometimes in the shower, sometimes before bed. Everything in his memory filled him with the kind of excitement he usually attributed to espresso.

He was probably fooling himself. In all likelihood, it wouldn't work out once they were expected to converse and act like civilized human beings. Maybe they'd enjoy one more nice encounter before going their separate ways. But Eli couldn't remember feeling like this with any other one-off in the past.

It was all so strange and ridiculous and wonderful and stupid, and that was part of the fun for now, although he didn't like how little he could control it or how silly he felt when he remembered all the reasons he *shouldn't* show up for the date.

Still, absolutely nothing was going to get in the way of his good day.

* * * *

Jules' wings draped over the back of the couch as he watched her with a mixture of amusement, disapproval and just the slightest bit of contempt that she would be getting into such a tizzy about meeting with a human

man. He'd made it perfectly clear that she was supposed to be doing that to the man, not the other way around.

Nova kept going back and forth from the racks they used as wardrobes and the mirror next to the bathroom. She was on her eighth outfit. This was ridiculous. She could cut her hair off, wear flannel, men's jeans and no makeup, and he'd still find her attractive. But the outfit mattered to *her*, which was something that Jules didn't quite understand. He got that how a girl dressed made a difference to how she felt, but he thought she was getting worked up over dressing for Eli, and that was only half right.

Nova had never done this before. She'd had plenty of sex, but she had never gone on a date. She needed to look just right so that the stars, sun, moon and earth would align for her to be just as impressed by what she saw in the mirror as she hoped Eli was when he saw her again.

She laughed halfway through pulling off the red button-up blouse. She sat down on the floor and buried her face in her hands.

"I have nothing to wear!" she howled in laughter.

"Do you want me to pick?" Jules asked, grinning when she parted her fingers to meet his eyes. "A man's perspective, as it were."

"Nothing slutty. I don't need help with that, and he doesn't need to see that much of my boobs while we're eating."

"Speak for yourself. I'm surprised he hasn't seen all your boobs already. Must be something wrong with the man if he hasn't torn your clothes off, public place or not." Jules' wings followed him like an elegant train as he joined her at their wardrobe.

"I just know what you'd prefer I wear."

"You don't give me enough credit. If there's anything else a sex demon is good for besides sex, it's knowing what outfit is appropriate for a venue. The packaging is sometimes just as important as content. For a man to make an impression, he has to touch all of a woman's senses."

"Don't give me that. It's easier for men."

"Not when you really want to make a visual impression." He went through her clothes, with a sharp clack for every hanger he pushed to the side. "I just don't bother with the public forum as much as you. However, as appealing as I am in college standbys, I'm irresistible when I bring out the tailored suits. So don't pretend I don't know it's about more than tits and ass for something like this." He pulled out a burgundy dress with wide straps over the shoulders but a devastatingly low neckline. "However, don't underestimate your tits, love. Even the stodgiest maître d' wouldn't toss you out of a restaurant if you improved the décor with those. Earrings, no necklace."

Nova gave him the side-eye as she took the dress.

"Do you think you're the first succubus I've lived with? I learned from them as surely as you learn from me."

Nova lifted the dress up and sighed. "It's perfect."

* * * *

Times like this, Nova wished she could legally drink so she could down a glass of wine before he arrived — *if* he arrived.

And she wished she'd been able to set the time later. It wouldn't have been reasonable for her to ask him to meet her at eleven in the evening for dinner, even with Meridian's later nights, but she could have hunted beforehand so that her skin wouldn't yearn for contact quite as much while she waited at her table. Fortunately, the server was a younger girl who wasn't at all interested in Nova, which meant she didn't have to field any flirting.

"Good evening."

Nova scrambled up when she heard Eli come up from behind. She smoothed her hands over the front of her dress like a nervous schoolgirl. Why were her hands so clammy? His attraction was a foregone conclusion.

But it wasn't really. Sexual attraction, yes. Nova was here for more than that, though, wasn't she? Hadn't that been why she'd given him a time and place for a date rather than an address and a phone number for a hookup? They'd already done the hookup thing. The fact that he was standing right there — in a nice shirt untucked over jeans, like a businessman dressing down for the evening — told her that he was here for more than that, too.

A man would do a lot for easy sex, but of Eli's ninety-nine problems, access probably wasn't one of them. He was an attractive man...and respectful. He held her chair out for her, then pushed her in. He had stubble, but his hair was neat, his scent clean and he treated her like a lady when he didn't have to, not after compelling her into a semi-public blow job.

A guy who knew he could have everything for free didn't act like a gentleman just because he wanted more. A guy who acted like a gentleman with a secret succubus simply was.

"Thank you," Nova said. "I wasn't sure if you were going to show."

"I wasn't sure, either — or whether you would."

"It would be pretty bad manners for me not to show up to the date that I scheduled."

Eli shrugged. "You're a lovely young woman. I'm sure you have many other things you could be doing with your evening."

"I managed to get my homework done and beat the rest of my boys away with a stick," Nova said dryly.

Eli took a few swallows from his water. "Did you already order something to drink?"

"I'm just sticking with water."

"I hear they have good local brews on tap."

"Then you should get one of those," she said with a half-smile.

Eli put his water glass down heavily. "Please tell me you're old enough to drink."

"Not quite yet."

"*Please* tell me you're old enough to be here with me right now," Eli said, a deep line between his brows as he rubbed his forehead.

"I'm nineteen." Nova laughed at the way that he winced. "What?"

"You're even younger than I thought you were. You realize you're more than young enough to be my daughter?" His face took on a pinched look, as though determined to age itself right before her.

"But I'm *not* your daughter."

"Less than half my age. What the hell are you doing here? Shouldn't you be going to intramurals and themed parties and study groups and getting your heart broken by boys your own age instead of me? I'm not ready for a mid-life crisis."

"Then don't have one. Besides, I think you're making an awful lot of fuss over who was president when we were born."

"I grew up in a time when the Internet was called the library and phones were plugged into the wall."

Nova reached across the table and traced her nails over his hand in a gentle circle before covering it. Anyone who had a passing interest in their table would know that her intentions were anything but pure, but fuck anyone who decided to judge them based on how smooth her skin was in comparison to his. She was a succubus. She was immortal. Suddenly, age didn't seem so important to her, not that it had been all that important before.

Eli stared at her hand covering his.

"I don't know whether how old we are is going to make a difference, and frankly, neither do you," she said. "Not unless *you* make it an issue right now. Maybe it will become a problem. We won't know until it does. But tonight is just a date, Eli, not an engagement party or a commitment ceremony. Right?"

"Yes," he said slowly.

"We're just here to have a good time with good food and good company. If something happens, great. If nothing happens, that's okay, too. But I think we're a little early into things for you to start worrying if our disparate experiences are going to be a long-term problem, don't you?"

"You're a psych major, aren't you?"

"Everyone seems to figure that one out pretty quickly," she said with a laugh.

Eli slowly turned his hand over underneath hers so that their palms touched. He grazed his fingertips over her wrist before grasping her hand.

She lowered her eyes before glancing back up at him, a hint of shy and sexy at the same time. "Besides, I've had my fill of boys my own age. They're always after only one thing."

He swallowed thickly. His gaze was drawn to where she leaned over, her cleavage generous where her breasts nearly pressed against the tiled table. The structure of the bodice gave her some support, but it couldn't conceal the natural shape of her breasts, making it abundantly apparent that she wasn't wearing a bra.

"Who said I'm not after that, too?" he asked.

She slid her hand away from his as she sat back to give him a different angle "Well, I assumed you weren't after *only* one thing."

Eli lifted his gaze back up to her eyes. The serious set of his mouth cracked a little when the corner lifted on one side. He still looked a little uncomfortable, however, as the waitress took their appetizer order and recommended one of the beers on tap.

"Tell you what," Nova said when the waitress left. "We try not to think about our differences tonight. We're just having fun, getting to know each other. Perhaps we'll have that one thing later. And *you* get to decide whether we have another date. Does that sound fair? Age is a big factor for a lot of people. I don't want to dismiss your discomfort. I just want to show you it doesn't mean anything to me."

He nodded. "Okay. I can accept those terms."

She relaxed and crossed her legs. "So, what is it that you do, Eli?"

"I'm in acquisitions, freelance."

"I don't know what that means."

"It means I find things that my private clients want me to find. I can't be more specific because of non-disclosure, but also because my acquisition base is too broad to define. Some might call me a buyer, others a hunter."

"Is this good work? Interesting, at least?"

"It pays the bills, although I have complicated hours," he replied. "It's all contract, so alas, no benefits, but my pantry bin isn't filled with cheap noodles, so I count that as a win."

"What did you want to be when you were a kid? I'm guessing 'acquisitions expert' wasn't on that list."

"I wanted to be a fighter pilot. I never wanted to be a lawyer, but law was what I got into during college. I did time as a paralegal, did really well, but I wanted out of that life. I'm much happier where I am."

"I like that you're doing what you love over what might make more money," she said.

"There are pros and cons to every decision. For instance, it doesn't make it easy for me to get to know someone, with my late nights, early mornings, afternoons spent asleep, most evenings working."

"Perhaps a college student is a good fit for you, then. Sounds like my schedule, except I suspect I get less sleep than you do." She was stretching the truth, since she'd stopped taking most of her classes, and that meant much more sleep. She attended the classes she cared about, but she stayed invisible for them, because she didn't want to test whether she was still on the attendance roster.

They already had chips and salsa at the table, but queso con carne arrived as their appetizer, and they gave the waitress their entrée order.

"What drew you to psychology?" Eli asked. "Aside from the fact that you'll never be short of clients."

"I had a rough time growing up. Nothing to fill a tell-all memoir or anything, but it got to the point that...that I wanted to help other people who were going through their own rough times. Nothing's worse than going through it alone and thinking you're the only one it's happening to."

"Sounds noble." Eli held up his glass. Nova grinned and clinked her water glass with his beer.

She was a little sad, though, because it *had* been a noble goal, albeit a fruitless one in the end, since some of her clients would have ended up treating her as a sex surrogate instead of a therapist. That might have been a legitimate thing in California, but probably wouldn't be in Texas in a human lifetime.

It stabbed her chest a little that she now knew beyond a shadow of a doubt that she wasn't going to achieve any of her dreams, even if she dropped her invisibility and took every class and then some. Demons didn't become therapists.

"Do you know what you're going to do with the degree?" he asked. "I know everyone over the age of twenty-one is asking you that, because they can't think of anything else to ask, but..."

"Oh, God, yes. It's funny because it's true. I'm still not sure what to do with it yet. There are a lot of options—schools, social work, public sector, private sector. Plenty of time to figure it out, though. I'm only a freshman."

Eli groaned, resting his forehead in his hand and looking across the table at her.

She licked her lips and grinned. "Sorry. I'll try to keep the keywords more age-neutral."

"A little old to be a freshman, aren't you? At the risk of violating my own wishes not to think about it."

"I'm on the old side of my year. My parents got to decide whether I needed to go into school early or late when I was toddling about. They decided on late. Hey, it meant I could drive before almost everyone else in my grade — not that it made much of a difference, since I don't drive."

"You don't drive? How, may I ask, did you get here?"

"It's this miraculous thing. You pay it minimal fare, and it shuttles you and a bunch of other people all over the city, and it's so convenient, even though there aren't any seat belts. I believe the locals call it a bus."

"Wow. I thought I was biting and sarcastic."

"You've never done either with me."

He swallowed and mostly concealed the wickedness in his grin as the waitress returned with their entrées. "Just you wait," he said softly, the rasp in his voice warm enough for the waitress to notice.

"Enjoy your meal," the waitress said before making a swift exit.

About halfway through their respective dinners, which caused the conversation to lag but not stutter, Eli asked, "You hear about the deaths on your campus?"

Fortunately, it wasn't odd at all for Nova to be focused on her angel hair pasta dish. She didn't have to look at him and lie, when she and everyone else on this planet knew she was a terrible liar. "I've heard a little bit, but not a lot. Are you talking about those three athletes?"

"The paper said there were more."

"I don't read the papers. Not even the campus ones. I should, but I don't."

"What are people saying about it? Are people worried? Doing anything?"

"Well, if it's only after guys, I don't have anything to worry about, do I?"

"Not just boys. There have been others. More men than women, but it's certainly not exclusive."

"I heard this group talking about it at breakfast. About how it's like a snake going through the pipes." She shook her head with a little laugh. "Maybe that's not too farfetched, the Speckled Band theory. We're not exactly Australia, but Texas has venomous snakes and spiders, too. I just find it hard to believe that a disease or creature bite wouldn't leave any marks or signs that it's been there. Another person called it a terrorist attack, which makes no sense. Another person said it was a government experiment of some kind of toxic gas. That one's more likely than the terrorist attack, but still...Meridian as ground zero for nerve gas tests? Seems implausible."

"What's your guess?"

She shrugged. "It's a college campus. The simplest answer is some kind of new designer drug. Didn't those guys have Rohypnol in their systems? Who knows what else was there that the standard tox screens can't detect? If that's the case, I still don't have to stay up nights. I angst over whether to take ibuprofen every month."

"I still think you should be careful," Eli said, his rough voice warmed not by attraction but concern. "Just like Rohypnol, a drug can be administered without your knowledge."

Her easy smile faded. "You don't have to worry about me. No parties. No Greek. Not a lot of friends to get me into trouble."

"You don't have a lot of friends? I find that hard to believe, a charming young woman like yourself."

"That rough time I had when I was younger? It followed me here. I like my classes, and I have a friend to watch out for me, but I'm mostly on my own. I like it that way. Much less pressure."

"If I didn't know exactly what you meant, I'd be insulted," Eli said with a roguish grin.

"It's not you I object to."

"I know. I don't have many people I'd call 'friend', either. It's probably much less shocking for you to hear that about me than it is for me to hear that about you."

Nova tilted her head in acknowledgement. He had a bit of the abrasive about him and a six-foot circumference of personal space that she was honored he'd invited her into, ill-gotten though her invitation had been.

"All the more reason why this date working tonight is even stranger than it already was," Eli admitted.

"Tell me about it. I can't help but expect disaster. Just my nature."

"Mine, too," he said quietly.

"There are some benefits to being a pessimist, though."

"What are those?"

"You're prepared for the worst, but when the worst doesn't happen, all the more chances to be pleasantly surprised."

Eli drank to that.

* * * *

They stayed at their table until closing at one in the morning, talking almost the whole time without any lull but for eating while the evening crowd trickled out around them.

Although Eli took up the check, Nova insisted on leaving their server a generous tip. The younger girl had surreptitiously stared whenever she'd come over, as though trying to figure out whether they were really here on a date and how she felt about it. However, Nova was either oblivious or indifferent to the waitress' judgment.

He found it truly unbelievable that a young woman as bright and engaged as Nova didn't have anything better to do with her time or anyone better to do it with. She talked about a rough past, but she had none of what he would consider the usual markers of trauma. He'd heard of late bloomers blossoming in college — although he intensely disliked flower metaphors — but there was either something very wrong with the way Nova viewed herself or she was keeping a pretty important secret from him.

Eli didn't begrudge her that. He had a few heavy-duty secrets himself, and it was only their first date. However, as first dates went, he was astounded by how well this one had gone — one o'clock in the morning, kicked out of the restaurant because they'd had too much to say and no need to go to sleep because of the uncommon hours they kept. Eli hadn't known he could talk that much, especially not to someone he'd feared he would only have a certain kind of chemistry with.

"So...do you want to get some coffee or call it a night?" Under cover of darkness, she must have thought he couldn't see her blush as her shyness returned. "I mean, if we keep talking, who's to say we'll have anything left to share next time?"

"Coffee sounds good." Eli slid his hands in his pockets, enjoying her sudden awkwardness. It made her seem more accessible, more her age but also more normal, so that the age thing didn't hit him quite as hard. Their conversation had been easy, but that didn't mean both of them hadn't been working hard to impress. As first-date awkwardness went, this was mild, endurable and surprisingly endearing.

"And by coffee, do you mean coffee? Or do you mean coffee, as in other things? We're talking a coffeehouse, right? So it's not like you're inviting me to your place for coffee, but even so, we kind of made it clear that we don't need four walls to do that thing that coffee's coded for…"

"I meant coffee coffee," Eli interrupted, although he'd considered just letting her keep going. "However, I'd understand if you wanted to go separately. You don't know me well. I'm sure your mother always told you not to get into strange cars with strange men."

"It's so late for that advice that it's already dead and buried." She bit her lip, unsure how he'd respond to that declaration. It alarmed him slightly, more *for* her than *against* her. However, it wasn't his place to ask, especially since he was the one interested in ravishing her at the moment—not necessarily in the car, but the more she looked at him like that, the more he wanted to.

"And I'm not exactly going to say 'no' to non-coffee coffee, am I?" he added. "Unless that's not the kind of coffee you're interested in tonight."

"Which car is yours?"

There weren't many vehicles left in the parking lot, but the area housed two restaurants and a strip mall, and employees were working late closing, so it was a reasonable question. Eli nodded to his truck. Without a word, she smiled, her gorgeous lips full and suggestive as she slowly headed to the truck.

At the passenger-side door, he slid his hands onto her shoulders and down her arms. The night was cool, but she was so warm. She'd never even put on a sweater in the heavily air-conditioned restaurant.

It wasn't the temperature of the air that made her shiver. He crowded her against the black-painted metal until she pressed her hands to the side of the truck, her breasts to the back of her hands. He kissed her hair, flipped up in a loose, casual knot.

The table had put distance between them, except for the caress of her hand on his at the beginning of the dinner, but now that he was close again, all the desires that he'd managed to keep at bay during the evening returned in full force.

"You never did say which kind of coffee you wanted," he murmured in her ear before lowering his mouth to her neck. He groaned when she bared it to him so that he could work his lips and teeth and just a hint of tongue down its length.

"I've been wet all night thinking about this," she whispered.

Fuck. He didn't say it aloud this time, but it was as though she knew exactly what he needed to hear for his cock to wake up completely. His jeans were too tight, and now he *swore* he could smell her desire. Eli moved his hips away from her. If he stayed against her ass for too long, he might not be able to control himself. He'd been selfish before. Although she'd seemed content, he would ensure that he didn't leave her unsatisfied tonight.

Her saying things like that wasn't helping.

It was all Eli could do to slowly turn her around in his arms and not shove her up on the truck door, yank open his jeans and fuck her right in the middle of the parking lot.

"Is that so?" He prided himself that the words came out steady.

She nodded.

"Because it's easily verified."

Nova's lips parted as he cradled and massaged the back of her neck in a possessive grip. But what made her cry out like a kitten was her skirt lifting over her legs as he tucked his right hand underneath and stroked up her inner thigh. No one would be able to see anything, but there would be no question to anyone watching what he was doing.

Eli was a private man. A hunter usually went about the world like a ghost. He'd never sought recognition or visibility, and all his sexual encounters with other women had been discreet, if not respectable.

But everything about Nova made his impulse for privacy fly out of the window. When he was close to her, he wanted her whether they were in public or not. If he could have, he would have taken her on the dirty floor of the restaurant. He fought not to have her straddle him right on the parking lot concrete, fought to do nothing but slip his hand under her skirt and cup her mound, mapping her folds through her panties with his fingers.

Dear Lord above and devil below, she was as wet as she claimed.

"Eli..." She moaned so prettily as he pushed against her clit to make her shudder.

"If I told you to take your dress off right now under this streetlamp, would you do it?" He stroked her over her panties with his whole hand again. She canted her hips to meet him.

Nova closed her eyes, her hands clenched against her shoulders as though afraid to move as he touched her.

"Look at me, Nova. I asked you a question. Would you take your dress off in the middle of the parking lot?"

Her eyes were so dark that they were practically black as she looked up at him. He felt dirty, mean, powerful and most important of all, trusted. It shook him like an earthquake when he realized he might actually be falling in love with the girl, which was exhilarating and terrifying in reeling turns. This was all wrong on so many levels, a series of unnecessary complications, but he couldn't convince himself to let go of her, to look away from those innocent yet not-so-innocent eyes.

"If you told me to," she said.

He reached into his pocket and clicked the button to unlock the truck as he withdrew his other hand from between her legs. Nova yanked on the door handle and pulled herself up into the cab, the skirt of her dress swinging around her legs. He got a glimpse of her panties as she bypassed the front seat and climbed into the back.

"Like you read my mind." With a fierce grin, he climbed in after her.

Chapter Eleven

He locked the doors before tossing his keys onto the driver's seat and grabbing a condom from the glove compartment. Then he braced his hands on the shoulders of the front seats and vaulted into the back, where Nova immediately reached for him, kissing him before he even sat down.

There was no need to stay quiet inside the truck. Her needy moans shot straight down his spine and sent lust through his body. He felt it in his scalp, in his fingertips where he slid his hands over her waist…hell, even in his knees, which usually gave him nothing but grief. His skin felt like glazed ceramic, as though his desire was too great to be held inside him as she pursued him and he met her, not giving her a moment's mercy yet feeling like he was the one drowning, nevertheless.

He gripped the loose knot of her hair where the band held it close to her head.

"Am I going to need to do this to you again?" he asked through gritted teeth, but he was as far from anger as he could be. "Or are you going to do what I say?"

Nova stroked his jaw, his neck, his hair. The lamb was actually trembling. "What do you want, Eli? I'll do anything,"

"You realize what a dangerous word that is, don't you? You've already experienced what I can do to you, and you throw around a word like 'anything'."

She trailed her fingers from his neck down to his lap, tantalizingly close to his erection. The weight of her hands on his jeans pushed them against his cock ever so slightly, hitching his breath. "*Anything.*"

Eli couldn't tell if she was foolish, adventurous or both—but some said that about hunters, too. He could hardly point fingers or throw stones, not when his cock desperately wanted to reward her for such a daring spirit—and himself, for finding her among the coal dust of Meridian.

What he really wanted to do to her required a little more space—a bed instead of a back seat. But he could improvise.

"Take off your underwear. Then lie down on the seat and spread your legs, Nova, your skirt high."

Nova pushed away from him into the next seat and lifted her skirt just enough to pull her panties down. He hooked a finger in them and brought them to his nose where they were dampened straight through.

She stared as he marked her scent like a bloodhound. Then he tossed them into the front seat where she couldn't reach them.

Eli shifted so that his back was against the side of the truck, his knee up on the seat. "I believe I gave you another command."

Nova lay down and raised the front of her skirt over her hips. She parted her legs as far as she could on the narrow seat, but there wasn't a lot of room.

"I said spread your legs. I want to see all of you without needing glasses."

"Where? I want to, but…"

Eli stopped her protests with a tickle to the bottom of her foot that had her giggling and jerking wildly away. She tried to keep her feet away from him after that.

"You're smart, Nova. I think you'll figure out what I want."

As he'd predicted, she eventually lifted her right leg so that it draped over the back of the seat while her left knee pressed against the driver's seat. She gripped her own thighs, displaying herself to him, but he brushed her hands away to confirm that she could keep the position without help.

"You're awfully flexible," he murmured.

"I guess there are some benefits to youth," she said, breathless as he leaned over her.

"Cheeky, aren't you?"

"Not usually." She bit her lip. "You bring out the worst in me."

He grinned. "You must be such a good girl if this is your worst. Are you telling me this is the bad girl?"

"Maybe not as bad as I can be."

"How bad can you be?" He still hadn't touched her, just let his gaze crawl over the pull of her breasts against the harness of her dress down to where her pussy glistened in the darkness, the streetlamp illuminating her in enticing contrasts.

"How bad do you want me?" she asked.

"Touch yourself. Show me what you want."

"Why won't *you* touch me? *Please*."

"We've both been waiting all night. Surely you're not telling me that you can't wait a little longer."

"I want you to touch me, Eli," she purred, sliding her hands over her thighs again to part them even more, suggestive of even more arcane feats of flexibility if he gave her what she wanted. "I'm so hot all over. I need…"

Eli wrapped his hand around her ankle and bit her thigh. Nova jumped. He didn't quite break the skin, but it hadn't been a soft little love bite. He softened the blow with a gentle lick and a kiss to the place where he'd left impressions.

"I told you I'd bite, little girl," he said against her skin. "You'll get me, but not until I see what you wish I were doing to you instead. Touch yourself, Nova…for me. You promised me anything."

"I did, didn't I?" Nova's fingers shook as she trailed them from her thighs to the center. She paused before reaching her folds, staring at the ceiling and swallowing in discomfort. "There's no way to say this. I don't really… I mean, I don't really know…"

"You're telling me that you've never touched yourself?" Eli asked in disbelief.

"Not never," Nova said. "Just…really not often. This sounds so ridiculous. I've had plenty of sex, but I rarely masturbated. We were always told it was a sin."

Eli tilted his head in amused confusion.

"Yeah, I know." She laughed, diffusing the tension a little bit. "The way we twist theology and laws into knots, right? I guess it always felt more purposeful to touch myself than to have someone else do it to me. If I just happened to fall on a guy's cock, that could be forgiven, but it was a greater sin to make the decision to give myself pleasure."

He affectionately rubbed her ankle. "And now?"

"I'm more purposeful about having sex with men." Nova brushed her fingertips against his lips. "It's silly for me to balk at touching myself in order to have sex with one."

"I hope this isn't a sin, because if it is, then we're going to sin many times tonight, little girl."

"You don't think it is," Nova said, although there was a dim question mark at the end of the sentence.

"The way I do religion would probably get me excommunicated from any church. So make your decision, Nova. You can leave at any time. You've always been able to. But if you want me tonight, I want to see you touch yourself. All the better if I can watch your discovery. Touch all the places you want me to touch you, and I might just follow the paths you've shown me."

She slowly relaxed against the seat, but her fingers still fluttered, uncertain, upon her inner thighs.

"If it helps," he said, "close your eyes and imagine that your fingers are mine."

When she closed her eyes, Eli stopped hiding his hunger, leered without restraint. She didn't look quite as debauched as she had when he'd shoved his cock deep down her throat, but this was only the beginning. It amazed him that she could deep-throat a man without problem, but ask her to rub one off and she lost her nerve.

Still, that meant that what was about to happen was indeed a treat. Whatever she'd done with other men — and he wasn't knocking her experience — this was new to her. This was all his.

Nova moved her fingers to either side of her folds, tracing upward toward her clit. As she arched slightly and caught her breath at her own touch, Eli adjusted himself in his jeans. They were entirely too tight over his erection, but he didn't want to take it out just yet. If he released his cock, he'd touch himself and likely finish long before he could really get started on her.

He couldn't do everything tonight, but she'd said it was up to him whether they'd get together again, and between the date and the sex, Eli definitely wanted a reprise, weird as this whole thing was, bewildering as she was, damaged as she was. Eli could accept damaged. He wasn't exactly unbroken. No childhood trauma or anything, but a man didn't hunt for fifteen years without seeing things he wished he'd never had to see. The things he'd gotten used to... He sometimes scared even himself.

However, now wasn't the time for introspection.

Nova circled her clit and used her other hand to lightly tease her folds. She shook her head, chewing on her lip as she disappeared three fingers into her cunt all at once.

"Ah...Eli, yes..." she whispered. "You'd be so much more than this, but I can imagine what you'll be like."

"You are a wicked, wicked little girl." He couldn't stop himself from smiling like a tiger as she rubbed over and around her clit. "What are you imagining?"

"Your tongue," Nova replied. "I'm imagining you licking me until I can't take it anymore. Until I scream so loudly, they think you're killing me in here. And I'm imagining your cock inside me, touching me in places that I can't. You'd start slow, torturing me, but..."

"But I wouldn't be able to hold back for long, would I? Look at you, no underwear on, in the middle of a parking lot, touching yourself—and anyone could sneak up on us and peer through the window. They'd see your legs spread like a whore's, your nipples trying to tear through your dress, your lips swollen from my kiss, your cunt wet thinking of me. Faster, Nova. Faster. Fuck yourself faster like you want me to."

If she was a bad girl, then he was such a bad man, because he thought he might cream his jeans without even touching himself or her as Nova delved deeper and deeper into her dripping pussy, faster with each dirty thing that he said about her. Her fingers on and around her clit became frantic until she let loose a series of gasping moans and lifted her hips to meet her hands, coming with his name on her lips.

He maintained his composure as best as he could at seeing her undone, nearly regretted that her first orgasm hadn't even been with him. "Give me your hand. I'm going to sample you before I taste your pleasure at its source, filthy girl. That's right. Give it to me just like that."

Eli sucked each finger clean of her juices separately. She struggled to sit up enough to watch, her free elbow almost under her back as he ran his tongue around the base of her forefinger, staring at her clit as he did so—making the connection between the two parts of her anatomy perfectly clear.

"Now..." Eli climbed down so that he partially kneeled behind the front passenger seat, at perfect eye level to view the lush terrain of her body. "Don't wipe your hands. I want you to take that wet, filthy hand and pull out your right breast from your dress. Don't take the dress off. Don't shrug it down your shoulder. Push the fabric aside and show me your breasts. Make it shine with my spit on your fingers."

"Eli..." she gasped. But she slipped her hand under the dress, pushing the V-neck to the side with her knuckles as she cupped her breast, then nudged the dampened cotton until her whole breast was exposed.

Her nipple wasn't much darker than her skin, but it was broad, and the peak was tight and flushed as she stroked around it, bent it back and forth, covering it with the wetness with which he'd coated her fingers until it looked like it had been tormented by his tongue. Suddenly, his mouth went dry, wishing again that instead of her touching herself, it could be him.

Patience. He was a patient man. He could fly all night. He could kill demons until the sun came up. And when he set himself to it, he could make love to a woman well into the dawn.

Nova made him want to tear off her dress and pound into her like the boys she'd dismissed, except none of them would have his strength. None of them would have his care or his stamina—although she tested that stamina, just his hand around her ankle and the way she rolled her nipple, tugging it out so that she suspended the full weight of her breast from it. He could practically see her on her hands and knees, her breasts swinging underneath her with a pair of clamps on those light, tightened peaks.

He wanted tears on her cheeks. He wanted to kiss them away. *Anything.* She would do anything for him. She would do it gladly. He could strap her in harness, and she would drool around a ball gag and allow herself to be tied to the bed, if he told her to. She would do anything he told her to.

"Pinch it," he said. "Twist it. Make it hurt. Make it so that you want to get away from yourself. Yes. You like that, Nova? You like the way it makes you feel?"

"Yes," she moaned, her eyes still closed. She winced with her teeth clenched as she pinched and twisted her nipple until she was crying out every time, her breast quivering from her writhing. Her other breast moved easily underneath its cotton, heavy against the side.

"You feel it in your clit, don't you?"

She twitched when she felt his breath on her folds. Her heat warmed his face. He'd heard of women in fever, but she was actually one of those people. He remembered her hot mouth around his cock as though it were happening right that moment.

"Don't stop," he said huskily.

Then he slithered his tongue through her furrow and closed his mouth around her clit. Although the leg over the back of the seat kept her open, he brought her other leg in to keep hold of it. Her thigh brushed his ear as he lost himself in her taste, her scent, her fever. Whatever she had, it was contagious. Tears almost pricked his eyes from how good it was, how sweet her juices, how delicious her reactions to his enthusiasm.

She stopped trying to keep her moans and cries quiet. They weren't behind a restaurant this time. The truck was good at blocking noise from the street, and it likely did the same to keep their sounds in. The sound wouldn't be muffled necessarily, but thinned, flat, not even a blip on the radar of a passerby, especially since they weren't exactly rocking the truck—yet.

Her head nearly fell over the side of the seat as all her wriggling maneuvered her to the side and her back arched to lift her hips off the seat.

"Enough," she begged. "I need…I need more. I need you. Right now. I need you inside me."

"I'm not finished," Eli said.

She frantically tried to push herself upright, Eli pursuing her pleasure the entire way. Her bun was askew, one breast hanging out and the other with its nipple protruding against the cotton in such a way that made its shape unmistakable. He couldn't believe that she hadn't even put on pasties, but she'd somehow saved this show for him alone, and again, he tasted his conquest of her. If he couldn't have firsts all the time, he could thrill in knowing that he was the only one she intended to please tonight. And please him she had, except that he hadn't told her to sit up.

"That's the point," Nova said. "I'm...ahhhh...I'm going to...too much...need you...ah *fuck*..."

He hadn't pleased her during their first encounter. She deserved at least two orgasms for that oversight, and he was more than willing to give her everything she needed and more. And now that she had disobeyed him by not waiting for his demands, he was going to give her this one no matter what. He went after her with his tongue like a lashing, a punishment that made her head hit the window and her breasts tremble as she pushed up away from him, then pushed down to force herself against her mouth, helpless against the arousal he wrought from her. There were those tears he wanted, dripping down her cheeks and hitting her bare breast, staining dark the purple fabric over her clothed breast.

"I can't..." she gasped. Then his chin was wet with a fresh draught squeezed from her cunt like juice from sun-ripened fruit.

She clutched at the back of her seat and the driver's seat, but then she rested a hand on the back of his head, tentative, tender but insistent, nonetheless.

He rasped his stubble against her close thigh and kissed it smugly. "That's my bad little girl."

Nova slumped against the side of the truck. The last time they'd had sex, he'd been wrapped, and the last time she'd had an orgasm, it had been at her own hand—there was no feed to be had. But even though he'd been technically feasting upon her for this one, she'd feared as she crested her climax that she could absorb his pleasure through her clit. Everything that she'd gone through, and she still didn't understand how everything worked.

She suspected Jules didn't actually know everything, but it would have been helpful for him to give her *all* the pertinent details. Instead, he let information trickle through as needed, and he wasn't there tonight for her to ask him questions. She'd known that she could drink a man through her mouth, take him if he was up her ass and in her cunt. But she hadn't known whether *any* pleasure where they were connected—*any* climax where he was close to her strongest erogenous zones—would be dangerous to him, her orgasm or his.

His energy had drawn into her in quick, thirsty swallows with her climax, but it relieved her once again that he seemed unaffected by it, same as when she'd given him that blow job behind the restaurant.

Of course, he wasn't *entirely* unaffected, still subject to the natural, involuntary power of her touch. But the only thing she cared about was not hurting him. The fear had crept up on her, catching up right before she'd lost control, and he'd been caught in her net, unable to *want* to pull away. Her magic had latched into him like the stinger of a parasite, but he'd felt no pain and she couldn't even manage guilt, because he'd felt so fucking good against her.

No one but Jules had ever gone down on her. The exhilaration of it was still novel and exciting, as much as touching herself while imagining it was him.

He had no way of knowing that it was her making him feel this way, but this man... She fervently believed that he desired her, even without her power. She'd seen him when she hadn't been close to him, when he'd been outside the sphere of her influence. She believed in him as much as she believed in God, believed he would be almost just as insistent, predatory, desirous, even if her power hadn't settled into his skin like their collective heat that warmed the previously cold air.

To say she was relieved she hadn't sucked his life force out of his mouth through her clit was an understatement. It allowed her to bask in the aftershocks and steady hum of her continuing lust as he eased her down from the highest point of her pleasure. But the more he stayed against her flesh — making her twitch away from the hypersensitivity in her clit following two orgasms that had focused on the poor, wonderful little organ — she whimpered, shaking her head again and pushing against his. But he shook his head back and flicked his tongue into her cunt to draw out and drink her juices before returning to her clit time and again.

When he finally pushed himself up, she wiped her eyes and cheeks on her arm, holding herself back from covering her face entirely. She burned hot to her ears, unsure about that hard look in his eyes and the cruel smile he gave as he took her in.

"My goodness. What a state you're in. You really are a bad little girl, aren't you, looking like that? Take a look at yourself, Nova. How does that make you feel?"

She was disheveled, the knot of her hair fallen nearly at her shoulder, the dress pushed away from the one breast, possibly stretching the fabric irreparably. Her covered breast was stained with her tears. Her hands had smeared her juices and the scent of her cunt all over the truck and into his own tousled hair. She slowly brought her shaking fingers to her bun and pulled out the rubber band. It was useless anyway, and she knew from the fierceness in his eyes that it made her look even wilder, more fucked, more the bad girl that he wanted of her.

"I feel dirty," she said softly. Her magic reached out to him of its own accord, the way a cat's tail curled to catch the leg of the human it rubbed against. It was a possessive feeling, and although he couldn't meet her with his own magic, she still felt completely and totally possessed by him.

He was strong. His hands were firm on her thighs, the thumbs almost bruising, and he looked at her like a coyote staring at a rabbit. He had no way of knowing that he faced and possessed a predator, but that's because, when she was with him, she didn't have to be one.

She didn't want to hurt him. She didn't want his last moments to be of betrayal. He would know as soon as his soul passed on that this little girl who he thought he'd thoroughly corrupted was a corruptor herself and that she was the one who had to be careful with him, not the other way around.

He made her feel human again — or at least he made her feel like she had when she'd thought she was human. He made her feel better than all those other boys, because he knew what he wanted but also cared what she wanted. He dominated her, demanded her submission to feed off her pleasure as surely as she fed off his. He made her feel like she wasn't the succubus.

But she couldn't let herself be fooled that she wasn't. As her magic caressed him, wrapped around him like a friendly serpent, she reminded herself how precious this was to her, how fragile. She needed to be so much more careful.

She stroked his slightly grizzled cheek. His eyelids fluttered closed, his lips parting. For a moment, he looked as vulnerable as he was to her—less hard, less calculatingly cruel. It wasn't a dark cruelty, though, what he offered her, but a tender one. With his eyes closed, it was only the tenderness that she saw as he leaned into her palm.

She couldn't catch her breath, as though he'd tightened his grip not on her thighs but her heart.

When he opened his eyes again, his pupils were so dilated that he could have been possessed. "I'm a mean, mean man, Nova, but you're definitely my dirty little girl," he whispered, bending forward. He pressed a kiss to the top of her breast above her nipple, where she suddenly wanted him more than anything. He drifted his mouth down, and his breath tormented it, but he didn't give in to her, even when she brought her breast forward in invitation, almost irresistible invitation. *Almost.*

He resisted. And somehow, that resistance was what made her cunt clench, dampening the fabric of her dress beneath it. He wouldn't be able to see that with the way her skirt had settled over the tops of her thighs, but she got the feeling that he somehow knew exactly how dirty she was, even in the places he couldn't see — all the way down to her soul.

He slowly released his grip on her thighs, his expression terrifying in its intensity and in the intensity of what he made her feel — protected, possessed, even loved, although surely it was far too early for her to think in such terms — not to mention dangerous. Jules' unbidden voice echoed in her ear, asking her with a kind of impish glee whether a human was really the best man with whom to throw in her lot — a man who couldn't ever know who she was and whose desire she would always question.

Nova shook her head against the doubts, against Jules. This wasn't love. It couldn't be love. And if it wasn't love, she didn't have to worry — just fun, sex with a man in a way that wouldn't drain the life out of him, that wasn't focused on revenge or sustenance. Sex with a man the way she would have sex with an incubus — except that his touch felt rawer, even in its calculation, without the additional manipulation of magic.

He ghosted his mouth up from her breast to her neck, her mouth. "Tell me you need me."

She reached down between her legs to cup the front of his jeans. She parted her lips to taste the air, to taste the need in his breath as she stroked its length. Her effort to stay composed lasted only a short while.

Nova grabbed his nice, light blue shirt and jerked him up from the truck floor back to his seat. She practically leaped on top of him from where she'd been sitting and straddled his lap.

"I need you, Eli. *Now*," she said in a semi-growl, halfway down the buttons of his shirt already. She reached into his jeans pocket and handed him the condom inside before resuming.

She hadn't been able to see anything more than the impression of his body against his clothes. She nearly ripped the seams of his sleeves as she yanked his shirt over his shoulders. His small nipples went hard under her palms as he fumbled to open his jeans and lower his boxer briefs enough to pull his cock from them with a strangled groan. He frantically covered his full, thick, flushed erection, his brows drawn together as though in pain to have to touch his cock in order to sheathe it.

Nova rewarded his haste, raising herself up and letting his hold on himself direct him. Then she sank down.

She threw her head back, moaning and trying not to howl. But the rasp of his own moans was so like a growl that she thought he wouldn't even blink if she did. The condom shielded her power from draining him, but it seemed to mean nothing when it came to the feeling of his cock stroking through her cunt, which practically molded itself around him.

"My... Mine," he grunted tightly as she pressed her half-clothed breasts against his warm flesh, hard to her soft, his arms inked and stark next to her unmarked skin. There was another set of tattoos near his hip and more on his back, but she didn't need to know those yet. All she needed to know was that he was large, firm, strong and as hot as she was, as though he'd absorbed her heat instead of her absorbing him.

He was as hot as Jules, but he was harder than Jules, larger than Jules. When he wrapped his arms around her, she felt caged, but when she moved over his cock, she felt powerful. She curled her arm around his neck and grasped the handle above the window for leverage.

They didn't go slow like she had gone with her fingers, feeling her way. She didn't need to feel her way around a cock, and she didn't want to wait. She thrashed her head from side to side as she rode him at a gallop, practically violent in spite of the clinging softness of her cunt around him. Her hair flicked over her shoulders, her bare breast in her face.

Their rhythm was off. She rocked her hips over him at a much quicker pace than he could thrust up, but part of that was because he couldn't take his eyes off her as she used him as thoroughly as he'd used her behind the restaurant. His breathing was shallow, his mouth parted, his neck and shoulders tense as he tried to keep up with her, but he didn't seem to need to keep pace or take over this part of their encounter, perfectly content to let her take the reins, to continue telling him in deed just how desperately she needed him. Even after two orgasms to his none, she needed him so much.

The huge truck rocked now. There could be no question what they were doing inside, two shadows upright and moving like lust-sick teenagers in a make-out spot.

Nova clenched her eyes shut. Her cunt was so sensitive and his erection so large inside her that she felt the same delicate contours that she'd mapped with her tongue, every ridge and vein, as she slammed him into her over and over.

Her breasts hurt from how hard she was moving. Her thighs ached, pounded against his hip bones. The sides of her folds were scraped by the zipper of his jeans. But she didn't, couldn't, wouldn't stop, because the pleasure in his erection felt so good purring through the intense, harsh pleasure in her pussy.

Eli tightened his hold around her, burying his fingers deep into her back and the broken moans of his orgasm filling her ears. His climax dragged her with him like a boat over a cataract. As soon as he'd finished, he yanked her down by her hair to surround him. She rocked her hips to move him inside her, but she released the handle and met his all-consuming kiss.

He combed his fingers through the tangle, rooting her to his fingers and massaging her scalp in a silent affirmation, a good girl now that the bad girl had gotten her pound of flesh.

Her bare breast stuck to the sweat of his chest. Her lower back was damp. Their faces glistened in the streetlight when he pulled his mouth away from hers, his gaze lingering again on her kiss-swollen lips. When they'd climbed in, the truck had been chilly from the mid-autumn cold snap that had passed through while they'd been in the restaurant. Now, it was like a sauna, the windows steamed up and dripping with condensation.

He extricated his fingers from the knots of her hair, touched her cheeks so gently that she almost wanted to cry again, but for a wholly different reason. When he smiled, all traces of the cruelty that had made her melt were gone, leaving behind a far more comfortable warmth.

"You're amazing, Nova," he murmured.

She gasped when she canted her hips again to bring herself closer to him. The movement of his cock strummed the harp of her pleasure all over again. "Not so bad yourself."

He traced her lower lip, and she lightly kissed his finger.

Eli drew her in again, as though he couldn't resist. He smiled against her lips, the kiss less possessive and instead almost protective. "We may never get naked, the way we're going."

She raised herself up, laughing a little as she settled next to him so that Eli could tend to the condom. "It's funny. I prefer not being completely naked. I was raised in a family that valued modesty. Yes, you can laugh if you want. It's only in the last few months that I've started wearing things that actually show skin, but I can't help it. I'm much more comfortable clothed. Then again, when we have sex in our clothes, those clothes do end up getting all messy, don't they?" she added, adjusting the front of her dress so that both her breasts were covered.

The material had stretched, but of greater concern for the moment were the not-innocuous places where she'd stained or soaked through the dress. Nova leaned over to the front seat to grab her panties and pull them on, although it was too late to save the back of her dress from her dampness.

Eli pulled his arms through the sleeves of his shirt, but she stopped him from buttoning it, touched his chest tentatively before pushing the sides open again.

"What?" He twitched at the softness of her touch.

"Just didn't have the chance to get a look at you yet. Not really." She chewed on the corner of her lip, her shyness returning. It always felt so superfluous when it settled on her like low clouds in an overcast sky. After all the things she'd done and wanted to do, why did something so small, even innocent, make her nervous?

"We were a bit preoccupied, weren't we?" He let her explore him but eventually closed his hands around her wrists. "If you keep doing that, putting on those panties was a futile gesture."

"Sorry." She clasped her hands in the lap of her skirt, her shoulders raised.

"No, don't be," he replied with a self-deprecating laugh that turned into a slight groan as he tucked his half-hard cock back into his pants and closed his jeans. "It's not *you*. I can't believe after all that, I was ready for another go. I just thought we could maybe save the next one for another night."

Her cheeks hurt from her smile. "So, coffee?"

"Coffee." He climbed into the driver's seat first to run the windshield wipers. She joined him right before he pulled out of the parking space.

"You're going to have to get it to go," she said. "I can't go in like this."

His grin turned wicked, but he nodded. Even though he'd turned the air conditioning on, color deepened high on his cheekbones, and he had to adjust himself one more time.

Chapter Twelve

These days, Jules regularly exclaimed that he'd never seen her like this, and none of the times were an exaggeration. Nova felt the difference as well. Her next date with Eli had been set a week after the last, and she was jumping the incubus almost every time they crossed paths, which was apparently what happened when she embraced the feast instead of approaching it with dread and sinking into a numb morass of depression afterward.

She'd found her true calling, even truer than becoming a psychologist. What was better than stopping the need for therapy before it started?

After a few nights flying solo to determine whether she could maintain consistency in her victims, she finally invited Jules to witness her in the flesh rather than just through frantic post-feed copulation.

He flew above her as she circled the dorms and fraternity and sorority houses. She watched the paths and parking lots as well. Even in their sleep, she found the young men she wanted, the ones whose hands left unwanted bruises in their wake, whose tongues carried a sharper cut than any whip, who washed blood or powder from their hands and didn't care whether the remains they left behind could be cleaned just as easily. Malice hung around them like the haze of alcohol that often accompanied it—not because alcohol was the cause of these young men's actions, only that it helped compel out of them what was already there.

In less than a week, Nova could find such men the way a shark detected a single drop of blood in the ocean.

The buffet of Jules' wings passed over her skin right before she swerved away from the dormitories and into the academic campus instead, gritting her teeth. She could guess what she would find based on location alone. It was October—midterms, when tests were taken and essays were due.

She homed in on movement in the Mathematics building. It wasn't in an office. The professor hadn't even bothered to give himself and his illicit tryst the illusion of privacy. He was making the girl get on her knees in his classroom.

Nova sensed no distress from the girl, but she did detect resignation and mild disgust. The girl had chosen this course of action, but she wasn't enjoying herself. The point wasn't her pleasure but to earn her way with his.

Nova might have spared him if he'd cared about the girl. After all, Nova lived in a glass house when it came to age disparity. However, there was no question that he was taking advantage of a truly disgusting tradition. This had been the girl's choice, but it should never have been an option.

As Nova swooped into the classroom in a whispered flurry of wings, Jules on her tail, she couldn't look at the professor and not see her priest. Memory of shame coursed through her like poison. The last month had had its share of guilt, but she'd lived a lifetime of a very specific kind of shame weighing her down, grain by grain, until she hadn't even known the weight she'd carried. She hated even more any man who spread that shame around — a carrier unaffected by the disease himself.

As the professor came, the girl coughed, struggling to swallow when he didn't let her keep the cum in her mouth or spit it out.

The professor had the audacity to pet the girl's head and thank her, reassuring her that her skill would be reflected in her grade. Although the girl smiled, any fool could see it didn't reach her eyes. However, there was a certain light in the professor's eyes as the girl put her shirt back on but walked out with her lipstick still messed up.

Nova squeezed Jules' hand hard enough to make him wince, but he jumped onto one of the desks like a gargoyle, eager for her revenge.

When Nova didn't go after him right away, Jules coaxed her closer to him and whispered, "You don't have to wait for him to go to sleep to kill him, pet."

Nova didn't jerk away, didn't move, but Jules had to sense how her body seemed to turn to stone underneath her flesh.

"And you didn't tell me that *before* I went out on a date?" Nova whispered back.

It was a large room. The professor had turned on some Chopin, and she and Jules were in the back. If the professor heard the hiss of their whispers, he probably thought it was something else — because why would he hear whispers at this time of night while staying late to grade papers and avoid going home to his wife? Nova could see his wedding ring from all the way up here, the douchebag.

"I didn't know you were going to pursue awake men," Jules said, "especially so soon. And you conveniently discovered that a condom is adequate coverage to block the feed. When they're asleep, it takes effort *not* to drain them dry. When they're awake, you need to work to drain them. You're ready to try because you're ready to kill, and you have the power to do it. On the brink of a willing feed, it's like standing under high-tension wires, sweetheart."

"A little forewarning would have been helpful to avoid accidentally sucking the life out of him," Nova snapped, quietly. The professor looked up, but of course he didn't see anything. "I was afraid I was going to when he... But when I didn't, I assumed I couldn't, and as it turns out, I could've killed him right then if I'd pulled hard enough? I know you have a system built around being the mysterious, attractive benefactor, but I need to know things *before* I *need* to know them, Jules."

He stroked the tail of her hair to help calm her down. "Well, now you know. And like I said, you still need to want to hurt them in order to really hurt them awake, pet."

"But I *could* still hurt him, and I'd rather not do that, okay? So fucking tell me about the damage I can do. You don't have to worry about me refusing to do that damage anymore...to the right people."

"I'll do my best." Jules ran his hands over her shoulder blades, where her wings had folded in with her declaration. "I don't always know what you need to know until after you need to know it, though. Remember, you're the one skewing the curve. Now, I want to see you work, and you don't even have to wait for him to fall asleep to do it."

She relaxed a little, leaning against the desk as he dipped his hand lower down her spine, stopping just short of her ass. She was wearing black cotton pants and a camisole, nothing overtly sexy, but it was still miles away from what she used to wear. He knew that better than anyone.

"I wasn't waiting for him to fall asleep," she said. "I was waiting for him to *start* falling asleep."

"What do you mean?"

"I mean that if he started nodding off, I was going to pull him under. That's what I did to those three boys. Sleep has them in its clutches long before they're actually unconscious." Nova paused. "Are you telling me that, in all your experience, you never knew about that?"

"I suppose I never had to. I either took them when they were awake or asleep, never pushed them when they were in between. That's...interesting. Very interesting...and incredibly attractive."

He managed to get her to smile at least, fighting back a giggle at his impromptu lasciviousness. He always seemed to want her out of nowhere, with little or no context. Nova liked it. Part of it was the sex demon in him, she knew, but after a month of playing the fantasy for the men she preyed upon, she'd learned the difference between a snow job and genuine desire. What Jules felt was genuine.

It gave her an extra swing in her step as she pulled off her clothes, even her shoes.

Of all the things she'd done so far, this felt the weirdest. She'd sat in a classroom just like this for several months. She couldn't help but imagine her classmates watching her as she shed everything, including the glamour that hid her from view.

At first, the professor didn't see her. The rest of the room was dark but for the bright lamp at his desk, which would cocoon him in its light, and because she was barefoot, she barely made a sound as she slowly descended from the top row.

The professor sighed, setting his blue pen down and leaning back in his seat. He peered into the shadows of the classroom.

He hadn't expected someone to be there. He nearly fell over, chair and all.

"What—what are you—?" Then he realized that she wasn't wearing a stitch of clothing. "W—How did you—? What are you—? Young lady, I s-suggest you get your clothes on r-right now."

Nova continued not to say anything. One step down at a time. Building the anticipation. Building the fantasy. Letting him see what he wanted. Her magic pulsed off her in heat waves so strong in her anger that sweat formed on her upper lip.

"Stop that. I think you should g-g-go. Are you hurt? Did something happen?"

Not a word. She spread her arms to display herself. Offer herself.

"Oh God." His cock had become an insistent tent in his tan trousers. He was too wide-eyed and hypnotized to try to conceal it from her in an effort at propriety, not that she expected propriety from him. A student-age woman showed up looking ready for sex, and a man like him didn't protest for long, magic or no magic.

The closer she came, the more he hyperventilated. Fog obscured his glasses, which he fumbled with when he could no longer see. By the time he removed them, he didn't need them anymore. She was close enough for him to see everything.

The back of his knees caught on his chair. He sat down heavily, his legs splayed to the sides.

She stepped in front of him, then leaned back against the edge of his desk and lifted herself to sit on the large calendar that acted as a blotter. Her buttocks slid against the most recent exam he'd been grading. It looked abysmal, based on the amount of blue.

Nova crossed her legs and stared at him, a subtle smile on her lips and a hyena's gaze upon his body.

The professor clutched at his shirt collar, unbuttoned it, loosened the tie as sweat dripped down his forehead and his quickened breathing turned to gasps. His cheeks were two blotches of brilliant ruddy color.

"Oh *God*," he muttered. "Oh God, oh God, oh God…"

All she had to do was show him the fantasy. She didn't even have to touch him, didn't have to make him touch her. He could crawl his gaze all over her, lingering and relishing, the way an art lover stands before a masterpiece in a museum. His cock made a damp spot on the khaki material from the combination of the girl's saliva and his renewed need.

Nova parted her legs and rested her feet on the armrests on either side of the professor, curling her toes to roll the chair closer, her folds exposed and spread enough for him to see the gleaming entrance of her cunt.

She was turned on as fiercely as ever — not because of the man in front of her, but from her own power and from knowing she had another man's eyes on her. Jules stayed invisible, but she felt his presence as surely as the professor felt hers without touching her. She couldn't tell whether Jules was close or whether he'd kept his higher vantage point. She thought he was close, though. She hoped he was. It would help with what she was going to do even more than her exhilaration at what she was doing — the kind of exhilaration a woman experienced doing what she was meant to do.

"I know what you want," she said.

The professor's eyes rolled back at the sound of her voice.

She ran her hands up her thighs and smoothed them over her abdomen until she could cup her breasts. The flesh plumped up, and between the cage of her fingers, her nipples caught against the webbing.

"You lust for a girl in your classroom to wait after class and offer herself to you — but not for compensation. You lust for her to lust after you, to dream about your cock inside her, to moan at the thought of your hands on her. You want her on this desk, her hair splayed" — she pulled the rubber band out of her hair to let it tumble over her shoulders, tickling the top of her breasts — "legs spread, nearly in tears because you haven't buried your cock deep inside her yet."

"God, yes," he breathed. He struggled with his belt as she lowered herself to her elbows, breathing heavily to push her breasts up for his captivated attention.

Once he'd dropped his belt to the floor, Nova ran her fingers over the flesh between her legs and whimpered.

The memory of her doing this for Eli surfaced for a brief moment before she shoved it down again. She didn't want to pollute the experience.

"You might not remember me, Professor, but I remember you. Perhaps you even thought of me a night or two." She had never taken one of this professor's classes, but she very much doubted he would be able to remember every single student in every single one of his large classes, even the pretty ones. "Well, here I am, sir. I couldn't hold back anymore. I couldn't wait. Fuck, do you see how much I want you?"

She brought her fingers to her lips to taste herself. Her mind flashed with an image of Jules watching her, then again with Eli. She shook her head just as the panting professor managed to get out of his clothes.

He wasn't in anywhere near Eli's kind of shape, although he might have actually been around the same age. He was scrawny in his shoulders and arms, soft in his stomach, with an academic's posture—which wasn't contemptible on its own, but the things he did turned everything average and unobjectionable about him disgusting.

Nevertheless, she still felt the sexual charge of him when he lifted her legs to his shoulders.

"God, you *are* real," he groaned and nearly came on her at that moment. She held him back, her magic gripping his balls so that his orgasm was dry. He fell forward, gasping against her breast. The action nearly bent her in half, but she could take it easily.

Nova bit her lip in spite of herself. Then she let herself like it. Like the boys, it would go better for both of them if she enjoyed herself, taught this professor in his last moments to take only what had been offered freely rather than exchanged.

He'd die with his lesson learned.

She guided his searching mouth to the peak of her breast. His cockhead probed against her folds as he eagerly took in as much of her breast as he could before withdrawing to focus the suction pressure on the hard little point of her nipple.

"Yes," she whispered for his benefit. "So good, Professor, so good."

He responded every time she used his title, every time she reminded him that she was a student and this was forbidden and oh so much more delicious because of it.

It affected her as well when she threw her head back and glimpsed the classroom, the ghosts of classmates past. Hadn't every girl imagined fucking a professor on his desk the way professors imagined the same now and then? Most of the time it was harmless, highly improbable, nothing more than a dream, not even a real fantasy.

Real life was better than fantasy every time. That was why a succubus was such a powerful demon, turning the fantasies into reality, even when the reality felt like fantasy.

"You're so warm," he groaned. He slid his cock through her folds as he rutted helplessly in the face of the reality of her—better than his most torrid pornography searches.

"God, yes, please, love me, touch me, just like that," she crooned.

He finally got hold of himself enough to kiss down her belly and settle back on his feet instead of bracing himself against her. He arranged her legs over his shoulders again, stretching her by leaning forward to test her flexibility. He licked his lips as he watched her move her fingers over her folds, her breasts pressed together between her arms. As he brought his cock to her cunt, her breath quickened.

"Fuck me hard, Professor. Fuck me across your desk. Let there be stains all over the exams where your students will touch them and smell them, never knowing that they're touching where their professor screwed a student until she came around his big cock. Come on, Professor."

After her last mention of his station—of his crime of passion—he grabbed the edge of the desk and thrust into her. His neck tensed, the cords standing out, as he ensured that she had a bumpy ride indeed. She encouraged him, writhing, gasping, moaning high to the rhythm of his thrusts—all things that he'd imagined or seen in videos aplenty, but hers were all natural, all sincere, even though she made him a better man for her with her magic, made the pleasure greater with her heat.

Her fingers on her clit went faster before she could stop herself, but she wasn't really trying to extend this more than she had to. Magic rippled over her like summer over concrete, as though she were nothing more than a hot mirage. The professor stared down at her, transfixed, trying to keep his eyes open, even though her cunt squeezing around him made his face contort and his eyelids flutter. He panted like a bull as he pushed into her. Her juices coated his erection, dripped down her ass to smear underneath her, wetting the pages. He kissed her knees, kissed near the place that Eli had bitten her, and she paused to convince him to turn his head away from it. He was easy to convince. It was all flesh to him, all something that he wanted.

Eventually, he moved his grip from the side of the desk to her breasts. He grasped her a little too tight, but she didn't care, nor did her nipples against his smooth, sweaty palms. His thrusts drove her across the desk, mussing and crinkling the papers underneath her and spreading the consequences of her pleasure—that would eventually fade, but he didn't know that. It was all the best kind of rough and messy.

The thrusts also jostled the desk so that the lamp swayed then fell onto its side, obscuring her body more, making it more the dream than stark reality. It didn't matter now. He had seen everything, committed it to his visual memory, now pounded the memory in through tactile confirmation.

The farther he pushed her, the closer her head got to the other end of the desk, until she was partially hanging over it, arching her neck with each cry.

Then she felt lips on her neck—not the professor's, because he still kept his kisses against her knee and inner thigh, his grunts of desperate effort high above her. Physical activity wasn't his forte. He was winded, his muscles aching, but his cock demanded greater stamina from him.

The lips on her neck traveled along her jaw to her open mouth. Jules' kiss was like drowning in a hot spring, shuddering all over her with an added boost of pleasure and desire. When he ran his tongue over hers, she bore down on the professor and grasped his arms. Her claws threatened to come out, but she didn't want to leave any marks, no matter how much he deserved them. She grew her teeth instead.

Jules growled low into her mouth when she raked her predator's teeth over his tongue.

"Who could resist you?" he whispered.

"No one," she replied. "God, professor, I'm going to come. I need you so bad. Need you so *hard*."

It wouldn't have mattered if every muscle in the rest of the professor's body had decided to cramp all at once. He wasn't going to slow down for anything.

Her ears filled with the sound of feathers as Jules spread his wings.

She pulled the professor down to her breasts again, even as he continued to use them as handles for leverage. The force of his hips jarred her almost all the way up to her ribs. He caught her right nipple between his teeth, and she cried out just before he surrounded it with the needy warmth of his mouth to muffle his groans.

Jules locked his lips over hers again as she held the professor's head to her breasts. Her entire body seemed to gasp in a long, powerful, drawn-out inhale. The professor shouted, his open mouth still over her breast. She *sucked*, pulling his cock deep into her, rippling with her climax, and took from both him and Jules.

She curled her blunt nails into the professor's scalp as she kept pulling the tangled strings of his energy into her, like wrapping hanks of yarned wool around a spindle. Nova panted, but while it took effort, it was surprisingly not difficult. It was just a matter of keeping the door open between them, all the flow entering into her where it wanted to be anyway.

The professor kept twitching as she extended his orgasm far beyond his own capacity. He laughed against her skin in euphoria, slamming his hips against her, even though his cock couldn't move out of her.

She absorbed every drop of his cum, the vibration of his laugh over her skin, his sweat, his joy, the quiver in

Jules' lips as he poured the sounds of his arousal at her predation down her throat.

Finally, with one final draw, the professor slumped over her.

Nova pushed him off and out of her with her knees on his shoulders until he collapsed in a slump onto the floor.

Now Nova was the one laughing, flying high from the professor's euphoria, as Jules jumped onto the desk and landed on her other side. He hit the professor with his foot, making a meaty sound right before he kicked the man away to take his place at her pussy, where he revealed himself in all his majesty, his black wings spread to their full span like those of a warrior angel, although the way that he looked down on her was as far from angelic as possible, just as predatory as she as he dug his fingers into her ass and lifted her whole lower half off the desk from the force of his thrust inside her.

Nova arched and screamed. The sound echoed in the empty room. She reached to the sides for something to hold, but there was nothing. Her wings unfurled underneath her, shaking her like she was in the middle of an earthquake until the tips of his wings met the tips of hers. Each pass of his erection through her cunt grated the flesh not with pain but with sharp fingernails of pleasure that seemed to rip through her body. His power was at its peak, as intense as it had ever been with her.

She met his challenge and watched his expression shatter, the black in his eyes spreading out into the whites as he seemed to double over in pain. They hit each other with the full brunt of each of their respective magics until they were nothing but mating animals, the sounds they made together enough to shiver the spine as well as heat the skin. She didn't have to be careful with her claws on his back. He didn't have to be careful with his teeth on her shoulder.

He was the one who finally caved. It probably didn't help that she had just fed, her spirit bloated with energy and renewed power. Still, in this contest, there were no losers. Jules screamed a ferocious howl as he lost himself inside her. She drank him in, riding his pleasure into her own. He took from her, and she took from him, the balance nearly equal. She drew him down for their mouths to meet, what they did too violent to be called a kiss until Jules softened his approach. All things sharp and hard became gentler, teeth giving way to the insistence of his tongue against hers.

Nova purred, arching against his body to convince him to lower himself over her entirely so that she could feel him on her as much as possible, blanketing her. She enveloped him in her arms to keep him against her.

"I could watch you fuck the bastards all night," Jules whispered against her lips.

He raised himself up so that he could stare into her eyes, his still completely black. He caressed her cheek, the places where her hair had plastered to her temple from sweat. Exam papers swept to the floor as he crawled over her, crouched like a beast above.

"I am *so* proud of you."

Chapter Thirteen

Brumley forwent the chair and planted herself right on Eli's lap. She slapped the rolled-up newspaper on his thigh as though chastising a dog. "You've been falling down on your job, Fray."

Eli dropped his breakfast burrito, tucked his arm under Brumley's legs and dumped her unceremoniously onto the bar floor. She giggled as her tulle petticoat flared out.

"I believe that's *you*," Eli said. "Classic projection."

She batted down the petticoat. "Listen to the therapist throwing around big words. When did you get so educated, caveman?"

"When I started reading more than newspapers."

"Touché, cutie. But maybe read a touch fewer books and kill a few more demons? Maybe? Possibly? Not like it's your job or anything." Brumley dusted herself off, then sat on his table instead, eating one of his tater tots. The menu called them 'hashbrown bites'. The bar owners were fooling no one, but Eli had long since stopped caring about which meal he was eating when.

Eli picked up his late-night breakfast burrito with one hand and the newspaper with the other.

UTM Professor Murdered in Classroom. Spree Suspected

Delightful. Professor caught dead with his pants down. If it weren't for the unnamed victims prior, Eli almost wouldn't care, except for the knowledge that succubi didn't just attack — they coerced. The professor must have dozed off at his exams. Eli read between the lines for more red flags.

The professor had been found with his clothes strewn under him. A girl, whose identity was being withheld for her protection because she was a student, had been brought into custody after having been seen by a janitor. Her DNA was being compared to DNA found on the body. She almost matched the description of the girl seen with the three boys before their murder, but Eli dismissed her as the succubus. If she'd left DNA behind, she wasn't the one.

No discernible cause of heart failure. By all accounts, the death had been natural. But now the deaths were becoming more sensationalistic, and they were hitting more and more prominent people. Three athletes at once, a married professor... These were not subtle or hidden kills. The succubus responsible was either recklessly clueless or so arrogant that she believed she'd never be caught out for her actions, not even with the media field day.

"College administrators better watch their backs...and their dicks." Eli threw the paper back onto the table so he could finish his burrito in peace.

"I gave you a solid lead for a single or couple causing quite the ruckus on the campus, and you don't even take it?" Brumley asked. "See if I do you a favor again, Fray."

"I didn't ask you for this one."

"You could have gone in last night, cleaned house and had enough time to get laid. What the hell were you doing?"

"My job," Eli replied, still paying more attention to his breakfast-for-dinner than Cam Brumley.

"Obviously not."

"I don't care about media attention. Any demon I find is a demon with a trail of bodies that never makes it to the papers. I got sidetracked from the university. It's not exactly a ground-breaking location, either. We clear out one infestation, another few are going to show up, like strays," Eli explained between biting and chewing. "So forgive me if I'm not in a hurry to go after the ones you showed me. I'll get to it—maybe tonight, maybe tomorrow. I'll even thank you for the heads up. But don't tell me how to do my job, unless you're interested in taking a stab at it your cute little self."

"A succubus hunting men isn't going to have much use for me," Brumley said. "Besides, I already told you I don't do sex demons. That's why I gave it to you in the first place."

"Do I tell you how and where to hunt vampires? Do I talk to you at all?"

Eli thought he caught the tail end of hurt before Brumley made her expression go blank. It hadn't even occurred to him that Brumley had made a point to be a royal pain in his ass because she might actually like him.

"Never mind. See if I tip you off again," Brumley said, sliding off the table.

"Brumley—"

"Go jerk off in a Chinese restaurant dumpster."

"Cam."

She turned on her high heel and crossed her arms, her matte pink lips pursed.

"I'm getting to it, okay?" he said.

"Whatever, dickweed. Don't go out of your way. Oh, wait, you're not." She continued her flounce and didn't look back.

Eli rubbed his forehead as he finished his meal, staring at the newspaper Brumley had left behind. He needed to let his stomach settle — flying on a full stomach was never a good idea, especially for whatever was below him at the time — but he might as well hit the university tonight. There was still more than half a week until his next date with Nova. He had plenty of time to get some demons slayed before then.

And there was no reason why he couldn't go out of his way for a few hours for a sure demon nest. No guarantees he would catch them, though.

University territory was a funny place to hunt. Not a lot of space for a demon to fly, so if he caught one of them mid-flight, the kill was all but certain. However, there were also a lot of buildings close together where the demons could spend most of their hunting time walking rather than flying. And those were the places that Eli couldn't hunt for them, couldn't do anything but wait and hope they came out on one of the sides that he happened to be watching at the time. Eli was confined to the rules of brick, stone and concrete. The sex demons weren't, half-apparition as they were, and that gave them the advantage on such a small but dense hunting ground.

That was part of the reason Eli preferred to not seek out a specific demon, no matter how richly the media vultures fed upon the flesh of their victims. When he wasn't looking for anything, he was far more likely to find something—like picking up change from the street. Hunting for something specific in a city like this was like trying to find a single rare coin in a freezer full of them.

It wouldn't hurt to spend a few hours looking, though. If the succubus was smarter than she seemed, she'd keep her head down for a few days. However, there had been no reported deaths of young women on campus since the last potential one recorded more than a week ago. He could seek the incubus. And if he didn't immediately kill it, he could follow it back to its nest.

Eli passed the bartender cash and tip and headed home to prepare himself for the evening. If he noticed Brumley at the darts board, showing up other vampire hunters with her deadly accuracy, he didn't let her catch him noticing.

* * * *

He flew over the campus that Nova attended, feeling as strong as a young man yet decrepit in comparison to the young men walking the campus in spite of the late hour. Like Meridian, it seemed that UTM never slept.

He vaguely remembered being that young. Oh, he had memories of university that were clear as crystal. It was the experience of youth that had gone fuzzy. His brain still thought he was in his early twenties, but whenever he was near twentysomething young people, they seemed indescribably young to him, immature to the core.

Nova had her moments when she acted or appeared her age. The rest of the time…she was just a woman, and he was just a man. That's what he hoped she thought as well, but it was harder to believe when he peered down upon the succubus' sampler plate of fresh, cocky young males, strutting even if they weren't in view of a corresponding female. What they had to be proud of, Eli didn't know. He bet they didn't, either.

Let them think that for a little longer. Life had a way of convincing little shitheads like that otherwise. He had been one once himself, he was sure, and losing that shitheadedness was a hard lesson. Some never did learn it, poor sons of bitches.

Still, youthful exuberance aside, he dared any of them to fly all night in golden wings. Their shoulders would give out in less than an hour, and even the non-smokers would be wheezing by then.

"I've had my fill of boys," Nova had said.

Eli wrapped that memory around his finger to recall every time he passed over another college undergrad.

He smiled, though, when he recognized Nova sitting on the roots of the large tree in the middle of the campus quad. She wasn't the only one there with a takeout drink, flashlight and textbook, but he couldn't help but notice that she was alone. He ached to see her all by herself, studying on a Friday night instead of out with other people. A party. A sports game of some kind. A movie. Hell, sidewalk bowling or old-fashioned hopscotch, if that was a thing these days.

She'd said that she didn't have any friends. He still didn't understand why. The people around her didn't even seem to acknowledge her existence. She wasn't exactly wearing the same jaw-biting type of clothes that she'd worn on the date—not much in the way of cleavage on the standard crew-necked university T-shirt she wore—but Eli was surprised there wasn't a single guy there surreptitiously glancing at her curvy profile.

Eli wished he could drop in like a guardian angel, but that was a complication no hunter needed, which was why most of them dated in the fold, if at all. And heaven knew he was no angel, after what they'd done together.

He flew past the quad toward the dormitories. The campus itself was more like a rectangle than a square, with the center consisting of the quad, student life and academic buildings. Dormitories bookended the university, which technically made patrolling the dorms a two-person job, but in the absence of another hunter, he started on the south side because he was already headed that way, then switched sides every thirty minutes.

Two hours passed before he called it quits and flew back toward the north side to return to his inner-city apartment. The university had been a bust, but he'd likely find one on his way back home.

Wait.

Eli dropped lower in the sky, riding the strong breeze. He thought he'd seen something near one of the smaller dormitories in the corner, just three stories high and open to the outside like a motel. It looked like one of the older buildings, although it was difficult to tell, since the city and the campus were all relatively young.

The gargoyles and angels here were smaller, innocuous little statues on the corners — probably only statues, too, since Eli had only ever seen the life-size or larger ones move, never the smaller. Of course, he so rarely saw any of them move that it was anyone's guess whether these were decorative or just unfortunate in size.

Eli swept around the other side just in time to catch the incubus flying in.

He swore, then pulled his wings back to dive down before sweeping them out again and landing on the roof. He became a gargoyle himself, still and quiet right above the third-floor room where the incubus had flown in. He'd get in closer, but midnight was still in the realm of early on a Friday night for these kids. Eli couldn't perch on one of the benches that lined the entrance pathways without risking someone bumping into him.

So he crouched on the roof to wait and hoped the incubus flew out the same way he came in, or else Eli was going to feel awfully silly in the morning. Incubi, of course, weren't vampires. They could prey in the daytime, although when one's food was juiciest at night, it was no wonder they joined their demonic cousins in nocturnal life. But Eli couldn't sit around waiting forever. Once the early birds started waking up and the incubus still hadn't come out this way, he'd have to assume that either the demon was taking a particularly drawn-out feed or that he'd left through another wall.

Fortunately, the incubus didn't know he ought to leave in another direction. Incubi were like humans in that regard. Even when there were more efficient alternatives and doors weren't a barrier, a demon would often leave the same way they entered.

As soon as the tips of the incubus' wings crossed the threshold of the rooftop, Eli jumped onto its back. He'd pulled his wings in, making himself dead weight, bigger and heavier than the incubus he brought down.

He let out his wings about ten feet from the ground to soften the fall, although the landing still jolted all the way up his body, like a single round of electrocution coming up through his feet. The incubus got the worst of it. He hit the ground on his abdomen, his breath knocked out, possibly with a broken bone or two if Eli was lucky. They didn't usually heal as fast as vampires, but this one had just fed, so Eli still needed to be on his guard.

It was instinct for Eli to check around him to make sure that none of the wandering student body could see the winged demon or the winged hunter or knew where those thuds had come from. Their gazes still passed right over him and the incubus, so Eli turned his attention back to the demon and took out two of his knives.

He approached the incubus with caution, frustrated that his boots had to disturb the browning grass beneath his weight. The incubus looked like it had just fallen from heaven, but that didn't mean that it couldn't resurrect right before him—a cowardly but effective move, like the opossums almost as prolific as rats in the area.

The incubus pulled his wings into his body and pushed himself up, hissing, his claws and teeth out, his eyes black with evil. He held himself hunched over, which could have been a fighting stance, but Eli thought it was because the demon was still hurt and healing.

"Who the hell invited you to the party, hunter?" the incubus spat.

Eli didn't respond. The incubus could attract attention from the students if he wanted. Eli couldn't afford to be noticed by anyone other than the incubus across from him, on whom the invisibility spell would no longer work tonight since they'd made contact—

which meant that Eli needed to bring him down, here and now. If he didn't, the incubus would disappear. Eli's biggest weapon was the element of surprise. Once he'd lost that, the incubus would be more cautious for a good while.

It had to be tonight.

The incubus tried to retreat, but Eli had longer legs and a longer stride, and the incubus quickly realized that he couldn't get away on foot. He could try to fly, but Eli's wings were visible, too.

Looks like you're going to have to fight, bud. You demons are lovers more than fighters, but that's why we're here in the first place, isn't it?

He thought of this incubus flying around the campus and getting a whiff of Nova's dreams.

Tightening his grip on the knives, Eli advanced upon the incubus with his teeth bared.

The incubus spread his wings and pushed them down just enough to lift off the ground in a flip above Eli's head. When he landed, he whirled around to kick Eli in the back under the wings, then on the side of his head. Eli grunted as he swept around as well, slashing his knives over the incubus' jeans. Eli cursed inwardly that he'd gone after the only covered limbs. Thick denim acted as a shield, making the first cuts shallower and slowing his momentum during the strike.

He got a few slices on the arms, but the incubus delivered a swift, harsh kick to Eli's leg. Eli flipped to the ground to avoid a broken femur before grabbing the incubus' feet and sweeping them out from under him.

The incubus landed on his hands and feet, then lunged at Eli like a dog.

Eli threw a punch with one hand, missed, but caught the demon's cheek with the other. The knife went in and came out easily, like stabbing through a stretched piece of fabric.

When the incubus growled, his teeth showed through the hole in his cheek. He slammed his knee up into Eli's gut.

"You're not welcome here," the incubus snarled in his ear right before he grabbed Eli by his wings and flung him about twenty feet away.

Damn, the little fucker is strong. What did he feast on in that dorm room? A whole sleepover?

Eli got a running start, then lifted himself into the air with his wings after the incubus, who was desperately fleeing back to the dormitory that he'd exited.

Eli buried his knives into the incubus' shoulders, right above the wounds where his real wings had been torn off. The sound was like two axes plunging into the same tree.

The incubus stumbled, hitting the railing that lined the concrete dormitory path. He used the railing to brace himself, grabbing the wrought-iron top like a bar and lifting his legs to kick out at Eli's chest. He missed and got Eli's diaphragm instead—which meant he didn't break any bones, but Eli completely lost his breath.

The incubus tried to reach the knives in his back—a process that pulled his flesh against the blades and tore him even more. But with students walking along the pathway on the other side of the fence, the demon couldn't scream as he worked one knife out, then the other, while Eli gasped on the ground, gulping in air but none of it going to his lungs. Blackness spread across his vision like an ink-bottle spill.

The incubus stood above Eli, the knives glinting moon-silver stained with red. It wasn't right that incubi and succubi bled as red as human beings. At least vampires had the decency to bleed darker, thicker blood.

Eli needed his breath back *now*. He couldn't control his limbs with his whole body focused entirely on sucking in enough oxygen to function, and the incubus wasn't going to show any mercy. Instead, Eli just lay there, rolling to the sides like a turtle on its back.

The incubus raised the knives above his head, the blades pointed at Eli's body.

Air rushed into his lungs. Eli took a huge breath and grasped for the sheaths at his chest. He pulled out two more knives, then thrust them into the incubus' abdomen just as the incubus drove Eli's knives halfway into Eli's shoulders. Eli bit his arm guards to keep from screaming, but the incubus didn't hold back this time. The sound was so animal that students ran out of their dorms.

"Where is it?" one of the girls asked. "Can you see it?"

"Is it coyotes?" a guy near her asked.

The incubus dug the knives into Eli's shoulders, but the harness acted as an obstruction. Eli's knives had no such obstruction, and when Eli forced them deeper, the incubus finally released the knives in Eli's shoulders and stumbled back.

This time, he let himself go through the railing, then through dorm walls until he was out of sight, weakened and hurt, but not fatally.

Eli, however, was in a sorry state on the ground.

Next time I'll stab the bastard first thing, as I'm falling on him.

He didn't want to pull the knives out. There was always the risk of infection by keeping them in, but in taking them out on his own, the risk of bleeding out was greater.

He needed to get away from the dormitory to call his patron without being heard. Students were still looking for the wild animal that had made such a terrible scream.

Eli grabbed the railing to climb to his feet.

The incubus hadn't been the most powerful one he'd ever fought, but it had certainly given Eli a run for his money. When a demon was used to hunting in the shadows, it usually didn't know how to defend itself as well as this one—which meant this one had probably dealt with Eli's kind before. This incubus had been a smaller man, well-muscled but slender. He must have been used to compensating for his size. That, and he knew his way around fighting with weapons, which wasn't all that common for predators who came with their own built-in protection.

Now the flying monkey knew he'd been found. And where he was holed up, he could probably heal himself and replenish his strength in a matter of hours, with a virtual cafeteria of young women just about to make themselves very vulnerable.

Eli stumbled to the brick building roughly fifty yards from the dormitory—a utility shed or something like that, locked. At least the walls gave him something to lean against as he pulled his phone from the satchel—nothing fancy, although he kept it silenced and protected in a container. It carried some of his dealers' contacts as well as a few emergency numbers.

Albert's was second.

"When the moonlight shines at a damsel's time, on how many tines does the moonlight shine?" the man on the other end answered.

"Albert, I have no time for your riddles that never make any sense anyway."

"Answer the question. How else can I know it's you?"

"Because if you didn't pay for all my gadgets, I'd tell you to shut the fuck up and get out here to help me. As it is, I'll just tell you to get the hell out here to help me."

"Answer the question."

"Oh, for God's sake." Eli had no idea the answer, but whether the answer was right was never the point. "The moonlight shines on two tines times two, for the tines shine brighter at tea for two. Now that you've made me spout that ridiculous nonsense, can you pick me up at the university, southeastern corner, near the three-story dormitory? I'll take off my charm when I see you."

"In a whisker's tick." The line went dead.

What does that even mean? Groaning, he slid down to the grass and kept his eyes on the dormitory. He doubted the incubus would come back out this way, but if he did, Eli could at least follow him back to its nest and hopefully eschew the hardest part of the hunt by getting the incubus and its partner later in the day. No better time to catch an incubus off-guard than asleep. Eli wasn't above using the same vulnerabilities on demons that demons used on humans. Some would call it poetic justice.

But before he could spot the incubus coming out his side of the dorm or flying off from the other side, Albert's black Cadillac approached the dormitories.

Eli deactivated the invisibility charm and pushed himself up, grunting against the forked lightning of pain that spread out from his shoulders.

Albert rolled down the passenger-side window. "You look even worse than you sounded. Get in the back. I have a waterproof mat on the seat back there, just in case of careless hunters like you."

"I'm touched," Eli said dryly, but he collapsed onto the back seat, closing the door with his foot. "And I'm not careless."

"Two knives in your shoulders looks like carelessness, Eli. The first-aid kit is on the floor. I'll have a look at the wounds when I get you to my house."

"You could have brought your healing potion with you. You just wanted a chance to lecture me."

"It's been a long time since one of our little talks, and Jeannie wants to say hi. You owe me for waking me up at this ungodly hour of the night."

"You shuffle around in your study into the ungodly hours right along with the rest of us. You can't fool me, old man."

"No, I never could."

Albert patronized a handful of hunters, four to six at any given time. He never patronized the same kind at once, so Eli was his only sex demon hunter—and the only hunter to whom he'd given wings.

He was an inventor, a tinkerer, a modern-day alchemist—not a witch. He didn't have that kind of power. He merely dabbled in mixing magic and science, had done so for most of his life. It drove his wife of forty years batty that her husband had a few mechanical bats in the belfry, but those mechanical bats had their moments of genius, which was why Albert was such a sought-after patron. Even if he wasn't quite independently wealthy enough to finance his hunters the way a few of the really fat cats of Meridian could, a hunter couldn't ask for better support.

Until about ten years ago, Eli had still had a working relationship with his father. Alzheimer's had taken that away, and two years ago, his father had passed. But ever since Albert had become Eli's patron, Albert had been like a second father, one whose absent-mindedness hadn't devolved into the elimination of memories and bouts of rage. Albert was good people, a hell of a handy guy, and if one of his hunters needed to be picked up anywhere in the city because of injury, car trouble, demon trouble or even drunkenness, Albert would put down whatever he was working on and drive over the speed limit to his hunters' aid. "*Protecting his investment,*" he called it.

His hunters pretended that was true, too.

* * * *

Albert helped him out of the wing harness and unfastened his pack. Then, without warning, he yanked the knives out of Eli's shoulders. Eli shouted obscenities at the wooden walls of the McMansion's attic.

"Stop being a toddler and take off your shirt, Demon Hunter Action Figure."

Albert's mousy brown curly hair was heavily weighted toward gray these days, and his rimless eyeglasses made him look like a professor or a mad scientist, but he was only one of those things.

"That's a wicked bruise," Albert said after Eli obeyed, wincing the whole time.

"I'm kind of distracted by the stab wounds at the moment."

"I'll give you a digestible anyway." He bustled over to his shelves. They'd been built as he'd needed places to put things, which meant they looked a bit like a complicated maze for a vertically inclined mouse, but Albert always knew where he'd put everything.

He came back with a handful of flannel cloths for Eli to clean his wounds more thoroughly now that the blades were out, a small vial of brown liquid that looked like coffee but tasted like chalk and a larger tub of stuff that looked like creamy green lotion. Wearing gloves like a good scientist, Albert applied it to the wounds after Eli had finished with the first step. Eli tossed back the healing potion, swallowing it as fast as he could.

"Care for something stronger to wash that down?" Albert asked.

Eli nodded while he tried to keep the potion in his stomach. He didn't ask what was in the unmarked liquor bottle that Albert gave him. If it was something that Albert had casked up in his basement, it was probably as good or better than anything he'd have to pay three weeks' salary on.

"Losing your touch or just a bad day?" Albert boosted himself onto the counter across from where Eli sat on a lower table. It was funny seeing a besweatered, bespectacled, pudgy old man kicking his feet against the counter cabinets. A foolish person would underestimate Albert when confronted with his childlike qualities. Eli was not a foolish person.

"Just a bad day, I hope." When Eli rolled his shoulders, he hissed at the pulling pain, but it was better than it had been. "The demon decided to get sophisticated and take my weapons. He was kind enough to give them back."

"I've been working on a silver-bullet revolver for my lycanthropologist."

Eli shook his head. "A gun is more dangerous for the people around me, especially if I happen to catch the demons in a populated area, like tonight. I'd mention the deafening gunshots, but I assume you've come up with a solution for that—or you're planning to."

"It's on the docket. I'm waiting, by the way."

"For what? I'm waiting for the stitching to stop so I can go home and recover, then go back tomorrow and the day after and the day after until I finally clean house on that campus." His shoulders felt like sun poured on him from behind, and his insides felt the same. Healing magic was comforting, soporific.

"Well, for one thing, you were out of your usual territory. You're an apartment and housing development kind of man. Since when do you scout out the student body?" Albert asked.

"I was following a lead. Another hunter set me on it."

"I greatly admire you, Eli, but you don't play well with others. You certainly don't let them point you in any direction. What's the other reason you wanted me to pick you up, other than potentially fatal injuries?"

This was why Eli never underestimated Albert. He could barely look a person in the eye, and when he did, his were magnified by those professor's glasses to comical effect. But he could see more while not looking than most other people could during a full-body scan.

"You found yourself a woman, didn't you?" Albert said.

Eli stared at his knees. "And there's the problem right there."

"What's that supposed to mean? Could you get arrested for seeing her?"

"No," Eli replied quickly.

"Then what's the problem?"

"It's awfully close."

"Ah."

"And I'm a mean old bastard. I'm still trying to figure out whether this is me being that mean old bastard or whether she's the big exception to everything I believed true."

"Lord help us, the son of a bitch *is* in love." Albert sighed. "Are you looking for a blessing from me? I believe a few goats and several oxen would be in order."

"We're not quite at the point of dowry exchange. We've only had one date. One and a half...I think."

"What percentage of your thinking is in your balls versus your brains?"

Knowing him, Albert was looking for an actual percentage.

"Roughly fifty-fifty, if I'm being honest," Eli replied.

"Promising." Albert gulped the rest of his drink. The ice clinked when he set it back down. "You went to the university to protect her from the big, bad incubus. A whole student population that big, and you wanted to save her more than stop the demon."

"God, is it really that bad?"

"It could be terminal if you let it. But alas, there's no medicine I can give you, no cure but time."

"I should end it, for my protection."

"Or hers, yes?" Albert said with a half-smile. "Age is just a number. My peers aren't representative of the world at large, so I know plenty of men whose wives are significantly younger. About three-quarters of those women are in the marriage for the rock, the divorce settlement, the inheritance or all three. There's still that one-fourth, though. My grandfather married a woman thirty years younger than him. Granted, they lived in a small town at the time, and he'd lost his first wife five years earlier. If your balls are calling only fifty percent of the shots with this girl who's got you discombobulated like a wonky hot air balloon, that's better than a majority of our sex in their early interactions with a beautiful woman."

Eli rubbed his head against a headache forming behind his left eye. "How do you know she's beautiful?"

"Because if she weren't beautiful to you, you wouldn't bother. I'll bet she's also a wildcat in the sack, yes? She's got to be to keep up with such a virile man for your age and more so than many of hers."

"This conversation is over." Eli gingerly got up from the table and pulled on his ripped shirt. It would at least get him home.

"Ribbing aside, you're not really worried about the fact she's so much younger than you."

"Could have sworn I was."

"If age mattered, you wouldn't have let it get to the second date—or the first date. You don't equivocate, Eli. Like most hunters, you're goal-oriented. If something doesn't meet that goal, it's blown away with the rest of the chaff. She might make you feel old, and she may have moments when you're reminded how young she is. But Jeannie is ten years younger than me, and I have those moments, too. Yet we somehow manage to love each other through it, because everyone's significantly different than their partner in some way. In fact, you've made bones about her age but never said anything about the fact that she's a woman and you're a man. If you want someone more similar to you, I'm sure there are plenty of hunters out there looking for someone like you."

"What have you been inhaling, old man?"

"It would make practical sense, of course, fraternizing with your fellows."

"Are you trying to convince me to turn gay?"

"Of course not," Albert said. "I'm telling you that being a hunter is a lonely life. When you're a natural person with a foot in the supernatural side of this city, it means being separated from the usual mass of humanity. They live in the light, work the nine-to-five, eat breakfast, lunch, and dinner, rise and fall with the sun, suffer the crowds and traffic and pedestrian crush to rub shoulders with people like them. A hunter doesn't do that. A hunter walks alone. I've never been one myself, but I've patronized enough to know. You think you'd be the only hunter to take what he needed, all things the same in the dark, no strings attached, before going back out into the fray? Pardon the pun."

"Is there a point to this, or are you in a philosophical mood?"

"I'm always in a philosophical mood, but that's beside the point." Albert hopped down from the counter. He had to pace a little before the stiffness in his legs and hips worked itself out. "The point is that many a hunter has gone to an early grave with little more than a cheap headstone and a pauper's funeral because there's no one to bury them. Like soldiers, you put your life on the line and risk your necks against the worst that hell sends after you, but soldiers have other soldiers to lean on, a hierarchy to depend on and the promise of an end if they survive their deployment."

He helped Eli strap on his armor, bag and wing harness once more.

"Hunters aren't like that. I've been in hunter bars before. A whole bunch of pathological loners drinking by themselves. It's dead depressing. The demon bars are much more interactive. Sometimes, though, on a rare occasion indeed, worlds collide. A hunter crosses paths with someone from the world they're protecting. In most cases, this relationship is doomed before it starts. You know all the dangers, but she doesn't. She goes through life in an optimistic haze, while you know what's lurking in the dark. That reaction you've had, latching onto the age difference... It's an urge to protect, recognizing something pure in her that's long since broken in you. It's not because she's young, Eli. It's because she's innocent."

"What should I do?" Eli asked, the rough banter giving way to an uncharacteristically honest question.

"You do what I did with my Jeannie. You meet her in her world. You figure out if you can love her there. Then you slowly show her yours. She doesn't have to be a part of it to love you back. She just has to know about it. You can still keep her as safe as anyone ever can be in this world. If she can't take it, you let her go and bear the pain in your heart on your own, as you bear the pain from the knives now — stoically, privately. It's a short, harsh, agonizing life, Eli. If you find someone to share it with, you've got the most precious thing in the world. If you let it go because she's still got a zit or two on her forehead, you're a fool. Are you a fool, Eli?"

"Sometimes."

"Your honesty is like my investment portfolio — much appreciated. Go out there, have yourself a little shared happiness, screw like rabbits and throw away all the rules that tell you under what arbitrary conditions you're allowed to have that happiness."

"I always love our little talks."

"Go away, smartass." Albert bustled Eli out of his attic study by the wings. "Fly the nest and be safe. Jeannie's in the library. Give her a kiss before you go. And promise her you'll come to dinner soon. She's feeling neglected."

"If she makes stew and pumpkin bread, I might have to move in." Already, Eli's stride was stronger as he descended the stairs.

"If you move in, I'll have to vet that young lady you've been talking about."

"No fucking chance."

Chapter Fourteen

For her second date — third date? — Nova chose her own clothes, a simple pair of fitted jeans and a black tank top with a gray screen of roses on the front and sequin accents, because the sequins made her feel special.

Jules again watched her with unfettered amusement as she went through her wardrobe, but when he offered to help, she turned him down. The first time her incubus partner helped her dress for a date with another man was helpful. The second time was just weird.

A few nights ago, he hadn't come home after dawn. And when he'd climbed into bed the following morning, he'd merely tucked himself against her, holding her fast against his body. She'd asked what was wrong, but he would only say that he'd gotten caught up in a dormitory and ended up sleeping there instead. He'd seemed shaken but wouldn't tell her why or even admit that was what he felt. She tried not to worry too much. After all, no limbs were missing, and he wasn't insisting that she stay in their little home to keep a low profile.

"Have fun, pet." He lounged on the bed instead of the sofa this time, resting on his stomach, which displayed the gouges on his wingless shoulder blades.

Nova crouched at the foot of the bed and pressed her lips against his. "I know I will." Jules nipped her lip lightly at her cheekiness. "Is there anything else I need to know about dating a human before I leave?"

"Make sure he wears a condom, and don't wear the poor man out. Lucky sod. I'd love to know what you feel like to a human being. I just content myself that I'm the only one who knows what you feel like to an incubus. Still, I hope you know what you're doing, Nova."

"I don't. Isn't that kind of the point?"

"Be careful."

* * * *

As lovely as an open-throated dress shirt had been on Eli, the gray T-shirt he'd chosen tonight did him even more favors. It wasn't skintight, but it showed the definition of every muscle in his torso nonetheless, and when he removed his jacket, she drank in the mouth-watering image of his arms, which nearly strained against the seam of the sleeves, though it was supposed to be a little loose.

Nova touched the tattoo on his left arm, a mandala centered on the top of his forearm but stretched out in either direction in a partial sleeve. His skin broke out into little bumps, the fine hairs standing on end where her fingers ran over the ink.

"Do they mean anything?" she asked.

"They're symbols of protection and strength."

"Do you have much need for protection and strength in the acquisitions world?"

"You'd be surprised." He graced her with a boyish grin that softened his rugged face considerably.

He'd shaved, too, which youthened him further. Nova hadn't been looking for him to make himself look closer to her age. Far from it. However, it was nice to see the harsher edges sanded away. He appeared more relaxed than the last date, more like he'd been after they'd thoroughly fucked each other in his truck. Nova considered requesting that they start there. Maybe the rest of the night could benefit from the haze of afterglow.

However, looking him over without shame, even with all the people around them, Nova thought that if they started with sex, they'd never get to dinner. She didn't have to suck the life out of him to do the kind of damage that was floating around her mind right now.

Nova suspected he could see some of the things she was thinking about, because when the hostess sat them down, he had to subtly adjust himself as they slid into a booth.

They went through the usual pleasantries — *How was your week? Have you ever tried this dish? Do we want an appetizer or a dessert?* — before Eli asked, "Have you heard any more news about the killer on campus? I figured if anyone got the news first, the university would get it quicker than the local newspaper or news circuit."

"Ha!" Nova scoffed. "If the local news hadn't gotten wind of the killings, I doubt our administration would have told us anything. Something about making us *feel* safe. They've ramped up campus security, but I think it's just one of those things."

"One of what things?"

"How long have you lived in Meridian?"

"Twenty years, give or take," he said.

"Do you know the stats on this city? Robust economy, sure, and a low petty crime rate, but unusually high sexual assault, homicide and suicide rates. They're law-bound to give incoming students the numbers, but they try to hide them in very small print, and they keep a lot of the crimes and deaths secret in the name of 'internal affairs' and 'our lawyers advise us not to speak on legal matters'." Nova shook her head. "Dear students, come to UTM for the awesome city experience, stay for the Halloween beheading or the refusal to do anything to make young women actually safe on campus. Some people in the Social Psych department did an informal survey a few years ago asking about women's experiences compared with what they report to the university and what they report to the police. It was pretty dismal."

"It's an old story, containing the scandal—like a nine-month vacation with Aunt Marjorie."

"Yep. It's all written in a university security report, filed, investigated by the Judicial Council and dealt with quietly, with the women pressured to keep their mouths shut. Of course, they don't say it that way. They say, '*Get treatment with our on-site psychologists – of which we have many. Learn to move on. The case is nothing more than he-said-she-said and unlikely to go anywhere in trial. Don't rake your life through the mud for a non-starter.*' Our Psych professor didn't give a crap about the university's reputation on the matter. She handed out the information when we reached the relevant section of the course. The university isn't thrilled about it, but as long as it stays out of the campus and local papers and she manages to hold on to tenure, there's not much they can do. Suffice it to say, the administration's all about obfuscating and creative wording, accentuating the positive, minimizing the negative."

"You'll find that's par for the course."

"Oh, I know. They have to sell tuition. That doesn't mean the cost of doing it isn't sickening on so many levels. Whenever money trumps lives, I just want to take out my sword. I don't actually have one, but I sometimes feel like I could make one out of thin air if I wished hard enough."

"I'm torn between telling you to never lose that sense of justice and telling you it would be better if you did," Eli said with a specter of a smile.

Nova pressed the toe of her shoe to his. "Let me have the day, Eli. I have plenty of time to become jaded and pessimistic."

"True. And I'm hardly the best person to advise you to lose your righteousness. Acquisitions might not sound glamourous, but there are other areas in my life where I do my part to fight against the bad things in the world. We all do a little. Only a handful of us ever do a lot. And if you can content yourself with your little piece of it, that might be the balance between unfailing optimism and unrelenting cynicism."

"Let's just say I've yet to find my balance. When it comes to the killings at the university, though, I'm not exactly losing sleep—not from what I heard about these last few guys."

Eli had a curious expression on his face, as though something she'd said upset him, but not necessarily from her saying she didn't care about the lives of the men she'd killed. "You think they deserved to be murdered?"

"I didn't say that. But I'm not going to waste a tear on it, either, if the rumors as well as the declared facts are true. Besides, they haven't determined that they're murders yet, have they? They're just suspicious deaths, right?"

"Apparently by natural causes, but the circumstances of the deaths are suspicious, yes." Eli tilted his head in thought. "Have you, by any chance, ever looked up the death rate for UTM? Not the homicide rate, but the *death* rate."

"I haven't. That's sneaky. You're thinking that these deaths might have been happening for a while?"

"I'm thinking that the first handful of murders this year were mostly of girls your age and never in the papers."

Their appetizers arrived, but Nova had trouble convincing herself to eat.

"I'm thinking," Eli continued, "that if the university is so eager to avoid bad press, they might keep the elevated number of natural deaths to themselves. This is a strange city, like you said, with strange numbers. Perhaps we could break this case wide open."

"*If* the local news runs with it."

It was an ongoing joke in Meridian that the city had an abnormal rate of certain terrible things, but their TV news circuit was one of the most upbeat in the country – either it was blissfully oblivious or someone was lining pockets with silver.

"Are you keeping yourself safe?" Eli asked. "I'll stop with the overprotective impulses, don't worry. I just want to know. Because, like you said, the men are getting the press, but more women at your school are dying, and they're neither warning you nor really protecting you."

"I know I look small, but I'm formidable. I sleep with a roommate and spend the rest of my time mostly off campus or in public areas with other people, although I'm not sure whether any of that helps. I think people get lost in the 'choose your own destiny' narrative and forget there's only so much a person can do against someone else determined to destroy your life. I suppose I *could* go around the campus with mace, five switchblades and an unlicensed gun. I could learn martial arts. Or I could never, ever leave the house..."

Her volume and pitch kept rising as her chest tightened. She clasped her hands tightly in her lap.

"That's not what I meant, Nova," Eli said.

"I know. Sorry. Lots of feelings. I can bottle them back up with food, I think. Probably an unhealthy plan, but I don't want the food to get cold, and the feelings aren't getting any warmer."

Eli covered her hand before she could take one of the mozzarella sticks. He lowered it to the table, where he stroked the back of her hand, then turned it over in his to trace gentle circles in her palm with his thumb — mirroring what she'd done to him, reassurance that made her thinned lips relax and loosened the constriction over her ribs.

"Was I being too parental?" he asked.

Nova scoffed. "No. Believe me. You were being human. I was being a bitch."

"You weren't. You're a passionate woman. You have been ever since I met you."

The way he said 'passionate' while continuing to stroke her hand warmed her even more. Her jeans suddenly felt like they pressed too closely to her folds and her clit, which tingled with the early stages of desire. Desire for *him*, damn the consequences. Because when he looked at her like that, with those darkened eyes and the softened severity of his face, he could order her to give him a striptease in the middle of the restaurant, and she'd do it. He *wouldn't* order her to, she was pretty sure—but the relevant part was that she would.

"Have you figured out what you want to order tonight?" the waiter said, interrupting their moment. This one wasn't quite as adept at hiding his curiosity about the way the two of them were touching, the charge in the air between them—not least because he was jealous, subject to Nova's charms but not the subject *of* them. Nova could read his fantasies as though they were dreams, could feel his reaction to her the way she felt the warmth of Eli's hand against hers.

Eli eased his hand from under hers and took hold of the menu instead to order.

Nova gave the waiter a flirtatious glance as she ordered to placate him and hoped he wouldn't take it out on Eli's dinner—mostly because the waiter was a skinny young guy and Eli could probably flatten him with one punch. He wouldn't, but like Nova's striptease, the important thing was that he could.

After the waiter had returned to the kitchen, Eli took a drink of his beer, then set it down soundly. "Nova, I'm only going to ask you this one more time. Any other discussion on the matter will come from you, if you want to discuss it."

Nova braced herself for further talk about her safety and how she was somehow solely responsible for it.

"Does it bother or disturb you at all that I'm old enough to be your father...and then some? I know it sounds like I'm hung up on the subject, but I just want to make sure before letting it go."

She let out her breath in a gust, laughing. "Sorry, not laughing at you. I was just expecting something else. It really doesn't bother me, Eli. If you had to pop a pill before we got it on, maybe I'd suggest we should see people more our own pace, but that doesn't seem to be a problem, does it?"

Watching Eli fight between amusement and horror at the same time was entertaining.

"No. No, that's not a problem. The Pope wouldn't need a pill with you."

Her smile must have been bright, because Eli responded with his own, in spite of his pointless worries about something so surmountable. It wasn't like he'd been there on the date of her birth or contributed to the child-rearing. And nothing she felt for him had anything to do with age, except that time had earned him some wisdom and that wisdom earned him respect. Time hadn't done the same for other people his age, so she figured it was more a quality of character.

"So what's the problem?" she asked.

"It's not me. I'm coming to grips with it, slowly but surely. I don't know you well, but I suspect it'll be worth it to give this a shot. And not just in the bedroom, I assure you."

"I'm assured."

"However, there could be a problem with other people. We shouldn't decide what we do based on other people, but let's face it. Our waiter's expression is going to be just one of many. There are people in this restaurant right now who have been glancing over to figure out whether we are what they think we are.

There will be judgment, silent or otherwise. If we do this, you'll have to swallow a daily draught of it. I've decided I couldn't give a shit, but are you ready?"

The table between them was too much. She could climb over it, but that was generally frowned upon in eating establishments. She could climb under it, but that might be too much scandal for the night. Instead, she slid out of her side of the booth and into his. Then she curled her fingers into the V-collar of his shirt. It was ridiculously soft cotton, a dangerous combination with the rest of him. She pulled him down to kiss her — nothing too explicit, although she rewarded his not giving a shit with a gentle but insistent tongue to his lower lip as they kissed.

When she withdrew, he initially tried to follow her, but she caressed his chin with her free hand, then drew her fingertips up his jaw before stroking the feathery hair near his ears.

"When I was younger, everyone around me talked about how sex was only okay under very strict, narrow circumstances. Everything else was bad. Then, when I started to grow breasts, these same people kept telling me that I was nothing but sexual. So that meant no matter what I did, I was all that was wrong and dirty and bad, even when I wasn't doing *anything*." It sickened her to say it out loud, especially to him, but she needed to make this clear. "Things have gotten a little better lately, but I don't think it's going to completely change any time soon. I've had to deal with everyone's disapproval for a long time. I have better things to do than try to get their approval when it's an exercise in futility."

Nova released his shirt. Under cover of the table and her body, she slipped a hand over the front of his jeans.

He clenched his teeth, struggling not to lift his hips more firmly against her palm.

"The only approval about our…arrangement that I'm going to care about is yours. And you've already made it clear that you don't care what everyone else here thinks about it. Whether they're jealous or just don't understand, that's their problem, not ours. I'm done making other people's problem with me my problem."

"Nova…" Eli closed his eyes as she kneaded him. The thick material of his jeans kept her from doing any more than that.

"Yes?"

Eli covered her hand with his, but to her delight and arousal, he didn't push it away. He guided her into a deeper massage over his cock.

"This has nothing to do with what we're talking about," he said, "but would you like to get our dinners to go? We can eat it on the way."

"On the way where? We've never made it thirty feet past a restaurant," she said with a smug grin.

"Well, we could go to your dorm, but I don't think that would give us much privacy." He squeezed her hand over him as his eyes sparkled with good humor. "Besides, I'm pretty sure I don't pass as a student anymore. No. I thought we could go home. To my home. My…apartment. It's not much, but—"

Nova smoothed her hand away from his cock and down his thigh, then kissed his neck. She could practically feel the condemnation from other people in the restaurant. It made her smile against his skin and bite. "I'm in. But only if we get a mint shake on the way. I have a craving…one of many."

"Whatever you want, Nova. *Anything* you want."

This time, when the waiter returned to the table, they didn't break away or pretend that their contact was innocent. Eli asked for their food to go and the check.

Chapter Fifteen

Eli dropped their empty to-go containers in the nearest dumpster to his apartment, then came back to Nova leaning against the passenger-side door, sipping her shake. She wasn't doing it suggestively on purpose, but the shake was thick and she had to really suck to get it out.

Eli stared at the hollowing of her cheeks for about three seconds before he pulled her to him by her hips and nudged the straw away from her mouth with his chin. He drank some of the shake from her mouth, groaning low and rough as he tasted her deeply, cupping her ass in his large hands, his fingers so close to her pussy, to where she suddenly wished she'd worn a skirt for easier access. Then again, at least the jeans forced them to slow down.

As did her hand, cold from holding her shake, when she slipped it under his shirt. Eli shouted in surprise, then pressed his forehead against hers as they tried not to laugh too loudly.

"Nova, would you do something for me?" Eli said.

"You know my answer to that."

He took a deep breath. Then Nova thought she'd melt against the truck from the way the sparkle in his eye became a glint, his warm smile a smirk. Being clean-shaven couldn't make him look innocent enough to soften the edge he acquired.

"There's a bag in the bed of the truck. I want you to get it and carry it up the stairs for me. It's not heavy."

"What's inside?"

Eli just continued to smile. A shiver trembled down her spine.

He opened the truck bed for her. She had to crawl to the locked trunk in the bed. He spanked her as she did, startling a slight cry out of her. She glared playfully over her shoulder before continuing to the trunk nestled near the cab. He tossed her the keys to open it. There were a few things in the trunk, but she focused on the multi-pocketed rectangular black bag, like something a cameraman would carry around.

He gave her a hand so that she could jump down without falling. "Follow me."

Eli used the stairs, which was its own form of torment, since he lived on the eighth and top floor. It was all Nova could do not to just call her wings out and fly up. She was used to walking, vehicleless as she was, but in Texas, there wasn't a lot of walking *up*.

"No wonder your legs look so good," she said, panting. Although the bag wasn't heavy, it started weighing on her shoulder after the fourth floor. She switched it and shifted over to the other rail.

"What's the reason for yours?" Eli asked.

"Clearly genetics. I don't work out enough for this."

"Do you trust I'll make every step worth the while?"

"Why do you think I'm doing it?"

Once they reached the top floor, Nova leaned against the wall. "Let me guess — end of the hall."

His smirk turned downright sadistic. "Yep." He wasn't even winded.

"There should be laws against people like you."

He bowed and swept his hand out in a classic 'ladies first' gesture. "Last one on the right."

She hitched up the bag and ran in her flats all the way to the end of the hall. He walked leisurely, though, twirling his keys on one finger like a gunslinger.

"Mind telling me why you ran?" Eli asked when he finally arrived at his front door.

"It was the only way I could think of to have time to catch my breath."

"Fair enough." He unlocked his door. "Set the bag by the bed, then stand in front of it. Would you like a drink? I have a coffee machine and Coke or juice in the fridge."

Nova drank the rest of her milkshake in response. His throat worked as she hollowed her cheeks again to get all of it.

"Then what are you waiting for, little girl?" he said in a dangerous purr. "Permission?"

She ducked under his arm holding the apartment door open and did as ordered, tossing her cup in the trash on the way. She was surprised to see that, although there was an open door to what looked like a bedroom to the right of the kitchen, the bed was actually in the living room. The lack of extraneous furnishing or decoration wasn't as surprising to her. She'd expected him to either be this economical or a complete slob.

"I spend most of my time outside my home, and I don't entertain. I use the apartment to work out and sleep, so I outfitted it for those needs," he said.

"Well, you don't entertain in such a way that you need more than a bed." Nova tucked her hands in her back pockets while he searched the fridge for something to drink. He chose Coke over beer. The hiss of the can was sharp in the quiet apartment.

At least, it was quiet until a small, black cat crept out from under the bed at the hiss and ran to the kitchen to meow for food in a pitifully tiny voice. Nova bit her lip to keep from unseemly squealing.

"Pardon me," Eli said lightly. "Princess must have her food."

If he was going to have a pet at all, a cat sounded about right. He filled a small dish with wet food and put it on the ground before stepping around the kitchen counter toward her.

"You misunderstand me," he continued, setting a black folding chair backward in front of the bed, then straddling it and crossing his arms over the back. "When I said I don't entertain, I meant never. I don't bring people home, Nova."

"You mean you don't—"

He barked a harsh laugh. "I've had plenty of sex over the years when I needed it. Don't worry, little girl. You haven't deflowered a virgin or even ended a long dry spell."

"So you often get blow jobs in alleys?" Strangely enough, that kind of hurt, although she was kidding when she added, "I thought I was special."

Eli took her wrist and eased her hand out of her pocket so that he could interlock their fingers, although his hold was loose. "It was a rare first. Traditionally,

I'm invited to their home or we meet on neutral ground—motel, hotel, cars. That one wasn't new."

"It's also practically a classic. I didn't believe I'd christened your back seat or anything."

"But not here. I don't bring anyone here—not friends, acquaintances, ships passing in the night. This is my home. It's always been just mine…and Cat's."

"You call your cat Cat." She didn't know how to respond to the other part except with a mixture of honor and shame. Her other hand was trembling, too, but she could keep that one contained in her pocket.

"Don't get me wrong. I'm not granting you access to some private sanctum that I protect with my life," Eli said. "However, I brought you here because, in spite of its beginning, I think we started this for more than just companionship. Or, if I'm being blunt, sex—good as it is. I'm not getting down on one knee or anything, but did I read this right?"

She nodded. "I think so. God, that's scary, isn't it?"

The harshness to his face gentled. "Glad I'm not the only one."

"I've never done anything like this before. I know that makes me sound super young. And so did what I just said there. But I wasn't allowed to date, and the boys I was with weren't looking for a *date*."

"I'm pretty sure you weren't allowed to do the other things you were doing, if dating was off the table." He caressed the back of her hand with his thumb, drawing her a little closer.

"I *know* it's hypocritical, but it felt like I couldn't help myself."

"So you've always been willing to do anything."

"Not in the same way. I guess when you're treated like nothing more than an object that's less precious each time it has sex, it's really no wonder a girl can get so confused."

"But you're not confused anymore?"

"Oh, I'm still confused. I'm just angry about it now," she replied with a self-deprecating smile. "And I know now that it doesn't make a damn bit of difference if I wear something like this or the bulkiest, most shapeless clothes that hide the fact I have legs and try to hide the fact that I have breasts. I got just as much sex back when I wore those things. But it's worth noting that the sex wasn't nearly as good, and it was *never* for me. Maybe because they could tell that I blamed myself for what they did to me, so they were content to blame me, too."

"Nova, no matter what I do to you, no matter *how* I do it to you…"

She shook her head. "Not you. Funny thing… It turns out that when you respect yourself more, it changes how people treat you — not that the way people treated me was ever okay. Like I said, Eli, I'm done with boys. You're not like them."

Eli turned her hand over and pressed his lips to her palm. He dragged his mouth up to her wrist, tasting the tracery of veins. She hadn't known how sensitive she was there until her knees buckled and she knelt before him while he saluted her wrist. Eli met her eyes with affectionate arrogance, but he also let her know that whatever their bedroom antics — in and out of a bedroom — there was nothing shallow or transient about their arrangement. His kiss was a promise — not of permanence but substance. After Jules embracing her for what she really was and teaching her how the way everyone had handled her before was wrong, this was the most important, significant, sweetest thing that anyone had ever done for her.

She shuddered when he finally gave her respite.

"Go to the bag, little girl," Eli said. "You'll find a blanket. I want you to put that blanket over the bed. When you're finished, you're going to come back over here and take your clothes off for me. I'm going to have you naked, Nova. I'm going to see everything you have to offer, show you everything I can give you and I'm going to make a mess of you doing it. Off the ground. The sooner you get naked, the sooner you get to come."

She scrambled to her feet.

"In theory," he added. When she looked back at him, he'd rested his chin on his arms. She couldn't tell whether he was kidding or not.

The blanket was maroon and felt like chenille. She tossed it over the covers, making sure it reached all four corners before she returned to the foot of the bed. She hadn't checked the rest of the bag, but she was beginning to get a picture of what it might contain. Her nipples pushed against her bra.

"Let's see you, Nova," he said softly.

After she pulled her tank top over her head, he undid his jeans, letting out a sigh of relief as he released his cock. Then he crossed his arms at his waist and removed his shirt. She wished she could have done it for him so that she could feel him under that soft shirt again. She told herself that this wasn't the last time she'd have a chance, and the body underneath it was well worth the sacrifice.

Under the canned lights rather than in the dark truck, she got an eyeful of just how delicious he looked, how well he treated himself, unabashedly drank in the sight of his naked torso and his cock, which thrust out hard from between his legs, arching until the tip was within inches of his navel. Her mouth watered again.

"You're staring. While I appreciate the wrapping, I don't think you're finished opening my gift, are you?" He closed his hand around his shaft and stroked, slow, little more than an acknowledgement of his need — and a way to display himself to her, either in thrilling intimidation or encouragement.

She swayed out of her jeans after taking off her sandals — which she'd placed on the chair between his spread legs to unbuckle. She'd dressed for eventually taking her clothes off, in a dark pink demi-bra and lacy shorts that enhanced more than contained her. She stroked the lace over her ass as she lifted an eyebrow for permission to take off the rest or leave it for him.

"Difficult to believe there are women out there as beautiful as you." Eli still steadily stroked himself to the sight of every bit of her. "Did I tell you to stop, little girl? Bra last. I want to see your pussy before your breasts. But this time, don't touch yourself. Tonight, I'm the only one allowed to touch you. Your body is mine. Is that clear?"

Nova nodded. She hooked her fingers in the sides of her panties and folded them down until they reached her knees and she could kick them to the side.

"Good. Now stand up straight, your legs parted slightly. Yes, just like that. Continue."

He licked his lips as she reached behind her and unhooked her bra. She held the cups to her breasts at first, plumping them over the edges while his breath grew ragged, his hand on his cock faster.

"Show them to me, Nova. Show me those gorgeous tits. Mmmm, there you are, love. God, those tits. I'll fuck those tits one day, little girl. You'll like that, won't you?"

Nova started to take her breasts in her hands to assuage the ache in her nipples but remembered that he'd told her not to touch herself. She dropped her hands with a whimper, bringing them behind her back so that she was on display only.

"Mmm, good girl. Tell me, Nova, are you averse to being tied up?" Eli asked.

"I've never been."

"Crawl back onto the bed. Lie down with your arms and legs spread. You'll hide nothing from me. Tonight, this body is my plaything. Look at your pussy, Nova. I've barely touched you and already you're practically dripping."

He grunted as his hand became a blur on his cock. Then, as she scooted to the center of the bed, he abruptly released himself with a fierce shake of his head. She could read his desire so clearly in his head — needing to come but not wanting to if she wasn't a part of it in some way. It didn't help that she was calling to him — not her, per se, but her body, in waves that she had no control over. It burned like a forest fire inside her, hotter than ever.

He walked slowly around the bed, inspecting her from all the angles that he could as he approached his bag of tricks. He rummaged through it until he found what he was looking for. Four leather restraints and four metal objects that looked like small clothespins.

"I'm used to using these at a specific hotel. As you can see, I can't strap these to the bed as I'd like," Eli said. "I can sling them on the posts, but if you really want free, you can just lift them over. However, it will please me if you leave them where I put them."

She nodded, biting her lip against a moan as he strapped the restraints to her wrist and ankle on her left side and stretched them open farther to hook them onto the posts of the bed. It would take a little reaching, but Eli was right. She could escape easily enough if she wanted to. But why would she want to? The peaks of her nipples were hard as granite. Her folds and her clit tingled as though still confined within her jeans, swelled as blood pulsed through her. All the places in her body were lighting up one by one from the fire inside her.

"As I'm sure you've already discovered, I have varied tastes when it comes to sex. I am not limited to control, but I enjoy it quite a lot, especially when a woman is more than willing to step into the role that you've adopted so easily. So far, we've played our games, we've learned new things, but I don't think I've really *challenged* you. I thought I would scare you away when I forced my cock down your throat, but you took me in as though you were made for it."

"I'd like it again," she murmured, low and rasping with her craving.

Eli had to swallow before he continued. His cock bobbed, now nearly pulled up tight against his abdomen, so hard that not even its heft could weigh it down.

"So I have to come up with new ways to push your limits, little girl. Some of them might hurt, but I think you'll enjoy them as much as I do. You have such capacity for pleasure, Nova...for passion, for desire, for letting lust set you free."

He bound her right ankle and wrist. Now she'd really have to work a little harder to get out of the restraints.

"If what I do to you is too much at any point, I usually start with a traffic-light system. If I check in and you're good, either say 'green' or moan if you can't speak. If you're nervous or something's not working, say 'yellow' or close your hand over and over on your right restraint. If something is too much, you can't handle it or you're scared, close your hand over and over on the left restraint or say 'red'. I'm giving you motions because sometimes…"

He traced her lips with his thumb.

"…sometimes your mouth might be otherwise occupied. I went by cues our first time, but now you know what you can do to stop me. That means 'no' and 'stop' are for you to say when things hurt or you're overwhelmed, but you're okay to go on. Does that make sense? Do you understand what I'm going to be doing?"

She nodded. Her abdomen felt flat and taut, her cunt a spring ready to tighten in coiled metal before release. He pressed his thumb a little past her lips, but he withdrew it before she could kiss or lick him.

"Very good." He sat on the edge of the bed, much more composed than his cock would have her believe. "Now, I'm open to requests. If you have any, this is the time to voice them, while you can still think well enough to share. I may sound like an arrogant jackass, but you know that I keep my promises, don't you?"

It somehow seemed so much dirtier to admit her desires than to just do them, but there was nowhere for her to lower her eyes in nervousness from speaking those desires aloud. She curled her fingers around the ropes, silky rather than rough, that connected the restraints to the bed.

"I don't want you to come inside me," she said.

"I can't hear you, Nova."

"I don't want you to come inside me," she repeated, perversely loud to her. Nova suddenly thought about the fact that this was an apartment. There was a bedroom between them and the next apartment, but that didn't guarantee that sound wouldn't travel, especially if the apartment walls were as thin as in the university dorms. "I want you to come *on* me."

Once she'd said it, it was easier to keep talking and look straight at him while doing it. Especially as Eli's eyes darkened again, the pupils abnormally large, the way men's eyes sometimes became around her. She wondered if it made them see more of her.

"You can come on me wherever you like, as long as I can clean it off with my fingers and taste you when you let me out of these restraints." She licked her lips pointedly.

His Adam's apple bobbed.

"And I can see from the way you're dripping like candle wax that if you don't screw my pretty little mouth right now, you're not going to last." She was almost certain she wasn't much better between her legs, but her body had been built to withstand desire as well as experience it. "Just remember to come on me."

"You're a pushy one," Eli said, catching her tongue between two fingers and making her squirm before releasing her. "But you've got a wicked tongue and an even more wicked imagination. Let's put that wicked tongue to use. I think you'll be a little less pushy with my cock down your throat."

He had no idea how much her mouth watered at that comment, or as he arranged the comforter under the throw blanket so that her head tilted back, or as he shucked his trousers and stood before her, looming like a giant. The cords of his muscles seemed strapped to him, layer upon enticing layer. She wanted to bite his flesh, lick him from the V of his hips to his collarbone, cling to his legs.

She supposed she should have guessed that he wasn't going to go about this the usual way, but she still exclaimed in surprise when he leaped onto his own bed with the energy and agility of a man half his age and knelt over her face at the head of the bed, her body spread out before him.

Eli caressed her jaw, the tender, vulnerable line of her neck and back up, then eased her mouth open. He had to hold his cock away from his body, one hand braced against the bed next to her breast as he slid his cock into her eager mouth.

She groaned in hungry delight at the taste and feel of his cock as bare as her body. The last time she'd had him in her mouth, he'd been wrapped, which meant that he'd either forgotten this time—which she doubted, given his relative composure—or he trusted her.

She had to make sure that his trust was never betrayed.

And she could trust *him* to do what he promised. Her touch affected him just as strongly as any, but his desire manifested in a far more dominant persona that relished in the power and pride of *not* losing himself in her or the fantasies that she offered—a more intense version of the man he already was. Jules was quite different, proud of inciting and exciting the both of them into a frenzy over and over and over again.

It was hard to think of Jules, however, with her mouth and the back of her throat full of Eli's erection, which strained her jaw and pushed heavy against the top of her mouth as his balls brushed against her nose.

The angle that he'd arranged her in ensured a clean line from her mouth to her throat. She didn't struggle, didn't gag, didn't need to. All she needed to do was run her tongue over him in encouragement, as though trying to draw him deeper.

But he was taking her so slowly, in spite of the harsh rush of air through his nose as he maintained an iron grip on his self-control. She arched with the not-yet-satisfied craving for all his cock, which curved her neck and put additional pressure on the head.

He grunted and thrust all the way in. She struggled with the restraints on her ankles in her effort to plant her feet on the bed as she writhed and moaned, the vibrations right where the cockhead was situated.

"Nova, love, if you want me to come on you, be still and don't moan for a second," Eli said through gritted teeth. He let his breath out in a rush, his chest heaving, his head hanging and eyes clenched shut.

He gently pulled back until the thick ridge at the edge of the head came near her teeth.

Then he pushed in again, this time going more quickly. Her throat felt so full, like she couldn't quite get enough air, but she didn't want him to stop...*ever*.

"Ah yes, just like that," he murmured. "Like swallowing a sword. Take me all in, my bad little girl. Moan again if you're green."

Nova did that and more, twisting her mouth over him and gently raking her teeth against the sensitive underside. Her breasts shifted over her chest as she turned from side to side in her enthusiasm. She clenched her hands into fists, but not over the ropes.

He shouted, his hips jerking as he fucked her mouth like she wanted him to, her saliva dripping down her cheeks.

Her whole body screamed because she couldn't. Her clit throbbed and her cunt tightened, tightened, tightened around nothing but didn't quite reach orgasm.

It was a close call when Eli yanked himself back and gritted out, "Close your eyes now."

His warm seed struck her face, concentrating on her mouth and cheeks, but some of it hit her chest in small droplets.

She opened her eyes when he traced her lips with his cum-coated cockhead. She eagerly obliged, sucking him like candy. He groaned at the intensity, and as she swallowed his semen, her fever grew, the sexual energy stored in his cum blossoming with new heat in her stomach. She turned her mouth away to moan high through her clenched jaw, raising her hips off the bed as her orgasm wrenched through her, strong but short and unsatisfying.

She didn't growl with frustration or anger—not when she knew that Eli wasn't done with her yet. He'd only just begun. And with his fingers gathering up his semen from her cheeks to feed to her like honey, so had she.

His cock stayed hard as she sucked at his fingers to get every last drop that he fed her, to take the power he'd willingly relinquished. He probed her mouth, curling his fingers to draw her head this way and that, stroking her tongue, her teeth, until there wasn't much left of him on her than the thinnest of layers, indistinguishable from her saliva, except that it still tingled where her flesh continued to draw it in.

Eli crawled over her, dragging his cock along her chin and neck, between her breasts, before he did an about-face and caged her body with his, staring at the places he'd marked as though the cum were still there—as though he'd defiled her and liked it.

Still holding his body above her, he ducked down to kiss her, tendered his tongue over all the places that he'd forced his cock in her mouth, his kiss languorous in contrast to her attempts to harshen it. When she nipped his tongue—not to hurt, but to spice his excruciating sweetness—he slapped the side of her breast, rippling it. He kissed her deeper at her whimper.

"A splendid idea, love," he whispered against her lips. He opened his eyes and grinned with such menace that she thought she was going to come again. "Now we can really begin."

Instead of coming, euphoric giggles bubbled out of her as he kissed down her neck where he'd left a damp line from his cock.

"Do you find me humorous?" He slapped her other breast and glared, but not seriously.

"No, sir," she said through her giggles. "I just feel really good."

He cut her laughter off as though with a mute button when he laid his head between her breasts and brought one nipple to his mouth, licking around it with nothing more than the tip, curling around it, probing at it…then closing his teeth over the bud. And this bite hurt.

He met her eyes as she cried out, pulled her breast up solely by the hold of his teeth and lashed the flesh with his tongue. She twitched—not wrenching away, because that would be even more painful—but she kept her lips resolutely closed so that she couldn't tell him to stop. Neither her breasts nor her clit nor her cunt seemed to care that it hurt. Her brand of lust accepted any kind of attention—even the pain was pleasure.

When Eli released her nipple, her breast snapped back, heavy, full and aching against her chest. He used the throw to dry her nipple off.

"Now," he said, grabbing two of the metal objects from the nightstand, "be very still for me."

She managed to tighten her body to keep from moving until he fastened the clamp on and settled back. Then she whined, pressing her flushed cheek against the throw. The clamp was as agonizing as his teeth, but it wasn't going to let her go like he had. And now he was drawing the other nipple into his mouth, worrying it and biting it just as much as the last one to harden the peak so that he could apply the second clamp.

Eli sat back on his heels to take in his work in progress. "You'll find that you'll feel better if you just scream."

"You have…neighbors," she gasped.

"I do."

Eli cupped her breasts, knocking the clamps with his knuckles. Even though they didn't bend very far, it felt like they'd been yanked. "Look at those lovely little nipples. So red. So sensitive."

He drew his palms down to her thighs, spreading them farther—an unnecessary gesture, because they were already open enough for him to see how her arousal hadn't abated. Just like the clamps magnified her sensations, everything between her legs seemed that much more intense after her first orgasm.

After his own first orgasm—and in spite of the fact his cock was as flushed and rigid as before she'd blown him—Eli appeared far too composed, not to mention smug, as he petted her pussy too gently to do anything but frustrate.

"How cute," he said. "The girl thinks she can hold back."

She stretched up to kiss his chest as he reached for the last two clamps. He flicked the nipple clamps in response, making her yelp.

"God, you've got gorgeous breasts. Ever since I saw the one, I've wanted to set them off with those clamps. And ever since I set eyes on your pussy, I've wanted to do this. Count yourself lucky that I don't think you're ready for one on your clit."

"You've got to be kidding." The tears had started with the flicks he'd given her nipple clamps. Now that the flood gates had opened, she couldn't stop them any more than she could stop her increasingly loud moans as he parted her folds and applied a clamp to each side at the same time he ghosted the tip of his tongue over her swollen clit.

"Oh God, oh my fucking God, ah, *ah, ah…*" Finally, she couldn't contain herself anymore. She screamed at the ceiling, her back an arc, although Eli held her thighs against the bed.

Eli sank his mouth over her clit, engulfing her, drowning her in such velvety heat in counterpoint to the pain of the clamps that she lost her words — or any desire to use them.

She was going to bring the whole apartment complex running into the room to see who was being murdered.

Eli knocked the lower clamps to the side to part the flesh and insert two fingers into the grasping entrance revealed. He laughed into her, the vibrations intensified by the metal, but he held her down with a firm hand on her abdomen as he violently thrust his fingers into her cunt. Her cunt begged him deeper, tightening around them as they curled and caressed, and Nova grasped the ropes of her restraints, but not in the open-and-close clenching motion that Eli had given her to tell him to stop.

Nova had become the creature again, and it frightened her that she couldn't rein it back in even if she tried, because he'd stripped away everything that held the demon at bay. Her teeth and claws went in and out. She thought her wings pushed against the skin on her back before she managed to hold them in, but the effort to do so also clamped her pussy around Eli's fingers, which had found a place inside her that made arousal explode in a constant barrage — until she feared she would shine too brightly or explode, scattering all light into darkness in her wake.

Instead, as he jostled the clamps on her labia every time he slammed his fingers into her, as he tormented her clit so sweetly and unrelentingly, as her breasts shook with her movements and made the nipple clamps tug on her, she expelled in a body-wracking release against his chin and hand, and against his neck and chest as well.

Eli kissed her belly under her navel and eased his fingers out.

"Now you know why we needed the blanket," he said as she settled back against the throw. She was crying and laughing at the same time, emotions wringing out of her like water from a rag.

"We're not done, are we?" she managed through the wracking sobs and giggles.

"Do you want to be? I think you can take more after you calm down."

"Calm down?" She felt like she would never stop crying. She'd flood this apartment like Alice with her tears, and she didn't have enough of her head together to be embarrassed. She could talk, relax the steel bar that had been her spine, but she was still the creature — the creature that could only feel rather than think.

"This ought to help." Eli opened the clamps on her swollen folds. They throbbed with ache, but her clit twitched little shocks of post-orgasmic pleasure as blood rushed through the places that had been pinched. She gasped in little moans from the release of pain. The clamps on her nipples became even more painful in comparison, though. She'd just been getting a hold on her sobs until he released her nipples as well.

Eli hooked his arms under her shoulders and held her through the rest of her emotional purge, his feathery soft hair tickling her breasts where he laid his head between them. She didn't care that he was getting the liquid she'd squirted onto him on her abdomen or that the breeze from the air vents cooled all the places she was wet, an especially strong contrast to her fever of desire that had not been slaked — not even close, in spite of her psychological exhaustion.

Eli rested his chin on her sternum. "Can I leave you for a second? If you think you can take more, I'll be right back, this time with an instrument solely for pleasure."

She rubbed her cheeks on the blanket on either side of her. The way that Eli had propped her head back gave her something more dimensional to rub against, which helped. "I can take whatever you dish out, Eli. I'm already broken. You don't need to worry about whether I shatter."

"We're all of us a little broken." He kissed her lips, just a simple touch, before crawling out of bed.

She admired his ass and the strength of his thighs as he went through his bag of tricks once again. She missed him, yearned for him, the moment his skin no longer touched hers, which told her she wasn't as strong as she pretended to be. She wanted to gather him tightly against her after he'd plugged something into the wall and climbed back between her legs, but she was still all tied up and at the mercy of his whim.

He stroked her thigh. "Are you all right, Nova? Tell me truly. Light check."

"Green with a side of vulnerable, I think. I'm just shaken, not stirred, and I…" She couldn't convince her tongue to word when he ran his hand up to her breast and tenderly massaged the abused nipple. Her eyes were mostly dry now, although her face was streaked with tears and the hair near her temples stiff with salt. But she felt herself sinking in quicksand before she could articulate it.

"Shhh." He set the new item down between her legs and stretched out beside her. His cock was a hard piece of hot iron against her hip, but he held her, stroked her, let her shudder out the emotional aftershocks. "It's perfectly normal to feel this way. Don't fight it. Just let it happen. You don't have to prove yourself to me."

"M-m-minute," she replied, turning her head toward him as she slowed her breathing. She thought the average person might fall asleep at this point from the powerful release of who knew what kinds of hormones, but her body wouldn't let her.

She wasn't satisfied. She needed him to come, and her cunt wanted more than just his fingers. In truth, she wanted him to stay inside so that she could drain him fucking dry—the creature did, anyway. But Nova wanted nothing to do with that particular wish of the creature within. She could hunt when she left. Eli was off-limits, period.

The closer she wanted him, the more he canted forward, his cock rubbing a wet line against her hip. His massaging strokes turned firm, the fingers pressing deep. His lips drifted from her shoulder to her mouth until she captured him like a lure with a fish.

"I want to see you," he murmured against her lips.

She lapped at his tongue. He groaned, lifted himself up to angle his mouth over hers so that he could take over the kiss, possess her, send his shadow deeper into her—though it was her darkness he should have feared, even as she capitulated.

The worst of her emotional outburst enhanced the kiss until it was as decadent as anything his fingers were doing between her legs—too light to be a stroke, too firm to be a caress, inciting, exciting, reawakening what had never really gone back to sleep.

When he pulled back and settled again between her thighs, she felt more like her old self again. She giggled as Cat jumped up to sniff at her nose and hair. Nova couldn't nudge her away, and Eli was too amused to do so, even convinced Cat to pounce upon the ends of Nova's hair as he pulled the rubber band out of it. Then Cat settled nearer to the pillows and proceeded to bathe herself.

Nova grew more anxious when she saw what Eli was doing with the rubber band.

"What the hell is that?"

Chapter Sixteen

"Don't tell me you've never seen a vibrator before," Eli said.

She could barely blink while telling a man to pull out and come on her, then blushed at the mention of a sex toy. He fell more in love with her with each passing minute. And as Nova had said, but with his own embellishment, it was fucking terrifying.

"I've seen a vibrator. That looks like something out of an infomercial," Nova said.

"Have you ever used one?"

She shook her head. "No touching myself, remember?"

He grinned. "Ah, yes. Your unusual system. Another first I can give you, although I warn you, this baby packs a heavier punch than most toys. I just want to turn it on and watch you go, see you in the midst of your orgasm without distractions. How many would that be for tonight? Be honest, little girl, how many times have you come tonight?"

Her blush didn't dissipate. "Tw-twice," she confessed.

"I suspected you had one after I finished with your mouth, but I wasn't sure."

Eli held up the massage wand in one hand and a washcloth and Nova's rubber band with the other. He covered the top of the machine with the washcloth and bound it to the wand with the rubber band, creating a small barrier between the vibrations and her. They'd be intense enough without becoming too much stimulation too quickly.

"I'm going to make you come one more time for me. The only request I have for you this time is that if you make a sound, it has to be my name. Let those nosy neighbors know exactly who's giving you this pleasure. Then I'm going to fuck you when you're finished and make you dirty like the bad girl you are. At that point, you can come with me or not. Something about you, Nova, makes me think that you will."

He brought the terrycloth-covered wand between her legs to stroke the bulb over her folds and sweetly glistening, dark pink clit. Then he brought it to her mound just above and turned the wand on.

Nova went from being replete and still to galvanized by what coursed into her. Cat ran off the bed from the loud motor, then glared at him from one of the stools in front of the kitchen bar. But Eli spared his cat a mere second, because Nova tensed all over, bucking up against the small circles he made with the rumbling bulb of the wand. And every moan that wrenched out of her, every breath she took, every hyperventilating gasp was his name.

He wanted to bury himself in the dripping pussy beneath the machine, wanted to still her breasts in his hands, wanted to bite that glorious, exposed neck, but instead he looked and didn't touch through the throes of her approaching climax. It wouldn't be long, rarely took more than three minutes when he brought out the wand, as though it was truly magic and reduced any woman to a squirming, wet bundle of pleasure. Men whose masculinity were insulted by toys missed so much, starting with what was in front of him right now.

He knew she'd come when she could no longer vocalize a name but just another shriek. Eli grinned at the thought of someone knocking on the door to tell him to hold it down or calling the police on him for disturbing the peace. If the officer saw Nova, he'd probably congratulate Eli instead of citing him.

Nova's grimaces went from being overwhelmed by pleasure to hisses of overstimulation. He abruptly turned the machine off, tossed it to the foot of the bed and positioned his leaking cock against her entrance. There was no friction at all. She was soaking wet and ready for him, clinging to his cock like hands, practically dragging him in through the last few spasms of her orgasm.

He kept her on the edge as he hooked his arms under her again and fucked her, his body tight against hers, his chest pillowed against her breasts. He embraced her, enveloped her as best as he could to give her the contact that she would need as well as to give himself the sensation of her blisteringly hot flesh against his.

He felt overstimulated, too, as though he were the one with the fever. Every touch seemed like too much, but this was good, good, too good everywhere their flesh met. He broke out in a sweat at her heat, the way it seemed to surround him, infuse him.

Then her pussy rippled around his cock and he knew he wasn't going to pull out of her in time. He just wanted to sink into her, deeper and deeper until she had all of him. If he could fuck her with his whole body, cover and smother himself with her juices, he would do it.

"Eli, now," she gasped, tossing her head back and forth as she pitched up.

He didn't think he was going to manage it until he shoved himself up, grabbed the base of his cock and forcefully pulled himself out. Two strokes to his gleaming, pulsing shaft, and he doubled over, strings of thick, whitish cum landing on her. Then his cock gushed the rest of his climax over the blur of his hand. He shouted with each wave until he fell next to her, panting, relieved that he had performed to the peak of his promise and ability.

Their dissonant breathing somehow aligned. He glanced up at her at the moment she looked down at him. Her smile made the flesh over his scrotum crawl in the best possible way.

He could go another round for this girl if she wanted to.

But he propped himself up, wiped his hand on the throw, then lifted the restraints off the bed posts so that she could undo the fastenings while he did the same to her feet.

When he turned back to her, he caught her drawing up threads of cum from her torso and consuming him, as she had the first time. He was unprepared for what the sight of her sucking her own fingers as though his semen were hot fudge would do to him.

She slowly pulled her fingers from her mouth and reached for him, her eyes unspeakably dark, although part of that was probably the angle of the lamplight and his shadow as he covered her again. Their kisses were soft but intense, the possessive quality gone, unless it meant they possessed each other equally. His heart thudded against his ribs. The bonds had been removed, the scene over, but Eli feared that he might actually kneel at her cunt again and declare fealty like a knight before a queen.

Not just terrifying. Dangerous. It was dangerous how much he felt, how *hard* he felt for her...and he didn't mean his cock, which stirred against her thigh but was too tired for now to make much of a showing. If anything, Eli was just proud that he had been able to keep up with her. Usually, the women he was with had to keep up with him. This had been a pleasant, if ambitious, surprise.

They dozed in and out on the throw, their skin cooling and drying off, although Nova remained warm to him. He briefly worried whether he'd been unsafe choosing bareback tonight, but she didn't seem sick. Her glow was healthy rather than feverish, her golden skin unashed under its natural color, no dark circles under her eyes. And he'd gotten an eyeful of her perfect little pussy, nothing untoward or unnatural there. He rested back against the blanket with her head pillowed on his arm and idly played with her breast with one hand — more affectionate than lustful. Her breasts were full, generous, as comforting as they were attractive.

"I think I'll take you up on that drink." Nova stroked his chest with gentle fingers. "No, stay there. I'll be right back."

He watched her as she climbed off the bed to head toward the kitchen.

What he saw dipped his lingering heat into a tub of ice.

He didn't have enough time to analyze how his protective, proprietary, possessive feelings toward her experienced such violent whiplash that he swore something snapped inside him, like the crack of a whip, and something else poured in where those feelings had been.

He lunged from the bed, grabbed her by the shoulders and shoved her against the wall with all his strength.

"Eli," she gasped, her cheek smashed against the plaster, "what—?"

"Don't you *dare* say my name."

He pinned her there with his hand on the back of her neck, staring intently as though it had been a trick of the light, a trick of his mind. He hoped with every sinew that those gouges on her shoulder blades would disappear. Never had he wished for human blindness more than at the moment he couldn't deny what she was.

How could I have been so stupid?

The way that he reacted to her touch. The way her eyes were so dark they seemed black...because they were. Her coloring had kept him from questioning it the way he would have with a fairer woman. Nor had he thought anything of her inspiring such lust from him with a touch when she'd done the same too far away for her to have much of a magical impact.

He had hunted covered from the very beginning. He'd never been directly touched by a sex demon, and hers wasn't the same impossibly intense weaponized magic which the succubi he hunted used to attack him. But he still should have fucking *known*.

"What's going on?"

The wicked thing had the audacity to tremble under his hand. She made it all so convincing. His gorge rose in his throat.

"Don't play games anymore. You can't fool me. I can see you plain as day."

Although her smashed face still exhibited some confusion and shock, her trembling abruptly stilled. "What are you talking about?"

"Your wings, demon," he hissed. "I see where your wings were torn off during your fall. There's no need to pretend, to be sweet or confused or fucking human. I hunt your kind. I know what you are."

He fumbled for the vampire kit he'd set on top of one of the book piles and pressed a smooth wooden cross between those eternal wounds. The skin didn't dissolve like it did for vampires, but Nova wrenched under his grip and cried out—in seemingly genuine surprise. He threw the cross down and shoved her harder against the wall, so close she gasped for air.

"What are you?" she asked. Now the demon thought she'd appease him with tears.

But he clothed himself from head to toe when he hunted for a reason. She was naked and so was he, his hold on her neck direct contact with a succubus whose defense mechanisms were rising like mercury in a thermometer.

It was all coming together. Her skin burned under his hand, still sizzled where he'd confirmed her demonic nature with the cross. What would Brumley say if she knew that a succubus had lassoed veteran demon hunter Eli Fray, and he hadn't had an inkling until he happened to see her bare back?

"You're the one I've been hunting, aren't you, succubus? You're the one preying on the men at the university, you and your partner with his women."

She had the perfect cover, youthful as she appeared. She might have even been telling the truth about her classes. God, he'd seen her in the quad just the other day, had feared for her safety when he should have plunged the silver knife straight into her unsuspecting heart. Had she been planning her next attack as he'd flown over her?

"You actually had the audacity to talk about those deaths as though you weren't *intimately* acquainted with them," he snarled.

Nova swung her arm around, claws out, and caught him in his side, tearing into the flesh. The second his hold loosened, she slipped out and backed away, her fingers curled defensively, not anger in her eyes but terror—and confusion. For a second, he actually believed that, even though she was undeniably a succubus, she really didn't have anything to do with the murders on campus.

"What do you mean, you hunt my kind?" Nova asked.

"Stop playing naïve! You killed those men!"

"They deserved it!" she shouted back.

"*No.* No, you do not dispense justice, demon. You dispense chaos. You spread temptation like a sickness, just like you tempted me. Were you laughing when you went back to your demon lover, laughing over the lovesick human you've been grooming?"

"I've been trying to protect you," Nova said, still backing up until her injured shoulders pressed against the glass balcony door. "What are you talking about,

285

grooming? I thought we were dating. I thought I could love you. I thought you —"

Eli backhanded her across the cheek.

He knew how deeply she'd sunk her poison into him when the sight of her shock and pain made his chest hurt, as though invisible fingers pulled at threads knotted through his heart and lungs.

This time, when she looked back up at him, anger intensified the black in her eyes. He saw the demon in her now.

"I don't talk with him about you because you're mine — because you're the most human thing I've done in over a month...longer, when I consider how inhumane my life was before that."

"Don't try to make me pity you, demon. It won't work." His throat felt as though someone had planted a large, spiky seed inside it.

"I did lie to you, but only about the kinds of things I can't tell a person who doesn't already know about these things. The part where I'm a d-demon." She struggled with the word, as though unaccustomed to it. "The part where I'm the one killing those men. Are you really a d-demon hunter? I didn't even know they existed."

Eli hesitated.

Any second he wasn't running for his knives in the other room or the gun he kept in his nightstand was another second that she suffused him with her magic, which hovered thick around her. Even the slap had left his skin humming, and his cock was half-hard. There wasn't anything he could do to protect himself from her if she touched him or he touched her again.

But she wasn't even trying to attack him. She was actually attempting to explain herself, as though there were a single excuse she could give for her demonic activity that would wipe her filthened slate clean. Why was she bothering with talk? Why wasn't she taking advantage of his weakness for her, the weakness she had cultivated herself?

"You're a demon," he said. "How can you *not* know that there are those who protect humanity from you?"

"I told you. I've only known I was a succubus for a month. It's been a difficult adjustment. All those stories from my past? God's honest truth."

"What do you know about God's honest truth, liar?" Eli spat.

"I was Catholic for almost nineteen years, and I'm still a terrible liar, even about the killings. I hated killing most of those boys. If I have to kill them, the ones I'm going to kill are the ones who deserve it. You were never on that list, Eli. You have to believe me."

"I can't believe a word you say. And you *won't* kill again. If you really want redemption, demon, I'll take care of that for you." He ran for his work room and grabbed a broadsword from the wall.

When she caught the gleam of the blade, her eyes widened and her wings emerged, revealing her faux-angelic form, the one he'd hunted from above most of his flying career. He couldn't pretend that seeing her like that didn't have an effect, with her gorgeous wings spread to fill the room and her gorgeous body framed by their wildness.

Eli knew what was coming before it happened, saw the caged animal look on her face, the same one on every other demon before he sawed their heads off or destroyed their heart.

Nova—this was the first time he had a name for the demon he needed to slay, and there was a reason most hunters didn't deal in names—slipped back through the locked sliding door and launched off his small balcony. No one but Eli and other eye-marked hunters would be able to see the naked woman flying over them as though the hounds of hell pursued her. He couldn't hope to catch up. After putting on all his shielding clothes and armor, then strapping on the pack and the wings, she would have had more than enough time to reach the nest she shared with her incubus partner.

"I don't want you to come inside me. I want you to come on me."

"I've been trying to protect you."

Eli dropped the sword, pressed his hands to the sides of his head as though he could cram the memories into a trunk and lock them away.

But although it wouldn't last, her juices drying powerfully fragrant on his skin and the blanket on the bed remained a reminder of all the ways in which he had put his life in her hands tonight. Yet she'd done little more than let him use her any way his smitten brain could devise and make it feel extraordinary.

"No," he snapped at himself in his empty apartment. "She made me love her. She only wanted to play with her food first. She's a murderer. A demon. A succubus. You almost killed her lover, and you need to kill her. You need to kill them both."

He yanked the throw off the bed, bellowing his frustration, still without a care for his neighbors. They wouldn't be disturbed again.

He turned off the lights and rested naked on the top of his comforter, exhausted but wired, angry but also in mourning, not to mention humiliated. He killed Nova. He killed her over and over in his head until he was sure he'd be able to do it in real life.

As dawn approached, his eyes stayed open, although he desperately needed to close them.

He'd have to put protection runes up in the corners of his apartment. He'd been complacent not doing it as soon as he'd signed his lease, but he'd never needed to use them before. A succubus had never known where he lived, because he'd never left them alive to follow him home.

And this one he'd invited straight in.

He was afraid to sleep.

Chapter Seventeen

Nova flew through the rose windows of Jules' home. "Why didn't you *tell* me?" she screamed.

Jules stood up from the wood-veneer table that he used as a desk. "Why didn't I tell you what?"

"*Hunters.* Why didn't you tell me there are hunters that go after demons? Why did you let me fly around and do all the things I've done once I stopped being afraid lightning would strike me down, when what I should have been worried about are actual people out there trying to kill me?"

Jules was stunned for almost a whole minute. "I was going to tell you, especially after one jumped me a few days ago. But we stayed in for a while, and I hoped he'd go away. They usually do. Did he get you on your way back?"

She shoved him. Jules stumbled back, shocked.

"No, you jerk! *Eli. He's* the hunter. And he said he's been hunting here. So when I asked you whether there was anything else I needed to know, *that* was the kind of information I was talking about. While I was being careful about not killing him, I could have been way more careful about him not killing me!"

Jules stiffened. "Did he follow you?"

"How could he have followed me? I was flying."

"When he attacked me, he had wings. Golden wings. I don't know how they kept him in the air — magic, I guess — but he flew after me."

"These are the things you need to tell me, jackass! But no, I don't think he was able to follow me. He wasn't wearing any clothes, and putting on wings probably takes some time. As far as I know, I wasn't followed, but I'm sure as hell not leaving this place anytime soon, no matter how much I want to throw you through the fucking wall. He could have *killed* me, Jules. I was so surprised that if he hadn't been just as surprised, he could have cut my freaking head off with the honest-to-goodness medieval sword he brought out before I escaped. He *knows* me. He knows my name. He knows my history. Even if he doesn't believe anything I've said to him, how much I..."

"Nova, calm down."

"How am I supposed to calm down? He knows I'm here, knows what I look like and he's mad as hell because he thought I was *grooming* him. If you could have seen how he looked at me..."

She batted his hands away as he tried to close them around her arms, but he was persistent, backing her against a couch and cupping her face to send waves of slow-burn arousal through her, which took all her tension and directed it into avenues of better use to him that made her more pliant and less provocative under his touch.

"The hunters talk a big game, Nova, but you're so much more powerful than he is," he said. "Their greatest weapon is surprise, and you won't be surprised anymore, will you? It's better that you know what your human is now instead of later, if you'd been unfortunate enough to fall in the kind of doomed love of great literature."

"What if I already did? You ever think about that?"

Jules stroked her tangled, flight-wild hair. "Loving that a man treats you the way you've always wanted to be treated doesn't mean loving the man. Given enough time, you'll learn that for yourself. For now, count yourself lucky and prepare yourself for what lies ahead."

"What are you talking about?"

"He's going to come after you. He's going to try to kill you again. You're going to have to kill him first."

* * * *

She and Jules flew with great caution off campus and into the city to feed and fill the reserves of their power to the brim. Jules didn't enjoy living in fear in his own territory, but he agreed that they'd be less likely found by Eli if they avoided their usual haunts.

Nova would enjoy taking a break from her usual heartless boys to drink instead from heartless men, except for the knowledge of why they were doing it.

"He probably has a spell or two up his sleeve to fly around the way we do and not make it into the newspapers, but he had to wait for me to come out before he attacked me, so I doubt he can go through walls like us. That's the way we'll win this. That, and you're in his veins now. He's embraced

your touch, your magic, and that makes him almost as susceptible as though you really had fed on him."

Going after cheating, closet-sociopathic men in their boardrooms and offices didn't quite give her the same sense of satisfaction as going after raping, closet-sociopathic boys and men on campus, though. Adultery was sinful, painful and traumatic but perfectly legal, and it just didn't feel right to her to punish it the same way. But she and Jules still left a path of bodies from the top floor down, because she had to take what she could get. Now, however, she was more aware of the fact that those bodies would be found and the suspicious circumstances publicly noted, catching the attention of a hunter...maybe even Eli.

If Jules had told her before that people tracked mysterious deaths like this, Nova might have been more careful with her previous kills. She wanted to be more careful about these, but Jules had told her not to worry. The hunters already knew about her, and staying in one place with a lot of people would keep them safer while also providing them a veritable buffet, which they needed more than secrecy.

While they'd discussed their options in Jules' attic, he'd stopped his frantic pacing, instead eerily still.

"Has he brought you to his home?"

"Why?" she asked.

"Isn't it obvious, pet?"

She raised an eyebrow, daring Jules to say it to her face.

"The easiest way to get to him is through his dreams. You'll barely have to ask yourself in. You'll get the feast that you've craved and will forever crave from him until you do it, and he'll no longer be part of the picture. We can lay low for a while in case he's put other hunters on our scent. Then we'll be able to resume our lives. That's the way it's always been."

She crossed her arms. "I'm not doing it."

"No violence, no pain, nothing but the pleasure he's always sought from you. You have something other succubi would kill to have – an address. Succubi are at the most risk, you know, since most hunters are straight men."

"And if I'm most at risk, you didn't warn me about them why?" Nova snapped.

"Because for every hunter, there are a thousand demons. We reproduce so infrequently, yet they die in greater numbers."

Ever the voice of reason to make her feel like she was overreacting – except she really didn't think she was. He didn't know what she'd had with Eli, what she had been trying to have. He hadn't been there when Eli had brought her into his home. He hadn't seen Eli's expression when he'd realized what she was.

"I hadn't told you about hunters yet because the odds of encountering one, much less dying to one, are low, even for succubi...especially in Meridian. I suppose they feel like they make a dent, but they're only a handful of soldiers at hell's gates. I wasn't keeping him from you, Nova. I just didn't want to alarm you. I wasn't intentionally putting you at risk."

"Well, you did. And you're not getting off the hook just because you intended better, Jules. You were reckless with me when I'd already warned you against that. I don't appreciate it at all."

She sat in the guest lounge on the first floor, four men's lives enriching her body like three days of good exercise and three weeks of a healthy diet. She thought about taking one more—she had room—but she decided to kick her feet up on the glass table, taking in the singular experience of being nude in such a corporate setting and surrounded by picture windows while a janitor buffed the marble floor.

She'd come a long way from the vague suggestion of cleavage making her hide in her room.

The problem was that she wasn't sure whether the place she'd ended up was a better one or simply adjacent, equally as extreme and even more damaging—for her as well as for the people around her, whether they'd earned the danger or not.

Jules descended through the ceiling, wiping lipstick from his mouth with the back of his hand. "You were probably more successful than me, but I think that'll do for the night."

She didn't reply, only stood and spread her wings. She expected him to follow but didn't wait for him to catch up.

They made it back onto campus without seeing hide or hair of the hunter, although if he had a spell concealing him like they did, they couldn't trust their eyes.

Before they could fly into Jules' home, Nova banked toward the dormitories.

"Nova!" Jules called after her. "It's too dangerous tonight."

But she'd caught a scent she couldn't ignore, and she needed this. She was pissed off, scared, horrified, mortified and sad. She didn't want to smell that perfume on any other woman.

Jules found her on the third floor, watching a young man try every argument under the sun to convince his girlfriend to screw him. Her resolve was weakening, even though her desire to put off the deed was not.

"What am I supposed to do about this, then?" The boy gestured to the prominent tent in his basketball shorts. "Come on. After everything we just did, what did you think was going to happen? How can you do all that and *not* have sex?"

"I'm sorry, Rog," the girl replied, her face pale. "I'm just not ready."

"We're practically already doing it anyway. The only difference would be that we wouldn't have our clothes on. It's the next logical step."

"I already told you, it's not that I don't love you or don't want to. I just don't think I'm ready."

"Come on, baby," the boy said, trying to get his hands up her shirt. "Just kiss me again. You'll feel it, and you'll want it as much as I do. Just give me a hand job or something, feel what it's like for me."

"I don't know." The boy either didn't see the way the girl went green or didn't care. "Hey, stop that. Why don't you go back to your room? What is it, two in the morning? I have an early class."

"Now you're just trying to get rid of me. That hurts, Jen. It really does. You have no idea what it's like for a guy."

Nova pulled in her wings but stayed invisible as she sank the fingers of her magic into the boy.

"Ah, man, just looking at you makes me feel this way," Roger said. "Baby, I'm so hard for you. Don't leave me like this."

"I think you know how to take care of it yourself," Jen replied, even as she played with the top closed button on her blouse. She wasn't warming to Roger, though, because Jules kept his distance, no longer protesting — because they'd be heard, but also because he could never resist watching Nova work. "I wish you'd stop pushing. It makes me think sex is all you want from me and I don't actually matter."

"If sex was all I wanted, I wouldn't keep going out with you, would I?" His eyelids fluttered as Nova bypassed his shorts and wrapped her hand around his cock. It had been hard to begin with, but now he was rigid to the point of wild distraction.

"That's mean, and it's unfair." Jen stopped playing with the button, but that didn't help Roger tear his gaze from her cleavage, ripe but not explicit through the open collar of her shirt.

"Whatever. Fuck. Fine, I'll go. If you want to be the last virgin in our graduating class, I guess that's your decision."

"Go fuck yourself."

"That's what I'm doing," Roger said, his hand on the door and Nova's no longer on him. "Because someone won't let me fuck her."

He hadn't done anything, but the stench of what he would have done still filled Nova's head. It was only her urging that had turned him away from that bed tonight—subconscious knowledge that he'd get some if he left, but it would be a lot more work if he stayed.

"You're a pig when you're horny, Rog."

"And you're a bitch when I'm horny." He slammed the door, heedless of the rest of the hall, who were trying to either study or sleep.

Nova followed him out, and Jules followed Nova.

Before Roger entered his room, where his roommate was already steadily snoring, Nova slipped through his walls, shed her glamour, pushed his comforter back and climbed into bed. When Roger came in and switched on a small lamp so he could see where he was going, he got an eyeful of Nova with her legs parted and both hands full with her breasts.

Roger's mouth fell open.

"Come on over, honey," Nova murmured, low enough that the roommate wouldn't be able to hear her, and for the purr to caress his skin, as intense as running her tongue over his balls. "I've got everything you've ever wanted. You don't want to die a virgin, do you?"

* * * *

When she returned to Jules' home after killing Roger, then another young man whose backseat companion had been unconscious and wreathed in a tequila mist, Nova fell in front of the toilet and threw up everything she'd eaten with Eli, from the takeout to the chocolate mint shake he'd bought for her.

Chapter Eighteen

Nova was rubbing it in his face. She was laughing at him. There was nothing in the morning papers, of course, but there would be tomorrow, and plenty of the carnage made it to the morning newscast.

She'd worn him out physically, but he still hadn't been able to sleep. Of course, he hadn't wanted her to catch him when he was completely vulnerable to her. He wasn't so foolish as to believe he wouldn't let her into his dreams the second she asked. But night was also his time to be awake, and he wasn't used to sleeping until sun burned through the curtains like the end of the world.

The morning newscast opened with a segment on the continuing mysterious deaths on the university campus, this time two young men, seemingly unrelated. An accompanying segment mentioned that there had been a rash of similarly baffling deaths at a law firm in Meridian Midtown. Clueless paranoid people gave their person-on-the-street comments.

Clueless experts weighed in, talking about the flu and the West Nile virus as well as Africanized bees and bee allergies. The Meridian populace was urged to call nine-one-one if they felt shortness of breath or other symptoms of an allergy or heart attack.

She must have known that he'd see the results of her handiwork. She'd even made sure that her partner had been there to kill a few women as well. No other incubus or succubus would be making waves like this while the city was on alert — as much as Meridian ever could be. Meridian news circuits wouldn't play this story for long, even if the deaths continued indefinitely. It would fade from sight, and thus from memory. Then the monsters could come out, anonymous once again and no longer feared in the most fearless city in the country, fearless the way that children were fearless, because it was young, too. Maybe one day it would learn.

It occurred to Eli that he might not live to see that day. He needed little more than kindergarten math to know that the reinforcements she'd fed upon last night might be too much for him to take.

"I've been trying to protect you."

Well, now she's trying to protect herself.

The news went from murder and mayhem to the line of thunderstorms supposed to hit after midnight, bringing with it the first under-fifty lows of the season. Eli's head stayed with the murders, trying to picture the sweet, ingenuous girl that he'd met as the lying, loathsome viper that she was.

He couldn't do it.

"I did lie to you, but…I've been trying to protect you."

He kept coming back to that, the way she'd seemed clueless about what a hunter was, the way betrayal had mirrored in her eyes...as though she deserved to be hurt when he'd been the one in real danger, his life in her hands, in her *body*.

It was all a ruse. He muted the television and interlaced his fingers behind his neck as he bowed his head. *An elaborate ruse to gain my trust, to be invited in. Playing with my heart like a pestilence demon playing with intestines. She's not a terrible liar. She's the devil's daughter, the offspring of the Father of Lies. She kept up that bewildered, terrified act to prey upon my sympathy. Nothing more.*

Then why didn't he believe it?

Part of him did. Part of him latched onto those thoughts like a man on the edge of a skyscraper. The other couldn't help but look down into the abyss.

What if it hadn't been a ruse? What if she hadn't been lying? What if she'd really only been a full-fledged succubus for a month and had just been looking for someone to spend time with? A succubus didn't usually bother with small talk, the getting-to-know-you portion of dating and relationships. She didn't have to, when a single touch was enough to get a man into bed.

But every touch, even in the filthiest conditions, had felt pure — the crispness of something fresh and honest and heartfelt, which was why he hadn't realized immediately what she was, and which could be just another layer to her treachery.

"I've been trying to protect you."

She hadn't protested him wearing his condoms. He mainly wore them because he wasn't interested in paternity suits or fevers and itching to slow him down, but it had also been grilled into him by his old partner, the sex demon hunter who'd mentored him and shown him the ropes before Eli had eventually availed himself of Albert's patronage.

And when he hadn't worn a rubber, she'd made sure he came outside her instead of inside, welcomed orgasms inspired by something other than his cock within her. A mere technicality that allowed them to enjoy that safely, but technicalities made the world go round.

She could have asked him not to be safe at any time. He'd been whipped up into such a state that he probably would have thought, *Fuck it, she's worth it.*

"You're the most human thing I've done in over a month. Longer, when I consider how inhumane my life was before that."

Eli had the day. He'd sleep in his truck outside a church if he had to, but he couldn't stay here.

* * * *

He started at the university, which was unsurprisingly unhelpful. When he asked whether they had a student named Nova Mendez—he was a lawyer calling on behalf of her family regarding a death—all they could tell him was that Nova Mendez was no longer a student at the university. When he asked why, they said they couldn't say. She was simply no longer enrolled. When he asked whether they knew where he could reach her, they told him they had no forwarding address, and if he was really calling on behalf of the family, he'd be able to get in contact with them.

Next, sitting in a diner with a large black coffee in front of him and his breakfast order on the way, Eli contacted Detective Dunn, one of only two police officers in the city who didn't have their head firmly ensconced up their ass. Most hunters who knew about them had the number to Dunn's private phone, used strictly for liaising supernatural cases.

"This is Eli Fray. I need you to look up a name for me."

"I'll have to get back to you on that. I'm in the middle of actual work here."

"Whenever you can, but I need it before this evening."

"Fray... I've heard of you, I think. You're one of Albert's golden children, aren't you?"

"That's right."

"I'll see what I can do. Who am I vetting?"

"Nova Mendez. I'm looking for a potential missing person report and any criminal activity." When succubi worked within the realm of the conscious, they sometimes caught solicitation charges or were fined for exhibitionism in public places. It was a place to start.

"I'll try to slide that one through," Dunn said, "but I can't make any promises."

"Thanks, brother."

Eli had finished his eggs, an English muffin and most of his coffee when his phone rang from Dunn's number.

"All right, Fray, I ran your girl. No criminal record, not even a parking ticket."

"She doesn't drive."

"There is a missing person report, although since she's not a minor, it didn't raise any alarms."

"Did the university or her family file it?" Eli asked.

"The university. Huh. According to the report, the officer in charge contacted the family, but he noted that they didn't seem worried or surprised. Turns out the kid wasn't close to her family, probably had been talking about getting away for years. You know how some kids get when they reach college."

"Yeah." Eli's palm was sweaty around his phone. "Thanks for the favor, brother. Can you do me another?"

"What?"

"Her home address."

Dunn paused. "That's stepping over a line, don't you think, Fray?"

"She's not there," Eli replied. "I just need to ask them a few questions. I won't bring you in it. I'll play the PI card, tell them someone from the university gave me the number. I think she's in trouble…serious trouble."

"If I hear something went lopsided with the family or the girl, I'm coming after you with a pickax and a hellhound. She's only nineteen."

"I wouldn't ask unless it was important."

Dunn hesitated again, then rattled off the address. It was in one of the neighborhoods right on the edge of Meridian, before the still-developing suburbs began. Modest, part of the old city before the boom. He'd hunted there before.

"Thanks, Detective."

"Hope things turn out right for the girl."

Eli took a breath. "Me, too."

* * * *

A woman answered the door. Eli had hoped that both her parents worked and the kids would all be at school or that Dunn had given him the wrong address. However, even though they shared nothing genetically, Nova favored her mother.

"Good morning. You must be Mrs. Mendez."

"We don't accept solicitations." The woman started to close the door.

"I'm not selling anything."

The woman warily kept the door open a crack.

"My name is Eli Fray, ma'am, private investigator." He pulled a PI license from his back pocket. Another gift from his patron.

"What do you want?"

"UTM hired me to find your daughter," Eli Fray said.

"Why would they do that?"

Eli blinked but barely missed a beat. "You might have heard about the series of unexplained deaths on campus. The university is being thorough, in case her disappearance is related."

"Covering their butts, you mean."

"I am well-versed in their habit of covering their butts, yes, ma'am," he replied. "I'm in the early stages of my investigation, and I thought I'd begin with members of her family, looking through her room for any clues as to her whereabouts before visiting the campus. I intend to talk to her roommate, her professors, her friends, anyone who might—"

"Nova didn't have any friends," Mrs. Mendez said shortly, but she opened the door. "Can I see your credentials again?"

Eli showed them to her. She wrote down his information on a notepad by their landline.

"Would you like some coffee or tea, Mr. Fray?"

"No, thank you. Mrs. Mendez. Did you say that your daughter doesn't have any friends?" Eli sat on the floral armchair that Mrs. Mendez offered him. His first impression of the woman was that she was quiet, modest, impeccably behaved. Although Nova had been less modest—in a multitude of ways—she shared a number of her mother's mannerisms.

Mrs. Mendez perched on the sofa against the wall. Above her hung a crucifix flanked by a pair of religious-themed prints. She tucked her clasped hands on her schoolteacher's black skirt. "When she was a child, she had several friends, but she withdrew in middle school. I scheduled activities with the youth fellowship at our church, hoping that it would be a good influence and provide a wholesome social circle, but she never tried very hard to make friends there, preferring a more secular sphere."

"A more secular sphere, ma'am?"

"Do you have children?"

"No, ma'am."

"I have three daughters," Mrs. Mendez said. "It is difficult to raise daughters in this world. I'm sure in your work as a private investigator, you've seen plenty of evidence of evil. My husband and I have done our best, but a parent eventually has to leave the rest to the child and to God. We hoped that Nova would honor her commitment to the Lord, but she always scrambled for the world's approval, which sank her into deeper misery every time. We've tried to save her from herself for the last ten years. Once she left our household for university, however, my husband and I let her go. She has God's Word, and she has the lessons that we gave her to protect her from the world."

Mrs. Mendez bowed her head. Lines at the corners of her eyes suggested that she knew how to smile well, but Eli hadn't seen a single one in connection with her daughter. It occurred to Eli that she wore gray and black not because they were modest, but because they were the colors of grief.

"When we heard she was missing, my husband and I weren't surprised, Mr. Fray. She's always been the most rebellious of our daughters."

"In what ways, specifically, did your daughter act out?" he asked. "Was she prone to running away, engaging in drug use, promiscuity?"

"Little more than rumors, but she only ever pretended at purity. There wasn't a day that went by after she became a teenager that we didn't have to send her back to her room to change, and she must have had her own hoard of inappropriate clothing, because her teachers sent her home, too. I believe Nova meant well, but she gave too much credence to what the world thought of her, wanted to please them by showing her body. And if she wanted to show her body, what other reason could there be but that there were boys to show it to?" Mrs. Mendez shook her head. "It wears a mother down, these constant battles. We never had as much trouble with our others. Nova more than made up for how easy they were."

She gestured to the side of the room with white built-in shelves on either side of the mantel, where family photos joined knick-knacks and fake flora. Eli approached them, studied each photo with detached, dispassionate curiosity. He came to several conclusions based upon Mrs. Mendez's comments and what he saw, but he didn't share them. He was, after all, a professional.

"So, you can't think of anywhere she might be or with whom?" he asked, still gazing at the pictures.

"I don't know where my daughter went, Mr. Fray. She hasn't contacted us since she left for college."

"Have you tried to contact her?"

"When the university called us to ask whether Nova had withdrawn from school and had simply not informed the university, we called her cell several times and left messages in her email inbox. But Nova never called or wrote us back. I don't know what more I can tell you. We have no idea where she ended up — or with whom."

"I notice that you refer to her in the past tense, never in the present. Do you believe she's dead?"

"My husband and I believe the world has claimed another willing victim."

Eli turned around, his hands behind his back. "May I see Nova's room now?"

"It's no longer her room. Her sisters split what she left behind for themselves, and the rest we donated or threw out. It's my sewing room now. Do you still need to see it?"

"When did it become your sewing room?" *After she left for college or after she disappeared, before you knew for certain she was dead?*

Mrs. Mendez pursed her lips. "I don't appreciate your tone."

"I apologize. I simply need to know whether Nova thought she'd be welcome home in whatever state she was or is in."

"We have a guest room," Mrs. Mendez said coldly. "Nova's room became my sewing room before her disappearance. She knew that was my plan for when she left. And now I think it's time for you to leave."

Eli allowed himself to be herded to the door. "I may have more questions as I continue with my investigation."

"A telephone call will suffice."

"I prefer in-person interviews."

"You are not welcome. I'll call the police."

"Is that what you told her? Did she ask you for help, and you told her not to bother coming home?"

"I said she never contacted us once."

The lock turning in the door was abrupt, sharp and final.

As he headed down to his truck, he couldn't shake the image of the Mendez family photographs. Husband and wife, two glowing daughters who looked like normal teenage girls—then Nova, standing near, sometimes even hugging her sisters, yet seeming miles away from them just the same. Her sisters' body language telegraphed subtle disgust that they might not have even realized they felt. Her own smile rarely reached her eyes—with none of the brightness that Eli had seen during their short time together.

And in every single one of the photos in which Nova was present, she was almost completely covered in dark clothes from neck to feet, even when her sisters wore shorts and brightly colored T-shirts in summertime.

It was clear that her family was conservative, modest, concerned with how appearance reflected religiosity. It was also clear that they were deeply, deeply ashamed of Nova—and that they'd deeply, deeply shamed her.

Eli had never thought about what human life had been like for the incubi and succubi that he hunted. They usually went through most of the years of their youth raised by human parents, perhaps unaware of what they were, but the people they called family obviously sensed that one of their children wasn't quite right. Then they became the demon, not only a trial but a culture shock, without time to slowly transition.

He'd known this was the case, but most of the demons he'd killed had been what they were for years, sometimes decades. They handled themselves too well, and they never tried to explain the rationality or moral virtue of their actions. They just fought back.

Eli didn't like that he was thinking about it now, that he was even for a second entertaining the idea that Nova might not be evil, even though she was a demon. That he was challenging the very foundation on which he'd built his life's work.

He closed his truck door and sat in the driver's seat without turning the vehicle on.

He could follow through with the investigation as he'd explained it to Nova's mother by heading to the university and finding her dormitory, maybe asking her roommate some questions.

Instead, he brought the engine roaring to life and headed the other direction, toward a more affluent part of town.

* * * *

Eli knocked on the grandiose front door, which Albert had outfitted with a griffin knocker. His excess wealth allowed him to indulge in every fantastic and eccentric whim that crossed his mind, with or without a trace of irony.

Jeannie answered the door. She usually kept more traditional hours than her husband, who sometimes forgot there were such prosaic things as clocks. She lit up when she saw who was on her doorstep.

"Eli, good to see you again so soon." She was taller and thinner than her husband and wore her gray hair in a bob with pride. If she colored her hair, it was only to make the gray more even, but Eli couldn't swear to that. "Come in. I can make you breakfast—or we have leftovers from dinner."

Some people offered such things to be polite, but Jeannie was a born hostess who felt neglected when a guest didn't let her take care of them. She and Albert had three dogs, five cats, three ferrets, any number of rats, a snake and who knew how many other pets that Eli wasn't aware of, but no children. Instead, Albert patronized hunters, and Jeannie made sure they were well-fed.

"Breakfast would be delicious. Is your husband up and about?"

"He went to bed sometime early this morning. I'd rather not wake him, but I realize that it's almost your bedtime as well. Do you need me to bring him out for you? You don't want to disturb him when he's sleeping."

"Oh, believe me, ma'am, I know."

It wasn't that Albert woke up like a bear in winter. It was that he slept nude and didn't always realize he wasn't wearing clothes when he climbed out of bed.

Albert met Eli in the kitchen, a maroon robe tightly tied around his rotund waist. Jeannie was in the middle of making a breakfast scramble, and Eli had accepted a glass of orange juice.

"Eli, my boy," Albert said, settling on one of the island chairs. "What are you doing here at this hour? No call?"

"I was out and about, and it wasn't important enough for a phone call, but too important to wait."

"Oh dear," Jeannie said. "Perhaps you should retire to the dining room. I'll bring you your food."

"I trust you," Eli said.

Jeannie nodded and went back to checking the eggs. The kitchen smelled like sausage, butter and garlic.

"I take it that this is a personal matter rather than a professional one," Albert said. "The young lady we spoke about before?"

"Both, unfortunately. In your years fighting against demons in your own way and through your patronage of others, have you ever known of a demon who wasn't evil?"

"My dear boy, how have you managed to live as long as you have and not realize that evil is a matter of degrees? I know hunters tend to function better in terms of black and white to make their job easier, but most of them die before your age as well."

"Are you telling me that there are demons that don't need killing?"

Albert rested his hands on the stone counter of the kitchen island. "Eli, you're a magnificent cowboy, but you're terribly reductive. If angels can choose to fall, is it such a strange thing to acknowledge that they can rise again? It's difficult, of course, and the more full-blooded they are—the darker, deeper hell-born monsters—the more likely they relinquished almost any chance of returning to the heaven from which they fell. But the ones who walk the earth have the chance to be influenced by the very people they're meant to influence, otherwise we wouldn't have gargoyles, yes? The gargoyles exist because a demon made a choice to claw their way back into their Creator's good graces. You know what gargoyles were. Did you forget what demons were?"

"But they have to become the gargoyle for us to know they've repented."

"It would be easier if that were so," Albert said. "If you came across a werewolf pack, would you slaughter them with impunity?"

"Some hunters might."

"But you don't."

"You won't patronize those who hunt werewolves for their pelts."

"Many werewolf packs, especially the urban ones, have learned how to live harmoniously with humans, minimizing their culinary impact. Several collectives and patrons have treaties with them."

"I've always hunted incubi and succubi exclusively," Eli said. "I don't have to consider the ethics of hunting the rest."

Albert peered at Eli over his round, rimless glasses. "Then you are questioning the ethics of hunting incubi and succubi."

After a beat, Eli answered, "Yes."

"Does this in any way relate to the young lady in question?"

Eli had to lower his eyes, unable to lie to such a direct question from Albert.

"I'm sorry to hear that," Albert said softly. "Have you handled that problem, or is this to determine how you will handle it?"

"She's still breathing, if that's what you're asking."

"I see. Are you questioning whether she's something you need to kill?"

"Yes."

"Eli…" Albert rested his hand on Eli's forearm.

Jeannie slid the scramble in front of Eli, but she apparently didn't take offense that Eli didn't dig in immediately.

"I'm afraid I might need specifics to help you—" Albert began.

"No. *Hypothetically*, is there a succubus who hasn't turned into a gargoyle that I shouldn't kill?"

"Hypothetically, I don't know, but there could be. Hypothetically, full-blooded demons almost always go full gargoyle when they choose to redeem themselves. Hybrids take a more curious route. Incubi and succubi are most often compared to vampires, for good reason, but they're more likely to go gargoyle than vampires because they have more demon in them. Vampires are too close to human, because, like the werewolves, they come from us, often against their will. Very few of them will grace the rooftops of Meridian.

"The incubi and succubi, though… They're curiously trapped between human and demon because, although they don't come from us. They're born from us, raised by us, often unaware of their demonic nature until it emerges. And while some of them embrace what emerges, others find the road far rockier. This young lady may have captured your heart, Eli, but it doesn't mean she must also capture your soul, if it is not her will to do so. The fact that you're here now, discussing such a personal matter with me, suggests that her nature might be a bit fuzzier than you're used to dealing with from such creatures."

"She's done terrible things," Eli said. "But she has justified them to herself."

"Haven't we all? Have you never questioned the violent work that I help you do? My dear boy, do you not even realize that if you walk in the darkness long enough, you start to carry it with you? When you mix money with duty, there is no helping it."

"Why patronize hunters if you think they're evil?" Eli asked, more snappishly than he intended.

Albert remained patient. "Because I have no doubt that the demons you kill needed to be killed. No doubt at all. In a war, sometimes the ones killed aren't necessarily true believers, even when they fight for the other side. Collateral damage is inevitable. But you follow no orders, Eli, not even from me. If you think she doesn't need to be killed, if you don't want to kill her, then don't. If you think she needs to be killed but you love her too much to do it, enlist someone else to take on the terrible task for you. There is no shame in that."

"And if I can't decide whether to kill her or not?"

"You don't have to take any action at all. You can simply leave her to the blade of whatever other demon hunter might cross her path. But there is another option."

"Which is?"

"If she's not too far gone, there is always room for rehabilitation. She may never be human, but that doesn't have to make her a monster. Some deaths might be inevitable, but yours doesn't have to be, and there may be certain...constructive outlets for a young woman of her talents, wouldn't you say?"

"Like punishing the wicked? Are you seriously telling me this?" Eli pushed away from the island, fighting against anger rooted in tendrils of uncomfortable, unfamiliar fear.

"There are men more wicked than any demon. You know that."

"But it's not for man to judge man."

"She's not of man. If there is a way to contain her magic, Eli, then you can show her, but succubi still need to feed—just as we do, which is why you should eat what my lovely wife gives you. And if your succubus must kill to feed, there are ways to handle that. That's all I'm saying," Albert said quietly. "That is the truce that many werewolves and vampires have made with our world—to narrow their feeding grounds to those whose loss is humanity's gain."

Eli pressed his hands against his forehead, pulling at his hair.

Albert patted Eli's shoulder. "You have many things to think upon, my dear boy. None of them are easy matters. You may need more than a day to consider them."

"I don't have a day."

"Then I suggest you have your breakfast and sleep in one of our guest rooms." Albert's tone brooked no refusal. "More problems were resolved in unconsciousness than in all the hours of stress-induced insomnia. Get some food to fuel your brain, then get some rest. I shall endeavor to do the same. Perhaps I'll arrive at a better solution, as well."

Albert wished his wife and Eli good morning, kissed his wife, gave Eli a reassuring squeeze on his shoulder, then went back to bed. Eli slowly returned to his seat, and although he had a hard time tasting what he put in his mouth, he ate it all, drank his orange juice and didn't protest when Jeannie showed him to the Blue Room.

Protection runes had been comfortingly carved into the wooden molding like art. It made closing his eyes much easier.

Chapter Nineteen

In his bed, Jules wrapped his arms around her, warm and tight, as though he feared she might try to run away.

"Do you remember when you first emerged?" Jules pressed a kiss to her shoulder. "I told you it wasn't the end of the world. It still isn't. A broken heart isn't such an uncommon thing. It's practically normal."

"Having your heart broken because someone else is a human being and you're not doesn't sound normal."

"Having your heart broken because you and your lover are different in insurmountable ways does. The important thing is that you caught it early. You might even recover quickly."

"Like a bad virus," she said dryly.

"Exactly."

"Jules?"

"Yes?"

She stared out of the decorative stone window, where the sun set violent pink behind the skyline. "Stop trying to comfort me. It's not working."

"What else did you have in mind, pet?"

She turned around in his arms, tangled herself around him, then whimpered as he took the hint and kissed her hard against the feather pillows.

He gave her great pleasure, but no matter how high her fever spiked, it couldn't thaw the cold rock buried in her chest or the others rattling around in her skull. Her climax pulled at him more strongly than his pulled at her, but the magic only slightly tipped in her favor now, leaving him gasping but far from unconscious or even winded.

Jules continued to rock against her in the aftermath, his cock still hard but his need greatly diminished. He kissed her until she nearly forgot why she was unhappy.

"What now?" Nova asked.

"We stop hiding. We lure the hunter to us by doing what we do best. If we wait too long, fear's poison will paralyze you. You aren't prey, Nova. You're an exceptionally powerful succubus, and you've nothing to fear from him. He isn't anything compared to you. Two demons against one hunter... It's barely even a fight."

"What if I don't want to kill him?" she asked.

"I can do it."

She gave him a look.

"Seriously. I'll keep my glee to myself and accept it as a solemn duty. I can do that for you. But I'm sorry, kid. This comes down to kill or be killed. There should be no qualms about killing him to protect yourself. That's just survival."

In spite of the feed and what she'd taken from Jules, Nova still felt pale, drawn, flesh stretched thin over bone. "You forget I was raised on a diet of martyrs and saints."

"You're not a martyr, Nova. You survive too well, and you were meant to thrive. That hasn't changed with one bad turn." He stroked a gentle line from her temple to her chin. "You ready to fly?"

"In a minute."

"You can't put this off forever."

"I just need to get dressed."

He propped himself up on his elbow as she slipped out of bed. "Really?"

"I notice you don't like flying without pants. And you've never had to fly with tits out before. It's almost as bad as running."

Jules bit his lip to keep from laughing. "Point taken."

* * * *

As she and Jules kept their senses attuned to the sky around them as well as the people below, Nova wondered whether she'd ever feel safe in the air again. They wore their glamour but had no confidence it would conceal them from the hunter. Instead, she relied on her body's ability to recognize him when he was close. She didn't know how close he had to be for that—probably too close—but it was all she had.

Jules followed her lead. It was her fight, her night, and he was far less picky about his food sources than Nova.

The fact that she was searching for prey of her own while Eli might be hunting her made her hot and cold in turns, as though she'd be caught at any moment with her hand in the cookie jar—and when she was, how could she deny her appetite? But if she wanted to convince him that she wasn't ashamed of who she fed upon, she couldn't show hesitation just because he disapproved.

Nova steeled her resolve, caught a scent, then dropped into a dive down to the Religious Studies building. She perched on a familiar ledge, peering through familiar wooden blinds at a familiar tableau that had her blood boiling.

Jules landed next to her. "Oh, how perfect." His wings brushed hers, sparks of furious lust crackling between them like static electricity. "Do you want me to stand guard or should we just open the windows?"

"Open the windows." Was that voice hers, that low, rustling, bestial growl? "Let anyone passing by know what he is."

They slipped through the glass and wood and landed behind the good Father's desk.

Nova didn't know which question haunted her most. Had Father Marcus always been the monster she saw before her now or had she been his trigger? The expression of pain and confusion on the girl's face as she twisted away from where the Father pushed her bra aside, whispering blame to her breasts between licks... It could have been a flashback.

"Don't you know what it does to a man when he sees your breasts?" Father Marcus took one of the girl's clenched fists, coaxed open the fingers to bring her hand to the front of his black trousers. "It's your responsibility to keep us safe and keep our thoughts pure, and you failed."

Nova pulled her wings in, then leaped onto the desk.

"Hey!" She dropped her glamour as the blinds folded in and the windows swung open.

Father Marcus stumbled back in shock. At first, there was no sign that he knew who she was, which was an insult in itself. Then again, she'd changed since the good Father had last seen her. She was definitely wearing less in the way of fabric than when Father Marcus had accused her of making him stumble. Now, she hoped she made him trip, fall and smash his nose in.

Then the good Father took a good look at her body, covered in little more than panties and an off-the-shoulder T-shirt, which showed the lacy top of her bra and certainly a generous expanse of cleavage. The windswept tangle of her hair framed her fury.

Revelation slowly dawned on him like the black sun of the apocalypse. She was all four horsemen to him as he cowered back against the wall of books, away from his victim.

Nova briefly turned her attention to the girl. "You. Nothing that happened here was because of you. Forget you saw anything. Run. *Now.*"

"Not you, Padre." Jules appeared out of thin air to grab Father Marcus before he could escape out of the office first. "You get to stay and have one last fling. The girl's not for the likes of you."

Nova wondered how she could have ever believed that he was a man of worthy cloth, how she could have admired him and hated herself all the more for her ability to break such a holy man. She wished she'd stumbled upon his continued monstrosities sooner. It would truly be a pity for Eli to interrupt her with this one.

The Father's tented pants hadn't diminished, despite his fear, and she wasn't even trying. He hadn't gotten what he wanted from her. She barely had to penetrate his mind to see how incessantly he'd touched himself since he'd almost had her, sometimes in places he shouldn't have had his dick out. The deeper she peered into the black void of his brain, the more she relaxed. She hadn't made him what he was. He'd been her trigger, not the other way around.

"You made me think it was *me*, you sanctimonious prick." Nova stepped off the front of the desk. "But even with magic oozing out of me at the time, it still wasn't my fault. *She* wasn't a demon, jackass. How many others have there been? How many other girls have you blamed for your own corruption?"

"We are all depraved, Ms. Mendez," Father Marcus said. "The difference between you and me is that I can repent."

"But you don't. You ask for forgiveness, but I see no repentance in you, no remorse. Maybe you can't help it. But that's between you and your God, and I hope you're ready to take it up with Him. You want me, Father? You want to finish what you started? I'm afraid you can't corrupt me anymore, and you can't make me ashamed of myself the way you did before."

As she approached him, she pulled the low neckline of her T-shirt down farther so that her bra was completely exposed. She shrugged one strap down, then tucked the cup underneath her breast.

The voluntary exhibitionism captivated him. He grunted when she lowered her mouth to lick her upthrust breast. Now Jules' hold on him wasn't necessary, although Jules didn't dare release him.

Father Marcus held himself up by the bookshelf, his breathing harsh through his nose.

"But I can make you think you're taking advantage of the dirty girl you think we all are," Nova said.

"Oh God," Father Marcus said as Nova lowered herself to her knees before him.

"Dirty girls need to be shown the logical conclusion of their sinful natures." She moaned as she ran her face over the front of his trousers, quite a cat-like gesture — but thinking about that made her sad, so she stopped. Instead, she worked her fingers down the fastenings. "Dirty girls need to be shown their place in the world under the divine authority of men. Should I kneel and pray, Father?"

"God, yes," Father Marcus groaned.

Nova pulled his briefs down. His weeping cock bobbed out. She purred as she took the base in hand and rubbed his damp cock against her cheek, sometimes catching it with her tongue.

"Oh, no, Father," she whimpered in a high, theatrical voice. "Don't. Don't do this to me. Don't fuck me. Fuck me. *Fuck* me, Father."

He grabbed her head and pushed his cock in her mouth, shoving past her teeth until he hit the back of her throat. He tried to force a rhythm from her, but she was stronger and her own rhythm faster until he had to let go of her and again grasp the bookshelves to remain standing as he drove his cock into her mouth over and over. It didn't matter how deep he went, she wasn't going to gag, but her mouth still made little wet noises every time she took him to the base.

"That's right, Father," she whispered into his mind while her mouth was full. *"Hard and fast. I don't want to linger with you, but for God's sake, make some noise. Be as*

loud as you've ever wanted to be in the sanctuary of your church."

The office filled with the priest's moans — sometimes telling her what to do, sometimes wordless cries when she twisted her head over him just right or swirled her tongue against the underside to caress just the right nerves, sending him reeling back against the bookshelf with a shout. The filthiest invocations dripped from his lips.

"Very nice, Father."

Nova slid a hand between her legs and under her panties to stroke her clit and her folds, some passes bringing her fingers to the sticky wetness of her pussy. It wasn't the priest making her so aroused, although she relished a cock on her tongue just the same. Nor was it Jules, although his presence kept her charged.

No, it was the small crowd she knew was gathering outside the window. The witnesses wouldn't be able to see anything, but oh, the things they could hear...

"Do you think that's him or someone using his office? I could swear it's Father Marcus' voice..."

"Should we tell someone?"

"He's breaking commandments, but we don't know if he's breaking the law. Besides, who do we tell?"

She tickled her claws along his high, tight balls, stroking them behind and worrying the little folds of flesh there until Father Marcus couldn't say anything anymore. All he could manage were his animalistic, deafening groans as she gave him the illusion of taking her innocence. In a way, he had. She'd had sex before he'd tried to have her, but she'd been innocent in so many ways, and she might have been innocent a little longer if he hadn't pushed her toward transformation. She would have been miserable, but she couldn't help but wish she still had that innocence — something precious to her precisely because she could never have it again.

Her teeth pricked his shaft. Father Marcus shouted, bucking, caught between pleasure and pain. As the thinnest trickles of blood touched her taste buds, something ugly sparked inside her — as ugly as it was beautiful and gaunt and wicked and sweet and dark and bright, a knot of contradictions, its skin leathery and its eyes glowing red behind the black. A creature. A *monster*.

It latched to Father Marcus' energy like the parasite it was and drew out an explosive orgasm that filled her mouth and shot down her throat, spreading out from her belly in all directions that had her squealing around his erection that was stoppering her mouth.

Halfway through the flood, Nova shut the door of the dam. It was as unpleasant to her as slamming her teeth down on her tongue. But Nova wrenched back from the priest's cock, gasping.

The priest slumped, his eyes half-closed and unseeing. But he still breathed, steady and even. He wasn't dead, simply unconscious.

Jules curled his arm around the priest's neck to keep him upright. "What are you doing? Finish him."

"I will." Her lips felt full, swollen, like the folds between her pressed-together thighs. "I just wanted to see if I could stop. It wasn't while he's sleeping, but…I think I can." She giggled, temporarily euphoric from the life force that had made it inside her. "Better for me to figure out how to do it with someone I *want* to kill. I'll be even better when it's someone I don't."

"He's under now," Jules said. "You can give him the dream to end all dreams. You can do whatever you want with him."

"No, you can't."

Nova jerked around. She couldn't see anyone, but papers fluttered from the desk, and bootsteps thudded on the carpet. "Eli."

"I'm disappointed in you, Nova."

"Do you know who this man is?" she asked.

"A priest. A man of God. Is God the one you're trying to spite by taking him?" He'd gone still. She couldn't see or hear him, but she felt him there, like a draft against her skin.

"This is the one who tried to take me when I didn't know what I was." As Nova stood, she didn't bother fastening the priest's trousers. His cock hung out, still semi-hard but somehow pathetic without her attention upon it. "Do you know what he was doing when I came in tonight? The exact same thing to another girl. Do you want to know how many others he's collected? Do you want to know how many others he's been forgiven for? And none of them were succubi. My magic might have sweetened the moment when he tried to do it to me, but I didn't make him. He deserves so much worse than me, Eli. He deserves honey and fire ants, but I'm what he gets instead."

"You're not going to kill him," Eli said.

"Why not?"

Silence followed her question, but it was a struggling rather than a sneaky silence.

"If I don't, he's going to do it to someone else. You know he will. Men like him always do."

"You mean a man who's like you?"

"A man can always deny me if that's what he wants," Nova said. "Arousal isn't the same thing as consent. There were times I didn't want to want it, but I did it anyway. But there were also times that I didn't want it, but it was done to me anyway, and I felt so good from it that everything got all confused. But those were boys. This is a man who told me to go to his office so that he could chastise me for inappropriate clothing that had caused a boy to feel me up during a worship service. You talked about grooming. What do you think he was doing to me and to every other girl who's been taken in his office or in the rectory of his other church?"

More silence. Sneaky silence. Invisible hackles rose on Nova's neck.

"When they accept you, they aren't asking for death," Eli whispered. He was throwing his voice. It seemed to be everywhere, but not yet close.

"Sex has always been able to kill. It's just a matter of how fast. If I have to kill, he's the kind of man it's going to happen to—*exactly* this kind of man."

"You're not going to let her have this one, are you?" Jules bared his teeth. "You're going to play righteous like all your kind do, with your pelts hung with pride next to your crosses and holy water. The whole lot of you are all the same. You're just like her, you know, destroying those you believe are wicked enough to die. But she *has* to feed. What you do is a choice, hunter, and was it ever something that kept you from a good, long, satisfying, shameless sleep?"

Jules whirled around with the priest almost throttled in his grip. He hissed at someone who Nova still couldn't see, but Jules' eyes had focused upon a form. "You try it, killer, and I swear the priest dies. We don't have to kill through sex, you know. A snapped neck is just as effective, and this one has such little resistance now that Nova's softened him up."

"Leave the man, Nova. Build up evidence, show the police," Eli said. "Let's go out into the open. Let's get this done."

"We have the advantage *here*." Jules shook the priest like a turkey. "Not another step toward her, killer. Nova, back up. He's got silver knives."

"I thought that was for werewolves." But she stumbled toward the entrance of the office, where there was more room to maneuver.

"It's not a full-system poison, but if he hits your heart, there's no way you'll recover."

"Or if I cut your head off," Eli said, still advancing. "Not much comes back from that."

A series of snaps crackled through the air, like someone jumping on bubble wrap. Then there was a rip, fleshier than fabric.

"You don't say," Jules replied.

Nova's mouth dropped open as Jules threw the priest's head at her.

But it struck something solid and invisible right in front of her. Eli fell forward with a shout, and his hand touched her arm. Suddenly, she could see him, covered from head to toe in black—covered so that demons like her couldn't touch him.

Eli whipped around toward the one responsible for killing the priest.

"Nova, fly!" Jules shouted.

She ran through the office door, pulled her glamour over her, then spread her wings to fly up through the classrooms to the roof.

She landed on the edge, crouched like the gargoyles and stone angels around her. When she peered down—

heedless of the chilly, wet air that swept over her bare skin—she scanned over the slowly dispersing group under Father Marcus' office window.

One of them sounded like she was on her phone with someone, her voice short and sharp as she answered questions rapid-fire. Across the grass on other pathways walked more students and a few adults, probably professors heading home. It wasn't really late on campus just because the sun had gone down, and the encroaching weather wouldn't be dangerous until the lightning on the horizon started flashing close enough to bring thunder a person could feel in their bones. This was Texas. People couldn't drive in such weather, but they didn't run for cover until the sirens started—and sometimes not even then.

Get out of there, Jules. Glamours aren't going to be much use when foot traffic reaches the office.

She wondered what the news would say this time when they found a headless corpse. Definite cause of death for that one.

Jules burst through the window over the crowd's heads, closely followed by Eli.

It was startling and, for a moment, arresting to watch Eli fly. His golden contraption glittered in the lights that lined the walkways. The wings certainly didn't look like they could keep him aloft, but they moved as easily as Jules'.

Jules doubled back into the building so that he could get Eli off his tail. Nova flapped her wings, keeping herself partially aloft as she ran over the incline of the roof, jumped over the statuary at the top, then ran back down and swept to the side, where she hid herself under her wings in shadow on an adjacent roof.

When she peeked out from under her wings, Eli was standing at the top of the Religious Studies roof. His wings were like those of the avenging angels on either side of him. He murmured something, possibly to himself or the statues around him. Then he jumped, spreading his wings to catch his fall, and sank into the courtyard between the four academic buildings.

No possible collision with innocent civilians back here. There were trees in every corner that stretched their branches toward the center, but Eli avoided them easily and landed on the decorative brick below.

Jules rustled the branches he'd concealed himself in as he tried to get the drop on Eli, but Eli had anticipated a possible attack from above. He swung his wings up, slashing them against Jules' belly like claws. Jules shouted, rolling to the side. The wounds were so clean from the thin slashes of metal that they bled freely and probably stung like a thousand paper cuts.

"You're not getting away from me again." Eli pulled out his knives once more. "You might be a conquest demon, incubus, but you're also more of a pestilence than Nova ever was. How long were you preying upon the campus before they started seeing a pattern only because you let *her* take center stage of the blame?"

"She needs to be center stage. A pig like you wouldn't know magnificence if it bit you on the ass, and since she probably did, that just proves my point," Jules snarled.

Eli lashed out, but Jules swept his own wings at Eli, obscuring his view so that he struck at little more substantial than feathers. Jules jumped forward and landed a solid kick of his bare foot to Eli's chest, sending Eli back as though catapulted.

"And how humiliating it must have been. A great, big, manly hunter such as yourself, realizing you'd been in the clutches of the very thing you've been slaughtering all these years." Jules curled his lip as he bent to pick up a pile of leaves to blind Eli again. Then Jules caught Eli's upper arms with his claws, tearing through the fabric of Eli's sweater where his armor didn't reach. He topped it off with a clawful uppercut that ripped the bottom half of Eli's mask. "How could you not know what she was? What kind of education does a hunter have to get before they give him his very first knives? Is it a correspondence course or a for-profit associate's degree?"

"You talk a lot, demon," Eli snapped. "Corruptors like you always do. So much to say, so little of value. Is that how you got to her? Said all the right things to convince her that it was okay to kill?"

He held his arms up at the next set of leaves that Jules swept in his face, then ducked to sweep Jules at his knees. They knocked together with a sound like acorns hitting concrete, and Jules tumbled to the side.

"You clearly don't know her if you think a little sweet-talking drove her to it," Jules said. "It was just a matter of finding the right victim, killer. Just like you. It takes a special kind of evil to fight evil, hunter."

"Then you admit what you are." Eli slammed his heavy boot on Jules' ankle. Nova flinched at the crunch of bone.

The incubus screamed, writhing in pain on the brick.

Nova flew down just as Jules got onto his good leg and flew up, his fists a flurry over Eli's face and shoulders in spite of the stabs and slashes of the knives.

Eli brought the heel of his hand, reinforced by the handle of the knife, up to Jules' nose with an even more disconcerting crunch. Taking advantage of the incubus' disorientation, Eli grabbed the back of his neck and brought the knife to Jules' flesh.

"No!" Nova landed her feet on Eli's shoulders, then jumped back to grab him by the smoother part of his wings, near his shoulders, where they wouldn't cut her palms. She shoved him to the side.

But although she curled her fingers to ready her claws, she couldn't make herself go after him. She should have. He was distracted, responding to her proximity even though she hadn't touched him directly.

Instead, she put herself between the two men, holding up her palms to warn Eli back. "Please, Eli, just let us go. We are what we are. You are who you choose to be. I think that's the difference between demons and humans."

"No," Eli said. "No, you still have a choice. It's a harder choice. And maybe that man deserved to lose his dignity and his head. I don't know. But you still have a choice whether you kill, whom you kill, how you kill them, why…"

"Pretty, pretty words, but they mean *nothing*," Jules spat, limping with his wings spread to avoid putting his weight on his broken foot. "You're fallen, Nova. There's nothing you can do to change that."

"How many other lies have you told her? As many lies as I believed she told me?" Eli fixed his gaze somewhere between her and Jules, keeping them both in his line of vision without meeting their eyes. "Fallen isn't forever. You may always be a demon, but you don't have to be fallen. There are other ways—ways that you might have already found. I can help you."

He held his hand out, covered in thin but sturdy-looking black leather.

"Come with me. I don't know exactly what to do, but I know someone who does."

"Do you know what hunters do to succubi?" Jules asked her, incensed as she stared at that open but shielded hand. "They skin them, scalp them, cut off the parts that fetch a price — your breasts, your teeth, your claws, your gorgeous wings. They leave the rest for the pestilence demons to devour. You're walking into a horror story if you believe he can help you."

Nova jerked back in shock. "Is that true?"

"Yes," Eli said. "And you suck people's lives out of them through their genitals, often by invading their dreams. Just your touch can be dangerous. Death isn't pretty, Nova, but hunters need to eat, too. Once the demon is dead, there's no reason to let what's left go to waste. It's an old and practical principle, gruesome though it may seem to you. If I were to kill you, which I don't want to do, you'd be dead before I did any of those things. But I don't want to do those things to you if I don't have to."

"How can I trust you, Eli?" Nova asked. "How can I trust you not to kill me the second you get a chance?"

"I'm asking myself the same questions."

"You can't seriously be considering anything this man is saying." Jules limped toward her. "*I* helped you. *I* showed you what you were. *I* showed you the world as it should be. I showed you everything you can ever be, everything you can ever have. I was there for you when this man turned on you in a heartbeat. Don't betray me for *this*, for the joke of human-demon love that can never happen, can *never* work. You'll only hurt him, if he doesn't hurt you first. You might not mean it, but it'll happen eventually. Desire will overwhelm caution. You'll be left with your lover dead on the sheets, and you'll have only yourself to blame, for trying to be something that you're not — for trying to be human."

"I'm not telling you to be human, Nova," Eli said. "I'm telling you his way isn't the only way. I believe you. I believe you don't want to hurt anyone. I believe that you do what you think you have to. I believe that you weren't trying to hurt me. I don't completely trust you, but I believe you. Please, Nova, come to me."

He held out his hand again.

Nova wished she could run...away, this time. But she was fairly certain that wouldn't make her safer. It would just delay a confrontation — if not with Eli, then with another hunter, one who wouldn't stop to negotiate.

She stared intently at Eli's hand as the first drops of rain darkened the brick around them. The thunder was now more than suggestion, although the storm hadn't quite hit campus yet.

Nova had never flown with wet wings before. She had a feeling it wasn't the easiest thing to do. She relaxed her fingers and furled her wings, although she didn't pull them in, then tentatively stepped toward Eli, not yet sure whether she was going to take his hand but at least wanting to show that she didn't think he would attack her.

"No!" Jules snarled, darting around her. "She's *mine*."

Nova was about to tell Jules that she didn't belong to either of them when silver and brown flashed in the glow of the single courtyard light.

Jules clutched at his scratched chest, where an arrow had embedded itself between his ribs.

"You bastard," he gasped at Eli. "You set us up. Run, Nova! Ambush!"

He landed on his bad foot, screamed even as he started to shake and fell to the ground.

"Damn, the tip must have only grazed his heart." The unknown woman's voice echoed in the courtyard from an unknown origin. "Still a good shot. Unfortunately, it's an excruciating death instead of a quick one. I can make it faster, dearie, if you just take a few steps back."

"I was handling this!" Eli shouted into the shadows. "I told you not to interfere unless I called for you."

Jules had gone ashen, with sickly, dark hollows under his eyes as he looked up at Nova with all the agony of a *Pietà*. She stumbled to him and fell to her knees, skinning them, but the minor pain didn't matter as Jules continued to scrabble at the place the arrow had entered him.

"I had to make a judgment call, Fray. Your head wasn't in the game. You let your heart rule the roost, and as much as I don't care about your guts splattered over the courtyard, I don't much fancy trying to kill two sex demons in your stead."

A young woman stepped out of the dark. For a moment, Nova thought she was hallucinating and having a nightmare at the same time. The woman looked like she'd walked straight out of some pop art version of the fifties in a plaid rockabilly dress and petticoat. She wore pristine, black, high-heeled Mary Janes and frilly ankle socks, hardly accessories that went with the quiver of silver-tipped arrows and crossbow. Her heavily made-up face was framed with a red ribbon that matched her lipstick and held her blonde hair back, where it spilled in wide ringlets to her shoulders. Not the appearance one would expect from a hunter at all, yet the cold, flinty set of her eyes reminded Nova strongly of the way that Eli had looked down at her when he'd discovered what she was.

"Nova." Jules' voice was little more than a rustle. He touched her lips until he no longer had the strength to hold up his arm.

He didn't close his eyes the way the dead did in movies. They just lost their light. She sensed his life leaving him like dust riding the wind of the storm.

The rain was soft but steadier now.

Chapter Twenty

"I was going to give them a choice!" Eli shouted at the woman.

"No. You said you were going to give *her* a choice. And since when did we give demons a choice at all?" the woman said. "Here I thought that when I pointed you in their direction, you wouldn't completely lose your nerve at the sight of a beautiful girl. I thought hunting these things pretty much inured you to the pretty. I've yet to meet a vampire who can thrall me the way you seem enthralled by this one. Did she touch you in the special place?"

"It's complicated, Brumley."

"I just made it simpler," the woman said brightly, her teeth blinding white against the red of her lips. "The way she's glaring, I'm pretty sure she's going to try to kill us."

"Oh shit," Eli muttered as Nova stood up from Jules' body. "Nova…"

"I don't know much about vampires. I don't know much about demons at all," Nova said, still gazing at Brumley. "I do know what I am, though, and I know what I can do. I'm not a vampire, so you don't usually hunt things like me, do you?"

"Bring it, sister." But Brumley's perfectly cultivated expression flickered, like a tiny crack in the face of a porcelain doll.

"He wasn't even going after you," Nova said.

"Not that it would have done anything to me if he had." Brumley smoothed a hand down her skirt, which in no way detracted from the solid hold Brumley had on the trigger of the reloaded crossbow. "Besides, it doesn't make a difference whether he was or not. I read the papers before I gave them to Fray. I know what he's done. I know what you've done, too."

Brumley raised the crossbow and pointed the silver-tipped arrow of it right at Nova's chest.

"Fray tells me that, according to you, those guys had it coming. The ones who made the headlines probably did. I'll give you that. What about the ones that were footnotes, demon? What about them?"

"They were accidents," Nova said quietly.

"You accidentally sucked their lives out through their dicks? You know, I've heard worse."

"I accidentally killed them. I was trying to feed without doing that. It's harder than it looks."

"I'm sure all the boys say the same thing."

"I changed my prey when I learned I couldn't control it yet," Nova said.

"Their families would be so comforted," Brumley said, "knowing you didn't really *mean* to kill their children."

Nova's lower lip trembled, but she gritted her teeth. If she started crying, she was going to lose focus and control, two things that were essential when staring down a hunter with a deadly weapon pointed at her heart.

Brumley tilted her head. "Interesting. Fray, can you recall the last time you saw a demon cry?"

"Cam, walk away," Eli said in a low warning.

"Occasionally, you get a vampire with a mate, and that's a tearjerker if ever there was one, although they don't exactly *cry*. I put the ones left behind out of their misery, because I'm kind that way," Brumley continued, ignoring Eli and instead stepping prissily toward Nova. By now, her ringlets were drenched, but her makeup didn't run and her petticoats remained festive and springy. "You need a little help crossing over, love?"

Nova abruptly darted forward, hissing.

"Nova!" Eli shouted.

Brumley's eyes widened in surprise, but she was a professional. She shot her arrow.

This time, however, the huntress didn't have the element of surprise on her side. Nova batted the arrow away. Then she batted the second one aside, grabbed the crossbow and wrenched it from Brumley's hand. She broke the mechanism with one squeeze.

"Nova, *stop*," Eli said.

But Nova kicked out to the side and caught him in the abdomen, briefly stealing his wind again and leaving more than enough time to strike Brumley's arms away when she tried to fight. The rain was making it hard to see and even more difficult to keep punches from sliding to the side, offsetting some of the hunter's momentum. And as poorly dressed as she was for a vampire fight, Brumley was even more ill-equipped for a succubus—especially since Nova had already known the second Brumley had stepped into the courtyard that the woman wouldn't have any interest in Jules.

The woman's dress reached her knees, but the sleeves were only half-length. So much vulnerable skin.

Nova locked her hands around Brumley's wrists and crowded her against the light post, then sent the full measure of her magic into the hunter.

Brumley's eyes nearly rolled back in her head, and she panted and moaned, rain alighting on her scarlet lips like dew. She struggled to get closer to Nova rather than away.

"While you were telling Eli how to do his job, you probably should have asked him for a few pointers if you were looking to change specialties," Nova whispered, less than an inch from the woman's lips. "Maybe then you wouldn't have let your lovely skin so close to a succubus whose friend you just killed in cold blood."

Nova wasn't sure how woman-on-woman feeding was supposed to work, since there seemed to be very specific, penetrative rules for incubi with women and probably with men. She let instinct drive her actions, her magic responding to willing prey.

She slipped a hand under the woman's petticoat. Brumley arched against the post when Nova reached her goal. She tried to kiss Nova, but Nova stayed just out of reach. Brumley whimpered, wrapped an arm around Nova's waist to try to bring them closer together. Again, Nova resisted—until her natural desire grew stronger than her uncertainty.

When Nova pressed her lips against the huntress', the huntress shivered and sighed as though finally tasting a long-awaited decadence. Nova played her like a harp until any thoughts of her profession had fled her mind. Then Nova filled those empty spaces.

"Nova." The strained voice came through like bad reception. "You have a choice. This is the time to show me you've made it."

She barely heard him. Her magic surrounded herself and Brumley like a cocoon as she sank it into the woman one silken strand at a time, preparing for the final draw. She hadn't gotten full satisfaction from the priest. After last night, she didn't need another feast, but how could she say no, especially when this woman had murdered Jules and tried to kill her not a few moments before? And the woman tasted so lovely, brimming with unresolved and untested desires and fantasies. Nova was almost disappointed she couldn't tap the well deeper than a storm-drenched session.

Brumley whimpered, such a pretty sound. Nova thought she looked more beautiful when she wasn't quite so perfect, wasn't just a painted face and costume. Undone as she was by Nova's kiss and the rain, she seemed much more accessible, much more touchable — in more ways than one. She was soft in a different way than some of the men Nova had taken were soft. There was a lightness and litheness to her limbs, a delicacy underneath the lean cords of well-maintained muscle that even the boniest man couldn't achieve.

"Nova, if you love me, you won't make me kill you."

Eli slid his gloved hand onto her shoulder. He wasn't going to lure her with the promise of his skin. It had to be a choice, not a trick. Even within the haze of lust, she understood that.

"*Please,*" Brumley begged when Nova pulled away from her lips again.

Nova withdrew her hand from under Brumley's petticoat. Brumley squirmed in thwarted desire, trying with all the language in her body to convince Nova to stay, but Nova slowly removed her hands from Brumley's skin and stepped back until the huntress couldn't reach her anymore. Eli did the rest, rushing forward and wrapping an arm around Brumley's shoulders from behind to haul her back and keep her from pursuing her own death.

"Cam," Eli said earnestly, jolting the woman like an ill-mannered child. "Cam, come on. Snap out of it."

Brumley stopped struggling against Eli and became completely still. Her glassy eyes brightened, then turned as stormy as the skies above.

"Fuuuuuuuck!" she screamed, leaning against Eli's hold on her, from lascivious to murderous in a matter of seconds. But there was no mistaking the fear mingled with the frustration. Brumley knew how close she'd been.

"You're out," Eli said. "You knew this was a risk when you wore your absurd get-up. She stopped. She's not going to kill you."

"I'm going to tear her limb from limb with my bare hands myself if you don't, Fray!"

Nova interlaced her fingers behind her back. "I won't hurt you if you don't hurt me." She stepped to the side until she reached Jules again, a slumped, wet mass. She crouched on the other side of him, never taking her eyes from Brumley but also guarding the body. "You don't get him. You don't make money off him. You owe me that much."

"I can take him to a drain. That's where the pestilence demons live. They'll dispose of his body," Eli said.

"How can I trust you?" she asked again.

"Let go of me, you big lovesick ass." Brumley yanked at Eli's arm. Eli loosened it, and Brumley ducked under, moving away from both Eli and Nova. There was no point to it, but she tried to smooth down her wet skirt into some semblance of put-togetherness.

"We had an agreement, Cam," Eli said. "She's mine to decide what to do with."

"I get it. She didn't kill me when she had a chance, and now you think it can all end happily ever after. I'm here to tell you it doesn't." Brumley flipped her soaked hair out of her face. Her makeup was finally starting to deviate from its sharp lines. "But an agreement is an agreement. I won't go after her or enlist anyone else to go after her unless you ask for my help again. However, if I see another murder on the front page, sister, you better make sure that death was worth it, because Eli's not the only sex demon hunter in the city. He's one of the fucking best, but he's far from only. And if you ever touch me again, I'm going to eat your heart while you're still alive. I've got rune protections you haven't even heard of, and you can bet I'll put a few on me so that what just happened never, ever happens again."

She turned on her heel, mostly concealing how shaken she was, and left the courtyard, the click of her Mary Janes duller against the brick with the persistence of the rain. The drops fell large and hard now, lightning almost constant, with all the violence of a cold front meeting the relative warmth of their autumn.

Nova felt naked as she looked up at Eli's dark form. "I wouldn't have tried to kill her if she hadn't killed Jules."

"She's so safe around hunters and most of the vampires she hunts that she forgot she wasn't safe with you," Eli said evenly. "She lives only because you let her, and now she owes you a debt. Is there a reason she shouldn't take that personally?"

He approached the body and crouched in front of it. "I met your mother today. She didn't know it, but she corroborated things that you told me. And you could have taken Brumley, put her between us and drained the life out of her right in front of me—but you didn't. You put your life at risk by saving hers. Let me help you trust me a little more. Let me take him to a sewer drain. No one can see us if you put your magic back up."

Nova slowly backed away from Jules' massive wings, giving Eli room to tuck his arms under the body and lift it with what seemed like preternatural strength.

Eli carried Jules out of the courtyard without another word. Nova followed him but kept her distance, far enough to get a head start in flight but close enough to keep an eye on Jules. Eli rounded to the back of one of the dormitories, where Jules' body wouldn't be seen by anyone passing by, now that his magic wasn't hiding him anymore. It wasn't the most dignified of places for a body to rest, but under cover of the storm, it was more dignified than having his body chopped up into pieces for fun and profit right before her eyes—not that she'd let that happen.

If Eli loved her, he wouldn't make her kill him, either.

He rested Jules partly in the drain, more arranged than road kill, but Nova still shuddered. She clenched her hands into fists as Eli fed Jules' legs into the drain, then wrapped the wings around Jules' body to make the fact that he looked human less apparent.

"The pestilence demons are quick. They'll take the body before the night is over," Eli said. "They're not the safest or most sanitary of beasts, but as long as they serve their purpose, they don't have to see the wrong end of a hunter's sword."

"You're just going to leave h— *it* here?" Nova asked.

"It's just a body." He seemed detached from her with all that armor, all those clothes. He could have been any tall, broad-shouldered man with wings and knives. But his voice was so his that it hurt to hear it come from the dispassionate warrior standing fifteen feet away. "Whatever a demon has—a spirit or a soul, I don't know—it's not in the body anymore. Headstones and memorials are for the living, not the dead, and you can have both, but your lover is gone."

Nova muddied her knees as she knelt near the body and plucked a handful of feathers from his wings. She had nowhere to put them, so she took a few thin locks of her hair near the back and tied them in a knot around the cluster of feathers. It held surprisingly well. She wouldn't be able to keep them there, but for now, she needed the brush of those feathers against her neck.

How am I supposed to do this alone? He'd never told her everything, and she didn't know where to look for another incubus who could show her what she was supposed to be—even if she didn't follow all of it.

For his size, Eli was eerily quiet as he came up behind her. She jumped to her feet, claws emerging but her teeth held at bay. He stopped more than an arm's reach from her.

"There's someone I want you to meet," he said. "It's a safe place—for you and for me, at least for now. In this weather, I recommend we take my truck. Even succubi can get electrocuted."

Nova didn't think it was possible, but she was getting more drenched by the minute—and not in a fun way. The cold wasn't quite enough to smother her fever, but it certainly challenged the heat. Her wings felt unspeakably heavy.

"What if I just want to turn around, fly away and never see you again?" she asked. "As long as I keep to a code, we can avoid each other. That would be our truce."

"Is that what you want?" Eli said, almost too quietly to be heard over the pounding rain around them.

He couldn't reach her from where he stood, but he was close enough that her magic met his desire, which sizzled on her skin like water hitting a skillet. He seemed to be deliberately keeping his posture unthreatening, but Nova couldn't determine whether he was doing that because he wanted to *be* unthreatening or because he wanted to *seem* unthreatening.

He's one of the best hunters of demons like me.

Demons like me... She stared at her claws, the full weight of their significance as heavy as a punching bag swinging back at her before she was ready. She was a demon. And he was a demon hunter. She was evil. He was good.

But was it so simple? Was it supposed to be?

If it wasn't so simple, where was she supposed to find the lines, when she trusted herself even less now than when she was human?

She stared at the rain as it ran down her fingers and gleamed on her claws. Then Eli put the straps of his wing harness in her hands. It was a heavy contraption, which explained the power in his arms, shoulders and back evident when he'd removed his shirt. In giving her the wings, he also gave her his knives. He could have had others strapped underneath the clothes — boots seemed like a good hiding place — but they wouldn't be as easy or safe to access.

"Now you have my weapons," he said. "You can tuck the wings at your feet and keep the knives against the floor. You can take some of them out and hold me at knifepoint all the way. You've done what you can not to hurt or attack me thus far. I trust that you won't try to hurt me now, despite the actions of my colleague. However, I won't lie. I didn't authorize the kill, but you were the only one I claimed."

Nova brought the wings and harness close to her chest as though embracing them. Her hair was plastered to her scalp and shoulders, her T-shirt molded to her body. Eli had to be profoundly uncomfortable in his get-up, but he moved as though all his clothes and armor weren't water-logged.

In rain, in sleet, in driving snow... It wouldn't surprise her if it were true. Real professionals trained for any obstacle.

Except for falling for something you're supposed to kill. Apparently, he hadn't trained for that.

She wanted to blame him for Jules' death. She wanted to blame him for the crystal layer around her heart — not nearly as thick as she thought it should be for the incubus who'd awoken her. She wanted to hate Eli for the fear he'd made her feel in his apartment, even though his own fear had been understandable.

She wanted to deny him and fly away, clipping his wings — if not permanently, then for a long time.

"At least we'd get out of the rain," he said.

Nova thought of Jules' home, but she wasn't ready to go back there. It had never been hers. She'd been crashing at his bachelor pad, nice though it was. Tonight, she'd be too much of an intruder, victim to too many of his ghosts.

The safest thing for her to do would be to take the wings and fly. Find her own nest. Accept the truce. She believed Eli would hold himself to it, otherwise he would have killed or tried to kill her by now. This was an awful lot of work just to net himself a succubus. There were probably easier ways.

"Out of the rain would be good," she said.

"You're not cold, are you?" It was more a wry statement than a question.

"Getting there, I think."

"My truck has heat. I don't care if the seats get wet."

I know. But now didn't seem the time for a dirty joke. There was part of her brain that hadn't and probably would never be touched by her human emotions or any measure of maturity. Nova was pretty sure that part had kept her alive to see the day when she'd know who she was.

I'm no longer what I used to be.

That didn't hurt nearly as much as it might have a few weeks ago. In some ways, as she followed a demon hunter through the cold storm, Nova felt freer than she had ever been. Nothing held her down anymore. Nobody could tell her what she had to do. She could choose on her own, accept the consequences of those choices rather than the arbitration of those around her with good intentions.

Good intentions didn't break shackles, only added more links to the chain. Circumstances outside her control had broken the shackles open, but it was her will that made her lighter, in spite of the heavy wing harness.

She climbed into the passenger side of the truck. Eli turned on the heat, dry and blasting cold at first but warming soon after he pulled away from the curb. There was no music. They drove in silence.

Chapter Twenty-One

Though the heater had dried them off somewhat by the time Eli pulled into the concrete-tiled, half-circle driveway, they stepped out and drenched themselves all over again because neither of them hurried under the high arch of the front porch. If anything, Nova lagged behind. This was a nice house, normal. It seemed shameless for her to just walk up to it in a large T-shirt and lingerie, Eli accompanying her in his ninja costume.

Eli, however, stood on the brick porch without self-consciousness as he ignored the doorbell and knocked on the door.

A lovely older woman opened the door, her mouth bright with a Texas smile that Nova knew from experience hid wariness.

"Come in. Come in, Eli. You never did have the sense not to stand out in the rain. Don't mind the carpets. Everything can be cleaned." The woman ushered both of them inside, as gracious as though Nova were wearing pants. "There are changes of clothes for each of you in the Blue Room. There's a bathroom attached, so you don't have to undress together. And if you enter my husband's dreams or intentionally seduce him in any way, young lady, we have a dungeon in the basement with silver-lined manacles. I wouldn't kill you, not when I could make your life a living hell. I'm retired, not safe. Do I make myself clear?"

The woman had the decency not to smile through the warning.

"Yes, ma'am," Nova replied meekly. She fidgeted with the hem of her shirt but fought the impulse to wring. That would just make her drip more water onto the foyer rug, which looked expensive against the hardwood. In spite of the woman's assurance that the water wouldn't damage anything, Nova was afraid to put that to the test.

"Albert's in his workroom, but let me know if you want me to herd him down," the woman said.

"You go on back to bed or *Late Night* or whatever you were doing, Jeannie." Eli had removed his mask, and he kissed the older woman's cheek the way a nephew might peck his aunt. "I'll get him when we're ready. Nova and I have a few things to talk about first."

"You know where the coffee machine is," Jeannie said, her gaze softer now that the warning was out of the way. Just knowing that someone could look at her like that—like a guest—after threating to torture her for eternity was somehow touching. "Something to warm you up on this chilly night. I'm surprised you didn't freeze to death out there."

"Thank you, Jeannie."

The older woman appeared reluctant to leave Eli alone with Nova. She rested her hand on Eli's wet forearm for a moment, then edged around them toward what looked like the main bedroom.

Eli held his hand out to Nova.

He was still wearing his gloves, but that would only protect him from the intensity of her magic. Proximity was enough for her arousal and awareness of Eli to stimulate him. Neither the cold nor the weight from the rain would have completely deterred an erection. She didn't have to look. His body practically begged her.

"Do you know what you're doing?" Nova asked.

"No fucking clue."

"Glad I'm not the only one." Her spine practically vibrated with tension and second thoughts, but she slipped her hand into his. The leather was still damp, cold on the surface, but his warmth permeated through.

He led her down the hall, past several rooms as elaborately decorated as the foyer, to a corridor behind the stairs. The Blue Room was at the end of the hall. He switched on the chandelier, which dripped with blue crystal. Two piles of generic-looking clothing had been folded on the dresser by the door.

"They don't do things by halves, do they?" Nova said.

"They are not subtle people, no. They find money amusing."

Nova raised her eyebrow.

"I don't need to apologize for them being independently wealthy, Nova. If they weren't, they wouldn't be able to patronize hunters like myself. Who do you think was responsible for the wings? I have little understanding of bird anatomy, engineering, physics or alchemy. All that comes from Albert. I'm fortunate to work with him."

He pulled his gloves off and tossed them onto the rug in front of the bed. Then he unstrapped his armor.

"So they finance demon hunting," Nova said.

"No. Although he sometimes supplements my practical expenses, Albert provides moral and mechanical support. He's not quite *that* wealthy, their affinity for elaborate home furnishings notwithstanding."

"Is it good work if you can get it, killing demons?"

"It's a living." He bent down to unlace his boots. There weren't any knives strapped on underneath that Nova could see. "Shitty benefits, though."

"Probably not much of a retirement plan."

Eli dropped his last boot rather than setting it down. It fell to the side, pouring a little rainwater onto the rug.

"I enjoy my work, Nova. I don't always get to rescue people before they're killed, but I do enjoy killing the demons before they can kill again. I'm not going to apologize for that, either." Eli determinedly raised his gaze to meet hers. "Most hunters I know are fulfilled by what they do, whether it's the money or the thrill or the righteousness they do it for. You haven't made me question the task as much as you might think."

"I didn't think I did."

"I'm good at what I do—killing demons, selling their parts, cleaning up the streets. And I'm not going to stop doing it. The question before us is what I'm going to do with you."

"I already offered what I thought was a viable solution to our problem," Nova said stiffly.

"It was one I considered. It's not the one I want."

"Then what do you want?"

"I want to keep doing what I'm doing, and I want you."

The man was direct, honest, aware of the flaws and landmines in his response, but he'd given it anyway. Nova could respect the balls it took to admit it.

"What if that's not possible?" she asked.

"That's not what you asked. I don't know if there's any way in hell, heaven or Meridian for this to work. I've heard of hunters hooking up with vampires or werewolves or witches, but they're closer to humans than a succubus. I've never heard of a sex demon hunter living the domestic life with a sex demon. You and I continuing where we left off, it's messy from top to bottom. It's a mistake—more for me than you. Although I guess we both sleep, don't we?"

"No, that's fair. Just a touch is enough to—"

He rested his bare hand on her arm.

"What are you doing?" she said, almost afraid to speak above a whisper in case she knocked some sense into him with volume.

"All my hunter instincts are telling me this is an unnecessary risk. But another side of me, one that your magic can't touch, is telling me not to let this go—not until I have a better reason than the demon and human divide to stop."

"But it's dangerous—" She couldn't finish her thought as he slid his hand down her wet arm to her wrist.

"Every time I go out, I put my life at risk. Now you know that you do, too. I won't be able to protect you from other hunters. I can't be with you when you're hunting and vice versa. Even if I trust that your killings are justified, that just means I leave you alone. But other hunters might not know or care. I can advise you on some protective charms."

"Like yours, in addition to my glamour?"

"Other than that, we're both on our own. We might as well view it as having two different and somewhat opposing jobs. What we were was all wrong before I knew you were a demon, Nova, but I couldn't get you out of my head, and I swear it wasn't just your magic. I've never had full-on succubus touch before, at least not more than a split second here or there, but you shouldn't invade my mind like you have when I'm not in contact or when I'm not sleeping. That was just you."

He stroked her wrist with his thumb, somehow more intimate than holding her hand. She swayed toward him but caught herself before she could sway right into his arms. It was one thing for him to touch her, another for her to touch him.

"I'm not saying this is going to work. It probably won't and probably shouldn't. If it doesn't, then your proposal's still on the table. You're quiet. Was it a lie, Nova, wanting me? Were you lying to me about that, too?"

"No," she said, little more than a breath.

She tried not to get close to him, made every effort to shut the most intense of her magic away — not a small feat when the closer he came, the more her body wanted him and the more her body did whatever it could to make him touch her more.

He eased closer to her on his own, almost looming in his dark clothes. He leaned in until his words brushed cool on her neck. "I brought protection."

"Aren't you afraid?" Of Brumley. Of his patron. Of other hunters. Of himself. Of the doubts and troubles that this had already raised and would raise. Of her.

He hesitated with his mouth near her skin. Then he pressed his lips against the cord. "Terrified," he whispered against her.

That was enough permission. She let her head fall back as he swept his arm around her and raised his mouth to hers. Once she released the restraint around her magic, it flooded out of her and swirled around them like a tornado, pulling them closer as the storm continued to rage behind the blue curtains that mostly covered the window. A hissing sound filled the air as fog surrounded them, not from a crack in the window but from their bodies, mostly hers. The cold water steamed from her and from where her bare skin met the moisture on his clothes and flesh.

She tugged at his sodden sweater, pushing it up away from his back until Eli impatiently grabbed the hem and pulled it over his head. Nova whimpered as he presented himself to her, as significant as a bared belly to a wolf.

He was the one who brought her hands to his chest when she couldn't, scared of herself, scared that his willingness would damn them both. Once she had her hands on him, though, she couldn't stop touching him. The rain made the flesh slick. He closed his eyes and groaned as she passed her thumbs over his small nipples. Then she slid her hands back up to take his face in her hands and kiss him again.

The only other break as he plundered her mouth was when he jerked her shirt off as well. He discarded it with the rest and made short work of her bra. She was reluctant to let go of him, even to undo his trousers, but when he pulled her abdomen against the front of them, suddenly the thing she desired most was just underneath. She yanked at the button before tearing it off, jerking the zipper down and shoving his trousers and his underwear down his hips.

He grabbed her wrists and pushed her back against the footboard, caging her to the dark wood. His gaze traversed her body greedily as though seeing it for the first time, because now he was seeing it for what it was — a demon's body crafted to entice and incite desire, a fantasy made flesh, but with the slight imperfections that made fantasy real.

It was more than her victims had ever seen. Whether awake or asleep, they'd only ever seen the fantasy.

"When I let you go, turn around," Eli said, his voice dropping into the edge of baritone. "And put your hands on the footboard. I've seen you plenty from the front, but I only got a glimpse of the back."

"I haven't seen enough of yours, either. What if I want to see yours first?"

"That's not how this is going to go." He released one wrist to slap her ass below the lacy line of her panties. He raised his hand to her chin, lifting it with one finger to stare into her eyes. "You do as I say, love, and you get a reward. I think you're a reward kind of girl, and you've always been so good for me."

The spanking hadn't hurt, more sound than substance. But she knew firsthand his strength.

Nova turned around, gripping the footboard until it groaned under her hand. The memory of the last time she'd presented her back to him was still fresh in her mind. A few days ago, she'd have known that any punishment he would dish out would involve pain, but not more than she could handle, and it would be so entangled with pleasure that the pain would be worth it.

She still believed any 'punishment' for disobedience when he used that voice and that severe mask would be harmless. Underneath her belief, however, was risk—risk that was very real for both of them and that hadn't been there before when they'd pretended to be normal.

Play wasn't just play anymore.

Which made things even more intense when Eli traced the line of her shoulders and trailed his fingers down to the blades. He cupped the wounds where her angel's wings had been torn away. She still had no memory of that day, whether it was thirty or three hundred or three hundred thousand years ago or why she'd chosen to fall when now she wouldn't dare.

Eli lowered himself to one knee behind her with a slight grunt.

"Step toward me a little. Arch your back. Yes, just like that." Instead of spanking her again, Eli massaged her ass and the backs of her thighs, his touch carrying more warmth than inspection, but his scrutiny burned like a laser. She held on more tightly to the footboard.

He peeled her panties down her thighs. They stayed at her knees as he spread her cheeks. All look and no touch, but her breathing became shallow as his sigh made the wetness there cool.

"Good girl," he murmured. "If you want to keep being my good little girl, Nova, climb up onto the bed, kneel and show me your wings."

Nova's head dropped, tears suddenly swimming along her lower lids. She sniffed her emotions back. Then she kicked off her underwear and crawled up onto the plush, powder blue duvet. It was like trying to crawl on a cloud. She hoped the cover was washable.

"All the way down to your feet," he said when she knelt in the center of the bed but kept upright.

She slowly lowered her ass to her heels. Then, with a deep breath, she unfurled her wings.

She was careful not to open them all the way. The room wouldn't hold them unless she wanted to send the tips past the walls, and she didn't want to break any knick-knacks or lamps. Her wings framed her body, the lowest point reaching the rugs on either side of the bed. In the light, the fact that the wings were gray rather than black was more apparent, especially against the blue palette of the room.

With her wings open, her legs trapped and her back to Eli, she was more aware than ever that she offered herself almost like a sacrifice. At any moment, Eli could jump onto the bed and plunge a silver knife into her heart from behind. Her wings blocked her arms and weighed her down. She wouldn't be able to react in time to stop the knife or strike back.

She heard the crinkle of foil. Then the bed shifted underneath her, rocking her slightly off-balance. Her limbs felt weak, liquid. Nova realized she was literally shaking, caught in the ambiguous place between fear and arousal until they seemed one and the same.

Instead of a blade, Eli pressed his lips to her back where her heart would be. He ran his fingers through her feathers, tested the strength of the limbs that emerged from her.

Then he rested his hands on her shoulders and pushed her upper body down, not shoving until she was almost all the way there. The duvet cushioned the impact — not at all like when he'd smashed her against the wall. Reminiscent, but replacing the memory with something kinder, intense but not angry, inherently dangerous but not implicitly so — not with his kisses counting her vertebrae all the way down, until he grasped her thighs, wrenched them open and jerked her ass up higher, which angled her head deeper into the duvet.

Her wings draped over her and the bed, and she felt even more like a sacrifice, at the altar waiting for her priest.

She didn't have to wait long.

He licked a firm line from her clit to her cunt, dipping his tongue in to taste her.

"You don't even need foreplay, do you?" he said into her thigh. "When did you start dripping for me, Nova?"

"I don't know," she said, muffled by the covers.

He slapped her ass again. This time the sting almost equaled the sound. She pitched forward, catching the duvet cover with her teeth.

"I think you're not telling me the truth, little girl."

"Whenever you're close," Nova managed to get out. The tears she'd tried to keep from spilling did so anyway, startled by the second spanking. "I can't help it. I've never been able to help it."

"Were you wet for her, too?" She heard the smirk in his voice as he stroked through her folds, focusing on her clit but sometimes teasing the entrance of her cunt.

"I'm wet for anyone who wants me. But not like when I'm with you — nothing like when I'm with you."

She spread her arms to align with her wings and grabbed fistfuls of the covers, gasping as he titillated the flesh outside her cunt with her own juices on his fingertips.

"You want my cock inside you." The rasp of his voice was more pronounced as he shifted closer to her. His cock, as hard as ever and already protected, pressed against her left buttock. He leaned over her, bracing himself with a hand near her head as he eased his fingers into her gripping pussy. "You want it inside so that you can strangle me, suck out my cum and more, revel as I succumb to you and give you more power than you already have."

He punctuated his harsh account with unforgiving thrusts of his fingers, continuing to rub his cock against her ass. The condom kept her from feeling all of him, but she still knew he'd be leaking pre-cum inside it, and it was such a thin barrier between them. Nova wrenched from side to side. All she had to anchor herself was her grip on the duvet. His thrusts were so hard, his knuckles almost bruised her swollen, aching folds, which felt only lust from his force and pulsed in a rhythmic, silent plea. He nearly bowled her over, lifting her hips over and over.

"No. No, Eli. I just want you," she moaned. "I can't have you if you die. Ah, *shit*." He abruptly changed the angle to rub against the place that had made her flood last time. She couldn't say anything else now. Her teeth grew, tearing the fabric of the duvet cover as she bit into it. She might have also gotten a mouthful of duvet down, because she thought she smelled feathers that weren't her own.

Right after Eli removed his fingers from her, he positioned his cock and drove home, slamming himself inside and stroking that spot again in the process. She gave a gravelly wail into her self-imposed gag.

He slid his hands — one slick with her juices and the other slick from the remnants of rainwater on their skin and the mist her body had made of it — down her arms to bind her wrists again as he covered her body with his. The more the surface of his skin met with hers, the more her magic fastened upon him, but he did it anyway, resting his mouth at the base of her neck, where he tested the flesh with his teeth as he pulled his cock back and shoved into her once more.

The position made her feel helpless, the weight and silky warmth of his strong body shockingly intimate, because in truth, he was the helpless one, even if she couldn't feed upon him with a condom on his cock. With every square inch, he opened himself up to her. She could tell him to remove all protection and bury himself inside her. She could kill him if she really wanted to, in spite of the unpleasant magical hum all around her that she instinctively knew would keep her from taking him in his sleep.

She didn't do any of those things, though. Nova couldn't call his name, but it resonated through her as strongly as if she spoke it aloud. Tears streamed from her eyes. The same rawness that made his fucking feel so good also opened her up to grief, despair, relief, ecstasy, all spiraling at once until it exploded inside her. She drew him in, drew him closer even though he was the one with a grip on her. Her wings fluttered like a thousand birds as her orgasm crashed through her. She was crying. She was laughing. She was shouting and sobbing. And through it all, he covered her, comforted her, filled her, held her, bit her, fucked her, gave himself to her, even if it wasn't his life that he gave.

Nova furled her wings back in, feeling smaller and more delicate as she did. Eli licked at the place he had bitten her, although he hadn't broken the skin. He rocked his hips, slow and deliberate, to extend the pleasure for both of them, but he eventually had to withdraw, leaving her empty once more.

"Stay right there. I'll be back," he muttered into her damp hair, which had curled from the combination of the rain and her heat.

He removed the condom and left into the en suite bathroom.

She thought about curling into a ball, but she didn't move, couldn't convince herself to move.

He's going to kill me. He's had me one last time, gotten me out of his system. He can get rid of me now.

Eli came back with a warm washcloth, which he used first to wash her face and neck, then between her legs. She whimpered at the sensation of being taken care of when she'd feared the worst.

"I'm not going to harm you, little girl," he said. "I give you my word that I won't harm you unless it's to defend myself. I'll mark it on my skin if that's what you ask of me."

He tossed the washcloth onto their wet clothes at the base of the bed. Then he took her in his arms and coaxed her onto her side with his long arms and legs wrapped around her, one hand covering her breast and the other firm on her hip. The wounds on her shoulder blades nestled against his chest.

"There's not much else I can promise you," he murmured into the extended silence and the white noise of the storm. "I know what you are, and you know what I am. I can't promise you that this will work or that we'll live happily ever after or that I can protect you. I can't promise you forever."

"I'm not asking for a promise, Eli. I'm just asking for now. To trust me." *To love me.* "For now."

He stroked his thumb over her nipple, an affectionate caress rather than a lustful one. "Close your eyes, little girl, and I'll close mine."

She closed her eyes.

* * * *

A few hours later, the squeak of the door woke her up. Eli also jolted awake, but like her, he stayed completely still. She couldn't tell if he opened his eyes all the way or kept them slits like her, pretending she was asleep.

Through the crack in the door, a bespectacled older gentleman dressed like an absentminded professor smiled, sad but gentle. His eyeglasses gleamed as he reached in to turn off the light, leaving them in darkness and lightning, although the worst of the storm had passed.

Nova settled deeper into the duvet and tucked herself closer to Eli. While she'd been sleeping, Eli had put a blanket between his hips and her ass, a small gesture of protection and goodwill, but the rest of him was still hot, smooth, strong and bare against her.

He stroked her cheek. "Good girl."

Want to see more from this author?
Here's a taster for you to enjoy!

Sanctuary: Winter Howl
Aurelia T. Evans

Excerpt

Renee took the last sip from her Samuel Adams and set the finished bottle down next to the first one. She smiled and nodded at Marie, who had come over to take the empty bottles and leave the receipt. There were no words between them. Usually Marie would chat to her customers, but she'd learned when she'd moved to Antoine five years ago that Renee Chambers would not look at her, half of the time wouldn't talk and the other half of the time would stumble through some painful attempt at conversation. Renee had got better as she'd come to know Marie, but it was still more comfortable for both of them when Renee didn't try to talk and Marie didn't try to make her.

Renee left the cash tip on the table, clenched the leash and slid out of the booth. Her legs stiffened when she saw Josh Beall and Marcus Levinson a few booths down. She had not seen them come in, and although she had heard their laughter, she hadn't recognised it as theirs. She would have to walk by them to leave. The warm body against her leg reassured her, nudged her in the right direction. She took one step, then two. Her knees loosened and let her walk. She instinctively — and fruitlessly — tried to hide in her long, light blue coat.

"…saw her at the supply store getting her checklist squared away," she heard Josh say.

"What's it been, two months since she last came down here?" Marcus asked.

"What does she do up there all alone, anyway?" Marcus asked.

"Roswell says she gets a lot of mail," Josh said. "He says she has help, but I don't believe it. She wouldn't let anyone up there. I bet she does it all herself. Completely crazy."

Renee closed her eyes and breathed in. She was not so egotistical as to believe that everyone in Antoine talked about her, but it was just her luck that she had to walk by these two rubes when they were. Neither was too far into his mug for slurred speech, but they were far enough that they couldn't gauge their volume.

"Maybe she does porn," Marcus suggested. "You know, video stuff."

Josh snorted. "Frigid bitch like her? Don't think so." He leaned forward conspiratorially. "Hey, what if we went up — ?"

"Hey, Renee," Marcus said, even more loudly then they had already been speaking. Josh turned around, his scruffy but reasonably attractive face lighting up with a sly grin when he saw her huddled against the booth table behind them.

"Speak of the scared little devil," he said, raising his glass. "Want a drink? You look a little tense."

Renee's eyes darted from Josh to Marcus to Marie to the door. At another nudge to her leg, and she stepped towards the door.

"Yeah, come on, sweetie," Marcus said, misinterpreting her direction. "We'll make it worth your while."

How? Renee thought. By drooling on me and trying to feel me up with all those smooth moves you've cultivated over the last ten years? She didn't say anything, of course, just kept inching along until she finally started past the table.

She lurched forward when Marcus delivered a hearty smack to her ass. It didn't hurt, but Renee could feel her face start to burn and her chest tighten. At least she could move her legs faster now that she was past them.

"Hey, now, none of that in here," Marie called from behind the bar. "Have a good day, Renee. Don't be such a stranger."

"You always run away," Josh shouted after her.

"I wonder why," Renee muttered, her tongue looser now that she was out of the bar and no one was looking at her. "Come on, Britt, one more stop before we go home."

"Hey, Mommy, can I pet the dog?"

Renee winced at the high frequency of the voice and hoped that the mother would know the appropriate way to answer her child. No such luck.

"Hello, miss. Can my daughter pet your dog?"

Antoine was not exactly a highly populated town, but it had a fair tourist trade, particularly downtown Main Street, which was described in most tourist guidebooks as colourful, cheerful, folksy, and unique. Renee did not know about unique or folksy, but many tourists liked to come by for the ambience. And like most townies, the Antoine population had both respect for tourist dollars and frustration with the tourists themselves.

Especially when tourists did not know a service dog when they saw one.

"I'm sorry, ma'am," Renee said, emphatically not looking at the woman. That sometimes helped, and the warm feeling of Britt against her leg reassured her. "She's working."

"Oh, I'm sorry... Hey, wait, you're not blind." The overly polite apology turned into a similarly grating voice of parental annoyance. "If you didn't want Lisa to pet her, you could've just said. There's no need to lie."

"I'm not lying," Renee said. In fact, she was a terrible liar, but that was not the issue at hand. "They do more than help blind people. Please... I need to..."

"Well, that's just rude, having a dog around when you're not really blind and then not letting a little girl pet it," the mother said indignantly.

"I'm sorry. She's working." The words came out short and clipped and curt, but Renee was not really that angry. Her throat was just tightening, and she could feel her shoulders curling in.

"Bitch," the woman muttered under her breath as she grabbed her daughter's free hand—the girl's other hand had been playing with Britt's tail. The little girl was lucky that Britt was an extremely well-behaved dog. The woman led her daughter across the street.

"Good girl," Renee whispered, rubbing Britt's ear gently. "Ready to go?"

She barely had to tug the leash in the direction of the grocery store. Britt had a deep bond with Renee, had been with her most of her life and been her service dog for about five years. She could feel where Renee wanted to go.

Renee admired Britt's beauty beneath the deep green service vest. So many people confused her for a

Siberian husky, and Renee understood the mistake. They were both northern sled dogs, but malamutes were bigger, with thicker fur. Britt was a little larger than average, and the darkest parts of her fur — set off by the usual white accents — were almost black. Malamutes were not traditionally service dogs. But Renee had loved Britt since the first time she'd met her, and the feeling had been mutual. There was friendship and respect between them, a connection that she had never managed to make with any of the people at school. It was really no wonder she spent all her time around dogs — she understood them and got along with them so much better than she did with most people.

With Britt in front of her, Renee felt secure in her steps. The sides of her coat hood blocked out her periphery, like blinders on a horse, and she felt a little more confident where she put her feet. Besides, with a large dog like Britt with her — a dog that was occasionally confused for a wolf — she felt more protected. Like a celebrity with a bodyguard, thankfully without the paparazzi.

They made it to the grocery store in about a ten-minute walk. That was what she liked about Main Street. Almost everything was within walking distance, so all she had to do was drive into Antoine, walk around a bit, then drive back home when she was finished, rather than drive from one place to another, and another, and another. Renee was able to stretch her legs after the long drive into town, and certainly Britt needed the exercise as well.

Renee did not need to go to the grocery store often, and she did not necessarily need to go now, which just went to show how much better she had become in public places. But she wanted to get a few treats to tide herself over before all her orders were shipped in. That was actually how she did most of her shopping — online through bulk providers. She had the space, the money and the resources, and most of the things shipped in needed to be shipped in bulk. Besides, it was such a long drive between Antoine and where she lived.

There had been a time right after her father had died when she could not even walk into a grocery store without panicking, a time when she could not walk off her property without feeling everything coming in to crush her, as if the entire world had a force field of inhospitality. That was what each successive building had felt like once she stepped out into the world — like a heavy, unpleasant curtain surrounded each of them, and it would take all her effort to pass through. And sometimes she couldn't.

About the Author

Aurelia T. Evans is an up-and-coming erotica author with a penchant for horror and the supernatural.

She's the twisted mind behind the werewolf/shifter Sanctuary trilogy, demonic circus series Arcanium, and vampire serial Bloodbound. She's also had short stories featured in various erotic anthologies.

Aurelia presently lives in Dallas, Texas (although she doesn't ride horses or wear hats). She loves cats and enjoys baking as much as she dislikes cooking. She's a walker, not a runner, and she writes outside as often as possible.

Aurelia loves to hear from readers. You can find her contact information, website details and author profile page at https://www.totallybound.com

Home of Erotic Romance

Sign up for our newsletter and find out about all our romance book releases, eBook sales and promotions, sneak peeks and FREE romance books!